PRAISE FOR JULIET E MCKENNA

"A writer to watch."

Vector on *The Tales of Einarinn*

"Brimful of magic and adventure."

Starburst on *The Tales of Einarinn*

"Her many characters are thoroughly engaging and her plots tight, well-paced and gripping."

Joanne Harris on *The Aldabreshin Compass*

"When a talented writer makes fiction seem like history, the book becomes an event."

Morgan Llywelyn on *The Aldabreshin Compass*

"Fully rounded characters, exceptional storytelling ability and quality writing make for a rich, entertaining read."

Stan Nicholls on *The Aldabreshin Compass*

"Magically convincing and convincingly magical."

Dan Abnett on *The Chronicles of the Lescari Revolution*

"At her best, combining politics, sudden, violent action, and a concern for the domestic."

Paul Cornell on *The Chronicles of the Lescari Revolution*

"Compelling narratives, authentic combat and characters you care about."

Stan Nicholls on *The Hadrumal Crisis*

BY THE SAME AUTHOR

THE TALES OF EINARINN
The Thief's Gamble
The Swordsman's Oath
The Gambler's Fortune
The Warrior's Bond
The Assassin's Edge

THE ALDABRESHIN COMPASS
The Southern Fire
Northern Storm
Western Shore
Eastern Tide

THE CHRONICLES OF THE LESCARI REVOLUTION
Irons in the Fire
Blood in the Water
Banners in The Wind

THE HADRUMAL CRISIS
The Wizard's Coming
Dangerous Waters
Darkening Skies
Defiant Peaks

THE GREEN MAN
The Green Mans Heir
The Green Man's Foe
The Green Man's Silence
The Green Man's Challenge
The Green Man's Gift

Juliet E McKenna

THE CLEAVING

ANGRY
ROBOT

ANGRY ROBOT
An imprint of Watkins Media Ltd

Unit 11, Shepperton House
89 Shepperton Road
London N1 3DF
UK

angryrobotbooks.com
twitter.com/angryrobotbooks
Double-edged Story

An Angry Robot paperback original, 2023

Cover illustration by Chris Panatier
Edited by Simon Spanton and Shona Kinsella
Set in Meridien

ISBN 978 1 91520 222 2
Ebook ISBN 978 1 91520 227 7

Printed and bound in the United Kingdom by TJ Books Ltd.

9 8 7 6 5 4 3 2 1

*With sincere thanks to Simon,
for starting such an interesting conversation,
and to Max, for encouraging me to pursue
this increasingly intriguing idea.*

BOOK ONE

CHAPTER ONE

A ring of stone walls and gates should mean safety. Nimue couldn't remember when she had last felt so uneasy walking through a town's crowded streets. It wasn't just that Winchester was unfamiliar territory, so very far from home. It wasn't only that the steep wooded hills loomed over these buildings huddled by the river, when she was used to Cornwall's wide unbounded skies. It wasn't even hearing the rasp of English instead of the Cornish tongue.

The looks she was getting from men she passed sent prickles of unease down her spine. She caught their leers in the corner of her eye, though she kept her gaze firmly on the beaten earth, sidestepping the garbage littering Market Street.

Nothing marked her out as more than any other maidservant. She had begged the loan of a drab, sleeveless surcote from the housekeeper at their lodging, the better to go unnoticed. Few men would realise her rose-coloured gown was far too fine to be worn with such a garment. They only saw a slightly-built woman of middling height, with wisps of long dark hair escaping the kerchief that covered her looped and pinned braids. Nimue wondered if she had made a mistake. Clothes that indicated wealth and status would warn these men to keep their distance. Instead, they might see her as prey.

These men were bored, turned out of the storehouses and workshops where they were billeted as soon as the working day started, and first light came early in late summer. The kings and princes they served were royally entertained at Uther

Pendragon's palace, but no thought had been given to the sizeable retinue that accompanied each noble. They loitered on street corners and outside taverns, finding their own amusement. More than that, these warriors were survivors of the recent wars. King Uther and his allies might be celebrating their victories, but these men had fought and bled for their liege lords. They had losses to mourn, and no one had considered what that would mean.

Nimue saw a beggar sitting in the gutter. He had lost one arm at the elbow, and stained rags bound his weeping stump. Despite the cooler air of the early evening, he was sweating and breathing heavily. With the heightened senses of the hidden people, Nimue could smell the sickly-sweet hint of rot in his wound. She walked on and averted her eyes. Later, perhaps, she might be able to leave her duties and come back to help him. Though she would need a guard to escort her, and permission to leave the King of Cornwall's lodgings after sunset. It would be hard to draw on her healing skills with some unsuspecting man-at-arms watching her every move.

She noted she wasn't the only one ignoring the suffering beggar. Visitors and townsfolk alike shunned reminders of the bloody battles. Merchants and farmers had watched sons and brothers answer their liege lord's summons, never to be seen again. The warriors who returned wouldn't want to remember friends killed and maimed on the battlefield. Too many would have seen the horrors inflicted on captives by the Picts. Idleness made it harder to keep such recollections at bay, so these men sought release from sleeping and waking nightmares in the brothels, and in flagons of ale, in dice and other games that too often turned violent. When their money ran out, they roamed further afield. Winchester's Watch, on their nightly patrols, found townsmen beaten senseless and robbed, and virtuous women raped and discarded in back alleys.

Thankfully, Nimue's unforeseen errand hadn't taken her into the back streets that branched off the high street as it wound up the hill. She reached the market cross and turned down the lane to the holy precinct around the Minster, overlooked by the royal palace. The twin threats of priestly displeasure and the brutal efficiency of Uther Pendragon's personal guard kept disorder out of this quarter.

Yesterday, King Uther had instructed his guests to rein in their men. King Gorlois had thrown the letter into the fire, demanding to know what right Pendragon had to give him orders. Even so, Gorlois had sent his squire, Melyas, to summon his knights. The Cornish king told them to tell their liegemen that if any of them were caught and hanged, those who had failed to stop them committing such crimes would be tied to the gallows and flogged. As Queen Ygraine pointed out, they were guests in Winchester. Any Cornishmen who abused their hosts disgraced them all, up to and including their king.

Nimue had some way to go before she reached safety. The lane was narrow and empty, deeply shadowed in the dusk. She heard footsteps behind her. Two men, she decided as she lengthened her stride, with a heavy tread that suggested they carried swords and wore the metal-plated leather armour of foot soldiers. They were walking more quickly now.

Her pulse quickened and her breath came faster. There was no question of the men succeeding in whatever they might intend to do to her. What should she do to stop them though? Killing one meant killing both, as neither could be left alive to tell anyone what they had seen. She had no time to dispose of two corpses, and dead men found so close to the Minster and the palace would cause uproar.

Some innocent might be accused and condemned for the murders, despite their desperate denials. Nimue could not right such a wrong without revealing herself. The thought made her blood run cold. These predators' fates might be well deserved, but a cascade of misfortune would plague her if guiltless men died for crimes they had no part in.

She tucked the small cloth bundle she carried inside her

sleeveless surcote, secured by her enamelled copper belt. With both hands free, Nimue could draw the shadows to her. She forced herself to work the magic slowly. Do this too fast and even the most dull-witted foot soldier would realise something unnatural was happening. Nimue could not risk some later accusation from men she wouldn't even recognise. Such an accusation could be used against Queen Ygraine and, through his wife, against King Gorlois.

Fortunately, her people's powers were strongest at twilight. The shadows thickened obediently, and Nimue reached through the darkness to find a corner tucked out of sight of passers-by. She must judge her moment carefully. She had to be close enough to the end of the lane for her pursuers to believe they had simply lost track of her when they emerged, blinking, into the lingering sunlight that gilded the Minster. She also had to stay far enough ahead that they wouldn't see her disappear.

The lane sloped more steeply downhill. Overhead, the jutting upper storeys of the houses drew closer together. The path narrowed as it skirted the rear corner of a building. That shallow dogleg was sufficient. Nimue gestured to cut an opening in the shadows. Taking a long, swift step, she passed through the darkness.

She emerged in one of the recesses between the chapels and chantries built along the Minster's north wall, where the wealthy dead sought forgiveness for their sins. The sinking sun bathed the far side of the great church in golden light, but she stood in deep shadow.

Nimue breathed more easily once she was sure no priests could see her. She had no quarrel with these devout men or their crucified god, but their blinkered view of the world could not encompass the reality of everything her hidden people could do. In her experience, men were unaccustomed to feeling inferior. Even those who swore vows of humility were apt to lash out when they faced uncomfortable truths.

Hitching up her skirts, she broke into a run. No one would question a maidservant hurrying to do her mistress's bidding, even a mistress as gentle and just as Queen Ygraine. No one ever saw the Cornish queen's ladies with bruised faces or hands scored red by a vengeful strap.

Uther Pendragon's palace lay to the west of the Minster. Its four towers were the only challenge to the majesty of the great church rising high above Winchester's roofs. The two buildings dominated this gravelled space bounded by broad streets on three sides and by the road that ran beneath the town's wall on the fourth.

Nimue passed the dour, square palace with watchful guards high on its battlements. She sought one of the substantial residences that lined the street beyond, built by the wealthy men of Winchester who sought advancement through proximity to their king. She could only imagine their chagrin reading the letters brought by the heralds Uther sent on ahead as he returned from the war in the north. They would have expected invitations to his victory celebrations, not instructions to vacate their luxurious homes to accommodate visiting kings and princes.

Nimue wondered how the wealthy artisans' and merchants' generosity would be repaid. Would it ever be repaid? Uther had no queen to keep track of such obligations and ensure those debts were honoured.

She ran up the outer steps of the long building where the King of Cornwall and his entourage were housed. Inside the tall oak doors, the pillared hall was thronged with men. The Cornish knights had comfortable lodgings around the town, but they preferred to spend their days with their brothers-in-arms, speaking their own tongue.

Nimue felt their eyes on her as she walked towards the dais where the high table stood. The stairs beyond led up to the private chamber above the house's storeroom and kitchen. This was nothing like running the gauntlet of lustful gazes on the streets. These men knew her as Queen Ygraine's trusted servant and would rebuke anyone who showed her disrespect.

At the top of the stairs, the bedchamber door stood ajar. Nimue heard King Gorlois speaking, though she couldn't make out his words. Ygraine's reply was clear enough.

"We will sit through Uther's feast, and we will give thanks to God tomorrow. After that, no one can object when we wish to return home while the last of the summer weather holds. You can say I'm pining for our little daughter. Morgana is very young to be left alone for so long."

Ygraine didn't sound perturbed, but Nimue knew the truth. The queen was devoted to her children, and Morgana was all the more precious now that Morgause and Elaine were so recently married and sent away to their husbands' distant realms. Though Nimue didn't imagine Morgana would be pining for her absent parents. Cornwall's princesses were raised to understand the responsibilities that were the price of their birthright's privilege.

Gorlois laughed. "You are as wise as you are beautiful, beloved. I can endure one last evening of Uther's bragging. Truth be told, we would have left far more dead on the battlefield without his masterful tactics. He has earned the right to crow on his own dunghill."

"The aldermen of Winchester would be hurt to hear you call their town a midden," Ygraine reproved him. "Though, granted, I imagine the streets are cleaner when they're not hosting so many horses."

Gorlois laughed again, and Nimue stepped back as he opened the door. He smiled at her. "That was quick."

Nimue answered him with a curtsey, and he went down the stairs. Cornwall's king was a handsome man, even well into his middle years with grey in his dark hair and beard and a little white at his temples. He was still a vigorous lover, as the discreet sounds of passion from the curtained bed proved while Nimue feigned sleep on her pallet on the floor.

The king was already dressed for the feast, wearing a long tunic rich with embroidery. Gold thread and seed pearls shone bright against the black wool. With his crown, he would look truly regal when he led his knights to Uther's palace.

"What did you find?" Ygraine stood by the window, looking out towards the Minster. The queen's gown was deep red broadcloth embroidered with garlands of golden broom flowers around the neckline, cuffs and hem. A belt of gold links studded with garnets emphasised her slender waist and the curve of her hips. Ten years younger than her husband, Ygraine was strikingly beautiful.

A gold net should draw her coiled braids back from her face, beneath the gauzy veil that her coronet would hold secure. Instead, the queen's long chestnut hair hung loose around her shoulders. The fine linen mesh beneath the gilding had given way in several places. There was no time to get the snood repaired.

"Red silk." Nimue held up the folded cloth.

"That will do." Ygraine sat on the stool at the foot of the curtained bed.

Nimue deftly plaited the vivid ribbons into Ygraine's hair before coiling and pinning the braids to frame the queen's heart-shaped face. She draped the translucent silk veil and positioned the gold coronet that was a more delicate version of Gorlois's crown.

"See to yourself." Ygraine went over to the table and took her pearl and gold earrings from the jewel coffer.

Nimue pulled off the drab surcote and made sure no street filth had stained her own gown's hem. She replaced the kerchief hiding her hair with a fine linen veil. A band of stiffened cloth held that in place, embroidered with pale pink sea thrift, a welcome reminder of Cornwall, where the hardy flowers flourished along the cliffs.

Ygraine grinned at her. "Let's get this over with and go home."

CHAPTER TWO

Nimue followed Ygraine down the stairs. Gorlois was deep in conversation with his knights. They wore elegant tabards of unbleached linen over their long tunics, emblazoned with the black-feathered, scarlet-beaked chough of Cornwall.

A dozen loyal men had accompanied the king, led by Sir Idres. Some had mustered ten foot soldiers from the manors they held, some twenty or more. The rest of Gorlois's force had said farewell high on the great ridge of the downs. While their king headed for Winchester, Sir Gauter led the weary Cornish army homewards along the road that passed Stonehenge.

As they reached the dais, Nimue wrapped Ygraine's cape around her mistress's shoulders and secured the clasp. Gorlois's squire, Melyas, appeared at his master's elbow with the king's black cloak and golden crown. When the boy was satisfied with the drape of the heavy cloth, Gorlois offered his hand to his wife. "Shall we go?"

Ygraine took his arm and they walked towards the door. Melyas and Nimue followed a few paces behind. Nimue glanced at the young squire. Melyas looked as if he would rather face a horde of howling Picts than the ordeal of serving his king in such exalted company.

They walked down the steps outside. Nimue considered telling the boy that no one would even notice him. As long as he didn't drop a full bowl into Gorlois's lap. She decided against saying that. Besides, Melyas wouldn't listen to a woman he assumed was older than his mother.

Nimue contemplated the back of Gorlois's greying head. She needed to find some time alone to borrow Ygraine's polished silver mirror, to assess the white threaded through her own hair and the fine lines she had drawn across her forehead. Older women might be invisible to youths like Melyas, but as Nimue had seen earlier, she could still catch other men's eyes. She didn't want anyone wondering why Ygraine's quiet servant didn't seem to age as fast as her mistress. Her reputation as a skilled herbalist would only go so far.

The Cornish procession skirted the grey stone palace to reach the great entrance facing the Minster. King Ryons of Gwynedd and his knights approached, wearing their kingdom's snarling purple lion with its lashing tongue and extended claws. King Vortepor of Dyfed and his retinue joined them. Dyfed's golden lion reared up on its hind legs, though the golden roses surrounding the beast softened that ferocity.

The men of Gwynedd bowed to Dyfed's raven-haired queen. Like Ygraine, Queen Sevira had received King Uther's invitation carried by his heralds sent by sea. Triumphant, Pendragon had spread word of the Picts' defeat far and wide. Like Ygraine, Dyfed's queen had taken ship for Winchester while the victorious army made its weary way southwards. Nimue had made sure to cross paths with her maidservant. The girl had artlessly confided that Sevira had to see for herself her husband was uninjured, after months of dreading widowhood.

Dyfed's queen was smiling as King Vortepor shared some joke with King Ryons. Short and stocky, dark of hair and eye, the two rulers could be taken for brothers. The Welsh knights saluted the Cornish contingent. Nimue was glad to see their long-standing alliances strengthened by personal bonds forged in the heat of battle.

A handful or more years younger than Gorlois, the Welsh kings deferred to Cornwall. He acknowledged their courtesy with a smile, and led them through the palace gatehouse. Torches blazed in brackets on both sides of the long arched passageway. Dagger-tipped metal gates hung ready to drop at either end. Trapped attackers would be slaughtered by crossbow bolts fired through slots in the walls, or by scalding water poured through holes in the roof. Uther Pendragon was merciless.

Tonight, his palace offered a welcome. The humdrum buildings along the outer wall were shuttered, but storehouse doors opened and closed as servants hurried to and from the great kitchen standing alone on the other side of the castle yard. Vast joints of meat would be roasting on spits in the great hearths while sweating cooks toiled over delicacies simmering on charcoal braziers. Savoury promise floated on the breeze, mingling with the perfume of rose petals scattered across the cobbles and crushed underfoot.

The great hall was easily twice the size of the residences offered to the other kings. The western third held Uther's personal accommodation, reached by a separate stair. The Cornish and Welsh kings headed for the other end of the long building, where double doors stood open as an eagle-eyed steward received his master's guests.

The noise within was deafening as everyone tried to make themselves heard over every other voice. Torches burned on the walls and sturdy candles lit the long tables. Nimue could only be thankful there was no need for a fire in the central hearth, to add the crackle of flames to the cacophony and more heat to the oppressive stuffiness.

The steward snapped his fingers at the underlings wearing Uther's fiery red, comet-tailed dragon on their green tunics. Lackeys bowed low and led the kings and their queens towards the dais. Pages directed the knights to their benches on the floor of the hall.

At the high table, attendants drew out the carved chairs to the right hand of Uther's empty throne so that Ygraine and Gorlois might sit. Seeing Melyas hesitate, Nimue unclasped Ygraine's cape and handed it to the closest Pendragon page. As the young squire followed her lead, his anxious eyes followed the boy carrying Gorlois's cloak away to some unknown peg.

The rest of Uther's guests arrived, and a flurry of activity saw everyone seated. Uther's heralds appeared through the door at the rear of the dais so promptly that someone must have been keeping watch.

A trumpet's flourish silenced every voice but Ygraine's, as she leaned forward to talk to King Lot. The red-headed ruler of Orkney was a lean and muscular man, wearing a purple surcote emblazoned with a double-headed golden eagle. He had been honoured with the chair to the left of Uther's throne.

"Does Morgause need–?" Ygraine realised Uther was waiting to make his entrance. She broke off, blushing with embarrassment. Lot's reassuring gesture promised her they would talk later.

Nimue noticed the crease between Uther's heavy brows as he came through the door and looked to see who had delayed him. His gaze lingered on Ygraine, unreadable, then he acknowledged the cheers from the gathering in the hall. The knights of every kingdom were on their feet. These fighting men knew they owed their lives to Pendragon's mastery of the battlefield. Britain's other kings remained seated, but their applause was no less sincere.

Uther smiled, triumphant. As the raucous applause faded, he walked to his throne. His emerald-green velvet tunic was adorned with the comet-tailed dragon worked in beads of scarlet glass that glittered in the shifting light of the torches and candle flames. Nimue noted the muscles cording his neck, the breadth of his powerful shoulders, and his sturdy thighs. She recalled the tales that praised his stamina as well as his devastating sword skills. Uther didn't leave the risks of warfare to his knights while he watched from afar.

He moved with the vigour of a man revelling in his prime. No hint of grey dulled his tawny-gold hair or beard. His features were strong rather than handsome, though his lips were full and sensual. Nimue couldn't decide if the glint in his dark eyes was arrogance or confidence. She didn't imagine such considerations ever troubled Uther, as long as his authority was unquestioned.

The king's loyal shadow walked unnoticed to stand between Melyas and King Lot of Orkney's squire. The lean man wore a long, unadorned black tunic with no rings on his long fingers nor precious chains around his neck. His pointed beard was clipped as close as his steel-grey hair, and his dark eyes were hooded in his deeply lined face.

Merlin's appearance had not changed as long as Nimue had known him, and that was longer than anyone here would ever guess. She wondered how old Uther's people thought his counsellor might be. She didn't imagine anyone would dare ask, or query why he served the king at table and in his private chambers, taking the place of a squire. His aura of ominous mystery quelled curiosity *very* effectively. As far as everyone in this hall and far beyond was concerned, Merlin's advice was vital for Pendragon's victories, and that was all they needed to know.

Nimue had no quarrel with Merlin cultivating his reputation of a sharp temper and a sharper tongue. Their hidden people each found their own way to avoid outsiders suspecting their magic.

Servants appeared with platters of roast venison and suckling pig. Stewards brought flagons of ale to the tables below and silver jugs of wine to the dais. Talk settled into an amiable hum as men reached for bread and the bowls of pease and vegetables.

As the kings and queens ate and drank, Merlin kept Uther's goblet and bowl filled and was ready with his napkin whenever the king wished to wipe his fingers. Still taut with nervousness, Melyas acquitted himself well enough, though Nimue could see he paid no heed to the conversations around the table. A good squire should be alert for useful gossip or news that his liege might not hear.

Not that she caught anything worthy of note in the tales of recent battles. The assembled kings praised each other's bravery and told the handful of queens how valiantly their husbands had fought. The women dutifully nodded and smiled, saying how proud they were of their beloved lords.

Even so, Nimue noticed Sevira of Dyfed's knuckles pale as she gripped her blue skirt beneath the table. King Ryons of Gwynedd was boasting how his swift action had saved her husband.

"That Pictish axe would have split his skull from crown to chin!"

"I don't believe the blade came that close," King Vortepor protested. "I'll grant the savage might have cut a few inches off my beard."

Lot of Orkney laughed, and King Ryons began an account of his men routing a mob of Picts before the foe could attack Ceredigion's flank.

At the centre of the table, Uther Pendragon ate and drank sparingly, and said little. He nodded and smiled as his allies complimented his tactical skills. Nimue was reminded of a satisfied cat who'd eaten his fill of mice and claimed the warmest spot by the kitchen hearth.

Food appeared in a seemingly inexhaustible procession. When the nobility had eaten what they wanted, the dishes were taken away, some empty, others half full. Nimue knew the town's poor would be gathering at the palace's rear gate, where the feast's leavings would be doled out. She wondered if the beggar with the suppurating stump would have the strength to join them.

Finally, silver baskets of honeyed sweetmeats arrived along with glass bowls of summer's berries shining like jewels in the candlelight. Fresh goblets were filled with pale, fragrant wines brought across the sea by merchants sailing from Brittany's ports. Ygraine waved away the sticky confections, but nodded at the offer of redcurrants and raspberries, and a modest measure of the sweet wine.

Gorlois smiled at his wife. "Do you suppose Elaine has grown used to such treats? Nentres of Garlot must fill his cellar with the choicest vintages carried down the great rivers to the sea."

"As long as he treats her with kindness and courtesy, she would be happy with spring water and plain bread."

Nimue knew Ygraine fretted. A husband's whims and moods could be very different behind closed doors. Elaine's letters seemed content, but those could be written at a husband's dictation. King or commoner, a man's word was law in his own household.

Nimue would remind the queen of King Nentres' visits to Tintagel when he sought alliance with Cornwall. They had agreed he seemed as genuinely well-mannered as he was well-educated. Add to that, before he agreed to Elaine's wedding, Gorlois had sent spies to the other kingdoms of Brittany. They returned without any cause for concern. Hopefully that would reassure Ygraine. It wasn't as if Nimue could tell the queen her scrying spells showed her Elaine was indeed cherished and content.

Uther Pendragon gestured to his herald. The youth raised his gleaming trumpet and the sound silenced every voice. Uther rose to his feet, squaring his shoulders and surveying the gathering with a hawk's merciless gaze. Nimue saw knights across the hall bracing themselves, ready to stand as soon as their host departed.

Then she saw Merlin made no move to draw Uther's heavy wooden throne back so the king could leave the table. The counsellor stood motionless, hidden in the shadows cast by the high-backed, canopied seat.

"Friends!" Uther raised his silver goblet. "You are most welcome! I am honoured to celebrate with you now we have crushed the menace of the Picts."

Loud hurrahs drowned out his words. These knights knew better than to get raucously drunk, but a good few were cheerfully uninhibited. Nimue saw a flash of anger in Uther's eyes. He did not appreciate being interrupted.

The herald raised his trumpet a second time but lowered it at Uther's curt gesture. Knights in the hall hushed their exuberant neighbours.

Uther raised his goblet to salute the assembled kings and the few queens. "As we enter this new era of peace, you have my solemn vow that I will always defend your lands and your people. I swear I will be even-handed as I mediate disputes between you. I will make laws for the good of all, from highest to lowest across these islands. As your high king–"

Lot of Orkney slammed his goblet on the table so hard that the dregs of his wine leaped up to spill over his fingers. "What are you talking about?"

Uther looked down at him. "I led your forces to victory. You told your armies to obey my orders. You yielded–"

"We gave you command of our men on the battlefield." King Lot was a few years older than Uther. He addressed the younger man like an impertinent squire. "You have no authority over our kingdoms now that the fighting is done. Do not presume to claim it."

Uther's voice hardened. "That is not–"

"You are king of Logres." Lot of Orkney's anger rang through the startled silence. "Your rule extends to the borders of Cornwall and of Powys and of Gwent in the west, and to the borders of Lothian and of Strathclyde in the north."

"The Picts would be ransacking Lothian and Strathclyde, and more kingdoms besides, if I had not led our assembled forces to put their realm of Alba to fire and the sword," Uther said, cold. "Who else could have saved you from such relentless foes? Who will you call for the next time you are attacked? Logres can raise an army with ten times the men of any other kingdom in these islands. That alone should command your fealty to me as high king of the Britons."

Nimue saw the other kings looking down at their hands or into their silver goblets. They avoided catching each other's eyes and refused to be drawn into glancing at Uther.

Pendragon went on. "If I am to answer your pleas for help, if I am to know how to muster and feed the forces I lead to save your necks, a single vision must oversee these islands. All the men I command, not only the foot soldiers of Logres, must obey a single voice. Otherwise, when war comes again, as it surely will, you will be left divided and conquered."

King Lot snapped his long fingers at his squire. He took his napkin from the boy and wiped the spilled wine from his hand. Nimue stole a glance at Merlin, hidden in the shadows. She summoned the sight of their people and saw a glint of satisfaction in his eye. Whatever was going on, Nimue realised Merlin was guiding events.

Lot of Orkney looked up at Uther. "Uniting to fight the Picts served the interests of your kingdom, just as we looked after our own. Now the blood shed by men of every realm has secured peace, we can all hope to prosper. We will respect your authority over your lands and people, just as you will respect our rule within our own borders."

He gave Uther no chance to respond. Lot stood and walked to the steps leading down from the dais. His knights with their surcotes emblazoned with Orkney's golden eagle rose from their benches and followed him from the hall.

CHAPTER THREE

Uther's face twisted with mingled disbelief and fury as Merlin drew the heavy throne back with one swift movement. Nimue wondered if anyone had ever noticed the wiry counsellor's inexplicable strength. Merlin followed as Uther stalked to the entrance to his private quarters. As the counsellor reached the door, he looked at Nimue, lightning-fast.

We must talk, tonight. I will set a candle in my window.

He left the hall before Nimue could answer his unspoken summons. Around the high table, the remaining kings wiped their hands and prepared to leave. Ryons of Gwynedd clearly shared Lot of Orkney's outrage, but most of the gathering looked uneasy. The few queens showed no emotion. Their opinions would not be sought and must not be offered. Down in the hall, no sound broke the tense silence.

Pendragon pages brought Ygraine's cape and Gorlois's cloak. The king offered the queen his arm, and they left the dais to rejoin their knights. Nimue saw Cornwall's noblemen were affronted, even insulted, by the notion that their liege lord should swear fealty to Pendragon. Equally outraged, the Scots and Welsh contingents glared at Uther's seated men.

The Cornish king, his queen and his knights returned to their lodging in silence. The men-at-arms were removing the benches and trestle tables to spread straw-filled pallets for the night. As the knights spoke to their liegemen, Nimue heard growls of indignation.

Melyas and Nimue followed Gorlois and Ygraine to their

bedchamber. Still without a word and scowling, Gorlois locked their jewels and crowns in an iron-bound coffer. Squire and maidservant took charge of their master and mistress's fine garments, while the king and queen discarded their sweaty underclothes for fresh linen to sleep in. Gorlois drew the canopied bed's curtains closed before he and Ygraine discussed the evening's events in low murmurs.

Melyas took Gorlois's tunic and cloak to the garderobe, then stripped to his shirt and kicked a wooden wedge under the door to secure it. Yawning, the squire dropped onto his pallet. Nimue had already taken off her rose-coloured gown and was pretending to be asleep in her linen shift.

A little while later, the boy's breathing softened and slowed. Ygraine was already snoring and Gorlois was a heavy sleeper. Nimue got silently to her feet. The keen night sight of her people showed her Melyas sprawled in slumber. Nimue took no chances though, weaving a subtle enchantment to make sure no one would wake until she returned.

She removed the wedge and lifted the door's latch. As she went down the stairs, she drew shadows down from the rafters to pass through the hall unseen in the moonlight falling through the tall windows. A good few knights and foot soldiers were still awake, and their murmured conversations had an ominous edge. Nimue made her way through the restless men as fast as she could, barefoot and silent. She had to talk to Merlin.

An ageing lackey drowsed on a stool by the hall's heavy outer door, one of the household who lived here year-round, while the wealthy merchant came and went. Nimue stooped to whisper in the old man's ear. His eyes opened, unseeing, and he rose to his feet. Thankfully the heavy latch was well-oiled, and he opened the door with barely a rattle.

The man staggered back to his stool and Nimue released him from the enchantment. Her heart pounded as she used the wedge she had brought with her to make sure the door stayed open a crack. Using magic to influence mortals wasn't forbidden to her people, but only the greatest necessity justified such assault, so those who had taught her insisted.

She hurried down the steps with the shadows wrapped tight around her as she approached the palace. Nimue didn't walk around to the daunting entrance where guards would still be wakeful. Instead, she wove enchantment into footholds like stepping-stones in a river, rising through the swirling night air. She used as little magic as possible, letting the breeze scatter the path like mist behind her as she made her way up and over the battlements.

A light shone in an unshuttered window on the topmost floor of Uther Pendragon's residence. That must be Merlin's chamber. Nimue's magic carried her there, and she hooked her arm around the central stone mullion to ease the demand on her magic. She must reserve enough enchantment to leave by the same route, and to get back to the Cornish king's bedchamber unseen.

"Merlin!" She hoped her low voice wouldn't reach some sentry patrolling the battlements.

The counsellor appeared, seeing through her concealing enchantment. "Your magic grows weak," he commented. "You should use your skills, or they will wither away."

"Move that candlestick." Nimue twisted to thread her feet through the narrow window and squeezed through at the cost of several painful scrapes. She let the shadows she'd gathered fall away as Merlin crossed to a table where a jug and several goblets waited. The gleaming silver was the only touch of luxury in this austere chamber. No tapestries softened the bare stone walls, and his bed was a thin pallet on a narrow wooden frame. An open chest held tightly packed books. Other coffers kept their secrets hidden.

"Wine?"

"No, thank you," Nimue said, impatient. "What does Uther think he is doing? Why are you encouraging him?"

She knew Merlin would have found some way to dissuade the king if this plan didn't serve his purposes. Did those purposes serve their hidden people?

A fist hammered on the door.

"Merlin!" Uther's bellow was unmistakable.

The counsellor gestured towards the garderobe. Chilled with fear, Nimue hurried to hide. If Uther saw her, she could not explain how she had got into the palace unseen, even if she wasn't recognised as Ygraine of Cornwall's maid. As soon as she was identified, she would most likely be accused of spying, or of sneaking into Merlin's chamber to seduce Uther's trusted servant.

She heard Merlin open the door. Her mouth was dry, and she wished she had accepted that offer of wine.

"My king." Merlin greeted him, deferential.

"You said they would fall into line," Uther spat.

Merlin was unperturbed. "I didn't say *when*."

"Don't play the fool with me," snarled the king.

"These things take time," Merlin said calmly. "Now we know where resistance lies, we can plan our next steps."

"What steps?" Uther demanded.

"A more subtle approach."

Merlin came so close to rebuking Uther that Nimue wondered whose idea that speech at the feast had been.

"You must persuade Gorlois of Cornwall that swearing fealty to a high king of Britain is the wisest and safest course for his realm. The other kings respect him for his many years of wise rule. He is Orkney's most trusted ally, more so now that Lot has married his eldest daughter. If you win over Gorlois the rest will follow."

"If," Uther said ominously.

"Show some humility and it should be simple enough," Merlin retorted. "Convince Gorlois that you will be the guardian of these isles, not some tyrant. Remind him that the Picts may be defeated now, but Alba is a vast realm. Your foes may be licking their wounds, but not all will die from fever. They *will* come down from the mountains again and his beloved daughter will be in grave danger as soon as the Picts attack Orkney. His first grandchild too, if the rumours are true. Gorlois will want Britain's armies to march to Orkney's aid under your proven leadership. He can guarantee that by acknowledging Logres' suzerainty. It will make no difference to his rule over Cornwall."

"Lot of Orkney is to have an heir?" The jealous edge to Uther's voice made Nimue uneasy.

"If Morgause bears a boy," said Merlin. "If not, she will doubtless be pregnant again soon. The girl will likely be as fertile as her mother."

How did Merlin know Morgause was pregnant? The young queen of Orkney hadn't even told her parents, not until those first perilous months were past and she felt the baby quicken. Then Ygraine would seek Nimue's advice on strengthening herbs to safeguard the unborn child.

"Gorlois has no son," Uther said sourly. "If a grandson of Orkney inherits Cornwall as well as his father's realm, that kingdom will rival Logres."

"Then you must win Gorlois over, so he will persuade Lot to swear fealty to you." Merlin was relentless. "The rest will follow his lead."

"They had better," Uther growled, "or I'll know your prophecy's worthless."

Nimue heard the door slam.

When Merlin appeared in the garderobe passageway, she challenged him. "What have you shown Uther of the future?"

"Nothing that a wise man could not foresee without enchantment to call on." Merlin crossed the room to look for something in his chest of books.

"But you have been using magic to look to the future." Nimue was certain.

Merlin rounded on her. "Why haven't you? Why are you

so afraid to use your skills? These wars between mortal kings
don't only threaten mortal realms. There is still wild sorcery
of wood and water, of metal and stone throughout these isles.
The hidden folk may have united to drive out the giants who
laid waste to this land, but you know how many of our people
resented being forced into hiding when the mortals reached
these isles."

"It was agreed–"

"Yielding is not agreement, and times change, even for the
long-lived. Our people see mortals suffer year after year as
constant warfare destroys their crops and herds. Some pity
them and say we should put an end to such strife. Others
see their weakness and long to seize this chance to regain
dominion over these islands. Use your magic to look beyond
your comfortable corner and you will see such dangers."

Merlin's words stung. Nimue felt her face redden. "I play
my part–"

"Do more. Convince Gorlois to swear fealty to Uther.
Persuade Ygraine this is the wisest course, for her daughters'
sakes and for their children to come. Convince her to use her
wiles in bed, to whisper in Gorlois's ear once she has satisfied
his desires."

"Why is this so important?" Nimue demanded. "What have
you foreseen?"

Merlin shrugged as he poured himself some wine. "You
know as well as I do that the future is as hard to read as a river
in flood."

"Which is why we are warned against trying to stem the
waters or heaving rocks into the stream to divert it. That's
what you're trying to do, isn't it?"

"You don't think his successes in battle have inspired Uther's
ambitions?" Merlin's hooded eyes were deeply shadowed. "If
I have seen a brighter future for these islands, why shouldn't I
offer advice to further the cause of peace?"

Nimue shook her head. "We cannot use enchantment to

advance a mortal's cause, however noble their intentions. Such interventions never end well."

"So we have always been taught." Merlin took a drink and gazed blandly at her over his goblet's silver rim. "Can we not test such assertions for ourselves?"

Nimue shivered, uneasy. The night was growing colder too. "What will you do, if Gorlois cannot be persuaded? If Lot of Orkney will not yield?"

"We will find another argument. Uther is destined to be high king of Britain. Scry the future for yourself."

"That still doesn't mean we should meddle," Nimue snapped.

"Then persuade Ygraine to persuade Gorlois – for all our sakes." Merlin's command turned into entreaty.

Nimue refused to be drawn. "I must go."

"Let me help you." He carried the room's single stool over to the window.

As Nimue climbed out, she felt their enchantments mingle. She realised how much stronger Merlin's magic was than her own as the obedient shadows hid her once again. Was he right? Did greater power come from working more enchantments?

This unseen pathway beneath her feet was as solid and continuous as a bridge, carrying her high over the palace wall. That support fell away as soon as the wall blocked Merlin's view of her. Nimue had to summon her magic quickly to get safely to the ground. As she hurried back to the Cornish lodging, she felt the last of her power ebb away. The door lackey was shifting on his stool as she stooped to pull out the wedge and slipped back inside. She dropped the heavy latch, but she didn't dare delay to drive the heavy bolts home. She could only hope the man would think he'd forgotten them and be too ashamed to admit his lapse for fear of a flogging.

If the man was caught out and whipped, Nimue's teachers had told her she would pay her own penalty in threefold misfortune, whether that was falling on the stairs, slipping on a wet flagstone, or being scorched by some flare of the hearth.

What calamity was Merlin risking, if he was using his magic to further Uther Pendragon's aims?

Debating that would have to wait until morning. Nimue was exhausted. She made her way through the drowsing men and up the stairs. Inside the bedchamber, she secured the door with the wedge and dropped onto her pallet. Sleep overwhelmed her.

CHAPTER FOUR

A hand seizing her shoulder startled Nimue out of a deep sleep. Instinctive magic kindled beneath her breastbone. She quelled it and opened her eyes.

"Wake up." Melyas was already washed and dressed.

She knocked his hand away, a little harder than the lad deserved. Gorlois and Ygraine were talking quietly behind their bed curtains, and the daylight through the unshuttered window was already bright. "Why didn't you wake me earlier?"

"I tried," the boy retorted.

Nimue reached for her gown, draped across the stool. "Is there water in the ewer?"

"Some." Melyas stood up. "I'm going to the kitchen."

Nimue stifled the urge to remind the squire she had to wake him four days out of five. As she struggled to her feet and headed for the washstand, her head ached and her dry mouth tasted foul. She emptied the tall jug into the wash basin. The water was cold, but that was welcome as she washed her unpleasantly sticky eyes.

Gorlois and Ygraine were still talking. The king didn't sound so cross and Ygraine was calm and reasonable. It seemed they were in agreement. But what had they agreed?

Nimue emptied the basin into the slop bowl and tossed in the linen cloth she had used as a towel. Dragging her gown over her head, she decided stockings could wait. She shoved her feet into her soft leather shoes and fastened her fiddly front buttons as she headed for the door.

Down in the great hall, barely half the trestle tables were set up for the day, and the floor was cluttered with men still in their blankets. As Nimue reached the dais, she saw one unfortunate mercilessly roused with a bucket of water. The hall was rank with musky odours, and her stomach roiled as she opened the door to the kitchen.

The scent of freshly baked bread was soothing. Melyas held a tray with a basket of fine white rolls nestling in linen, a plate of sliced beef and a dish of dark red preserves. He nodded at the table. "You can bring the ale."

Nimue picked up the heavy flagon and the horn cups. As they walked out on the dais, Melyas glanced at the soldiers down in the hall. "That lot can thank too much ale and wine last night for their thick heads this morning. What's your excuse?"

For one heart-stopping moment, Nimue thought he knew she had left the bedchamber. Then she realised Melyas would have roused a hue and cry if he had woken to find her gone, if only to save his own skin. Did he think she had somehow drunk herself tipsy while she had been serving Ygraine? Nimue decided she didn't care.

"Their graces will be wondering where we are." She led the way up the stairs.

In the bedchamber, King Gorlois stood by the window, gazing across Winchester's thatched roofs. Queen Ygraine sat in the bed, with the curtains drawn back.

"Ah, good, breakfast." Gorlois smiled before nodding at his squire. "Hot water for washing, as quick as you can."

Melyas set the tray on the table. Before Nimue realised what he was doing, he took the flagon of weak ale and the cups from her. "As quick as you can. I'll serve their graces."

Nimue glanced at the bed. Ygraine met her gaze with the slightest of nods. Nimue curtsied to the king. "By all means, your grace."

She went back down the stairs. Ygraine would find an

opportune moment to remind the boy it wasn't his place to give orders to her maid.

Urgent bustle down in the hall drove such thoughts out of her head. Knights clapped their hands to hurry men setting up the last few tables. The old servant who guarded the door was climbing the steps to the dais, clutching a letter.

"From Pendragon, for Cornwall's king." He thrust a sealed scrap of vellum at her.

The man's lip was swollen and split, and his cheek showed the mark of a heavy blow. Someone must have found the outer door unbolted. Nimue guessed this vile headache was the price she must pay for the suffering she had caused.

"Thank you." She took the letter straight to Gorlois. "King Uther sends word."

Gorlois wiped his hands on a napkin, took the letter and cracked the wax seal. He scanned the few lines and looked at Ygraine propped against her pillows, eating a bread roll spread with honeyed fruit.

"We are to be honoured with a visit – at any moment."

Ygraine crammed the last bite into her mouth. "Melyas, hot water, now!"

By the time the boy came back with two heavy, steaming jugs, Gorlois and his queen had finished their hasty meal while Nimue laid out their clothes and jewels.

The king was dressed before Nimue finished brushing out Ygraine's night plait. "You may join us downstairs when you are ready, my love. There's no need to hurry."

Ygraine was surprised. "You don't want to receive Uther here in private?"

"Whatever he has to say to me, he can say it in front of my men."

Nimue saw the glint in the king's eye. As she braided her mistress's hair, she wondered if Uther had taken Merlin's words last night to heart.

"Have you had any breakfast?" Ygraine asked her.

"Me? No, your grace." Nimue fetched a fine linen veil and the enamelled silver band to hold it secure. The blue flowers and green leaves complemented the blue of the queen's gown and the green of her belt.

"Eat something." Ygraine walked over to open the door to the staircase.

They could hear masculine voices below, but Nimue couldn't make out the words. The mere thought of using magic to eavesdrop on the kings' conversation made her nauseous. She went to fetch a small vial from the chest that held her remedies for hurts and ailments, emptied it into her ale and drank it down. Her headache and queasiness receded. At least some of her talents were useful this morning.

The voices below grew louder. Ygraine looked at Nimue. "We had better go down. As soon as Uther takes his leave, start packing. The king intends to be on the road home today."

"Yes, your grace." Nimue twisted her own hair into a knot and snatched up her veil as she followed Ygraine out of the room.

In the hall, all eyes were on Gorlois and Uther, sitting at one end of the long oak table seemingly relaxed in high-backed chairs. Melyas had fetched wine and cakes from the kitchen and Nimue was relieved to see the disarray in the hall had been cleared. King Uther's escort sat with a handful of Cornish knights drinking ale.

Ygraine approached the two kings. Uther was talking with the stubborn expression of a man repeating himself. He was clearly used to getting his own way. Who in this realm would stand against him?

"Lot of Orkney must agree that swearing fealty to a high king will safeguard his kingdom. Surely you can persuade him. He has always respected you, even before he married your daughter."

Uther showed none of the deference that Merlin had advised. His tone was somewhere between giving Gorlois orders and chastising an underling.

"The Picts will regroup in hidden strongholds. They *will* return to the fight and sooner than Lot of Orkney expects. Do you trust him to keep your daughter safe? Are you willing to gamble with her life? With the lives of any children she bears?"

Nimue saw no hint in Uther's face that he knew Morgause was pregnant. So, Pendragon was an accomplished liar.

"My lord. Your grace." Ygraine picked up the wine jug and topped up Gorlois's goblet and then Uther's. "Are the honey cakes not to your taste? Shall I send for something else?"

Nimue had seen Gorlois's weathered hand tighten on the armrest of his chair. He relaxed his grip and whatever harsh rebuke Ygraine had feared for Uther went unsaid.

"No, thank you, dear heart. We need nothing more."

Uther wasn't looking at Gorlois. His hawk's eyes fixed on Ygraine, unblinking. Nimue's mistrust of Logres' king deepened.

Uther's fist clenched as if he wanted to pound the polished oak as he addressed Gorlois. "Unity under resolute leadership will deter the Picts or anyone else who might attack from overseas. Logres is the largest kingdom in these isles. No other realm has the resources to take up this role – this duty. You simply agree to obey a high king in time of war. Your rule over your kingdom remains absolute, as long as peace lasts." He reached for his wine and drank it down.

Gorlois left his goblet untouched. "I have told you. I will not agree to this proposal. Now, if you will excuse me, we will be taking the road home today."

He rose from his chair and offered his arm to Ygraine. She managed the briefest of curtseys to Uther before Gorlois drew her away.

Nimue saw an instant of fury blaze in Pendragon's eyes. That was a third warning, she noted. The hidden people had learned long ago to heed any sign repeated threefold.

She followed the Cornish king and queen up the stairs as Uther and his men strode towards the great door. Pendragon's shoulders were stiff with irritation.

"The sooner we're on our way home, the better." Gorlois waved a hand at Melyas as they reached the bedchamber. "See to things here. I must speak to Sir Idres."

"My cloak, if you please. The grey one." The queen gestured at the garderobe door as the king left the room.

"Your grace?" Nimue fetched the lightweight wrap.

Ygraine looked at Melyas as Nimue draped the soft wool around her shoulders. "If my husband returns before me, tell him I have gone to bid farewell to Sevira of Dyfed."

Nimue donned her own cloak and followed her mistress. Down in the hall, Gorlois and Sir Idres were nowhere to be seen. They must have gone to alert the other Cornish knights billeted with their men around Winchester. Gorlois wouldn't entrust his thoughts on Uther's visit to writing which might be retrieved and read by unfriendly eyes. Vellum was hard to ignite and slow to burn, and few fires were lit outside kitchens in the heat of summer. Ygraine would carry word to Dyfed's queen. Sevira would share this news discreetly and the other royal women of Wales would tell their husbands in the privacy of their marriage beds.

The summer sun was strong, though a breeze softened the gathering heat. Ygraine took the path past Uther's palace, walking fast towards the street to the east of the Minster where the Welsh kings were lodged. Nimue wondered if Uther had hoped to stop the kings of Britain uniting against his plan if he kept them inconveniently far apart. Then she wondered if that been his scheme, or Merlin's?

"Your grace, are you going to pray?"

Ygraine spun around, disconcerted to hear Uther close behind them. "Your grace? No." She swiftly recovered her poise. "I am merely taking some air."

"Then let me escort you." Uther didn't let Ygraine reply before he took her hand and tucked it under his elbow.

Unable to free herself without insulting him, she forced a demure smile. "Your grace must have far more important duties."

Uther smiled like a man who had won his throw of the dice. "This is a pleasure, believe me."

He started walking. Ygraine had to go with him. The two men-at-arms looked at Nimue, unsmiling. One gestured, ordering her to follow her mistress.

She did so, her face expressionless. Inside, she was seething. *How dare these men–*

Then she saw Uther had steered Ygraine off the main path, taking the fork that led to the Minster.

"You would be well advised to spend some time in prayer." Uther spoke like a kindly father rebuking a daughter. "Let us both beseech God to grant your husband the wisdom to do what is best for Cornwall and for Britain."

Ygraine's back stiffened. Uther went on.

"The sooner he comes to his senses, the better. For your daughter Morgause most of all. You must agree. You are as astute as you are beautiful."

Ygraine didn't reply. She tried to ease her hand free, but Uther clamped his arm to his side. The queen would have to fight to get away.

They walked onward. Nimue's anger burned hotter, but Ygraine would have to continue this charade. Still, Uther would have no excuse to detain them once he had said his prayers. He couldn't force Ygraine to say amen to whatever he declared either, not in front of the priests. They drew closer to the Minster. Nimue heard the monks chanting within the looming stone walls.

"Well, your grace?" There was no pretence of good humour now. Uther's face was hard as he released Ygraine's hand. "Will you be sensible and persuade your husband to acknowledge me as high king? What must I do to convince you?"

Ygraine still didn't answer. Uther grabbed the queen's shoulder.

"I will have an answer." He tightened his grip and shook her.

Ygraine yelped, astonished. "Let me go!"

Uther shoved her off the path, forcing her along the south face of the minster. Chapels and chantries jutted out from the ancient masonry here as well. He pushed Ygraine out of sight, ignoring her protests.

Nimue drew a deep breath to shout for help. Let Uther explain himself to the pious priests. Those who worshipped the crucified god might believe women should be silent and obedient, but that didn't mean men could do whatever they wanted without consequences.

A heavy blow struck her between the shoulder blades, sending her staggering forwards. Before she could recover, Uther's soldiers seized her arms and dragged her after the queen.

Uther had forced Ygraine back against the lichen-spotted masonry. His hand was braced beside her shoulder, his muscular arm blocking her escape. He leaned close and Ygraine shrank away as Uther's lips brushed her cheek with an unwanted kiss. Pendragon closed his eyes as he inhaled Ygraine's perfume like a starving man offered a meal.

Nimue glared at the men who held her. One had his free hand on his sword hilt and his hot eyes dared her to try intervening to save Ygraine. The other man turned his back, standing guard at the entrance to this hidden space. He would never know what had hit him if Nimue chose to snuff out his life. She could kill them both as easily as quenching a candle.

Could she kill the king, to keep her magic secret? What would the consequences be for her, for Logres and the other realms? What had Merlin seen of Britain's future, that kept him so loyal to Uther? What part had he played in Uther crossing their path just now? Uncertainty held her back, for fear of making this perilous situation worse.

Uther caught Ygraine's chin with his free hand, forcing her to meet his gaze. "Leave that old dotard to his follies and I will crown you as my high queen. I long to take you to my bed. Let me make love to you with vigour that you can never have known. You need only say the word and I am yours to command."

He looked down. His finger brushed the silver clasp fastening her cloak. For one horrifying moment, Nimue thought he was going to cup his hand around the queen's breast. Ygraine's frozen pallor showed she feared the same.

Uther smiled, and stroked Ygraine's flank to rest his palm on her hip. He stepped closer still. Ygraine's eyes widened. So did Uther's wolfish grin. Nimue could tell her mistress felt Pendragon's erect manhood pressing against her thigh.

She clenched her jaw so hard that her teeth ached. She could whisk herself and Ygraine out of this trap in the blink of an eye. Her enchantments could hurl Uther and his men to the ground. But she couldn't burden Cornwall's queen with her secret. She couldn't throw Winchester and the whole realm of Logres into chaos. Merlin might be reckless with his magic, but Nimue kept to their people's customs. She wouldn't give those who resented mortal men any excuse to torment innocents with wild sorcery.

Scarlet-faced, Ygraine shoved Uther's chest. Caught unawares, he took a pace backwards. Ygraine slapped his face with a blow as loud as a whip-crack.

"Let me go!" Tears of fury spilled from her eyes.

"By all means, your grace." Uther stepped further back, smiling as he raised his hands high and wide.

His warriors withdrew. Ygraine reached for Nimue's hand, and they hurried away.

"Which way, your grace?" Unease ran up and down her spine like fleas from a verminous cloak. She fought the urge to look over her shoulder in case rough hands reached for them again.

Ygraine's voice shook. "Back to the lodging."

Nimue's fears faded as they walked away, but she saw curious glances from men and women crisscrossing the space between the Minster and the palace.

"A moment, your grace." She steered Ygraine into the shelter of a stone buttress and stripped off the queen's veil. The pale linen was dirty and scuffed by the stonework. She handed Ygraine the enamelled circlet and bundled up the cloth. "Please turn around, your grace."

As Ygraine did so, Nimue used the soiled veil to brush flakes of lichen and nameless smudges from her dove-grey cloak. She pulled off her embroidered headband and set her own veil on the queen's head.

"I can do this." Ygraine secured her circlet while Nimue tied up her own hair in the grubby linen. She would look more like a peasant than a royal servant, but that was better than going bareheaded like a whore. What mattered was foiling gossip spawned by passers-by seeing Ygraine dishevelled.

"Ready?" Ygraine drew a resolute breath.

Nimue nodded. "Let's go."

The women walked back to the lodging. When they reached the stone steps, Ygraine turned to Nimue.

"Go and tell Sevira of Dyfed we are leaving today. Tell her what Uther said to Gorlois – but not the rest. Not yet."

The queen plucked at her skirts and ran up the steps to safety.

CHAPTER FIVE

Nimue looked at the lofty wall ringing Uther's palace. She walked towards the smaller rear gate, where servants came and went, where the town's beggars were fed, and where Uther's men would sally forth if anyone attacked the main entrance. She would take Ygraine's message to Sevira, but there was something she had to do first.

A guard watched people passing in and out. Evidently, he knew their faces. He raised a hand as Nimue approached. "What's your business here?"

"I am Nimue, attendant to the queen of Cornwall. I need to see Master Merlin. Send word to him if you wish. I'll wait."

Nimue's expression must have warned the man not to challenge her. He looked around, raising his fingers to whistle for a page boy. He coughed as he swallowed the sound. "Here's the counsellor now."

Merlin came striding across the cobbles. "Let her through!"

Nimue pushed past the soldier. Now she could see Merlin, they could talk mind to mind.

So, you saw what happened. Were you keeping a watchful eye on Uther, or are you spying on Queen Ygraine?

Merlin answered her with a penetrating gaze.

Not here. We need privacy.

Nimue nodded. She followed Merlin until she realised they were heading for Uther's apartments. Her throat tightened at the thought of coming face to face with him or his men.

Where is he?

Elsewhere.

Merlin went up the stone steps. Nimue followed him inside to a small hall with tapestries on the walls and an oak table ringed by high-backed chairs. A dozen heavily annotated maps were scattered across the polished wood. Stools flanked a hearth swept bare for the summer.

Merlin ignored the broad staircase and opened a door in a wood-panelled wall. Nimue followed him into a library that few kings or monasteries could equal. There must be a hundred books, maybe more. Some rested on sloping shelves beneath the window, where a couple lay open to be read. More were stacked flat underneath. All were secured with an iron bar threaded through the ends of their chains and fastened with a lock at either end. Nimue didn't doubt those locks needed different keys. Uther assuredly kept one and she guessed Merlin held the other. Who else did Pendragon trust?

The counsellor waved a hand and subtle heaviness in the air told Nimue that no one would hear their voices beyond this room.

"How long has Uther lusted after Ygraine?" she demanded.

Merlin shrugged. "She caught his eye at the victory feast."

"Then find him a willing whore or a biddable wife of noble birth to give him sons." Nimue glared at him. "So, were you scrying after Uther or Ygraine?"

Merlin scowled, deepening the furrow between his steely brows. "I was watching Uther. He has many talents, but subtlety isn't one."

"What was he thinking, waylaying her like that? He needs to learn he can't always get his way. You need to teach him."

"That's no easy task." Merlin waved that away. "You must convince Ygraine to keep her mouth shut, to keep the peace. Uther never meant to insult her. She should be flattered by his ardour."

"Only a man could say that," Nimue said with contempt.

"How many women has he forced because they were too scared to say no?"

Merlin didn't answer that. "I will try to persuade him to apologise. Let that be the end of the matter. Uther is too important to Britain for some quarrel over a woman to divide him from his allies. For all his faults, he is the best hope for a peaceful future. I have foreseen it."

"You said the future is as hard to read as a river in flood." Nimue threw Merlin's words back at him. "Why entrust Britain's fate to one man who lets his passions rule him? An alliance between the kingdoms would surely serve far better? Persuade Uther to bring his fellow rulers together as equals in a council. They can debate–"

"Debate on a battlefield gets everyone's throat cut," Merlin said, scornful.

"What if someone cuts Uther's throat?" Nimue retorted. "An outraged husband perhaps? What if an arrow skewers him in some melee? You risk Britain's fate on one throw of the dice. Pendragon has no sons, nor a daughter whose husband might rule. He has no acknowledged heir. If he dies, *when* he dies, the lords of Logres will rip this realm apart as they fight to claim the crown. Our kindred who resent these violent upheavals and those who long to rid these islands of mortals will seize their chance in such chaos. If there must be a high king of Britain, let him be a man with a dynasty to follow him."

"Uther has no equal as leader in time of war." Merlin shook his head, stubborn. "Those who might attack must see that, whether they come sailing from overseas or venturing out of the hidden places. Convince Gorlois to let Pendragon have his title if you want to see peace in these isles. Uther will listen to his elders and allies. I will see to that."

Merlin went over to the window, using one long, bony finger to turn the pages of a book that lay open on the shelf. He was avoiding her gaze, Nimue realised. He had his own doubts about Uther.

"I must go. My mistress sent me to tell Queen Sevira the Cornish are leaving today."

Merlin looked at her. "And–?"

"And to tell her Gorlois will not agree to Uther's demands. Don't worry," she added sourly. "I shan't tell her your master laid rough hands on my queen, for Ygraine's sake, not for his."

She didn't wait for Merlin to answer, turning to leave the library. Outside, to her relief, no one challenged her presence within these walls. As she left through the main palace gate, the guards only questioned people coming in. Nimue made her way swiftly to the Dyfed royal residence. She was escorted to the private chamber where Sevira and her maidservant sat by the window working on their embroidery. Nimue delivered her message.

The queen of Dyfed nodded. "Please tell Queen Ygraine I will be sorry not to spend more time with her, though I understand her eagerness to return to her child." Sevira smiled. "Let your mistress and your king know it will be our pleasure to welcome the princess Morgana too, if their graces of Cornwall wish to visit us before the autumn winds make the sea crossing unwise. Or they might come in the spring?"

"I will tell her, your grace." Nimue curtsied.

Sevira waved her away, and Nimue walked briskly back across the Minster precinct, keeping a sharp eye open for Uther or his two men. Meantime, she considered Sevira's needlework. The sturdy linen had looked like swaddling to Nimue. The queen of Dyfed couldn't know if she was pregnant yet, but she must be hoping her reunion with King Vortepor would be blessed with a baby.

Nimue frowned as she passed Uther's palace. Pendragon had no queen, so he had no legitimate children, and he'd sired no bastards either, as far as anyone knew. Some cowards refused to acknowledge such offspring, to placate the crucified god's priests, but there had never been a whisper of a woman leaving Uther's court to conceal such a secret. Was he even capable of fathering a child? One coupling could be all it took, as hapless maidens discovered. She should have pressed Merlin harder about Uther's lack of an heir.

Outside the hall where the Cornish contingent were lodged, she saw every knight and man-at-arms had arrived. Horses, pack-mules and carts filled the road and shouted orders cut through the murmur of conversation. Nimue hurried into the hall and up to the king and queen's chamber. Ygraine and Gorlois were nowhere to be seen. Cloaks, gowns and tunics were heaped on the bed while a basket of freshly laundered under-linen stood on the table. The royal travelling chests gaped empty as Melyas dithered amid the chaos.

"You look like the donkey who starved to death because it couldn't choose between two bales of hay," Nimue said caustically.

Melyas stared at her, wide-eyed. "Did Uther really lay rough hands on our queen?"

"Where did you hear that?" Nimue demanded.

"King Gorlois told the whole household. Uther accosted our queen, to browbeat her into taking his side. He would not let her go on her way, seizing her arm to force her to hear him out. You were there. Is it true?"

"Do you question our queen's word?" Nimue rebuked him.

Ygraine would have told Gorlois the whole revolting story. There were no secrets between them. It didn't surprise Nimue that the king had chosen to share this pared-down version though. As Melyas had shown, some men always doubted a woman.

"Look lively!" She clapped her hands as the boy flushed with anger, embarrassment, or both. "Must I do your work as well as my own?"

Melyas began packing. In less time than Nimue had feared, the royal luggage was carried down the stairs to the waiting carts. She seized her chance to put on woollen stockings and boots for riding. Melyas went on ahead, weighed down with a jewel coffer under each arm. Nimue followed with her own bag and her chest of herbs and tinctures. Outside the empty, echoing hall, Melyas headed for the carriage where he and the king's jewels would be guarded until they reached Tintagel. Nimue didn't envy the boy the jolts from every rut and stone in the road. Cornwall's king and queen were already on horseback, surrounded by armoured knights.

"Mistress!" Sir Idres led over a palfrey, saddled and bridled, so Nimue could ride behind Ygraine. He held the placid animal steady while Nimue secured her bag to the saddle and mounted.

Satisfied that everyone was ready, King Gorlois nodded. Sir Idres raised his hand and Cornwall's herald blew his horn. The column of men and beasts began to move.

Nimue wondered if Merlin had foreseen this.

CHAPTER SIX

At Tintagel, the sea was ever present. Even in the calmest weather, the waves were heard lapping against the rocky walls of the harbours on either side of the headland while gulls soared high above with their thin, mewing cries. When the storms swept in, the crash of the surf fought with the roar of the gales that rattled shutters and slammed doors snatched from unwary hands.

Today, the skies were clear. The morning had been fresh with a hint of autumn, though the trees along the coast were still densely leaved and green. Now the afternoon sun turned golden and Ygraine's sheltered garden was warm and fragrant with flowers, herbs and fruit. The brambles allowed to claim one wall were heavy with blackberries and Nimue gathered the day's bounty. Ygraine was tending her beloved roses as the last blooms faded.

Gorlois strode through the arch, looking thunderous. Nimue looked for Melyas, but the boy was nowhere to be seen. Gorlois had something to tell Ygraine which he did not want to become castle gossip. Melyas was never knowingly indiscreet, but he could be careless.

"My lord?" Concerned, Ygraine tossed her pruning knife into the basket of dead roses.

"Sit with me, beloved." Gorlois walked to the bench on the far side of the garden.

Nimue continued picking the blackest berries to fill the red-glazed bowl cradled in the crook of her arm. A simple magic carried Gorlois's words to her ears. Not that he was likely to object if she had been within earshot. Both king and queen trusted her discretion.

"Uther's army has crossed the Tamar." The king vented his fury with a wordless growl.

Nimue knew Sir Idres's scouts had been tracking Uther's army since it had become clear this was no peaceful progress along Logres' southern coast to reward his knights for their courage in the war with the Picts.

"He truly means to attack us?" Ygraine's voice shook. "Cornwall has done nothing to offend Logres. It was Uther who insulted–" She bit off the rest of that sentence.

"Uther has lied to his knights, and they have shared his falsehoods with their liegemen," Gorlois said with cold precision. "He claims you sought his protection from my violent tyranny. Allegedly mindful of the church's teaching, Uther did not think he should come between a husband and his wife. It was only after I dragged you from Winchester that he repented of his hasty decision. A man whose wife goes in fear of him has broken his sacred vows to love and honour her, so he says."

The king didn't hide his contempt. Nimue shared it, though she didn't imagine Uther had crafted such deceit. This reeked of Merlin's conniving.

"He said what?" Ygraine was blank-faced with astonishment.

"His army believes they are marching to your rescue." Something undercut Gorlois's exasperation. Not fear, not yet. Frustration, that was it.

Nimue contemplated the tangled bramble thicket. Evil rumours were like the spiteful tendrils that crept through the garden's flowers and shrubs. Low to the ground, wiry stems spread unseen until someone caught their foot or snagged an unwary sleeve. The tips of tiny thorns would break off as they brushed a wrist or forearm. Nimue would see where they had pierced the skin, when their victim came to her for a salve to quell the redness and itching. Gorlois knew Uther's claims would be nigh on impossible to stamp out. His insidious lies would fester like filth in an untended graze.

"This is intolerable." Now Ygraine was angry. "I must–"

"Whatever you say will be dismissed, dear heart." Gorlois reached for her hand. "Uther and his henchmen will say I have forced you to defend me. That you dare not defy me, for fear that I will cast you aside and you will lose Morgana."

Nimue guessed Gorlois's spy had told him this was already being said. Merlin was cunning enough to foresee Ygraine's protests.

"How can we throw these lies back in Uther's face?" she demanded.

"I will muster Cornwall's army and meet him," Gorlois said bluntly. "Pendragon has led an armed host across my border without my leave. I will insist he departs and swiftly. He will soon learn that every Cornish hand will be raised against him if he tries to advance. With luck, he will realise he has overreached and retreat without any bloodshed."

Nimue continued to pick plump blackberries. She didn't imagine Merlin was leaving anything to luck.

Ygraine had her doubts too. "What if his price for peace is you swearing fealty to him as high king?"

Gorlois shook his head. "I will not yield to his bullying, and I will send trusted messengers by sea to the Scots, the Welsh and the Irish to tell them what Uther is doing before I march."

"He must know this will turn every kingdom against him," Ygraine cried. "This proves Lot of Orkney was right. It is utter folly."

"Whatever else Uther may be, he isn't stupid." For the first time, Gorlois's wrinkles deepened to betray his age. "It's not too late in the year to fight, if he can force us into a battle, but with autumn nigh, our allies cannot march to our aid without risk of getting bogged down on the roads. They certainly can't chance the seas with ships carrying men and horses." Gorlois heaved a sigh. "The sooner we march, the sooner we can send Pendragon back across the Tamar with his tail between his legs. I must be on the road before sunset, dearest."

He kissed Ygraine and departed. The queen sat watching him leave the garden. Nimue waited for a count of five and then hurried over. Merlin must know this outrage would cost Uther the enmity of his fellow rulers. What could be worth paying such a price? "Your grace?"

Lost in thought, Ygraine took a moment to respond. "It seems Uther is not content to merely insult me." She told Nimue what the maid had already overheard.

Nimue looked down at the bowl of blackberries. "If you'll permit me, your grace, I will take these to the still room. I'll make sure Melyas has everything he needs to treat minor ailments or scrapes as they travel." He must be gathering the king's gear. He would do that efficiently. The boy longed for the day when Gorlois would make him a knight.

Ygraine stood up. "If my lord is writing to his fellow kings, those couriers can carry my letters to their queens. It's time they knew what manner of man Uther truly is and how he vilely he abused me in Winchester." She picked up her basket and knife. "Go and see to your tinctures and salves."

As they went through the arch in the wall, Ygraine went straight on, taking the path that led past the chapel to the royal apartments on the sheltered, landward side of the headland. Nimue turned to her left, passing the storehouses that overlooked the haven far below the steep cliffs. She headed for the cluster of buildings to the north, where the constant breezes carried away unpleasant scents and sounds from the household's mundane activities.

There was ample space at Tintagel, and the headland's cliffs meant that the castle had no need of an encircling wall. The fortifications were on the far side of the narrow neck of land that linked this natural fortress to the coast. Gorlois's loyal men-at-arms only allowed expected guests to advance to

the gatehouse barring access to the headland itself. Vigilant
sentries kept watch there day and night, looking out across the
land and the sea.

Above the northerly cliffs and the open waters, the still room
stood next to the brewhouse and the laundry. They shared one
of the headland's three wells, and a single store of firewood.
Nimue had claimed this sturdy thatched building for her own
long ago. These days, a trifling enchantment ensured that no
one would ever wonder how long she had been at the castle,
when they came in search of remedies for their ailments or
treatment for cuts and bruises, scalds and burns.

She had never meant to stay. She had only ventured onto
the headland in the first place to see what the newcomers
were building. She wanted to see how mortals' boats and
endeavours might encroach on the caves and cliffs where her
own people lived hereabouts. Seeing little cause for concern,
she had come back from time to time merely to confirm that all
remained well. As the years passed though, she realised news
of eerie encounters would be brought here to Cornwall's king.
The mortals might not understand what they met in the wild
places, but she would. Nimue could intervene, to smooth away
trouble before anyone came to grief. She spent more and more
time at Tintagel, until she realised it had become her home.

She put the bowl of blackberries on the table and swiftly
mashed the fruit with a wooden spoon. She set up a frame to
hold some cheesecloth to catch the seeds with an empty bowl
beneath it. She tipped the dark pulp into the cloth and stuck
the wooden spoon into the fruit. Any visitor would find her
diligently forcing the aromatic fruit through the coarse weave,
preparing one of the syrups that made her medicines palatable.

At the far end of the room, well away from the door, shadows
hid her workbench from curious visitors. Nimue filled a silver
bowl with water from a jug. Dipping a quill into a pot of ink,
she let a single drop fall. The ink hit the water and a dark
shimmer spread across the surface. The bowl reflected a scene

countless miles away. As Nimue had hoped, Uther's army had
already halted to make camp. The days were growing shorter,
and many tasks must be done before the light faded.

Armoured men surrounded a cluster of tents. Sentries
patrolled the perimeter, though these warriors weren't
expecting attack. They were inspecting their gear, from their
boots to their helmets. Some sharpened swords, and here
and there a loose strap was repaired with a thick needle and
waxed thread. As she watched, Nimue saw more than the
simple reflection of their presence. Her spell showed her faint
glimpses of each man's aura and of the shifting colours that
indicated a corrupt or a noble spirit. She saw their vital spark
more clearly. One man's essence was dulled by injury or pain.
The warrior beside him shone with vigour as a bowl of pottage
renewed him.

Cooking fires glowed beneath great pots hung from iron
tripods. Quartermasters sent the women and strays who
served them to fetch water from the nearby stream or sacks
and barrels from the carts that followed the marching men.
The shaggy ponies that drew those wagons were hobbled and
allowed to graze. Their rough coats were thick with dust stirred
up by countless feet.

Nimue bit her lip. It seemed Uther had summoned every
knight and his liegemen from the fiefdoms of southern Logres.
That can't have made the king popular, when these men had
barely returned from the war with the Picts, but no one would
gainsay Pendragon.

On the far side of the camp, horses were taken to drink
further down the stream. Squires tied their lords' mounts to
picket lines, checked their feet, and began to groom them. Men-
at-arms brought armfuls of fodder, doubtless stolen from some
peasant's holding. She considered causing some panic among
the animals once the dusk thickened. Enchantment at such
a distance would be a challenge, but Nimue was reasonably
certain she could stir up an eerie noise to unnerve these steeds.

What would that achieve? Some horses might be lamed or suffer worse injury, but Uther's knights would commandeer replacements from a nearby manor. Add to that, the innocent animals didn't deserve such suffering. The young squires might be hurt, or flogged for their carelessness. None of them deserved that. These men had no more choice about marching against the Cornish than the dumb animals they tended. Add to that, Nimue had no wish to suffer the penalty for whatever pains she inflicted.

Their leaders bore the guilt for this venture. Nimue focused her magic on the largest tent. The crimson, comet-tailed dragon flapped on the pennant outside. This was where Uther slept and held his councils of war. Unfortunately, there was no way for her scrying to penetrate the oiled canvas.

Fortunately, she had other spells. The hidden people frowned on using enchantments to spy on one another, but Nimue decided Merlin had forfeited such consideration. She was also coming to the conclusion that he was right. The more magic she worked, the easier and stronger her enchantments became. Taking a small bronze bell on a fine chain from its hook, she held it over the silver bowl and flicked the golden metal with her fingernail. A pure, sweet note rang out. As the bell's chime faded, faint voices strengthened.

"How soon can we bring the Cornish to battle?" Uther demanded.

"Soon," Merlin assured him. "I have seen Gorlois's messengers leave Tintagel. He is mustering his men."

"Are you certain?" Uther pressed him. "These arcane arts of yours…"

"Has my sorcery ever failed you?" Merlin didn't wait for an answer. "I followed the first messenger to Sir Gauter's manor. His men have already gathered, forewarned by Sir Idres."

So, Merlin had revealed far more of his magic to Uther than merely offering him some so-called prophecy. He had betrayed every custom of their hidden people. As Nimue's shock faded, she wondered when this forbidden alliance had been made. How much did Pendragon's prowess in battle owe to Merlin's scrying? When was he going to pay the threefold price? Then she wondered if he had betrayed her, telling Uther an enchantress served Ygraine.

"We must advance fast." Pendragon insisted. "If Gorlois can hold out until the winter storms, we will be forced to retreat. I cannot be sucked into a siege where the rest of the Cornish can harass us. Every day will bleed us of men and resolve."

The still room door creaked, tugged by the thread of magic Nimue stretched across the path to warn her if someone approached. But she needed to learn all she could.

"If we're still here in the spring, we risk a war on two fronts," Uther warned. "Orkney will attack our backs as soon as Lot can get his army here by ship. There's every chance the Welsh will come to Gorlois's aid."

"You will have everything you desire by spring," Merlin assured him. "Everything I have promised will unfold just as it should."

His conviction chilled Nimue to the bone, but she had no more time to listen. Hanging the bell on its hook, she emptied the silver bowl into the drain in the rocky floor. Before her visitor knocked, she was busy with the blackberries.

Princess Morgana came in. As the king's daughter, she had no need to wait for permission to enter any room in this royal fortress. She was allowed to go where she wanted, having outgrown the need for a nursemaid more than a year ago. The child knew every inch of Tintagel, and everyone who lived on the headland kept a watchful eye on her, as well as answering her endless questions. When marriage took the princess far from here, as it had taken her sisters, she would know every trick and detail of running a royal household. Self-possessed at six years old, she had her father's dark hair, tidily bound in two long braids, as well as his determined chin.

"What are you doing?" She barely glanced at the table, looking around instead.

"Dealing with these blackberries." Nimue saw the girl's eyes take in every detail of the still room.

Bunches of dried herbs hung from the rafters, and bowls and flasks were stacked on a broad shelf beside the window, close by the unlit charcoal brazier. Morgana's gaze lingered on the jars of honey and of lard beside Nimue's pestle and mortar. She looked at the mysterious vials of thick green glass, set in neat rows on a much higher shelf and sealed with wax and linen.

"I heard voices. Who were you talking to?" she asked with an echo of her father's authority.

"Myself," Nimue said tartly. "It's often my only hope of intelligent conversation. What brings you here, highness?"

"I'm looking for kittens. It's the time of year for late litters."

That was true, though it was unlikely to be the whole truth. Morgana was already used to keeping her own counsel without telling actual lies. She'd learned that from her mother and elder sisters.

"There are no cats in here," Nimue assured her. "They'll be in the storehouses hunting rats and mice."

"The dairy is only across the yard. Cats like cream and cheese." Morgana walked forward, intent on the workbench.

"Stay there, highness," Nimue said firmly, as she stirred the blackberry pulp. "You don't want to get splashed with this juice. Your maid will never get the stains out."

The little girl stepped back hastily, smoothing the pale linen surcote over her russet gown. Truth be told, the surcote was there to catch the stains and smudges that children seemed to collect, but Morgana invariably stayed clean, even though she roamed over Tintagel's broad headland once Ygraine released her from her daily lessons.

"My lady mother is upset and my father the king is making ready to leave again." Her composure faltered.

Nimue left the blackberries and checked that her own hands were free of juice. "Then help me fill a basket with things he might need on his journey."

That should help stop the child fretting, and princess or not, every girl should learn the uses of healing herbs.

CHAPTER SEVEN

Days passed. Nimue found Morgana following her at every turn. She could only scry at night, to see how far Uther's army had advanced. She had no chance to listen to his conversations with Merlin in hopes of hearing their plans.

Granted, the princess spent her mornings with her mother. Ygraine taught her daughters to read and write and how to draw up a household's accounts, as well as fine embroidery and how to play the small harp. Nimue was expected to be in attendance, tidying and mending and doing countless small tasks in the queen's private hall.

Ordinarily, Nimue would have time to call her own in the afternoons. Ygraine would meet with Tintagel's stewards, or the women who presided over the dairy, the brewery and the laundry. Occasionally, the queen enjoyed some leisure with her own books or music. These were no ordinary days though. Morgana clung to her mother, and when Ygraine insisted on some privacy, the child felt her mother's maid offered the next best reassurance. Nimue saw the little girl sensed Ygraine's apprehension.

Sir Idres's couriers brought letters, saying King Gorlois was avoiding a pitched battle with Uther's army since Cornwall's host was significantly smaller. Pendragon's greater numbers weren't all to his advantage. The Cornish army was far quicker to move through countryside which every man knew like the back of his hand. Logres' host was more cautious. Every unfamiliar rock or tree might hide some lurking foe. Every passing day brought their Welsh and Scots allies closer, while loyal Cornishmen harried the invaders, denying them time to rest. Nimue had seen this for herself.

That was all well and good, but she was starting to dread what she might see each time she used her scrying bowl. Step by reluctant step, Gorlois was forced to give ground. Now, after days of manoeuvring, Uther had seized the road to Bodmin. Gorlois had no option but to retreat to his castle at Launceston. This morning's messenger brought the news that Uther was laying siege to the Cornishmen.

Ygraine had gone to Saint Hulanus's chapel to pray in solitude. Nimue wondered if the crucified god would tell the queen why Pendragon was doing the one thing he had been so set against. Frustrated, she longed for a chance to eavesdrop on Merlin and Uther.

In the still room, Nimue sorted through the comfrey Morgana had helped her harvest from the queen's garden. The child's hands were grubby, though there was barely a smear of soil on her surcote.

"Will the men of Logres lay siege to us?" she asked in a tight, small voice.

When the courier came to the queen's hall, the princess had been silently copying the passage of scripture that was her lesson for the day. Evidently, she had listened as Ygraine read the letter to Nimue. The child had learned from her mother and sisters that royal women were expected to speak when they were spoken to, but that didn't stop them using their ears.

"I doubt it." Nimue had seen no sign that Uther was preparing to split his forces. If he did that, he had no chance of seizing either stronghold. He wouldn't commit all his men to attacking Tintagel either. As soon as he turned his back on Gorlois, the king's army would escape from Launceston. The Cornishmen would retreat further down their peninsula, to stay out of his reach until their allies arrived. Then Uther's men would have nowhere to run, as enemies attacked from all sides.

"Uther knows this fortress cannot be taken," she assured Morgana, as much as herself. "We have fresh water from our wells, and food to last out the winter. Boats can bring us whatever we might need, and Pendragon's men cannot stop them."

Well, they could cut down trees and make trebuchets to fling rocks at the fortifications. Much good that would do them. Nimue was ready to use enchantment to warp and crack any siege engines, to ensure missiles missed their mark. If Merlin's magic assisted Uther, her strengthening skills would defend the innocents in Tintagel.

"Now," she asked the child briskly, "what is comfrey good for?"

"It promotes healing in wounds when used in a poultice," Morgana answered. "Taken in a medicine, it helps bones to knit. It strengthens weakened lungs and troubled stomachs."

"Very good. Now, we will hang these roots up to dry, as well as some of the leaves. We'll use the rest to make salve. We tear them up and pack them into a jar like so. Then we fill the jar with this oil that comes from far overseas."

"As far as Brittany?" Morgana watched intently.

"Much further away, highness." Nimue reached for the flagon of olive oil that traders from the sun-drenched south swapped for Cornish tin. "The leaves must steep to draw out the virtues of the herb. We need to heat the jar, but not too much. A wise woman who lived even further away devised a way to do that. She was an alchemist called Marie who lived in a land called Egypt."

"Where the Virgin Mary and Saint Joseph fled." Morgana watched Nimue take a copper pan from its hook.

"That's right." Nimue caught herself just in time. She had been about to light the charcoal in her brazier with a touch of magic. She must never do that with the child present. "Now, let's go and beg an ember from Mistress Eseld."

Thankfully, the fires in the brewery were lit today. When

the brazier had been kindled, Nimue set the copper pan on the coals and half-filled it with water. She stood the jar of oil and leaves in the pan.

"What happens now?" Morgana asked, expectant.

"We wait until tomorrow." Nimue managed not to laugh at the child's startled face. She remembered her own impatience when she was first taught the healer's arts. "These things take time, highness. When the oil is imbued with the essence of the comfrey, we will strain out the leaves and thicken the salve with beeswax."

The need to tend to the brazier overnight would be her excuse to come back once Ygraine and the child were in bed, so she could scry.

"Let's see what other herbs we can harvest." She picked up her basket.

By the time the sun was setting, more pots of leaves and oil stood in the warm water. The strain in Morgana's face had eased, and as the breeze shifted to bring scents from the kitchen, Nimue saw the child's eyes brighten at the thought of food. She finished cleaning her knives while Morgana scrubbed the tabletop. "We've done a good day's work, highness. Let's wash our hands, and make ready for dinner."

Ygraine was in the queen's hall when they arrived, sitting in a window seat and looking out at the cloud-streaked western sky. She smiled at Morgana and held out her hands. "What have you been doing, dear heart?"

The princess ran to her mother's embrace, eager to share every moment of her afternoon. Nimue kindled a spill at the small fire in the hearth and lit the candles on the table. The evenings were turning colder as the year edged closer to winter, and the jewel-hued tapestries could only do so much. Movement by the door caught her eye. She saw the hall steward had come to see if the royal ladies were ready to dine.

She went over. "Have there been any more letters or messengers today?"

"No, none."

Nimue saw her own disquiet reflected in Breock's face. On one hand, no news was good news. Word of Uther's victory would arrive as fast as a whipped horse. On the other hand, no reassurance from Sir Idres or from Gorlois must mean the siege at Launceston was drawn mercilessly tight.

Ygraine looked over from the window seat. "You may serve us now, thank you."

"At once, your grace." Breock nodded and retreated.

A loin of pork from autumn's slaughter had been roasted to succulence, served with a dish of pease and apples, and a loaf of soft, white bread. Once Nimue had filled her mistress's bowl, and the princess's, Ygraine invited her to join them at the table.

The queen wasn't inclined to conversation. As she ate, and drank a cup of cider, her eyes were distant. Morgana didn't seem to notice anything amiss. The fresh air had given the child a hearty appetite and a full belly made her sleepy. Her eyelids drooped as she ate a dish of blackberry posset until a sudden yawn took them all by surprise.

Ygraine was startled out of her preoccupation. "Let's get you to bed, sweetling."

The bed in the chamber where Morgana now slept alone had been warmed with a cloth-wrapped brick from the kitchen hearth. As the queen knelt to share her daughter's night-time prayers, Nimue supervised the kitchen maids clearing the table in the hall. She was adding wood to the hearth when Ygraine returned, closing Morgana's door quietly behind her.

The queen covered her own yawn with her beringed hand. "I will have an early night myself."

"Your grace." Nimue took a candle from the table and followed Ygraine into the second bedchamber at the rear of the hall. Once her mistress was in her night gown, Nimue brushed out and replaited her hair.

Ygraine smiled as she settled against her pillows with the book of poems Elaine had sent her from Brittany. "Thank you."

"Sleep well, your grace."

After making certain the fire in the hearth was sinking, with no risk of spitting embers setting anything alight, Nimue left the hall. Outside, night had fallen, and Tintagel's paths and yards were empty. Here and there, golden light glowed behind a window's shutters. The fortress's men and women were taking their well-earned ease after their day's labours. Most of them, anyway.

The warriors standing guard on the inner gatehouse were alert. Torches burned on the battlements of the fortifications on the landward side of the narrow path beyond. Sir Gauter had been sent to command Tintagel's garrison while the king was away. The loyal knight inspired as much respect as Sir Idres, and Nimue had no doubt that well-hidden scouts watched every approach to the fortress. Any spies that Uther sent this way were unlikely to return.

She took the path to her still room. With no need for a lantern, she saw the cloak-draped figure coming up the last stone-cut steps from the sheltered haven well before he saw her. Gorlois? How could the king be here? Reaching safe harbour in the rocky haven below was a challenging task for a skilled seaman in broad daylight. No one risked it in the dead of night. Gorlois would never ask such a thing. Except, apparently, he had.

The king slowed as he saw her. He nodded curtly. "Good evening to you."

Skirting around her, he walked faster. Nimue saw him take the path to the queen's hall with lengthening strides. The shiver down her spine had nothing to do with the cold night breeze.

The king hadn't asked after the queen or his daughter. Their welfare was always his first concern. He hadn't asked Nimue how her day had been. Where was Melyas? Nimue looked down the path to the haven. The squire was nowhere to be seen. Something was wrong. Very wrong.

She hurried after the king. As she approached the queen's hall, she heard the soft thud of the wooden bar dropping into the brackets inside of the door. The entrance was barred against... who? These buildings would only ever be barricaded as a desperate last resort, if invaders got past the landward fortifications and overwhelmed the gatehouse. That had never happened yet, and Nimue had sworn it never would, not while she drew breath. So Tintagel's doors were left unsecured in case of sudden illness or the ever-present hazard of fire.

More and more uneasy, Nimue walked around the hall to the shuttered window of the queen's bedchamber. She heard low voices, and a touch of magic sharpened her ears.

"Beloved?" Ygraine was incredulous. "How–?"

"Come here," Gorlois commanded. "I must have you."

"I – wait – Morgana–" Something cut off Ygraine's confused protests.

Gorlois's voice thickened with lust. "I have dreamed of this moment."

Horrified, Nimue fled. She ran as fast as she could to her still room. A wave of her hand warded the door. She hurried to fetch her scrying bowl, wringing water from the air. She tore the side of her fingernail with her teeth. There were hazards in using blood for this magic, but she had no time to lose.

She swiped her bleeding finger through the water. The ripples stilled and she saw the queen's bed. Ygraine lay on her back with her chamber robe ripped open. The king was on top of her, one knee between her thighs. Nimue couldn't see his face as he claimed Ygraine's bare breasts, nuzzling, sucking, licking. Her hands tightened on his shoulders as she yielded as a good wife should. Nimue grimaced as she saw Ygraine's consternation. From everything she had ever heard behind the royal bed curtains, Gorlois was a patient and considerate lover.

Now he was in brutal haste. He had shed his cloak and tunic, but not his shirt nor the braies where his woollen hose were tied. He used one hand to pull up his shirt. Linen tore as he shoved the braies off his buttocks and down his hairy thighs. His hand forced Ygraine's knee aside, to get both his legs between hers. He thrust forward and Ygraine's confusion turned to distress as the king–

Nimue gasped as she saw the man's aura in a lightning-fast flash. Deep, sullen red betrayed his anger and resentment, just as quickly shifting to putrid yellow denoting impatience. The shimmer faded to the sickly green of jealousy before vanishing altogether.

It was as if the spell had opened her eyes. That wasn't Gorlois's greying hair falling forward as he rutted like a beast. Uther Pendragon's tawny locks lashed Ygraine's anguished face. No wonder he had seemed so distant when they met on the path. He hadn't known who Nimue was. He hadn't spared her a glance in Winchester, not at the feast nor when he and his men had waylaid Ygraine. A maidservant was of no more account to Uther than the dust of the path.

Nimue watched Pendragon rear up on his knees to rip his shirt off over his head. Ygraine pressed outspread hands against the mattress, trying to raise herself up, trying to say something. Merciless, Uther clamped a palm over her mouth to stifle her protests. His other hand mauled her breast. As he forced Ygraine back against the pillows, his face twisted with brutal lust. His hips drove into her, over and over.

Nimue swept the scrying bowl aside. It hit the floor with a sour clang as Nimue headed for the door. Merlin entered. He gestured and the door slammed behind him.

Of course he would be here. Nimue knew masking Uther with Gorlois's face could only be Merlin's doing. He hadn't counted on her scrying revealing the truth, as such magic always did. "What is this vile deceit?"

"What needs to be done." He was unrepentant.

"What does that mean?" Nimue spat.

"That is none of your concern." Merlin folded his arms as he blocked her way.

"Let me pass!" she hissed.

"To do what?" he challenged her. "Break down the door to the queen's private hall? How will you do that without help? Who will you enlist? How will you explain that you must force your way in because King Gorlois has returned in secret to bed his beloved wife, and you want to – what do you want? To intrude on their marital bliss? Because you cannot have seen anything else that's a cause for alarm. You cannot confess to your scrying, not if you wish to remain here with no one suspecting your magic."

Infuriated, Nimue raised a hand. Merlin grabbed her wrist. Nimue slapped his face hard with her free hand. Merlin's grip tightened and he swung his fist to answer with a blow of his own. Nimue barely managed to knock his punch aside with her upraised forearm. Merlin caught hold of her other wrist. Now they were stuck fast. Nimue could not free herself, but Merlin dared not let her go.

"What good can you do?" he demanded. "Who will believe it, if you claim Uther is here, when they can see Gorlois with their own eyes? Granted, he's been unable to restrain himself, but any man returning home must be forgiven a little roughness when he claims his lady's embrace."

"A little roughness?" Nimue was revolted.

"Think of the child." Merlin's dark gaze held hers. "Break down that door and Morgana will think her beloved father has returned, only to see him leave before daybreak. Don't think that Uther will try to comfort her."

For the first time, Merlin's grimace betrayed the merest hint of shame.

Nimue stopped struggling to free herself. "You're going to leave? Both of you? Before dawn?"

"Do you think the queen will thank you for revealing her humiliation to the whole household? Shouldn't you leave her some dignity, to let her put this unpleasantness behind her? She might even persuade herself this was some nightmare born of fear and longing. You would do your mistress a service, if you use your skills to blur her recollections, to convince her this was a dream."

Merlin shook Nimue with sudden savagery.

"Or will you tell her she has been violated by Uther by means of magic? Will you explain you know this thanks to magic of your own? Will you tell her you inveigled your way into this fortress long ago as a spy listening for news of Gorlois's liegemen encountering wild sorcery? Can you deny your true loyalties are with your own people, first and foremost? How much will that betrayal add to Ygraine's distress? And you'll be banished from Tintagel. Ygraine is a devout daughter of the church, and the crucified god's priests hate our people. You won't be at her side to help her come to terms with what is to come."

Nimue wanted to protest, but curse him, Merlin was right. She would be cast out and condemned and she would be alone. Her own people would shun her, suspicious or contemptuous of one who had spent so long living alongside mortals.

He drew a deep breath and spoke more calmly. "I know your honest affection for Ygraine and her children. Believe me, your mistress will soon need you more than ever. The child will need you. Their lives are going to change and only you will be able to help them. Reveal your magic and you cannot–"

He broke off, as if some noise distracted him. Nimue hadn't heard a thing. Merlin released her. Nimue reached out to grab him, to shake some answers loose. Her fingers brushed his sleeve as the door flew open at Merlin's gesture. He took a long stride into the darkness.

Nimue hurried after him, but the sorcerer was nowhere to be seen. There was no sign of Uther Pendragon. Around her, Tintagel's halls and workshops slept. Nimue's furious impulse to wake everyone withered and died. What was she going to shout? Help? No one here could help her.

The night breeze traced cold lines down her face. She hadn't realised she was crying, from mingled rage and fear over what she might find in the queen's hall. She hurried there all the same. There was no sound within. Was the entrance still barred against her? No, the door swung open at the touch of her trembling hand. The dying embers of the fire offered a little light. A cat had sneaked in to curl up in the warmth close by the hearth. There was no sign of anything amiss.

Nimue's heart pounded as she crossed the threshold. She walked past the hearth on silent feet. The brindled cat didn't stir. Nimue opened Morgana's door a crack. That was one blessing at least. The little girl slept sprawled beneath her blankets with her night plait half-unravelled.

At the queen's door though, a soft and desolate sound told Nimue Ygraine was weeping. Uther must have left as soon as he had slaked his foul desire. Merlin's magic must already be carrying their boat safely over the restless sea.

Sick at heart, Nimue turned away. She could offer the queen no comfort without impossible explanations. She returned to her still room where she had blankets stowed beneath the workbench. This wasn't the first night she had slept on this floor.

CHAPTER EIGHT

Wide awake before birdsong welcomed the dawn, Nimue gave up any hope of sleep. She put away her bedding and headed for Ygraine's hall. She looked eastward, hoping to draw strength from the rising sun amid the scudding clouds.

She halted, aghast. The dawn light showed an army massed along the coast overlooking the headland. Pendragon's army, flying Uther's banner. Sharpening her eyes with a little magic, she sought out the sentries on Tintagel's gatehouse and on the fortifications beyond. Gorlois's loyal men were at their posts, though their frantic pacing showed they could not understand why the men of Logres weren't attacking.

Nimue hurried to the queen's hall. Cold dread hollowed her stomach. If Uther and his army were here, where were King Gorlois and his men?

She entered the hall. "Oh, highness–"

Morgana was out of bed, still in her nightgown and playing with the brindled cat. She looked up and smiled. "Have the herbs steeped?" She pronounced the unfamiliar word with care.

Nimue looked blankly at the child. Then she remembered the copper pan on the brazier with the charcoal beneath it dead and cold. "Oh, highness–"

The wind carried the raucous cry of a signal horn across the headland. Nimue clapped her hands. "Can you get yourself dressed, princess? Quick as you like."

Morgana ran a hand over her tousled plait. "My hair–"

"I will see to that. Just get dressed." Nimue heard hurrying feet outside. The first to see the enemy menacing Tintagel were coming to Ygraine for guidance. Nimue could not allow her mistress to be caught unawares, not after...

"Quick, quick." She ushered Morgana into her room. Barely pausing to knock, she went into the queen's bedchamber. "Your grace..."

Wrapped in a blanket, Ygraine sat in the north-facing window with a view of the chapel. "Yes?"

"The enemy is here."

"Logres?" Ygraine's eyes widened. "What are they doing?"

"Waiting beyond the outer fortifications."

"He didn't say–" Ygraine drew a deep, shuddering breath. "I will wear the russet gown, and the gold and garnets as well as my regent's crown."

"At once, your grace."

As she fetched the queen's garments and jewels, she noticed the chamber gown the queen had worn last night lay discarded on the rumpled bed. Ygraine had fetched a blanket from a storage chest. The queen had washed as well. That was clear from the basin and water jug.

Ygraine didn't say a word as they followed their familiar routine. Last of all, Nimue settled the crown on Ygraine's veiled head. This was not the delicate gold coronet she had worn in Winchester as Gorlois's consort. This heavier, more solid circlet was identical to the Cornish king's, to remind everyone in his absence that she ruled with his authority and his trust.

Ygraine rose from the stool and tears glistened in her eyes. "Morgana–"

"I will see to her," Nimue promised.

They left the bedchamber. The queen's hall was full of people seeking reassurance. Voices rose in a clamour of questions. What had happened to their king and to Cornwall's warriors?

Ygraine raised a hand to command silence. "We must wait for a messenger."

The hush lasted barely a moment before the same questions began again, seeking answers no one could give.

Nimue hurried into Morgana's room. The princess was dressed and trying to unplait her tangled locks.

"Let me do that." Deft with brush and comb, Nimue teased out the knots and braided Morgana's hair. As she tied the princess's ribbons, abrupt silence fell out in the hall. She gave Morgana a swift hug. "Stay here, highness. Quiet as a mouse." She hated to leave the silently anxious child, but her place was at Ygraine's side.

Out in the hall, the queen sat straight-backed in the carved chair at the head of her table. Her clasped hands rested on the pristine linen cloth. Someone had fetched firewood and stirred the central hearth to life. Someone else had lit every candle they could find. Ygraine's jewels and her crown glinted gold as errant drafts stirred the flames.

A herald on one knee bowed his head. He wore Cornish livery, but Nimue couldn't tell if he had come from Gorlois's army or Tintagel's outer fortifications. She wished she had heard what he just said.

A knock rattled the door. The men and women of Tintagel stared, their faces taut with fear. Something far harder and heavier than a hand struck the planks a second time.

Ygraine's shoulders stiffened. She gestured and the herald scrambled to his feet. The queen raised her chin. "Enter."

Merlin strode in, carrying a staff of ash wood. A bearded knight in Pendragon livery followed. The man was unarmed, and his head was uncovered. Nimue had seen him in Winchester, one of Uther's inner circle. She couldn't recall his name.

Merlin halted and the knight dropped to one knee.

"Sir Ulfius." Ygraine acknowledged him.

"I bring news from Launceston, your grace," the knight said, unemotional. "The dawn before last, Cornish sentries saw King Uther ride out from his encampment with a handful of men. My liege lord wished to satisfy himself that the siege was drawn tight around the castle. King Gorlois led a small force of his own out of a hidden gate. He was intent on pursuing Pendragon and ending this war through single combat. I grieve to tell you, your grace, that your husband was slain in the skirmish. King Uther's forces seized Launceston Castle and Cornwall's army has surrendered to Logres. Your last duty as queen is to agree terms with this realm's new ruler."

Shocked voices protested. Ygraine raised a hand to quell them.

Sir Ulfius rose to his feet. He spoke with more authority. "Cornwall's army has surrendered, and little blood beyond your king's has been shed. Be thankful for that. You have my word that your husbands, sons and brothers are unharmed, for the present, at least." He looked at Ygraine. "What happens next is up to your queen."

"Leave us." Ygraine stared at her clasped hands, her eyes unseeing.

Those closest to her chair looked at each other, uncertain. Several glanced at Nimue.

"Leave us!" Merlin brandished his staff. "Do as your queen commands!"

"Do not presume to speak for me," Ygraine said coldly. She looked around the hall. "I will hear this knight out alone."

After a tense moment, Tintagel's people filed out. Merlin watched them, not hiding his satisfaction. As he looked back at the queen, his gaze met Nimue's. She silently challenged him to try dismissing her. Merlin looked away. Nimue felt his magic ensuring the most assiduous eavesdropper would hear nothing from inside the hall.

"What–" Ygraine cleared her throat. "What happened to Melyas, my husband's squire?"

"The fool boy saw Gorlois fall and tried taking on Uther himself. Three swords cut him down." Sir Ulfius smirked.

If Nimue had been within arm's length, she would have slapped his foul face and taken the consequences.

Ygraine contemplated her hands. "If King Gorlois is truly dead, then Sir Mark of Castle Dore–"

"–is his heir, I know," Sir Ulfius interrupted. "He's some cousin to Gorlois in the third or fourth degree? Hardly a strong claim to even a minor throne. We captured him on the road to Bodmin. If he is proclaimed ruler of Cornwall, his reign will last for as long as it takes him to die, hanged from the battlements at Launceston."

The fire crackled softly. Finally, Ulfius's silence forced Ygraine to look at him. Her bloodless lips were pressed tight together.

Ulfius smiled with triumph. "Unless you marry Uther Pendragon, High King of Britain."

Ygraine was lost for words. Nimue's eyes narrowed as she saw something familiar in Ulfius's expression.

The knight continued. "It is a simple enough decision, your grace. Make peace, marry Uther, and you and Morgana will live in luxury in Winchester. Sir Mark can inherit Cornwall's throne once he swears fealty to Pendragon. Those brave and loyal men who followed Gorlois can return to their farms and fishing villages, to their loving families' embrace. Unless…"

He shook his head with barely a pretence of regret. "Defy the high king and everyone in Tintagel will be hanged or thrown from these cliffs. Every captive in Launceston will be hanged. We cannot leave enemies alive to harass our rearguard when we march to defeat Lot of Orkney. We will be forced to make war on him next and that will be your doing."

He paused with that same satisfied, secretive smile. "Unless Lot sees this new settlement bringing peace to Britain, guaranteed by your wedding to Uther. He will hardly make war on the man who has married his wife's mother, who stands as a father to her young sister. For his part, Uther will be content for Lot to stay out of sight and out of mind."

Ygraine's whisper shook with anger. "I will not–"

"Do not answer in haste, your grace," Ulfius warned. "Force Uther to march against Orkney, and believe me, Pendragon will prevail, then he will insist King Lot and his family swear fealty to him as high king. If they refuse?"

The knight shrugged. "A high king cannot be defied. Uther will be forced to put them to the sword. Do you want to wager the lives of Morgause and the child she carries against Uther's record of victories?"

Ygraine shook her head blindly, rejecting everything that Ulfius said. The knight chose to take this as agreement.

"Very wise, your grace. Very well, we–"

"How did my beloved lord die?"

"Bravely," Ulfius assured her.

"Answer me this." Ygraine demanded. "You say my husband died yesterday, shortly after dawn–"

"Then how did he visit your bedchamber last night?" Ulfius chuckled.

Ygraine stared at the knight, dumbfounded. Ulfius grinned at Merlin. Now Nimue recognised that feral smile. Merlin waved a hand and Uther Pendragon stood there, gloating.

Ygraine gasped. Merlin shot Nimue a warning look. Did he think she would try to kill Pendragon? Nimue wished she could strike the brute down, but that would reveal her own magic to the queen. Add to that, she would most likely die as Merlin retaliated. Then no one would protect Ygraine and Morgana from this villain's – these villains' – evil schemes.

"Your grace." Uther bowed low. "Though must we be so formal, after last night's intimacies?"

"You – you–" Ygraine choked on disbelief and revulsion.

Uther laughed. "You may as well marry me now. I have one of your rings as proof that I bedded you. The sapphire ring that Sevira of Dyfed admired. She will know it for yours and believe me when I say how I got it."

"You thief!" Now Ygraine was furious.

"You will show me more respect when we are married, my lady." Uther scowled, his mood changing as swiftly as a storm cloud covering the sun. "If you force me to lay waste to Cornwall, if you insist on dying here with your daughter, do not think you'll be remembered as a martyr. You will be condemned as a wife who betrayed her marriage vows. I'll offer your ring as evidence that you seduced me in Winchester, when you begged me to save you from Gorlois's brutality. Alas, I will be appalled to have learned too late that you lied, and I made war on Cornwall for nothing. The mothers and wives of those who die in Launceston will spit on your grave. Once you are dead, I can say what I wish."

He held up a hand. "What will your daughter Elaine believe, I wonder? She's in distant Brittany, but news crosses the sea as easily as a bird in flight, or at least as fast as trading ships sail. What will King Nentres of Garlot think when he learns his wife's mother was a faithless whore? Elaine will be disgraced. Perhaps Nentres will set her aside. A husband must trust his wife."

"What of a wife's trust in her husband?" Ygraine hissed. "How could any woman trust a man who resorts to rape by means of sorcery?"

If the queen thought she could wound him, she was mistaken. Uther smiled.

"Doesn't knowing how easily I did that convince you? How can you stand against me when my advisor is a sorcerer holding the secrets of past, present, and future?"

Merlin gestured and Sir Ulfius's face and voice replaced Uther's. He looked steadily at Ygraine.

"I will leave you with one last consideration. Merlin has the gift of prophecy. You will bear me a son, thanks to last night's coupling. Marry me soon and no one will count the days as they rejoice that my line is secure. Sit here alone as your belly swells and everyone will wonder what really happened in Winchester. I will tell my tale, and when the child is born everyone will see that I sired him. Your disgrace will be complete. I will claim my heir and your only refuge will be a nunnery."

"Why?" Ygraine cried out. "Why are you doing this?"

"Merlin foresaw I would defeat the Picts and be proclaimed high king. He foresaw you would bear me a son who will be a still greater king of Britain." Uther's conviction was absolute.

Nimue looked at Merlin. He gazed steadily back. Nimue gritted her teeth. How dare he defy every custom of their hidden people? As for using lies and sorcery in a mortal king's service? How had Merlin come to this?

Ygraine was still defiant. "What will your loyal knights think if I tell them you consort with enchanters?"

Uther laughed. "You think they don't already know? You think I would wear this face without Sir Ulfius's permission?" He stroked the knight's luxuriant beard, grinning.

Ygraine rose and headed for her bedchamber without a backward glance. Uther looked at Nimue and his smile broadened. "Tell your mistress to send word when she's ready to wed me."

He left the hall. Before Merlin followed, he glanced at Nimue.

Do not let her delay too long. Whatever he says, his patience will not last.

Nimue had no idea what to do. Then Morgana's bedchamber door inched open, and Nimue saw the child's terrified face. Her blood ran cold. What had Morgana heard? Merlin's magic ensured no one outside the hall could have heard Uther and Ygraine, but the princess's bedchamber had been within the bounds of that enchantment.

CHAPTER NINE

Days passed with the army of Logres camped along the coast. This wasn't a siege. Unarmed men and women could pass freely in and out of Tintagel. As Nimue walked along the southern cliffs, she saw wagons bringing provisions and fuel to the headland.

Those carts carried other things. Prisoners in Launceston who could write sent letters on scraps of vellum provided by Uther's castellan, along with pens and ink. The men said they were not mistreated, that they had food and water. Every day, Tintagel's families learned who among their husbands, sons and brothers still lived and who had died of their wounds.

Nimue walked towards the queen's hall. She knew the captured men begged their families to beseech the queen. Ygraine could set them free. Everyone from the Tamar river to Land's End knew King Uther had offered to marry Gorlois's widow. Once they were wed, there could be peace with Logres. Cornwall would be ruled by King Mark after he swore fealty as Pendragon's vassal. Queen Ygraine could safeguard their interests in distant Winchester, and there need be no more bloodshed.

Inside the queen's hall, Morgana was playing with the brindled cat, dragging a lure of gull's feathers along the floor. Once again, Nimue decided to leave her be. If Morgana asked her questions, she would answer honestly, but until then…

A maidservant was laying tinder and kindling in the hearth. Another swept crumbs from the table, now that the queen and the princess had finished their breakfast. The two girls watched as Nimue headed for the queen's bedchamber. She knew what they would ask if they dared. When would Ygraine accept Uther's offer of peace, for the sake of her dead husband's people? It wasn't only Pendragon's patience wearing thin.

Inside the bedchamber, Ygraine was by the window, gazing at Saint Hulanus's chapel. Nimue silently hoped they weren't going to spend another day in prayer. It wasn't as if the crucified god's servant whose bones lay beneath the altar could offer any guidance.

"Good morning." Ygraine greeted Nimue with a small, sad smile. "How is Endelyn?"

"She passed a comfortable night, and I redressed her burns. Her leg shows signs of healing." The foolish girl had strayed too close to a fire and her skirt had caught alight.

"Some good news at least."

"Your grace?" Nimue looked warily at the queen.

"Once, every dawn was a reason for hope, at least until my dream of bearing Gorlois a son was washed away by blood and tears." Ygraine sounded utterly defeated. "It seems that Uther was right. There's no denying that I am with child."

"Your grace? After such a dreadful shock, some delay, perhaps a lengthy one…" Though Nimue had known the truth since that foul day when Uther had boasted of what he had done. Her magic had shown her the faint presence in Ygraine's womb that might one day become a child.

Ygraine shook her head. "After bearing three daughters, and enduring more losses besides, I know these changes in my body too well."

"Nothing can be certain, not yet," Nimue said carefully. "There are still steps you could take."

The queen knew as well as she did which herbs served women whose hopes of a child had faded, and whose womb must be encouraged to cleanse itself in case some sad remnant festered. Those same herbs could relieve a woman of a travail she could not bear, well before any new life quickened within her.

Ygraine bit her lip. "I have considered that, and thank you. But this child may be Gorlois's son, or perhaps another daughter."

"Indeed, your grace." Though Nimue doubted it. Merlin wouldn't make such a mistake.

Ygraine glanced towards the chapel. "Only the Almighty knows if I will carry this child safely and see it born alive. Only He knows its father, so I must put my trust in Him."

She looked at Nimue, resolute. "The fates of many others are in my hands. While I am Cornwall's queen, I have a duty to act in the realm's best interests. Help me write to Uther. If he wants this wedding, he can agree to my terms."

Nimue bowed her head. "I will carry your letter to Pendragon myself."

The queen's blunt message didn't take long to compose. Ygraine read through the final fair copy and signed her name, Nimue stood ready with sealing wax and a flaming taper. She let a drop of wax fall onto the vellum, red as blood. Ygraine pressed her signet ring down, to prove that she and no other had written these lines. Once the swiftly cooling wax was firm, Nimue folded the letter, and the queen sealed it again.

Ygraine looked as if some great burden had been lifted from her. "Take it. I will walk around the cliffs with Morgana. We have both spent far too long cooped up. Come and find me when you have Uther's answer."

"At once, your grace." Nimue picked up the letter and left as Ygraine went to see what Morgana and the cat were doing.

At the gatehouse, Nimue found Sir Gauter deep in conversation with Rewan, one of Tintagel's sergeants-at-arms. The gate stood open. There was nothing to be gained by barring it.

"Mistress Nimue?" Sir Gauter was surprised to see her.

She held up Ygraine's letter. "Her grace sends word to Uther Pendragon."

Sir Gauter reached for the sealed vellum. "I will take it to him at once."

"I am to carry it myself." Nimue wasn't going to miss this chance to see Merlin.

Gauter frowned. "Surely–"

"You don't imagine any man of Logres will keep me from Uther? Everyone in his army has been waiting for our queen's answer." Nimue waved at the sprawling encampment. "They'll be eager to head home before autumn turns to winter."

Sir Gauter looked defeated. "I suppose so."

Nimue walked across the neck of land that overlooked Tintagel's twin harbours. The boats were tied up securely as the season's gales grew stronger. She reached the outer fortifications, and the Cornish warriors allowed her to pass through the open arch. Nimue had seen more spirit in whipped dogs.

She walked up the path to the knot of Logres' men-at-arms who were standing watch. She greeted them politely in English. "Good day."

"What's good about it?" one man muttered, sullen.

Nimue addressed the sergeant. "I have a letter from Queen Ygraine for your king."

He held out a hand. "Give it."

Nimue shook her head. "I have been ordered to hand it to Pendragon myself, and to wait for his reply."

The sergeant sneered. "Your queen's wishes mean nothing, woman."

"Your king's orders mean everything, however." Merlin appeared behind the men. "You were told to bring him any messenger from Tintagel immediately."

The sergeant protested. "I was going to, as soon as this old hag–"

Nimue walked past him. She noted the soldiers' apprehensive glances at Merlin – at least when the black-clad sorcerer wasn't looking their way.

"Finally." He offered Nimue his arm.

So, he had been keeping watch with his magic for any sign of Ygraine's reply. Did his sallow face and those shadows beneath his eyes mean he had been losing sleep over it? Nimue certainly hoped so. She ignored him as they walked through the camp. She noted the bruises on the women and strays where these brave warriors had vented their frustrations on those who couldn't fight back. The grass had been trampled into mud and the air was tainted with the stink of middens. Drifts of ash and splinters were the only trace left of the trees that had flourished here. Logres' army would leave a lingering stain on Cornwall.

Didn't Merlin worry about making enemies of the hidden people who had lived in these woods? Of those who lived in the waters? They would know he was responsible. Was that why he looked so drawn? She wondered how he intended to settle that debt.

His thoughts were elsewhere. "How has it taken you so long to persuade Ygraine to see sense?"

Nimue wove magic to make sure they were not overheard. "You may use sorcery to bend others to your will. I remain true to our people."

"I serve our people in all I do."

"So you say. Time will tell. It always does."

Nimue was pleased to see red rise on Merlin's angular cheekbones. He would never convince her that his motives were pure, and it seemed he had some struggle to convince himself.

They walked in silence to Uther's tent. As she followed Merlin inside, Nimue saw a curtain divided the sleeping quarters from an outer, canvas-walled chamber where Uther was deep in conversation with his loyal knights. They sat in a half-circle on camp-stools, even the king. Sir Ulfius was at Uther's right hand and the knight smirked when he saw Nimue. She guessed he thought Uther wearing his face into Tintagel had been a grand jest.

Pendragon clapped his hands. "Leave us."

The English knights departed. Uther smiled at Nimue, repellently smug. "I take it your mistress has realised she has no choice?"

Wordless, Nimue handed him Ygraine's letter. Uther cracked the seal and read the queen's terse message.

He looked up, scowling. "What is this nonsense? She thinks she can make demands?"

He rose to his feet and loomed over Nimue. She held her ground, still silent.

"Does she imagine Gorlois's allies will save her? She cannot be such a fool, when she's had no word from them for so long?"

He gestured towards a trestle table piled with parchments. Nimue looked at them since that was what he expected. There was no real need. Scrying had shown her Uther's scouts intercepting every courier trying to reach Tintagel. Relieved of their letters, they were sent home to warn their liege lords. Intervene in Cornwall and they would face Uther's wrath next.

Ygraine knew what such silence must mean. She had sent her own messages to the kings of Dyfed and Powys, as well as to distant Orkney. With Cornwall as good as lost, Gorlois's loyal friends must retreat and bide their time rather than let Pendragon pick them off, one by one. Brave men who knew the few possible, perilous routes had climbed down Tintagel's cliffs at low tide. They had escaped along the coast unseen, and carried the queen's words away, safely locked inside their heads.

"Well?" Uther's face darkened.

"If I may?" Merlin plucked Ygraine's letter from the king's hand and scanned it. He pursed his lips.

"She wishes to see King Gorlois and his squire Melyas buried before Saint Hulanus's altar. That is no great concession, my king, and it will reflect well on you, to treat your fallen foe with such respect. That will console the Cornish and those who visit his grave will inevitably be reminded that Gorlois defied you and lost. She wishes to arrange Morgana's marriage as she sees fit..."

"The girl's of no value now her father is dead." Uther waved the princess's fate away. "But she wants to stay here until my son is born."

"That might be wisest," Merlin said judiciously. "The journey to Winchester is long and tiring, even in the fair weather of spring and summer. Insisting the queen travels as winter draws on, in these uncertain early days of her pregnancy? Why risk her health and your child?"

"You promised me my son would be born safe and well," Uther accused him.

"True, but I did not say where," retorted Merlin.

Uther glowered. "Did you foresee he will be born at Tintagel?"

Merlin shrugged. "What of it? Everyone will know the boy is yours."

That might be so, Nimue thought, but Merlin wasn't answering Uther's question.

The king didn't seem to notice as he paced back and forth. "She wants my oath that I will not claim my rights as her husband, even on our wedding night. I am not to visit her bed until she invites me?" This seemed to anger him most of all.

Merlin's response startled Nimue. "Are you surprised? Your rough wooing may have won her, but you must live with her as man and wife. She must learn to trust you before she can love you." He shrugged again. "Does that matter? Your union has already been consummated, as everyone will soon see. Ygraine cannot hide a growing belly."

Nimue bit the inside of her lip to stop herself clawing Merlin's face with her fingernails. Rough wooing? Uther had raped the queen, thanks to Merlin's sorcery. That surely meant they would pay the threefold price, sooner or later. Nimue fervently hoped she would see it.

Merlin was still talking. "To secure peace across Britain,

you must have peace in your household, my lord. As long as Ygraine is seen to be content, no Cornish troublemaker can raise any force against you in her name. Indulge her and she will come to respect you all the sooner."

Uther shook his head. "I cannot keep this vast army idling until the bitch has whelped. Firewood is getting scarce, and the weather grows colder by the day."

"Indeed," Merlin agreed. "Your knights and their loyal men must return home before winter. They can carry the news of your glorious victory and of your mercy to your vanquished foes. The tale of your wedding will be told and retold when their families celebrate Yuletide. Meantime, Ygraine's people and the whole of Cornwall will become used to a new lord in Tintagel. King Mark can have Launceston Castle, but you should retain this fortress as the high king's residence. Your presence will remind everyone that they owe you their lives."

Brisk, he refolded the queen's letter. "When spring arrives, we will send heralds to spread the word that your marriage is to be blessed with a child. Logres will rejoice and you can return to Winchester in high summer with your son and heir."

"Indeed I will." Uther savoured that prospect before he turned to Nimue. "Tell your mistress I will let her have her way, for now at least." He glanced at Merlin. "I will teach her obedience in due course."

"Indeed, your grace." Merlin bowed low. As he straightened up, he took hold of Nimue's elbow. "By your leave, I will escort Queen Ygraine's woman back through the camp."

Uther laughed unkindly. "I'm sure her virtue is safe. Not even these men are that desperate."

Nimue allowed Merlin to usher her between the tents and the fire pits, back towards Tintagel. She wove another muffling veil of magic. "You didn't foresee where this child would be born?"

"That didn't escape you?" Merlin shook his head, rueful. "I originally saw the boy born in Winchester, but that was when Uther had wooed and won Ygraine rather more gently, after Gorlois's death in a hunting accident. Alas, my king is not a patient man. Once I told him what was to come after his victory over the Picts, he chose to secure his legacy sooner rather than later."

The two of them chose to deny Ygraine any choice in her own future, Nimue thought furiously. But there was nothing to be gained by challenging that. Not here, and not now.

"Not that it matters where the child is born," Merlin insisted. "In every future I have seen, the boy Arthur becomes high king of the Britons. That's what I must secure. Unless he wears his father's crown, these islands will be ravaged by invaders and plagued by wild magic. You cannot want that any more than I do."

Nimue nodded. That seemed to satisfy him. They walked to the edge of the camp in silence.

As she passed back through Tintagel's gates, Nimue considered what she had learned. Merlin might have foreseen some inevitable destiny for Ygraine's child, but if Uther had taken a different route to reach that future, who was to say what else might have changed? What might Merlin have overlooked or dismissed as irrelevant?

As she crossed the narrow path high above the noisy seas, Nimue felt the first faint stirrings of hope.

CHAPTER TEN

At long, long last, Nimue saw Winchester's walls rising above the thatched roofs of the humble cottages straggling along the dusty road. She realised with some surprise that it must be close on a year to the day since she and Ygraine had last come to Uther's capital. This was a very different arrival. They had made the long journey overland rather than travel more swiftly by sea, disembarking in the sheltered waters of the Solent and taking that last easy day on foot.

Loyal Cornish men and women had flocked to greet their former queen in those first few days on the road. To Nimue's surprise, Uther had been content to take a step back, to allow everyone to see that Ygraine had recovered from the trials of childbirth, and she was wearing the rich gowns and jewels of a cherished wife.

Other unspoken questions were answered. The baby had Uther's colouring and his unformed face already showed a hint of his father's strong features. Nimue saw the veiled disappointment on countless faces. They had been hoping Gorlois had left their queen a son. Now that dream was dead, and King Mark was proving a loyal Pendragon vassal, well aware he owed his life and his crown to Uther.

Ygraine's other ties to Cornwall were ruthlessly severed. Sir Gauter was ordered to attend King Mark's court in Launceston rather than escort Ygraine. Sir Idres had been sent to his manor and forcefully advised to stay there. Sir Ulfius was installed as Tintagel's castellan.

Once they crossed the river Tamar, English crowds had greeted them, rejoicing to see their king's heir. As the royal household travelled from manor to manor through southern Logres, Uther had taken charge. He carried the baby from Ygraine's carriage himself when they arrived at each night's lodging. While Nimue and the queen's servants were escorted to their room, Uther claimed the seat of honour in their host's hall, to accept congratulations on his son's birth. The child was only returned when he needed feeding or cleaning, or when Uther was ready to sleep.

Ygraine made no objection. She said nothing when Uther declared the baby would be christened Arthur. She told Nimue this infant was Uther's child foisted upon her, not Gorlois's son born of love. She would do her duty to God as his mother only because he must be considered innocent of his father's sins. Ygraine was true to her word and the child thrived.

But now this interminable journey was over, and they would soon be trapped in Uther's palace. Apprehension knotted Nimue's stomach. Uther would expect Ygraine to be more than a wet-nurse. Nimue could only hope that as long as Ygraine gave the infant suck, Uther wouldn't beget a second child when he insisted on his rights in their marriage bed.

She reined in her patient palfrey. The long line of wagons, riders and pack animals was slowing as they approached Winchester's lofty west gate. Above the mismatched entrances, Nimue could see the guardroom where Uther's soldiers were ready to meet any attack. Armoured sentries kept watch from the battlemented walk running around the city's walls.

"What's wrong?" Morgana's arm tightened around Nimue's waist. The little girl was riding pillion behind her. Everyone had agreed that was the best solution to her tendency to vomit after a few miles of being jolted inside the queen's carriage.

"We'll have to wait to enter the city. Can you see the gate, if you look around me? There's the big arch for carts, and that little arch is for people who are walking."

She patted Morgana's wrist, ready to grab hold if the child gave any hint she was about to slide down to the cobbles. Winchester's daily life went on, even if the King of Logres had returned. Carts and beasts tried to leave through the gate while those eager to enter the city advanced. Men shoved and shouted while women and children tried to avoid being trampled or knocked into some wagon's path. Morgana would have to learn this place was very different to Tintagel. She could not go where she pleased amid so many hazards.

"Do you think he's alright?"

Nimue knew Morgana wasn't asking about her half-brother. She had seen her mother's lack of interest in the baby and followed Ygraine's lead. She was anxious about the brindled cat she had refused to leave in Tintagel. Moppet rode in the queen's carriage in a basket, and Morgana kept him on a leash when each day's journey was done. Nimue was surprised the animal hadn't seized some chance to run away, but he was still with them, and Morgana dutifully dealt with the basket's soiled straw every morning and night without complaining.

"I'm sure he'll be fine, but you had better keep him indoors when we reach the palace. You don't want to get lost, either of you." There were doubtless cats in residence, and Nimue didn't imagine they would take kindly to an interloper. "Hold tight now."

The advance guard had cleared the gate with shouts and the menace of drawn swords. The royal cavalcade started moving. As they passed through the angled arch and made their way down the steep high street, Nimue gave the palfrey her head and the deft animal placed her hooves carefully. The queen's carriage followed close behind, the weary horses threatening to baulk at the commotion surrounding them. Winchester's residents were throwing open their shutters to cheer their liege lord's return. Nimue heard Ygraine's stable master soothe his beasts with soft Cornish words.

Thankfully, they soon reached the broad street leading to

the palace. The king's personal guard spurred their horses and Nimue saw Uther in their midst with his comet-tailed dragon banner flying from a rider's spear. The horsemen galloped through the open palace gate, greeted by glad cries and raucous horns.

Mules to the rear made their displeasure known with loud braying. Their handlers answered with ripe curses. Even Nimue's imperturbable palfrey threatened to bolt and Ygraine's stable master had his hands full holding back the carriage horses. Morgana's arm tightened around Nimue's waist as they passed through the gatehouse.

As they emerged from the shadows into the evening sunlight, no one within the encircling wall paid them any attention. Uther's men led horses and mules to their stables. Heralds had ridden on ahead, giving the palace cooks ample time to prepare a feast. The scents of roast meats and fresh bread made Nimue fiercely hungry. A moment later, she felt queasy, recalling that fateful night when Lot of Orkney rejected Uther's ambitions.

What was done was done. Now she must do all she could to keep Gorlois's widow and daughter safe. She spoke to the stable master driving Ygraine's carriage in Cornish. "Follow me."

She urged her horse past the great hall and towards the entrance to King Uther's apartments. To her grudging relief, Merlin stood on the steps. The counsellor had come and gone without warning throughout their journey. Sometimes he had been absent for days. At other times, he rode at Uther's side from dawn till dusk. Occasionally he spent an evening with Ygraine and the baby. Nimue hadn't had a chance to talk to him alone.

The carriage halted and the Cornish women who attended Ygraine got out. One passed the swaddled baby down to another's waiting arms. Merlin strode forward to be certain the child was well.

Nimue turned to Morgana. "Get down, sweetheart."

The youngest of the Cornish maids was coming to take charge of the little princess. Morgana slipped down from the palfrey's rump and seized the girl's hand. The princess dragged her towards the palace servants unloading the queen's baskets and coffers. Everyone could hear her cat was loudly displeased.

Nimue dismounted and gave the palfrey's reins to a boy who'd appeared from somewhere. She was intent on catching Merlin before he disappeared, but to her surprise, he was striding towards her. His dark eyes were bright, and his thin lips curved with satisfaction.

"Where are the queen's chambers?" she demanded.

"On the floor between Uther's rooms and my own. She may greet any visitors in the king's hall beside the library. She need only notify the captain of the watch, to let him know who is expected."

So Ygraine's comings and goings would be watched and reported to Uther.

"My mistress will be stiff and weary. She will wish to bathe. Whom do I send to the kitchens for hot water?"

"Everything is ready," Merlin said, impatient. "Get her dressed for the feast as befits Uther's queen. Hurry up."

He hurried away with his black robe flapping. Nimue watched him go with a powerful urge to use her magic to trip him.

"Nimue?" The queen got out of the carriage. Concern deepened the weariness in her face. "Where is Morgana?"

"There." Nimue pointed at the child and her maid carrying Moppet's basket.

"Ah, yes." The queen's smile came and went. "What did Uther's crow have to say?"

"That you are expected to attend the king's feast." Nimue grimaced. "Suitably attired."

"Uther's hunt was successful, so he wants to show off his trophies." Ygraine shrugged. "With luck, he'll spend the rest of the night drinking with his lickspittles."

"As you say, your grace." Nimue followed Ygraine up the steps.

At least Merlin – or whoever the counsellor had instructed – had done a good job preparing their rooms. The queen's chamber was comfortably furnished, and a steaming bath was fragrant with revivifying herbs. As soon as Ygraine settled in the water, Nimue went in search of the queen's clothes. She found the Cornish maids unpacking gowns and linen in the room next door. Ygraine's jewel coffers stood on a table.

"Mistress. Please–" One of the girls looked up, anxious. "Could we send for some pallets and blankets and sleep up here? So we're on hand if her grace or the princess needs us."

Nimue saw the women's dread of this unknown place. The thought of being split up in the servants' quarters was terrifying. She knew how they felt.

"That's a very good idea, Wenna." She tried to offer them a reassuring smile, but she had no more idea of what tomorrow might bring than these girls did. What about the day after that? "Take the sage green gown, and the gold with agates to our mistress."

She left before the maids could ask any more awkward questions and found two more spacious rooms on this floor. One had been set aside as a sitting room for the queen and the other was for Morgana. The child sat on the bed, playing with her cat, while the youngest Cornish maid unpacked her belongings.

"Derwa, where is the nursery?" Nimue had seen no sign of a cradle or anything else that an infant might need.

"Downstairs, in the room beside the king's bed chamber."

Nimue supposed she shouldn't be surprised that Uther would put his own wishes above everyone else's convenience. Perhaps he would reconsider when he realised how seldom the baby slept through the night. She had told Merlin time and again the infant needed a settled routine.

She smiled at Derwa. "Please fetch the baby as soon as

you're done here. The queen will dine in the great hall tonight. She must feed the child before she dresses."

If Merlin objected to the delay, Nimue would ask if he wanted Uther to hear his precious heir wailing with hunger. She returned to the queen. Once out of her bath, Ygraine sat in her chemise while Nimue braided and coiled her hair. They heard the baby's whimpers. Derwa wasn't carrying the infant though. An English nursemaid brought him into the room. At least the woman looked old enough to have borne her own children. Nimue hoped she had experience of lulling a wakeful baby in the small hours of the night.

Ygraine unlaced her chemise to offer the baby her dark nipple. The child sucked heartily as he always did. Nimue seized this opportunity to change her own clothes. It wasn't long before the baby had fed from both breasts and drowsed in Ygraine's arms. She handed him to his nurse, still without a word.

Nimue helped her mistress to dress. When Nimue picked up the fine silken veil, she realised Ygraine no longer had a crown or a queen's coronet. As Gorlois's widow, she had no claim to the Cornish royal regalia, and besides, Uther had sent every heirloom to King Mark. What was to hold the queen's veil in place?

"Uther is waiting."

Merlin's voice from the doorway startled them. Nimue wondered how long he had been there, and if he had used magic to conceal himself. Such questions could wait. He held out a finely wrought gold diadem. Nimue went to take it. Not a full circle, it was nevertheless sufficient to hold the silk secure.

Ygraine turned to Merlin, her face unreadable. "We are ready."

The queen followed the counsellor down the stairs to the king's apartment, and Nimue followed Ygraine. Uther waited for his new wife, wearing the heavy crown of Logres. It bore no resemblance to Ygraine's diadem. Uther had not chosen a consort to share the burdens of his rule.

Scowling with impatience, Uther thrust out his arm.
Composed, Ygraine rested her hand upon it. She allowed the
king to escort her to a second, narrower staircase at the heart
of this building. Nimue realised this led to the door at the
back of the great hall's dais. She glanced upwards and made a
mental note to discover where the door from these stairs to the
queen's floor might be.

Merlin opened the door. The knights of Logres greeted
their king with a deafening roar. Uther smiled broadly as he
walked to his canopied throne. He made a show of pulling out
Ygraine's chair with a courteous bow. That was no different to
the others around the table. Uther's queen's place was at his
side and no more.

Food was swiftly served. Conversation rose down in the hall
and along the high table. Nimue knew she should take this
opportunity to get the measure of the English nobles. Ygraine
must cultivate friendships in this hostile place. Unfortunately,
the queen was the only woman present tonight. Add to
that, weary after a long day in the saddle, it took all Nimue's
concentration to serve Ygraine without spilling anything. The
king's expansive gestures didn't help as he ate and drank and
told tales of his campaign against Cornwall.

Uther had invited knights who hadn't taken part in that
war, and those who hadn't been summoned to visit and hunt
in the months he had spent at Tintagel. Nimue tried at least to
remember their names. She could find out where they lived
in the next few days. That would give her an excuse to talk to
the palace's servants as she sought her own allies. Other than
that, she heard little of any use. The knights were primarily
interested in enjoying the abundant delicacies and washing
them down with fine wine. Few of them spoke to Ygraine, and
Uther made no effort to introduce her.

Nimue wondered if that discourtesy prompted the return of
the crease between Merlin's brows. As he stood behind Uther's
throne, his dark eyes darted back and forth. Nimue saw him

glance at the knights seated towards the end of the table. From time to time, the men concealed brief exchanges behind their raised goblets. She wondered if Merlin used magic to hear what they said. She wondered if she should do the same.

The evening dragged on. Down in the hall, the celebrations grew raucous. On the dais, roast meats and robust red wines were replaced by honeyed pastries served with golden vintages. Uther was in no hurry to leave as he shared jokes and stories with his men.

Nimue wondered if she saw a few hints of impatience in their faces. As long as the king was present, the knights had to remain. Before she could decide, Ygraine tapped Uther's forearm. He looked at her, surprised. Had he forgotten his wife was beside him?

Ygraine leaned closer to make sure he could hear her. "May I have your permission to go to your son? He will be hungry by now."

She offered Uther the smile they had found convinced him his queen was content. As long as he was getting his own way, he could be persuaded that all was well. Through these past months at Tintagel, Nimue and the queen had learned how little Pendragon knew of women.

Uther nodded and Nimue hurried to pull back Ygraine's chair. Ygraine curtseyed as a dutiful wife should and Nimue did the same. Uther was already embarking on a fresh anecdote.

Ygraine heaved a sigh of relief as Nimue closed the stair door on the hubbub. "Fetch the baby. One of the girls can help me undress."

They retraced the route they had taken to reach the hall. Ygraine went on up the main stairs, while Nimue followed the sounds of a fractious infant to the prince's nursery. The nurse was walking to and fro, rocking the hungry baby.

"Let me take him to his mother." Nimue reached for the child. "If you please, could you do me a great favour? The queen wishes to keep her women close until we're all more used to the palace. They need pallets and blankets, and I don't know who to ask."

"I can see to that." The woman smiled amiably as she handed the baby over.

A knot of tension in Nimue's neck eased as she took the baby to Ygraine. Not every Englishman or woman could be their enemy. By the time she emerged from Ygraine's chamber to take the baby back downstairs, the nurse had been as good as her word. A trio of lackeys carried bedding into the room beside the queen's.

Nimue returned the prince to his nurse and the most ornate cradle she had ever seen. The woodcarvers who served the Minster must have made this pinnacled and impractical monstrosity. She was still amused when she returned to the queen's floor and checked on Morgana. The child was fast asleep with Moppet curled up beside her, so Nimue went to her own bed. Ygraine was already snoring. As Nimue settled on her pallet, exhaustion swept over her in a smothering wave.

Some unaccountable time later, she was shaken awake. Her eyes snapped open, and she stiffened with fear. Merlin crouched beside her. He had no more need of a candle than she did, and no need to speak aloud.

Come with me. Uther is deathly ill.

CHAPTER ELEVEN

By dawn, the king had stopped vomiting and purging, but only because he had nothing left to spew or shit. Nimue stood by the open window getting a breath of fresher air when the bedchamber door opened. Merlin had returned.

"How is he?" He looked at the canopied bed until he had seen Uther's chest rise and fall.

"If we cannot get him to drink without heaving the liquid straight back up, he will sink and die."

"We? You're the healer," Merlin challenged her.

"It would help if I knew what I was trying to cure." Nimue wasn't about to take the blame if Uther did not rally. "Was there sickness in the palace before we arrived? Are summer fevers rife in the city?"

Merlin looked blank. "I don't know."

"Find out," Nimue said curtly.

If Uther had a squire, she could send the boy on such errands. But Pendragon had no inclination for instructing some hopeful youth in the ways of warfare and courtly manners. She and Ygraine had agreed he was far too impatient to make a good teacher.

She snapped her fingers to get Merlin's attention. "Tell the kitchen to send more boiled water, and tell the laundresses I need fresh linen. Fetch me wine in a stoppered and sealed flagon. Bring it yourself, with a clean goblet, a silver one."

Merlin left without a word. His lean face was drawn with anxiety. So, he hadn't foreseen this turn of events, Nimue

91

concluded. That was no consolation. If Uther died... The consequences for Ygraine and Morgana, and for their faithful Cornish servants didn't bear thinking about.

She left the room to fetch her coffer of tinctures and potions. The nursery door opened, and the prince's maid looked out. The woman looked weary to the bone.

"Should I take Prince Arthur to his mother's chamber? In case the miasma of the king's sickness spreads?"

"You may as well." Nimue didn't believe this illness was carried by foul air, but the infant would be less disturbed upstairs, and the Cornish girls could watch him while the nurse slept.

The woman fetched the oblivious baby, swaddled in a basket of woven straw no different to a peasant child's bed. They walked up the stairs together. Nimue left the nurse to explain her arrival as she went to find her medicines in the queen's sitting room.

Ygraine came to join her. "What ails the king?"

"I think he's been poisoned. Do not eat or drink anything sent from the palace kitchens until I have assessed it."

Ygraine bit her lip. "I would not wish that on him, even if..."

"No," Nimue agreed. "Let us see how he fares now the worst spasms have passed."

"We will stay up here." Ygraine gestured towards the room where Morgana was sleeping. "Until we know, one way or the other..."

"Indeed." Nimue took several small jars down to Uther's chamber. Merlin had evidently terrified the palace servants, as far more boiled water and linen than she might possibly need swiftly appeared. Nimue added a scatter of herbs to a basin of hot water. She stripped back the light sheet draped across Uther and washed the unconscious king. His sturdy frame was formidable, but Nimue knew those corded muscles, veins and sinews were so starkly visible because his body was wracked with thirst.

Uther's limbs were heavy and as limp as his shrivelled manhood. He did not react to the touch of the wet cloth or to the pungent herbs. Nimue pinched a fold of skin on his flank between her thumb and forefinger. She pinched harder and twisted. Uther stirred and grimaced, though only for a moment.

What had caused the vomiting? There was no hint of a fever in his skin, or the rank sweat of summer sickness. She looked at him with the sight of her people. Merlin said Pendragon and his heirs would save Britain from wild magic, but Nimue saw no hint of sorcery at work. That was some relief, as she had no real idea how she might counter such malice with her own magic. On the other hand, Uther's vital spark was as dull as a guttering candle. His aura was the faintest sheen of tarnished silver.

"How is he?" Merlin brought the wine she'd asked for, still in its wax-sealed earthenware flagon.

"Very ill." Taking the flagon and the goblet, she mixed a draught of wine, hot water, honey and a pale powder from one of her jars.

"What's that?" Merlin demanded.

"Wine and honey to strengthen him, and camomile should help him keep it down. Lift his head, gently."

Merlin did so. Nimue held the goblet to Uther's lips and tipped a little into his mouth, watching carefully to see if he swallowed it. The apple in his throat moved.

"He's sucking it down." Merlin was relieved.

Nimue wrapped his hand around the goblet. "Get him to drink as much as you can but stop if he starts to cough. Get liquid in his lungs and you'll kill him."

She left the room before Merlin could object. She had heard feet coming up the stairs. That rattle and clink of crockery must mean breakfast had arrived for Ygraine and her maids.

"One moment."

The two lackeys and the maid might not know who Nimue was, but they recognised a voice they should obey. They stood

patiently as she lifted the dish covers on their trays. She found
frumenty cooked with milk, and the cracked and swollen grain
was enriched with fresh cherries and shreds of dried apples
from last year's harvest. More apple had been stewed slowly
with honey to go with fresh baked bread, and a dish of pale
butter. The maid carried tall jugs of milk. Everything looked
and smelled enticing, and Nimue's magical sight showed her
nothing amiss.

She looked at the apprehensive servants. "Is there any other
sickness in the palace? Anything outside the walls?"

"Sir Brastias and Sir Jordan have been taken ill," one of the
lackeys offered.

"And Sir Baudwin, mistress," the girl piped up, "but there's
no word of fever in the city, not even in the back alleys or
down by the river."

Nimue recognised the names of some of Uther's most loyal
and trusted knights. They had been sitting well apart around
the high table. They couldn't have shared spoiled meat with
their king without anyone else falling ill.

"Sir Lardans and Sir Pinel and some other lords are waiting
in the great hall." The second lackey sounded dubious.

"I will tell Master Merlin. Follow me."

Nimue led the servants up to the queen's chamber. She
answered Ygraine's questioning glance with a nod to tell her the
food was wholesome. She didn't return to the king's chamber,
heading for the inner staircase instead. There was no one else
to be seen. Was that Merlin's doing, or did Uther customarily
demand such privacy? Nimue didn't know and she didn't care.
She was simply grateful as she sat on the steps in the darkness
behind the door that opened onto the dais.

Closing her eyes, she used her magic to seek out other
presences in the building. She sensed Merlin in the king's
bedchamber and made very sure to veil her magic from him.
The last thing she needed was the enchanter coming to see
what she was doing. She could also feel how weak Uther's

hold on this world truly was. If Nimue drew him into the perilous spell she was working, even by accident, his life could be snuffed out.

She turned her attention to the servants who had carried their trays upstairs. They would soon be leaving, so they were no use to her, but the queen and her maids had gathered to share their breakfast. Nimue felt their devotion to each other like a soothing warmth. That smaller, brighter presence must be Morgana, while the dancing wisp of animal vigour had to be her cat, doubtless hoping for milk.

Nimue left Moppet and Morgana well alone, along with the baby prince and his nurse. She drew a delicate thread of their vital spark from the other women and wove these together in her cupped hands. That was enough to kindle her spell. She reached through the wood and wattle wall with her sorcery and found a handful of men close by. There were others, further away. She guessed the knights had brought some liege men who were sitting by the great hall's far doors. Good. She would make use of them and spare the women up above. These men had more vigour to start with, and it was no concern of hers if they found they were unaccountably weary for the next few days.

When Nimue opened her eyes, a mouse sat in her cupped hands. A moment later, she saw herself through the mouse's eyes. She fought a rush of dizziness as she jumped down to the floor. Then she squeezed through the gap under the door to the dais and the unpleasant sensation faded. Instead, a mouse's fears threatened to overwhelm her, just as her long-ago teachers had warned. She could not stay in this form for long without risking her sense of her true self.

Five bold knights had claimed the benches closest to the steps leading up to the king's table. Mouse-Nimue crept to the edge of the dais. She made herself as small as she possibly could as the hall became impossibly large and terrifying. Every instinct of the form she wore urged her to flee for some crevice and safety. Fighting those impulses, she crouched to listen to this conversation and to commit the men's voices to memory. A mouse's eyesight was lamentably poor, and her magic could only improve it a little. Everything beyond the closest table was a blur where any number of predators might lurk. Mouse-Nimue trembled.

"It has to be poison," a lord with a shaved head insisted. His yellow surcote bore an armoured gauntlet embroidered in black. He had never come to Tintagel. Nimue would have remembered him.

Another unknown knight agreed. "It must be, to strike down Brastias, Jordan and Baudwin in the same night." His blazon was a sheaf of wheat on a dark green weave.

"Poison is a woman's weapon," the first lord said emphatically. "The Cornish bitch is not resigned to her fate, however sweetly she simpers and smiles. Uther cut down Gorlois and took her as his prize. She must long for revenge."

"She is bound to him by the child. Anyone who looks at the whelp can see he is Uther's son," one of the other three pointed out.

"If she wished to murder Uther, why wait?" the knight beside him wondered. "If he died at Tintagel, her household would back whatever story she told, whether she claimed the king fell ill with some wasting sickness or fell from those cliffs."

Mouse-Nimue wondered if Ygraine had ever contemplated such vengeance. In her darkest moments of despair through the cold of winter, she had considered paying the threefold price. Only fear of men like these seeking revenge had stopped her.

The wheat sheaf knight answered the doubter. "Ygraine is no fool. She would know she would be accused and condemned to burn at the stake once the child was born."

The shaven-headed lord nodded. "If the king dies here, she can cast suspicion far and wide while she holds Uther's palace in Prince Arthur's name. Uther's loyal men will flock to his infant son's banner."

"Do you want to be ruled by a woman?" the wheat sheaf knight demanded. "What will become of Logres with her as regent for a mewling infant? Invaders will land along our shores before the summer is out."

"Unless Uther's counsellor rules from the shadows," the shaven-headed lord said dourly.

"You share our doubts about Merlin's influence, don't you?" the wheat sheaf knight chimed in.

The three other knights exchanged glances.

"Why did she poison Sir Jordan, Sir Brastias, and Sir Baudwin?" The shaven-headed lord shook his head. "She knew they were as close to Uther as brothers."

These two were the enemy, Mouse-Nimue decided. They were spinning lies into a rope to lash Ygraine to an executioner's stake. She wished she could see their auras, to get some hint of the motives that drove them, but she couldn't hope to do that with these weak, animal eyes.

"How did she do it?" The one who'd sat silent so far spoke up. "Poisoning four men on her very first night in this palace?"

"A queen can always find cat's-paws to do her bidding. We'll find the culprit in the kitchens after a few scullions have been put to the question," the wheat sheaf knight assured him.

Because pain and fear would secure whatever answers he wanted. Mouse-Nimue's whiskers twitched with terror at the thought of torture. She had to fight the urge to flee.

"I hear Sir Baudwin has rallied. Let us hope that Uther recovers," the doubting knight said.

The shaven-headed lord laughed harshly. "With the queen's own healer tending him? She'll sit on her hands while she watches him die, or she'll hasten his end."

"Whatever we may suspect, we have no proof," one of the others protested. "What are we going do?"

"Stand ready," the shaven-headed lord replied.

"Wait for our signal," the wheat sheaf knight advised.

Mouse-Nimue had heard enough. She scurried back across

the dais and squeezed under the door. The body she had left behind was sitting stiff and still on the stairs. She climbed up her own skirts to curl up in her own cupped hands. A moment later, she was herself again, and the mouse was a scrap of shadow melting into the darkness.

She took a moment to reacquaint herself with hands instead of paws, long, straight legs, and the lack of a tail. When she was sure she was steady on her own feet again, and muffling her steps with a skein of magic, she hurried up to the king's floor. Merlin sat at Uther's side. The king was no longer so deathly pale, and his aura was a little brighter. Nothing indicated he had vomited again, or that the honeyed wine had passed straight through him.

"Whose blazon is a black mailed fist on a yellow ground?" She didn't bother greeting Merlin.

"Sir Pinel. Why do you ask?"

"A wheat sheaf in gold on green?"

"Sir Lardans." Merlin rose from his stool. "What's going on?"

"Where were they last night?"

"I believe they were both down in the hall."

Nimue nodded. The villains would want to be seen where they could have no opportunity to tamper with food served to Uther and his allies. It wasn't only queens who could bribe underlings to commit their crimes.

"What of it?" Merlin demanded.

"They are in the great hall, supposedly waiting for news of Uther. They're striving to persuade the knights with them that Ygraine poisoned the king."

Merlin shook his head. "She would never be so foolish."

"But he has been poisoned, and I'll wager so have Sir Brastias, Sir Jordan and Sir Baudwin. Why are Pinel and Lardans so confident Uther will perish?" Nimue challenged him. "Why are they the first to suspect poison? Because they are behind it."

Merlin stared at her for a long moment. "Make sure he survives then."

He left the room. Nimue gritted her teeth so hard her jaw ached. She had thought the worst fate Ygraine faced was life as Uther's wife. A future as his widow at the mercy of these Englishmen would be far more perilous. A future that hatred and suspicion would surely soon cut short. Nimue had never been so sorely tempted to try scrying into the future, to see where she might frustrate these men and their evil plans.

Though Merlin hadn't foreseen this turn of events. She should save her magic for more immediate uses, such as keeping Uther alive. For one thing, whatever debt the king owed for Merlin's assistance in raping Ygraine and killing Gorlois must still be paid. Falling victim to a poisoner wasn't the same.

She mixed another goblet of honeyed wine and camomile and warmed it with a hint of magic as she added herbs to balance the humours in the king's blood. Little by little, she persuaded him to swallow it.

The morning passed and Merlin didn't return. Only the Minster's bells calling the monks to prayer broke the silence. Eventually Uther's ominous stillness shifted into true sleep. He drew deeper breaths and his waxy pallor ebbed. Some time after midday, Nimue heard footsteps. She turned to see Ygraine in the doorway.

"How is he?" The queen did not enter the room.

"I believe he will live, if we can save him from being poisoned a second time. I told Merlin what I suspect."

The enchanter would doubtless take the credit for saving Uther's life. Nimue didn't care. She would rather not have the king know he was in her debt. Having Merlin under such an obligation was a different matter.

"When should we–"

Commotion outside interrupted Ygraine. She stared at Nimue, startled. Both women hurried to the unshuttered window. Down below, they saw men and women looking in all directions as shouts echoed around the palace. The stamp of booted feet heralded armoured men running along the battlements. Nimue heard the crash of the portcullises securing the palace entrance. The Minster bells began ringing a raucous alarm.

A scream ripped through the summer afternoon. A man fell from the wall walk with an arrow jutting from his face. A rain of deadly shafts soared over the fortifications. In the castle yard, those too slow to see the danger collapsed, skewered. Some thrashed, screaming. Others were dead before they hit the ground. Everyone else ran for cover.

Nimue glanced at the silver bowl she'd used to wash Uther. She couldn't scry with Ygraine here. How could she find Merlin? What was he doing? Why was Uther's palace under attack?

CHAPTER TWELVE

A clatter inside the room startled the women. Uther's flailing hand had knocked the silver goblet off the bedside table.

Shivering, Ygraine shook her head. "I can't–"

"Go. See to your children. Reassure your maids."

As Ygraine hurried away, Nimue approached the bed.

Uther opened his eyes. "What–?" He coughed and winced.

"Let me get you some watered wine."

Uther's hand seized Nimue's wrist painfully tight. "I hear battle," he said thickly.

Nimue could hardly deny the clangour of the Minster's bells and the shrieks and yells of fighting outside. "The palace is under attack. I have no idea who the enemy might be."

Uther released her and struggled to sit up. "Where is Merlin?" he rasped.

"Saxon raiders have landed on the coast, my liege." The black-clad enchanter appeared in the doorway. "They are attacking Winchester from the south in force. A small detachment have scaled the city walls closest to the palace."

"Who leads the defence?" Uther tried to kick away the sheet that covered him.

Merlin's answer shocked him into stillness. "At present, no one, my lord, though your warriors are fighting valiantly. Sir Baudwin, Sir Brastias and Sir Jordan were struck down with the same sickness as you."

With the same poison? Have any of them died?

Nimue stared at Merlin, but he wouldn't meet her eye.

"Fetch my armour." Uther swung his legs off the bed and tried to get to his feet. He barely managed to stand before his knees buckled and he sat down heavily.

"Your grace, you are in no fit state to get up," Nimue protested.

Ygraine's situation would hardly be improved if Pendragon collapsed and died before he reached the great hall's door.

He glared at her. "Give me something to lend me strength or get out."

"Your grace, a moment." Merlin hurried to retrieve the goblet from the floor and filled it from the wine flagon.

"Sir Pinel, Sir Lardans and some others are waiting for news," Nimue said quickly. "Let me fetch them, your grace."

As soon as the loyal knights saw Uther was alive, they would rally to him. Lardans and Pinel would do the same, if only to save themselves from suspicion.

"No." Merlin replied instead of the king. "They were here earlier, but Sir Pinel and Sir Lardans are nowhere to be found. I am told their men left the city last night."

"To join the raiders attacking us now?" Uther demanded.

"Alas so, my liege." Merlin handed him the wine. "It seems this is a long-planned attack."

Nimue saw the shimmer of magic around the goblet. Merlin shot her a warning look.

"You must be seen leading Logres' forces, and soon," he told the king. "The defence of Winchester will fail if your people believe you are dead. This is why these enemies seek to trap you in the palace. You must win this battle and take the fight to these invaders and the traitors in league with them."

"He cannot fight," Nimue objected.

"Silence, woman!" Uther drained the goblet and tossed it to Merlin. This time he managed to stand for a count of three before the bed saved him from hitting the floor.

He struggled to his feet again. As much as Nimue detested Uther, she could not deny his courage.

"Get me as far as the stables, and we'll see if I can sit on a horse. If I can't stay in the saddle–" He staggered, fighting to keep his balance. "I'll go to battle in a cursed horse litter if I must."

Merlin handed him the refilled goblet. Nimue realised with a cold shock that Uther must know the wine was enchanted, and he didn't care. As he drank, Merlin found the naked king under-linen, hose and a tunic. Nimue joined him, as if she intended to help. She caught hold of the enchanter's black sleeve and used her magic to sting him with a rebuke.

This is madness.

Merlin's dark eyes were hooded, and his lips pressed tight together.

This is how it must be. I have foreseen this day.

But Nimue felt desperation thrumming through his sorcery. Fear hollowed her stomach.

What have you foreseen for my lady and for the princess? What about the baby?

Merlin turned away, carrying clothing to the king.

Uther was steadier on his feet. His face was still drawn, but from a distance, the king's summer tan could be taken for good health. He dismissed Nimue with a gesture. "See to your mistress, woman."

She left the room. She had to obey the king. Besides, Merlin wouldn't tell her anything, and Uther wouldn't listen to a word she might say.

Uther's choices would seal his fate, and so would Merlin's. Nimue would keep Ygraine and her children safe. If Merlin was using sorcery so recklessly, she could use enchantment for her own purposes. There could be no penalty for protecting the innocent.

She ran up the stairs to the queen's rooms and found all those who had come from Tintagel gathered in the sitting room, including the stable master and the grooms. Ygraine was hugging Morgana. White-faced and uncomprehending, the prince's nurse sat in a corner, cradling the baby and unable to understand the heated debate in the Cornish tongue.

"Your grace, we can get away," the stable master insisted. "We have harnessed your horses and the carriage is ready by the rear gate. That's not under attack."

A maid protested. "You think Pendragon's men will let the queen pass?"

"If we tell them he's ordered her to take his son out of danger. That one will vouch for it if she knows what's good for her."

The stable master flung a hand towards the nurse. She flinched, hearing the threat in his tone. Nimue couldn't work out who favoured this desperate plan, or who opposed it.

"Silence!"

Everyone stared at her, dumbfounded. Nimue saw anguish and uncertainty in the queen's eyes, and Morgana's terror. "Your grace–"

A roar outside interrupted her. Two maids and a groom rushed to the window. The groom turned, his jaw slack with awe. "The king."

Nimue forced her way to the window. The boy was right. Uther's gleaming armour was unmistakable, and the herald riding at his side carried a pennant with the comet-tailed dragon. How had he appeared on horseback so fast? That could only be thanks to Merlin's magic.

A dozen knights joined the king, each leading their men-at-arms. More loyal warriors advanced along the battlements, carrying tall shields of woven wicker. They sheltered Uther's archers as their merciless arrows drove back the Saxon invaders below, driving them back from the walls, Uther's army marched towards the great gate. Shrieks of panic died away, replaced by shouted commands.

"If the king–" The maid had stopped talking.

Nimue turned to see everyone frozen in place. Not motionless from fear or surprise, but held by magic. Merlin crossed the room, intent on the baby in the nursemaid's arms. Quick as thought, Nimue stepped into his path.

"Out of my way." He tried to shove her aside.

Nimue drew on the solid stones of the walls to resist him. Merlin could not move her. "What are you doing?"

"I must take the child to safety."

"Why? What have you foreseen?"

Merlin hesitated, but scowling, he answered her. "Uther will win this day. He will hold Winchester and he will slaughter these invaders. He will not win this war though. He will be dead before winter. This is my only chance to save Prince Arthur. I must save him to save Britain."

"Without his mother? What will become of Ygraine if Uther returns from today's victory to find his son gone?"

Merlin shrugged. Furious, Nimue realised he had no idea. "You haven't made the least effort to see what her future holds."

"She has you to save her, doesn't she?" Merlin snapped. "She will not miss the child. She has never loved him, not since she realised he is Uther's son."

Nimue couldn't deny it. As she hesitated, Merlin reached for the child. Nimue snatched the baby from the blank-faced nurse's arms. She nearly dropped him when she realised the infant wasn't wholly under Merlin's spell. Prince Arthur gazed up at her wide-eyed, as he sucked on a fold of swaddling.

Merlin reached for the child, pleading. "If I do not take him, he will be killed when his father dies."

The ring of truth in his words chilled Nimue. "Let's make a bargain then."

Merlin wasn't expecting that. "What do you mean?"

"I'll give you the child in return for these other lives." Nimue gestured at the Cornish servants. "Use your magic to ensure all eyes slide over them as they leave the palace. Veil them from every foe until they reach home."

Merlin scowled. "If I must, though I doubt Ygraine will be welcome in Cornwall."

"That's not your concern." Nimue looked at the English nurse. "What about her?"

Merlin drew an impatient hand across the woman's unseeing eyes. The nurse got to her feet and left the room with the slow gait of a sleepwalker. "She will remember me taking the baby to safety on Uther's orders. Now, let me have him."

"Only if Ygraine agrees." Nimue unpicked the threads of the magic that snared the queen.

Ygraine trembled as she saw everyone else in the room held in unnatural thrall. "What is this sorcery?"

"Your grace, forgive me." Merlin bowed low. "King Uther commands me to take his son to safety, but Nimue will not give up the child unless you agree."

"Nimue?" Ygraine's gasp contained countless questions.

"I have magic of my own, your grace." Nimue was shaking. She had never disclosed any hint of her true nature to a mortal before. What would she do if Ygraine cast her out? "I have only ever used it in your service and for good. I swear."

"That is true," Merlin interrupted, "and she drives a hard bargain besides. She says she will only let me take Prince Arthur away if I see you safely back to Cornwall."

"What–" Ygraine stared at Nimue.

"If you wish to keep the child, we will find some refuge together, your grace." Though Nimue had no idea how she might do that with Merlin in vengeful pursuit.

Ygraine looked at the baby in Nimue's arms. Commotion outside battered the tense stillness around them.

"No," the queen said slowly. "He was never mine and he never will be. Arthur is Uther's son, and that means some men will gladly kill him before he takes his first steps." She looked at Merlin. "I may not love the child, but I would never wish him harm. Do what you must to keep him safe."

"Always, your grace, I swear it." Triumphant, Merlin held out his hands.

Nimue didn't relinquish the infant. "Do not try to find us. Not me, the queen or Morgana. Give me your oath on that."

"You have my word."

Swear it on your magic.

I swear by the hidden secrets of our people. But you must do the same. Never seek to find Arthur.

You have my word, on my magic.

Nimue gave Merlin the baby. He vanished. Ygraine yelped, clutching Morgana. The little girl squirmed, glassy-eyed. Nimue felt the enchantment in the room melting away. She quickly bolstered the spell with her own magic, to keep the servants unseeing and unknowing, just a little while longer. Ygraine watched her, fearful.

"They will remember Merlin taking the baby away on Uther's orders, and with your permission. They will believe it is the only way to save your son. Let me take you and Morgana far away," Nimue begged. "If you return to Cornwall, Uther will pursue you. Him or someone worse."

Ygraine turned so pale that Nimue was afraid she might faint. Then the first of the maidservants staggered as the spell's hold slipped away. More frequent use had strengthened Nimue's magic, but she couldn't hope to equal Merlin.

"Your grace?" As far as the stable master knew, his conversation with the queen had barely been interrupted.

Ygraine looked at Nimue, beseeching. The queen had no idea what to say. Nimue clapped her hands briskly.

"Now the baby prince is safe, do your duty to your queen. Take the carriage out through the rear gate and leave Winchester by the road to the west."

Nimue ushered the men and women towards the door. She used ruthless enchantment to stifle questions and objections as soon as she felt such thoughts form. She had never intruded on any mortal's mind so mercilessly before. It was far easier than she imagined. She could herd this gathering like sheep. Worse, she felt the thrill of wielding such power over mortals. Imposing her will was so delightfully easy...

"Travel as fast as you can, and don't draw attention to yourselves. If anyone asks for the queen, say she has gone on ahead, or that she will follow the next day." That should start enough rumours to confuse Sir Pinel or anyone else who might pursue Ygraine's servants with evil intent.

The queen looked away, freeing herself from Morgana's arms. She hurried towards the table where her jewel coffer stood.

"You will need silver for the road." Ygraine found two soft leather bags that chinked softly with coin. She handed one to the stable master, and one to the eldest maid. "Share what's left between you, when you reach Cornwall."

"Your grace–" The maid burst into tears.

"We will be safe," Ygraine assured her, but Nimue saw doubt cloud the queen's eyes.

Another of the maids was grizzling. Nimue could feel her hold over them start to slip away.

"Go, now," she commanded. "Do not stop to gather possessions. Travel as long as you have daylight. Never question what you are doing. You must do this to keep your queen and the princess safe."

The servants hurried away and Nimue closed the door.

"What – what–" The queen was shivering so violently, she couldn't speak.

Nimue closed the jewel coffer and secured its clasps. Ygraine wasn't going to leave here destitute. There were gifts from Gorlois in there that Ygraine cherished, as well as his mother's jewels which should go to Morgause, Elaine and Morgana. She looked at the little princess, wondering how she might reassure her. To her surprise, the child looked more thoughtful than scared.

"Take your mother's hand, and take mine." Cradling the jewel coffer in her other arm, Nimue reached out towards her.

Morgana did as she was told. Nimue wove her spell. She drew the power she needed from everyone within the castle's wall. She had never worked such a reckless enchantment, but she discovered it was simplicity. The sensation was glorious, as intoxicating as fine wine.

As her sorcery swept them away, she lost all sense of time. Nimue felt herself falling into chaos. Terror scattered her wits. Frantic, she fought to regain her hold on her magic. Her feet hit the ground so hard, she was jarred from her heels to the top of her head. Trying to shake off sickening dizziness, she heard gulls cry overhead. The wind on her face was warm and moist with the scent of the sea. Nimue opened her eyes.

"Where are we?" Ygraine looked around, disbelieving.

They stood by the high tide mark in a sheltered bay ringed by grass-crowned sand dunes. To Nimue's profound relief, there was no one there to be startled by their inexplicable arrival. "This is Brittany, your grace. We are somewhere in the kingdom of Garlot."

At least, she fervently hoped so. If her magic had carried them somewhere unexpected, she would deal with whatever problems arose. "We have to decide what tale to tell, when you seek refuge with King Nentres."

For the first time in a long time, Nimue saw the queen's eyes brighten. Ygraine drew a deep breath of the clean, salt-scented air.

"Nentres is a brave and honourable man, and he owes nothing to Uther." She laughed for the first time since Gorlois had died. "He won't turn us away, for Elaine's sake."

Morgana pulled her hands free and walked around them both, leaving a wide circle of footprints on the wind-blown sand. She looked back at Nimue.

"Magic brought us here?" The child was intrigued.

"Yes, but this must be our secret," Nimue said hastily. "No one can ever know."

BOOK TWO

CHAPTER THIRTEEN

"What news from Logres?" Morgana swept into Nimue's chamber. Her fashionably long sleeves flapped as she adjusted the ivory combs holding back her dark hair. Her long tresses reached to her slender waist, unbound as befitted a still unmarried maiden. The creamy woollen gown was buttoned to a decorously high neck, but the tight fit enhanced rather than concealed the curves of her breasts and hips.

"There are English ships in the harbour?" Nimue was surprised. The winter had been mild, but few mariners would risk the crossing before the equinox gales were safely past. "Any letters will have gone to your mother. I imagine they will be more requests for permission to court you."

Though Nimue knew King Nentres favoured a match within Brittany for his sister by marriage, or perhaps further afield on this side of the sea. Elaine and Ygraine agreed. They had turned their backs on Britain after Ygraine had arrived in Garlot fifteen years ago.

"There are no ships with stupid letters," Morgana said, impatient. "What have you scryed?"

Nimue looked at her, uneasy. "Have you been trying to work magic again?"

Morgana grinned, impish. "I don't know if I've seen the truth or some reflection of my own imagination. I need to know what your spells have shown you."

"Men dying," Nimue said bluntly. "What else do I ever see?"

If she thought that would dissuade Morgana, she was

mistaken. Whenever Garlot's courtiers speculated discreetly about the English princess's future, the word most often whispered was "headstrong". That was hardly unexpected, they murmured, since she had grown up without a father's guiding hand.

"What men and where?" Morgana persisted. "Let's try scrying together."

Not for the first time, Nimue recalled a warning from a teacher long ago.

Use your magic sparingly, and always with caution. You can never know what consequences could follow. Throw a stone into a still pool and there's no telling what you might stir up.

She should have paid more heed to such wisdom when they had first found sanctuary here. But she had wanted so badly to offer Ygraine the comfort of seeing Morgause safe and well in distant Orkney. The queen had known the truth of her skills, so what could be the harm? She might never see her daughter in the flesh again with Logres' hostile lords dividing them.

After that first time, why shouldn't Nimue scry for news and not just for the queen's peace of mind? They enjoyed seeing Morgause and her growing family thrive, though of course they pretended to be surprised and delighted when letters finally reached Elaine, announcing the births of Lot of Orkney's sons. Gawain was swiftly joined by Agravaine. Gaheris and Gareth followed soon after, both of them within the same year. Most recently and unexpectedly, Mordred had arrived.

Nimue sought other news without the queen at her side. At first, she had feared pursuit. She had seen Uther's victories as his army drove off the Saxons. He crushed the traitors who had enticed those sea-borne raiders to attack Winchester. As Merlin had predicted, Pendragon waged merciless war on his enemies with Sir Ulfius and Sir Brastias by his side. Then sickness or perhaps poison had struck Uther down as he celebrated in Westminster. He was dead before the year was out, just as Merlin had said.

So Ygraine and Morgana were safe. The knights who had once united behind Uther fought among themselves to claim Pendragon's empty throne. Every spring for a decade and a half, once the days grew longer than the nights, rival armies marched. Rivers and fields ran red with blood until winter's approaching chill put an end to such mayhem. Through the cold and hungry months, men who had survived those battles succumbed to lingering wounds.

Nimue wondered if Merlin saw the same, and if his conscience troubled him. She wondered where he was hiding and how Uther's son fared. The child would be on the verge of manhood now, if he still lived. She did not look for him though, true to her word.

Here in Brittany, in recent years, merchants' ships brought appeals from rival lords eager to wed Morgana, so her father's royal blood might add lustre to their ambitions. Ygraine handed their wheedling letters to Nimue, to be scraped clean of ink and the vellum reused. She never replied.

The kings of the Welsh and the Scots guarded their borders and kept their own counsel as Logres' warring lords' fortunes ebbed and flowed. If the English wished to slaughter each other, that was not their concern. Lot of Orkney's letters said as much to Nentres of Garlot, who told his ally that Brittany's kings felt the same.

"Well?" Morgana demanded.

"Very well." If she didn't agree, Nimue knew Morgana would try to scry on her own. "Fetch the ewer."

She went to the chest where she kept her powders and tinctures as well as other treasures. Nimue had established her reputation as a healer soon after their arrival, and the lords and ladies of Nentres' court valued her services highly. She easily earned enough coin to buy whatever she might desire. Merchants brought luxuries to Brittany from unimaginably distant places. Her chamber was comfortable with bright tapestries and an opulent canopied bed.

She set the silver bowl on the table and turned to Morgana for the ewer. The young woman smiled, and water pattered into the bowl, wrung from the air and scenting the room with the sea.

Use your magic sparingly, and always with caution. You can never know what consequences might follow.

It had never occurred to Nimue that a mortal could work magic. With the crucified god's priests so set against sorcery, she'd never imagined that any would try. But Morgana paid no heed to priests, not since the Minster's clergy had counselled her to accept her mother's marriage to Uther as their god's undoubted will.

Nimue hadn't realised how closely Morgana studied every spell she saw worked. Too late, Nimue realised she should have foreseen that possibility. Morgana had been an excellent pupil as she learned the intricacies of healing herbs.

Nimue narrowed her eyes. "Where did you learn to do that?"

Morgana smiled sunnily. "I met a wise woman in the woods some days ago. We fell into conversation and one thing led to another."

There was wild magic in Brittany. Nimue sensed hidden folk in the lakes and forests, though she stayed well away from such places. Could Morgana feel their presence too? The child had been exposed to powerful sorceries when she was very young after all. Who had she stumbled across? Or had one of these strangers sought the princess out? If so, why? Remembering Merlin's chilling prophecies, Nimue longed for time and solitude to think this through, but Morgana was already holding a quill over the water-filled bowl. The drop of ink at its tip swelled and fell.

Nimue wove her enchantment. Initially, the water resisted her because Morgana had already begun her own spell. For a few moments she could only see their two faces reflected, side by side.

Morgana had grown into a beauty, and anyone who had known Gorlois would see his firm jaw and his shrewd eyes beneath her dark, arched brows. She was far more her father's daughter than either of her sisters. Perhaps that was why Ygraine was in no hurry to see his youngest child married, and lose this daily reminder of her beloved husband.

Nimue looked barely older than the princess. Before they made their way from the beach to Nentres' castle, she shed the mask of years she had worn at Tintagel. As she explained to Ygraine, this would enable her to serve Morgana far longer. The only people here who had known her in Cornwall were King Nentres and Queen Elaine. They had no reason to doubt Ygraine's word that this Nimue was a niece named for the loyal aunt who had served Gorlois and his queen.

That was the story they had told when they first arrived, with little Morgana sworn to secrecy. Nimue didn't know what secrets Ygraine might have shared with her second daughter since then. Elaine was the child who most resembled her mother, and they had grown closer with every passing year in Brittany. Ygraine was devoted to the grandchildren whose births she had attended: Prince Galeshin and little Princess Elaine.

The water in the bowl rippled and stilled. They saw the castle perched on Launceston's hilltop overlooking the river valley. The trees were still bare of leaves, but yellow clusters of celandines and coltsfoot brightened the dull green of the meadows in the sunshine. King Mark's standard flew from the castle's highest vantage point, and they could see armoured sentries patrolling the battlements. Pennants fluttered beside tents pitched at regular intervals along the mile of road between the town's walls and the closest bridge. When warmer weather arrived, Cornwall's men would repel any English violence that spilled over the border.

King Mark had swiftly reclaimed Tintagel when he heard of Uther's death. He garrisoned the stronghold and paid his respects at Gorlois's grave before returning to Castle Dore. He had written to King Nentres, seeking news of Ygraine and Morgana, when he learned their servants had returned unscathed from Winchester. Once he knew they were safe, King Mark held aloof from Logres' quarrels as the years passed.

Nimue scanned the bustling figures around those tents along the road, and the men marching back and forth across the bridge. All seemed peaceful enough. Nimue looked for a tall, lean figure clad in black. She had kept her word. She had never tried to find Uther's son. She had never sought out Merlin, but if she were to catch sight of him while scrying for something else? She might glean some clue as to what he was doing.

Speculation had run rife, even here in Brittany, when word spread of Merlin's absence from Uther's final campaign. There had been no news. Rumour was slower to fade, but in time people's attention turned to other concerns. These days, Nimue wondered who remembered the dead king's mysterious counsellor. As far as she was concerned though, Merlin's misdeeds were far from forgotten or forgiven.

Morgana nodded with satisfaction as she gazed at the bowl. "That's precisely what I saw."

"You need to be careful, princess." Nimue tried not to scold. "Untrained enchantments easily get out of hand. That can be dangerous–"

"I will be careful." Morgana left the room. Not before Nimue saw a flash of annoyance in the princess's dark eyes. She didn't hold out much hope of learning who had been teaching the young woman these spells now. She should have held her tongue until she had persuaded Morgana to confide in her.

Nimue sighed. Behind her, someone chuckled. Her heart pounding, she spun around.

"Good day to you." Merlin spoke as though they had seen each other only the night before.

"You–" Nimue was lost for words.

There was no sign of the years that had passed on the lean enchanter's face. His cropped grey hair showed no sign of receding, and his beard was still trimmed to a point. As lithe as always, he wore the same unadorned black robe. "Morgana has grown into a most desirable woman. I trust Queen Ygraine is well?"

Nimue gathered her wits. "You swore not to seek us out. Leave us alone."

"I kept my word until I felt your enchantment brush against my own just now, assessing Cornwall's readiness. Evidently, you share my concerns. Where do you think the first battles of the year will be fought?"

"Englishmen's fates are no concern of mine," Nimue said forcefully.

"Not even your mistress's son?" Merlin raised his eyebrows. "Has she never wondered what became of her baby boy?"

Nimue hesitated. She saw a wistful, distant look in Ygraine's eyes on every anniversary of the child's birth. Like Morgana and Elaine, Nimue had learned not to question the queen's low mood when the seasons turned to the day when she had given up her son.

Merlin took a seat at the polished table without waiting for an invitation. "I don't suppose you remember Sir Ector. He was seldom at Uther's court. He is an honest man and kind, and his wife lost a newborn child to a summer fever a few days before Uther was poisoned. I took Arthur to them to be fostered, though I never told them he was Uther's son. I think I eased her grief by giving her a new baby to put to her breast."

Merlin shook his head, regretful. "I hoped this strife in Logres would have burned out by now. Most of the realm's knights are weary of fighting, and they fear their sons will be snared in the same endless bloodshed. The time has come for us to act."

He looked expectantly at Nimue. She gazed back at him, unmoved. Irritation fleeted across his face.

"Sir Ector and like-minded knights will gather in Westminster at Candlemas. They seek some path to lasting peace. They will not succeed without a new king on the throne. They will unite behind Arthur. He is Uther's undisputed son, and the crown is his birthright."

"I imagine a great many will dispute that," Nimue countered. "However strongly he resembles Uther, he could be some bastard. The crucified god's priests deny a child's rights unless his parents exchanged vows in front of their altars."

Merlin grinned. "You can attest he is Uther's true-born son. You can swear you attended Ygraine in childbed." He frowned momentarily. "You will have to disguise yourself with a suitable weight of years, but enough of Uther's knights saw you with the queen at Tintagel or in Winchester."

Nimue shook her head. "He is a barely whiskered boy, raised in some backwoods fiefdom by a knight of little renown. What can he know about ruling a kingdom? Logres' great lords won't swear fealty to an untried youth."

"They will." Merlin smiled, smug. "Each one will imagine they will get the chance to mould him into the king they wish him to be."

Nimue was repelled. "While you intend to do that yourself."

Merlin spread his hands. "I seek no power. I have no interest in amassing wealth or lands or enriching any allies or family."

"Then what do you want?" Nimue demanded.

"A king to defend the Britons against wild and vicious magic."

Nimue wondered where Morgana had gone. She fought to keep her face expressionless. What would Merlin do, if he learned the princess had discovered how to work scrying magic from one of their people in Brittany's woods? Was this the threat he had foreseen? If so, how could she keep Morgana safe from him?

Merlin had other concerns. "Without Arthur on the throne, I can tell you what the future holds with no need for enchantment. Another year of pain and misery. Another year of carnage will follow, and another after that. Needlessly shed blood will be on your hands, if you refuse to end this ceaseless warfare."

"How dare you blame me?" Nimue felt sick.

"Dare you risk the consequences for Cornwall if the fighting spreads?" Merlin rose to his feet. "What of Orkney if the Picts decide Logres' disarray offers them the opportunity to strike at long last? What will you tell your queen if she sees Morgause widowed and left unprotected with five young sons?"

Nimue hesitated. Could Merlin's plan to crown Uther's son succeed? Maybe not, but months of manoeuvring around a new king's claim had to be preferable to another year of battles? If the lords of Logres met to talk instead of fight, calmer counsels might prevail.

Merlin tried a different argument. "Does the boy not deserve to know who his father was?"

Nimue was shocked. "You haven't told him?"

"I haven't had a reason." He shrugged. "But the time has come, don't you agree?"

"Perhaps," she said slowly.

"Should I ask Queen Ygraine to give you permission to help her son secure his throne?"

"No!" Nimue didn't want Merlin anywhere near Ygraine, and especially not Morgana.

He smiled, triumphant. "Come to Westminster at dawn on Candlemas then."

Before Nimue could say anything, he vanished.

CHAPTER FOURTEEN

The weather was clear and cold when Nimue stepped out of the shadows. The Candlemas sky was pale gold above the stark black outline of Westminster's abbey. The great church stood at the heart of this riverside enclave bounded by ice-fringed streams and brushed by the tides, but the islet housed far more people than the community of monks.

Uther had not been the first king of Logres to build a hall in the shadow of the abbey. More nobles had followed to build houses to use when they had business with London's merchants and moneylenders. Those wily and wealthy men sat watchful behind their walls a short distance down the river. Sometimes they were invited to Westminster when the noble lords held a feast or a joust. Nimue had travelled here a few times with Gorlois and Ygraine.

She contemplated the Pendragon residence where Uther had died, those long years ago. Was that why Sir Ector had summoned his fellow knights here, or had Merlin suggested this meeting place? She wondered who had claimed the lofty hall after Uther's death? Perhaps the monks had taken it into their keeping to prevent battles breaking out on their doorstep?

There had been no lights behind the long shutters when she had scryed to make sure she would arrive unobserved. The windows were still dark and the roof vents showed no smoke rising from a rekindled fire. Everyone was still asleep. She started walking towards the great church.

She wondered what Prince Arthur would say when she

vouched for his parentage? What did he know about Uther
Pendragon? What had he been told about his mother? Would
he give Nimue some message for Ygraine? The queen had told
her to tell the boy she had never forgotten her last-born child.
She had only given him up to be sure he was kept safe.

Nimue had told the queen why she was coming here.
There was nothing to be gained by keeping such secrets.
If Arthur succeeded to his father's throne, that news would
reach Brittany as soon as the first ships sailed in the spring. Of
course, that meant telling Morgana, but the princess showed
no interest in Uther's son.

Nimue huddled in her hooded cloak and walked carefully
over the frost-glazed cobbles, to stay warm and to keep up the
pretence of old age that she wore. She rounded the east end of
the abbey, wondering what Arthur might ask about Ygraine's
swift marriage to Uther after Gorlois's death. How could she
possibly explain the foul deceit of that night at Tintagel? She
would change the subject, Nimue decided.

She stopped so abruptly she nearly slipped on the ice. A
pavilion stood on the north side of the abbey. Not to give
anyone a night's shelter; that was clear from its looped-back
sides. Everyone would see what was within once they got
close enough. Four knights stood watch to say how close that
might be.

Nimue walked slowly forward. She'd had no reason to scry
on this side of the abbey. Now she regretted not taking more
time to see what awaited her. She would have expected to
find hapless men-at-arms standing watch through the bitter
darkness. Instead, she realised, these were young knights who
had recently won their spurs after serving their liege lords as
squires. Those lords were doubtless still tucked up warm in
their feather beds.

Even at this early hour, the knights weren't alone in the
churchyard. Men and women who served the monks and the
noble halls were arriving from their humble dwellings beyond

the shallow streams where the Tyburn divided as it reached the Thames. Nimue walked faster to join the tail end of a gaggle of women wrapped up in humble homespun. She veiled her fur-trimmed wool cloak with an illusion to match. She already looked older than the eldest of them, so Logres' lords would see the woman who had served Ygraine at Tintagel.

These women paused by the tent. Their awed murmurs reminded Nimue of the sleepy coos of doves roosting up in the abbey eaves. These knights were guarding a marvel. Nimue stared and wondered what Merlin was plotting.

A massive square block of white marble stood as high as a tall man's waist. A blacksmith's anvil was set on top of it. A splendid sword's hilt jutted from the dark iron. Nimue realised the blade had been driven right through the metal and into the stone beneath. As she read the gilded inscription on the side of the anvil, she felt the unmistakable frisson of magic.

Whosoever pulls this sword out of this stone and anvil is the true-born king of all Britain.

"Had a go yet, Sir Kay?" one of the cloaked women called out. "Will we be bowing down to you before the day is out?"

A dark-bearded young knight scowled. He wore two golden bird's wings outspread on his blue surcote. "Be about your business, hag."

The women laughed and made no move to leave. Nimue eased herself between the two at the back of the group. One looked at her with mild curiosity.

Nimue asked her question first. "When did that marvel appear?"

The other woman was surprised. "New Year's Day. You must have heard."

"What we hear isn't always the truth of it," Nimue said quickly. "I wanted to see for myself."

"I wonder what we'll see after morning prayer," the first woman remarked.

"What do you mean?" Nimue prompted.

"You must have heard." Now the first one was startled. "The true-born king will be revealed, so everyone has been saying for days."

"Noble born, but raised humble, so the word goes. A king who understands a commoner's struggles and fears. A king who'll make peace at long last, God willing," her friend said fervently.

"If you haven't heard, what brings you here?" The first woman's curiosity was turning to suspicion.

Nimue realised these weren't servants hurrying to their duties. They had come to see the spectacle, whatever that might be. She summoned a spell to hide herself. As the women gaped, she wiped all memory of this encounter from their minds. Still invisible, she walked away through the gathering crowd, and out of the churchyard. She didn't let her spell unravel until she reached the grass-fringed streams.

Nimue bent to pick up a shard of ice. Her anger melted it, but she had seen Merlin walking along a narrow street overhung by timber-framed buildings. Now she could sense him, and he wasn't far away. Quick as thought, Nimue stepped through the space between them.

Merlin halted, startled. He recovered fast. "I am glad you're here in good time. Let's go and see Sir Ector and Arthur together."

He waved a hand and the illusion of homespun wrapped around her blew away.

"How dare you!"

Merlin didn't answer. He headed for a nearby house and knocked on the door. A man in his middle years with a greying beard and thinning hair opened up. He was already dressed for the day, and his blue surcote was emblazoned with two golden wings. His resemblance to the young knight Sir Kay was obvious.

"Sir Ector." Merlin greeted him warmly, before turning to introduce Nimue. "This is the lady who will swear to Arthur's parentage."

"Come in, come in." The knight stepped back into the candlelit warmth. He bowed to Nimue, but he struggled to hide his doubts as he looked at Merlin. "You think the word of an ancient maidservant will be enough? We've been at this since midwinter."

Nimue already suspected Merlin hadn't told her the whole story. Those women had said the stone with the sword had appeared weeks ago. Before she could demand to know what was going on, Sir Ector bustled Merlin back out into the street and closed the door behind them.

Nimue would have followed them, but she heard footsteps on the steep wooden stairs to the upper floor. A young man, barely more than a boy, came down into the hall. Even in this dim light, he had Uther's height and colouring, though it would be a few years before he gained his father's broad shoulders and muscled thighs.

Clean-shaven, his plain brown woollen tunic had no embroidered symbol from a noble family line. He wore a thick shirt against the cold, with winter hose and sturdy boots. His clothing was clean and well-made, but not luxurious, like this house. Nimue recalled the women in the churchyard saying the new king had been raised in a humble home.

The youth was surprised to see her. "Good day to you, mistress. If you please, where's my – my foster father?"

"Outside, talking with Master Merlin."

The youth glowered. "They say he was Uther Pendragon's counsellor, but no one has seen him since before the old king died. Now he's back, but they say he hasn't aged a day."

Nimue saw he was apprehensive, even afraid. "What has he said to you?"

"Nothing. No one tells me anything. Not even my father – my foster father–" The boy's face reddened with anger, embarrassment, or both.

"I didn't mean to do it," he burst out. "I was only sent to fetch a sword for Kay, when we were here for the New Year joust. I passed the sword in the stone on my way and there was nobody there. I only wanted to see what it felt like. All the knights had tried to pull the blade free, and none of them could do it, so how was I to know? I put it back, at once."

Arthur stared at Nimue, truculent. "I wish I'd never touched the cursed thing. I wish I'd never told Father – Sir Ector – what I'd done. Then I'd never have known he isn't my father, and Kay's not my brother. Did you know that?" Injury rang through his words. "My whole life has been a lie."

As he scrubbed angry tears away with the heel of his hand, Nimue saw a heart-rending glimpse of Ygraine as she had looked so long ago. Then Arthur's anger burned brighter and he looked like Uther.

"When my father – I mean, Sir Ector – made me show the other lords, they said some sorcerer's trick didn't matter. They weren't going to be ruled by a bastard. Merlin swears I am true-born. He said he had a witness to prove it. Is that you? Who am I, really?"

Before Nimue could answer, the door to the street opened, and the sound of the abbey's bells followed Merlin and Sir Ector into the house.

The enchanter clapped his hands. "The monks have finished their first office of the day. Let's show the people what you can do, Arthur, and claim your crown."

The youth looked to Sir Ector for guidance. The knight nodded, grim-faced. Arthur set his jaw and squared his shoulders as he walked past Nimue. She was guiltily relieved that she need not answer his questions. Not yet, anyway.

Arthur walked on ahead with Sir Ector. Merlin followed, beckoning Nimue. Irritated, she hurried to his side. For one thing, she didn't actually know how to get to the abbey after using her spell to join Merlin.

"Don't snap your fingers at me. I am not your servant," she hissed.

"Follow my lead, and tell the truth, no more and no less."

"I do not tell lies," Nimue said pointedly.

Merlin ignored that. His attention was fixed on Arthur. Nimue was more interested in Sir Ector. What manner of man had reared Ygraine's son? What was his wife like, if she still lived? No one had mentioned the woman. Had she taught Arthur his manners? The boy had greeted her politely, even on this stressful day.

On the other hand, Sir Ector's elder son, Kay had been brusque to the point of rudeness with the women by the stone. Perhaps the young knight could be forgiven after a long, dark night standing watch in the cold. His life had been upended as thoroughly as Arthur's. He no longer had a younger brother, but a potential king.

The older knight rested a reassuring hand on his foster-son's shoulder as they walked. Nimue saw fatherly concern as he glanced at the youth, and while Ector's voice was too low to hear what he said, his tone was kind.

They crossed Tyburn's shallow stream and returned to the churchyard. The waiting crowd had more than tripled, with monks and priests among the curious populace. A substantial number of knights had arrived, each one with a sizeable retinue.

Most of the nobles were strangers, though Nimue did recognise Sir Ulfius, Sir Baudwin and Sir Brastias. Their grey hair and deep lines carved on their faces by relentless warfare were a shock. She wondered what Uther would have looked like, if he had lived. Not so battle-weary, if he had kept the peace as high king. For the first time she wondered if Gorlois and Lot of Orkney had erred when they chose to defy him.

Sir Ector walked up to the pavilion and embraced Sir Kay. Arthur hung back, staring at the ground to avoid catching anyone's eye. Sir Ector addressed the crowd, though not everyone looked his way. Most of the knights were watching Merlin with scarcely veiled hostility or outright suspicion.

Sir Ector cleared his throat. "My lords, you have seen this

marvel performed, some of you several times. Now the people will see it for themselves."

He nodded at Arthur. The boy looked more like Uther than ever as he climbed onto the marble stone. His face was unreadable as he took the sword's hilt in a practised grip. Sir Ector had taught the boy to be a warrior, whatever else he had learned.

The knights standing guard retreated. In one swift movement, Arthur pulled the blade free of the anvil and the stone beneath. Standing high on the great block of marble, everyone in the churchyard saw him do it. He saluted the growing crowd with the gleaming blade. His face was still expressionless.

The common folk clapped their hands and stamped their feet. Gleeful voices shouted.

"The rightful king!"

"The king is here!"

"We have a king again!"

Arthur was startled into an unexpectedly charming smile. As he lowered the sword, the joyous uproar redoubled. He laughed and the crowd laughed with him.

Nimue looked at the knights. Sir Ulfius looked thoughtful. Sir Baudwin was grinning while tears ran down Sir Brastias's hollow cheeks. Some of the younger nobles shared the crowd's elation, though a number of their older brethren made no attempt to hide their disdain.

Merlin sprang onto the white stone with an ease any man would envy. Abrupt silence fell as he seized Arthur's hand and raised the blade high. "Uther Pendragon's lost son has proved himself by doing what no other man could. Will you kneel and swear fealty to King Arthur and see peace in this land?"

A few voices shouted emphatic agreement. More than half the common folk sank to one knee and mumbled some sort of oath. The knights remained on their feet, defying the boos and cries of shame from the crowd. Nimue wondered if the nobles realised how deftly Merlin had outmanoeuvred them. If they denied Arthur's right to the throne, they were rejecting the populace's choice of their king.

Merlin said something to Arthur. The boy looked uncertain, but he used the sword to point to Sir Ulfius. Silence fell once again.

"You wish to speak, sir knight?" Arthur's voice was high and tight.

Sir Ulfius looked warily at Merlin. Then he looked at Arthur and smiled, rueful. "Sir Ector is an honest man, and he says he took you in as a helpless infant and raised you with no idea who your father might be. Those of us who fought with King Uther can see the blood tie in your face, but there are many degrees of kinship."

The other knights nodded, some readily, some reluctantly, as Ulfius raised his voice above the crowd's murmurs. "Master Merlin promised us proof of your royal parentage."

"I will make good on my word." Merlin's pointing finger picked out Nimue.

She realised why he had stripped away her shabby disguise. No one could discount her as some pauper paid to tell lies, seeing her deep-dyed maroon cloak and the opulent sable that trimmed it.

"Stand forward, Mistress Nimue," Merlin commanded. "Sir Ulfius, this witness to Prince Arthur's birth was known to you in King Uther's household."

The ordinary folk standing nearby retreated as if she had burst into flames. Anyone standing between her and the assembled knights hastily scrambled out of the way. As cross as she was with Merlin for dragging her into this masquerade, Nimue was pleased to see astonishment and unease in Sir Ulfius's eyes. Was he afraid she was going to tell everyone how he had helped Uther rape and trap Ygraine with foul sorcery and Merlin's connivance?

She looked at Arthur. Standing high on the white marble, the youth's face was almost as pale as the stone and his mouth was taut with anxiety. He was guiltless in all this. Nimue decided to tell only as much of the truth as the boy could bear.

She addressed him as if no one else was present. "Prince Arthur, you are the true-born son of Uther Pendragon and his wedded wife, Queen Ygraine. I swear it on my life and my honour. I attended your birth in the fortress of Tintagel, far away in Cornwall. These men see your father in your face, but I see your mother as well."

She cleared her throat. "Your parents brought you to Winchester when you were a babe in arms. Your father's enemies soon tried to kill him with treachery and poison." She glanced at the knights closest to Sir Ulfius. "Sir Baudwin, Sir Brastias, you were poisoned too, as I recall. I was sorry to learn that Sir Jordan died."

As they acknowledged her with nods, other nobles recognised her. Several knights began urgent, low-voiced conversations. Nimue turned back to Arthur who was standing still as a statue.

"Uther left his sickbed to drive off the Saxon invaders. Master Merlin took you from the palace, afraid that evil men would try to kill you while the king was away. He swore you would only be safe if no one knew where you were hidden. My mistress, your mother, only gave you up to save your life, before I persuaded her to flee to save herself. She has never forgotten you, I give you my word. She will be glad to learn you were raised by a respected and honourable man."

Better Sir Ector than Uther, Nimue guessed the queen would say. Nimue still wanted to know about Sir Ector's wife. Ygraine was bound to ask what manner of woman had taught her son his earliest lessons. That would have to wait though.

Nimue fell silent. She heard muffled, sentimental weeping here and there. Then a gasp ran through the crowd. A blazon was appearing on Arthur's unadorned tunic. Embroidery silks, gold thread and glittering red glass beads appeared out of thin air. Uther's comet-tailed dragon took shape faster than mortal hands could ever have worked the design. Magic was at work, plain for all to see.

Nimue shot a furious glare at Merlin. How dare he flaunt such sorcery? But he was looking at Arthur, as triumphant if he'd been the boy's father himself.

Abruptly, Nimue dropped her gaze. Had anyone had seen her reaction and wondered at her anger? Had she betrayed her own familiarity with magic? She glanced sideways through her lashes and saw she need not worry. Now she had said her piece, no one was interested in some old woman.

"Well?" Merlin shouted when the Pendragon symbol finished embroidering itself. "Will you see your new king crowned?"

The common folk roared their agreement. The crowd surged forward, and Arthur was carried off on the shoulders of two burly men. There was no danger of him falling. Far too many people clustered around. The crowd headed for the north door of the abbey. Nimue saw several black-clad servants of the crucified god fighting their way through the throng. She guessed they were trying to warn whoever was in charge what was coming their way. As for Sir Ector and Sir Kay, she lost track of them completely.

Faster than she thought possible, the churchyard was deserted. Overhead, the abbey bells started ringing in celebration to be carried far and wide by the breeze. Those summoned by the peals would spread this momentous news as fast as eager tongues could relay it.

Merlin jumped down from the marble stone where the anvil stood. No one glanced in his direction and Nimue realised he had woven a spell to turn eyes away from the two of them.

"I take it someone has Uther's crown ready in the abbey?"

Merlin ignored her sarcasm. "Uther died close by, so the monks held it in safe keeping. The day is ours, thanks to your help."

"The day, perhaps, but what's to come?" Nimue wasn't

convinced he had achieved as much as he thought. "Look over there."

Most of the younger knights had gone into the abbey where the crowd had now hushed, presumably in deference to the priests and their prayers. At the edge of the churchyard though, older nobles conferred in twos and threes. Some looked resentful while a few shrugged, ready to make the best of things. Others dared to look hopeful. Nimue guessed they longed to see peace restored.

She feared they were doomed to disappointment. The knights who would never accept Arthur were obvious. Their faces twisted with hostility and their gestures were violent. Nimue felt a chill that owed nothing to the frost when she recognised Sir Lardans among them.

"How many of Uther's enemies still live to hate his son so fiercely?"

"Enough for me to know they must see he has magic to call on, to compel their obedience." Merlin's glare dared Nimue to challenge him. "Wild enchantment still threatens Logres and we cannot fight foes on two fronts. Arthur must be the unquestioned king."

Nimue nodded, mute. She must return to Brittany and convince Morgana to abandon her pursuit of magic.

CHAPTER FIFTEEN

"So what do you make of this young king?" Lot of Orkney sipped his wine.

"His desire for peace seems genuine," King Nentres observed, "along with his wish to know his true family. He has shown his lady mother and his sisters every courtesy."

Nimue still couldn't tell if Garlot's ruler approved or disapproved of his newfound brother by marriage. She did know he had come to Camelot for this late summer feast to learn all he could to share with his fellow kings in Brittany.

Nentres set his fine glass goblet down and looked around the long room. The fresh-cut stone was the colour of cream, and soot from candles hadn't yet stained the ceilings. Tapestries of hunting scenes hung on the walls, bright and unfaded, and the furniture gleamed with polish.

"What do you make of this place?" Nentres raised his brows at Orkney's king.

"What was wrong with Winchester?" Lot said tartly, "or Westminster?"

"He says he wants a fresh start. To step out from Uther's shadow." As so often, Nentres' tone was neutral.

Nimue was less sure about Lot of Orkney's reasons for accepting Arthur's invitation. Morgause swore her husband was willing to agree a formal peace with Logres. That might be so, but no one knew if Arthur intended to revive his father's claim to be Britain's high king.

Nimue was busy with needlework at the other end of the

room with Ygraine, Morgause, Elaine and Morgana. The queen had seized this chance to be reunited with all three of her daughters. For her mistress's sake, Nimue was relieved that Arthur had invited them to this new castle, Camelot. Cruel memories would besiege Ygraine in Winchester, and in Westminster.

The royal women had other concerns as they sat with their embroidery, on low chairs comfortable with cushions. Nimue released the magic she had been using to eavesdrop on the two kings as Queen Elaine's curiosity snagged her attention.

"Could Master Merlin really have built this castle with sorcery?"

"It couldn't be done without magic. Arthur has no coin to pay masons and carpenters, never mind weavers or anyone else." Morgause was as practical as ever. "He spends every penny he gets in dues from his liegemen fighting those lords who still defy him. Think how long it takes to get a storehouse reroofed, never mind finishing a project started from the foundations up. Arthur has been king for scarcely half a year, and he can already call this vast labyrinth home."

She looked at her husband. "There were always rumours about Merlin, so Lot says. Evidently those suspicions were correct."

Elaine looked at Nimue. "Did your aunt share such gossip?"

"Never, your grace." Nimue kept her eyes on the chemise she was hemming.

Elaine persisted, turning to Ygraine. "Did you hear any talk, Mother?"

Morgana interrupted, waspish. "If Merlin's magic was the secret behind Uther Pendragon's successes, perhaps our dear brother should use his counsellor's talents on the battlefield instead of on a building site."

Nimue glanced up and their eyes met for a moment. When she had returned to Garlot, Nimue told the princess how Merlin expected his displays of enchantment would force the rebellious lords to yield. So much for that. She had also warned Morgana that Merlin was convinced that wild magic would threaten Arthur. He would crush any hint of such enchantment without mercy. To her intense relief, Morgana had taken that to heart. Nimue hadn't sensed her attempting any spells for months now.

Ygraine sighed. "How can Logres ever be at peace, if these lords refuse to accept Arthur as king? I don't understand why, when they acknowledge him as Uther's true-born son."

Nothing could bridge the gulf of those lost years, but the queen had been glad to find her unknown son grown into an honourable and conscientious young man. He was very young though. Nimue hoped Arthur's character was strong enough to meet the challenges he faced.

"With or without Merlin's magic, our brother has won every battle thus far," Elaine said comfortably. "Sooner or later, no one will be left to defy him."

Nimue wasn't so sure. King Mark of Cornwall was expected to join them at Camelot, but he had been delayed on his journey, according to his apologetic herald. None of the Welsh rulers were here. Lot of Orkney was the only Scots king who had accepted Arthur's invitation. He made it clear that was for his wife's sake, and because his son Gawain was now Arthur's heir, at least until the young king married and had a son of his own.

"Let's hope the hold-outs surrender before the common folk decide their trust in Arthur is misplaced. His victories have been costly for them." Morgause looked up as the door to this sitting room opened.

"My lady mother." Gawain of Orkney hurried in and closed the door. "Your grace. Your grace. Your highness." He greeted Ygraine, Elaine and Morgana with practised courtesy. "We have heard–"

The door burst open as the rest of the Orkney brothers arrived. Agravaine was at their head as he usually was, whether Gawain was there or not. Gaheris and Gareth followed, inseparable as always. Mordred trailed after them, divided from his brothers by their longer legs as well as by the years between them. The only one of Morgause's children with her dark locks, the little boy was barely old enough to serve as a pageboy. The older boys were already squires to King Lot's liegemen.

Agravaine was red-faced with excitement, which clashed horribly with his flaming hair. "King Arthur is going to fight Sir Pellinore in single combat."

"What did you say?" his father demanded, striding towards them.

"King Arthur got word this morning." Gawain warned his brother off with a glare. "Malcontents are plundering nearby villages, led by Sir Pellinore."

King Lot snorted. "He always was a troublemaker."

"Griflet stumbled across them," Agravaine piped up. "He barely escaped with his life. They say Sir Pellinore wanted to send his head to the king as a message."

"So much for Arthur's day out hunting," Nentres commented. "Perhaps we should have ridden out with him."

"King Arthur went in search of whoever had half-killed his squire." Gawain addressed his father. "He and Sir Pellinore agreed to settle the matter between themselves. Griflet has just arrived back to have his wounds tended."

"Where were you, to hear all this?" Lot looked sternly at his eldest son. They resembled each other even more strongly than Arthur brought Uther to mind. The most noticeable difference was Gawain's hair and his boyish attempt at a beard were as bright as polished copper. Lot's head was snowy white as he approached his three-score years and ten.

Lot had forbidden Gawain's request to spend his days with the king's knights instead of his brothers. Gawain hadn't taken that well, already touchy because he was still only a squire. Arthur was a year younger, but he had been dubbed a knight by Sir Ector moments before his coronation.

The door opened again to reveal Prince Galeshin and Princess Elaine. The little girl was grizzling, and her mother sprang up. "What's happened, sweetheart?"

"We got lost," wailed little Elaine.

Both children tried to explain. Lot's four elder sons were talking to their father, all trying to be heard over their brothers. Nimue couldn't make sense of anything.

Ygraine touched her arm. "I am tired. I need to rest before the feast tonight."

"Assuming we're not holding Arthur's wake before crowning Gawain as king," Morgana muttered as she stowed her sewing away. "Let me help you, mother."

"Help Elaine with the children." Ygraine had heard Morgana's quip, and she didn't appreciate it.

Morgana rolled her eyes, but she did as she was asked. She gathered up Mordred and followed Elaine and her children out of the room. She'd told Nimue the Orkney boy had her sympathies. Morgana had been a youngest child with much older siblings.

Ygraine got to her feet and rested on Nimue's arm as they made their way to the door. The queen was starting to feel the weight of her years despite Nimue's discreet enchantments easing her sore joints.

"Oh, that's better," she said fervently, as Nimue closed the door on Agravaine arguing with Lot. "I had no idea that boys are always so *loud*."

"Let's be grateful their rooms are in a different tower," agreed Nimue.

She agreed with Morgause. Camelot could only have been built with magic. There was enough accommodation in this vast castle for every king of these isles and a retinue. Though Ygraine and her daughters were the only noblewomen in Camelot at present. Arthur's loyal knights left their wives and children safe in their own castles before marching to fight.

Thankfully, Ygraine's private chamber was directly above

the sitting room. As the women reached the stone spiral that curled up from the castle's yard to the tower's topmost turret, heavy feet hurried up from below. Sir Ulfius appeared.

"The kings of Orkney and Garlot are in there." Nimue jerked her head at the door.

Ulfius looked at Ygraine with undisguised loathing. "This is your fault, you faithless bitch."

"What?" The queen gaped at him.

Nimue restrained an urge to send the knight crashing back down the stairs, hopefully to break his neck. But that risked betraying her magic. Arthur's people might be used to Merlin's sorcery, but if Nimue was ever forced to use enchantments, she wanted the advantage of surprise.

"Uther dragged himself from his sickbed to save you and his son, but you ran away," Ulfius spat. "You gave his son to that bastard Merlin and condemned us to years of war because we thought the boy was dead. If you had stayed, no one could question Arthur's claim. If he dies now, we'll be ruled by Orkney, and that will be your fault too."

Ygraine was too stunned by the knight's hatred to reply.

Nimue retaliated. "I hear you are King Arthur's chamberlain. How long will you hold any honoured post at his court, when he hears you have insulted his lady mother."

She didn't wait to hear Sir Ulfius's answer, ushering Ygraine up to the sanctuary of her chamber. She slammed and bolted the door. As she helped Ygraine to the bed, and took off the queen's shoes, she felt her trembling. Ygraine wasn't frightened though. She was furious.

"Men always find some way to blame the nearest woman for their mistake. Can you find out where this idiotic duel is happening? Can you make your way there through some spell?"

"I can." Nimue hadn't expected this.

"Stop Arthur from getting himself killed." Tears trickled down Ygraine's wrinkled cheeks. "I cannot bear the thought of Morgause's sons wasting their lives on these pointless battles."

"I will do whatever I can, your grace."

Nimue left Ygraine lying on the bed with her weary eyes closed. She poured water from the ewer into the queen's wash basin, added a drop of perfume, and looked for Merlin. He'd be at Arthur's side. She found them under trees that ringed a forest glade. Arthur was fully armoured and quenching his thirst from a water skin. Merlin wore the same black robe as always. Two contingents of armoured men faced each other across the grass.

"So much for a day out hunting." Nimue had no doubt that the young king had known Sir Pellinore and his forces were in the area. Perhaps the malcontents were testing Camelot's readiness as they planned some attack. Regardless, Arthur had gone hunting these interlopers.

Nimue fixed her attention on Merlin, using her sense of his magic as a beacon to guide her spell. She stepped out of the shadow of a mighty oak some distance from the glade. Making her way towards the roaring men, her enchantment ensured all eyes would slide over her. At least the clamour wasn't aggressive. She heard cheers of encouragement and anticipation.

As she drew closer, a musk of sweat and metal undercut the summer fragrance of the greenwood. She reached the edge of the trees and circled around to get a clear view of the glade, now turned into an impromptu lists.

King Gorlois had never been interested in jousts. If loyal men were to risk injury or even death, he said, they should do it for some worthy cause, not for purses of silver and the cheers of the mob. King Uther had excelled in such contests and regularly hosted tournaments. His loyal knights must have told Arthur tales of his father's triumphs. Did the young king want to prove he was Pendragon's worthy heir? Did he know who he faced? Sir Pellinore had an enviable record at such tourneys.

Arthur readied his horse on one side of the glade. Merlin

looked up as he spoke to the king. Arthur nodded impatiently and lowered his visor. The comet-tailed dragon shone bright on his shield, and he couched his lance with a degree of skill that reassured Nimue a little. His horse fretted and snorted, with its ears eagerly pricked. The beast was used to jousting, and from the splinters of wood on the ground, these combatants had already ridden at each other.

At the other end of the rope line set up to divide them, Sir Pellinore adjusted his shield straps. His blazon was rows of small blue crosses on a yellow ground. Several young men wore blue surcotes with the same design of crosses embroidered in yellow. If Nimue remembered right, Pellinore had four sons not much older than Arthur, as well as a daughter. If their father killed Arthur today, Pellinore would doubtless claim the crown of Logres as the spoils of victory. These youths would defy Lot of Orkney's sons, miring another generation in bloody rivalry.

Both men spurred their horses. The crowd's roar startled birds from the trees. Hooves thundered on the bruised turf. Each man's lance met the other's shield dead centre and brutally hard. Green wood, freshly cut from the forest, cracked and shattered. Arthur and Pellinore swayed in their saddles, fighting to recover their balance.

Arthur's horse stumbled, spilling him to the ground. Arthur scrambled to his feet, unharmed. Cheers and groans divided the onlookers. The young king drew his sword, and Nimue recognised the blade drawn from the stone in Westminster.

Sir Pellinore wheeled his horse around and tossed the remnant of his lance away. He drew his sword and rode towards Arthur, intent on attack. The king stood braced with his shield raised and his sword ready. The king's men howled their disapproval. Sir Pellinore slowed and turned his visored face towards his followers. Their loyalty was muted, and Nimue saw disbelief on several faces. Surely their liege lord wasn't going to fight in such a dishonourable way?

A squire wearing Sir Pellinore's blazon saw some signal and ran forward to hold his liege lord's horse. Pellinore dismounted and advanced to meet Arthur on equal terms as the onlookers cheered.

They circled each other. Nimue wondered how equally they were matched. Sir Pellinore had decades of experience in tournaments as well as fighting on Logres' battlefields. How much would those years weigh him down? Arthur had the vigour of youth, and this past half-year of battles must have honed Sir Ector's training.

The combatants met in a flurry of blows. Swords struck shields time and again. Both men were as deft in defence as they were attacking. Each twisted and thrust with their shield, as much a weapon as their hacking blades.

They broke apart and circled. Nimue saw smears of blood on each man's armour, though she couldn't tell where they were wounded. Neither man moved as if he were injured. Sir Pellinore attacked with undiminished vigour and Arthur matched him. They hammered at each other, unrelenting. The onlookers stood silent now, as they willed their sworn lord to victory.

King and knight broke apart after another agonizing exchange. Now, they moved more warily. Each man was slower to raise his shield. As battle resumed, their swords slid over scars marring those painted blazons to land bruising strikes on their foe's arms and shoulders. Their swords might not penetrate their opponent's armour, but the padding beneath could only do so much to soften such blows.

Nimue couldn't begin to guess who might win as the brutal bout went on. The summer sun shone bright overhead and the day grew hot as midday approached. Onlookers shared water skins, and she discreetly cupped a handful of water from the air to ease her own dry throat. Thirst might fell the king or the knight rather than a blade. Both men must be sweating freely, and they were more bloodied. The impact of their swords would be splitting skin beneath their chain mail now that they were too weary to evade their enemy's strokes.

Sir Pellinore launched another attack. Arthur raised his sword to block it. The blades met with a sour note. Arthur's sword broke in half. A gasp circled the glade pursued by taut silence. Nimue saw naked disbelief on Merlin's sharp-featured face.

Sir Pellinore thrust his blade under Arthur's chin. The blood-smeared steel slid into the narrow gap between the king's helmet and breastplate. Pellinore could stab him through the throat in the blink of an eye. Arthur stood motionless with his arms outstretched. He dropped the hilt of his broken sword.

The silence was absolute as Sir Pellinore's chest heaved, his breath rasping. Nimue bit her lip. If the exhausted knight staggered, if some cramp caught him unawares, he could kill Arthur by accident.

Arthur didn't move a hair's breadth. Nor did Pellinore's blade. The rebellious lord's voice rang out strong and clear, even muffled by his helmet.

"Yield or die."

Slowly and carefully, Arthur unstrapped his battered shield. He let it fall to the ground with a dull thud.

"Never."

Lightning-fast, Arthur recoiled from the sword's point at his throat. He forced the blade upwards with his metal-gauntleted hands. Sir Pellinore was thrown off balance, only for a moment, but that was long enough. Arthur ducked down and charged forward. He wrapped his arms around Pellinore's waist. The knight smashed his sword down, but the blade glanced off Arthur's armoured back. Before Pellinore could raise his arm again, Arthur knocked him off his feet.

Pellinore landed hard. Arthur was on top of him. Pellinore struggled, trying to throw the younger man off, hampered by the shield still strapped to his arm. Arthur knelt on the knight's elbows to pin him to the turf. That freed his hands to pull off Sir Pellinore's helmet.

The older man's hair was soaked with sweat. His face was mottled red, and he blinked bloodshot eyes as he stared up at Arthur. Everyone waited to hear what the king might say.

No one found out. Was Arthur's balance uneven? Did Pellinore feel some tremor of weariness in the younger man? Nimue could only guess. The wily old knight dug his spurred heels into the turf. A heave of Pellinore's hips tossed Arthur straight over his head.

Arthur skidded across the grass. He recovered quickly, scrambling onto his hands and knees. Not quickly enough. Sir Pellinore was on his feet and the older knight still had his sword. He planted a foot on the king's back and forced him flat.

Pellinore leaned forward and pulled off Arthur's helmet. He set his sword's point in the hollow where the king's backbone met his bared head. Pellinore didn't say a word. Arthur had made his choice.

The sword's hilt slid from Sir Pellinore's slack fingers. He slumped to lie senseless across King Arthur. For a long moment, everyone stood in stunned silence. Then Merlin was running across the grass. Pellinore's sons were nearly as fast. Nimue ran too, using magic to be the first to reach the fallen men.

Arthur was struggling out from under Pellinore's limp body. Seeing Nimue on her knees beside his fallen foe, the king's brow creased. "You? How are you here?"

"Later." She wanted to know how he could see her, but that could wait. Right now she had to stop a bloodbath. The assembled men were shouting and jeering. Both sides claimed victory in this duel, and they were ready to fight to secure it.

Nimue straightened Sir Pellinore's arms and legs. He was breathing and she could hear his heart beating, raggedly but strong enough. She ran a cautious hand over his head, afraid that she would sense a raging torrent of blood from some burst vessel in his brain. That could explain this sudden collapse. Instead, she felt the magic scattering the knight's wits. Merlin's magic. Nimue looked at him, furious. He was unrepentant.

Later.

Two of Sir Pellinore's sons arrived. The first snatched up his father's sword, ready to attack Arthur.

"Don't," the other said sharply.

"Is he dead?" Arthur struggled to his feet. For an unguarded moment, he looked horrified.

"No," Merlin said firmly. "Sir Pellinore was overcome by heat and exertion. He will recover in a few hours."

Arthur looked at Nimue. She nodded, reluctant. Merlin doubtless knew the effects of his own spell. He could have killed Pellinore outright. She wondered why he hadn't.

Merlin addressed the crowd. "This matter is decided, as Sir Pellinore agreed. King Arthur has prevailed. His rightful claim to his father's throne has been proven once more."

He looked at Sir Pellinore's sons. Their eyes were fixed on their father, desperate to carry him away.

"Well?" Merlin demanded. "Sir Aglovale? Sir Lamorak? Will you honour your father's oath, when he swore to abide by this outcome? Will you kneel to your king?"

Sir Lamorak had picked up Sir Pellinore's sword. He glanced at his brother. He must be Sir Aglovale, the eldest and heir to Lystenois, Nimue belatedly recalled.

Aglovale held out his hand. Lamorak surrendered their father's blade. Aglovale raised the sword to salute Arthur and sank onto one knee. His brother knelt beside him.

Slowly, the fallen knight's liegemen knelt to acknowledge Arthur as the victor and their king. A few voices in Camelot's ranks raised a cheer of sneering triumph. Arthur cut them off with a gesture and a ferocious scowl.

"As soon as he is recovered," the king said hoarsely, "I will welcome Sir Pellinore to Camelot as my honoured guest. The noble knight will retain his lands. His sons' rights of inheritance will not be challenged by anyone on my account. I fought today to secure peace in Logres, nothing more."

Nimue thought he wanted to say something else, but Arthur was shaking with exhaustion.

Merlin saw it too. He used his fingers to whistle like a stable boy. "A horse for the king, as quick as you like. We will return to Camelot."

His glance told Nimue to take herself back to the castle. Defiant, she stayed where she was. If he wanted her gone, she wanted to know why.

Amid hearty cheers, a fresh horse was led forward for Arthur. Merlin helped him into the saddle, offering his cupped hands for the king's foot. Nimue stepped close enough to hear what Arthur said for Merlin's ear alone.

"Will they follow me now the sword from the stone has been broken?"

"I'll find you a blade to equal it," Merlin promised.

Nimue wanted to know he what meant by that. She also knew if she asked, he wouldn't answer. For the moment then, she would go back to Camelot and reassure Ygraine. Since no one except Arthur and Merlin had seen her here, no one would see her spell carry her away.

CHAPTER SIXTEEN

Nimue woke just after dawn the next morning. She succumbed to the temptation to lie still for a few moments, warm and comfortable. In Camelot, even servants were provided with feather beds, and Ygraine was still asleep on the other side of the chamber. The castle was quiet. Arthur's victory over Sir Pellinore had been celebrated late into the night. Astute squires and maidservants would wait to be summoned rather than risk rousing a knight who had a sour stomach and a thumping head.

She wondered how Merlin intended to secure a blade for Arthur to equal the one the king had pulled from the stone. She didn't think he would be visiting a master swordsmith.

She rose to wash and dress. As she closed the chamber door, she used a touch of magic to secure the bolts behind her. After yesterday's confrontation with Sir Ulfius, she wasn't leaving the ageing queen at anyone's mercy. She felt a qualm as she realised she was working casual enchantments so readily now. Had this path led Merlin so far from their people's wisdom?

The year was closer to autumn's equinox than to midsummer. Nimue relished the cooler air as she stepped out of the tower doorway. There were no servants in Camelot's great castle yard, though watchful sentries patrolled the battlements between the tall round towers along the long curtain wall. They were drawn from Arthur's own men-at-arms and from the contingents that followed each knight and visiting king.

Nimue headed for the great keep at the castle's heart. This

was King Arthur's residence, and Merlin had claimed the topmost floor, just as he had done in Uther's palace. No other counsellor had such constant access to the king. As she walked towards the keep's entrance, the great door opened, and Merlin hurried down the steps.

He halted, scowling. "Whatever you want, I don't have time for it."

"What's your hurry?" If he wanted to get rid of her, Nimue wanted to know why. She decided on a different question. "Pellinore should have killed Arthur yesterday. You used magic to save him when you know such interference never ends well."

Merlin's brows arched. "You interfered to carry Ygraine and Morgana away to Garlot. That seems to have worked out very well."

Nimue could hardly deny it, but she persisted. "You keep saying wild magic threatens Logres, but you're the only one I see using enchantments. Arthur's reign has hardly brought the peace you promised, to justify betraying our people and letting mortals see the boy pull an enchanted sword from a stone."

Merlin waved a hand, dismissive. "Peace is within our reach now that Sir Pellinore is defeated."

"Really?" Nimue challenged him. "Plenty of knights still hold out against Arthur. Will you use magic to defeat them too? How will you guarantee his people's loyalty now that the sword from the stone has been broken?"

Nimue saw Merlin hadn't realised she had heard what Arthur said. She waited for an answer, but before Merlin replied, the door to the keep swung open. Arthur appeared, lightly armoured for riding. He halted, surprised to see Nimue. "Mistress? Is my lady mother–?"

Merlin answered quickly. "Queen Ygraine is well, your grace. I have asked Nimue to join us, to bear witness to the bargain that will secure your kingdom. As you know, she wields her own enchantments to keep your family safe."

Arthur smiled at her. "Thank you for everything you have done for my mother and sisters."

"Your grace." As Nimue curtseyed, she shot a furious glance at Merlin.

How dare you betray me to him?

I do what must be done. You will soon see that more of our people agree with me than cling to the old ways.

Arthur was oblivious to the tension between them. "We had better hurry if we want to ride out without half my father's liegemen following."

"Indeed." Merlin led the way to the stables.

The grooms they roused were curious, though no one asked where the king was going so early in the day. These men were wary of Merlin. Nimue saw two lads in the shadows, whispering behind raised hands. Her hasty magic caught their last word, and it made her blood run cold.

Wizard.

Rumour of magic was one thing. Tales of the uncanny had long been explained away as coincidence, or imagination. Now that Merlin was openly acknowledged as a sorcerer, he put all the hidden people in danger. What mortals didn't understand, they feared. Where they saw unearned advantage, they resented it. What they feared and resented, they attacked.

Witch.

That's what they would call her as they condemned her to death, if Arthur betrayed her enchantments to anyone else.

Nimue mounted a chestnut palfrey and urged the smaller horse after the men as Camelot's main gate opened. Merlin and Arthur rode stallions, one black and one bay. Their hooves were loud on the wooden drawbridge that spanned the dry moat circling the castle.

They cantered down the road. Nimue murmured encouragement as her mount did her best to keep up. She was wholly unfamiliar with the lands around Camelot, and she didn't want to get lost before she found out what Merlin was doing.

The road wound between forested hills, cutting a line of beaten earth across the turf. Here and there, a glimpse of smoke above the treetops showed a village had been hacked out of the woodlands. Axe strokes echoed through the oaks, and they passed several swineherds watching over foraging pigs. Nimue wondered why Merlin had convinced Arthur to build his bold new castle so far from Winchester or Westminster. She couldn't believe this had been the boy's idea.

As they passed a lightning-struck elm, she felt the brush of enchantment. They were leaving the mortal world. Merlin's arrogance left her breathless. How dare he bring Arthur into the hidden realm? Did that answer her earlier question though? Had Merlin built Camelot within easy reach of a crossing between the mortal world and the unseen? If so, why?

They rode on and soon reached a broad lake's shore. The waters were so still that the hills and woods encircling them were reflected without a ripple. The air was rich with magic. Nimue felt the thrill of infinite possibilities at her fingertips. Did Arthur feel the power that surrounded him, as awe-inspiring and as perilous as a thunderstorm? Did he know Merlin had transgressed by bringing him here? More to the point, what was the wizard planning?

The two men pulled their horses up. Nimue halted her palfrey some distance away and wrapped her reins painfully tight around her hand. That should help her resist, if her other senses were beguiled. Had Merlin warned Arthur to be wary of whatever he saw or heard?

Merlin pointed at the water. "There."

Arthur stood in his stirrups with a gasp torn between eagerness and apprehension.

A sword rose from the centre of the lake. It appeared point first and so swiftly that the water barely stirred. The hand holding the hilt emerged, slender and delicate. The forearm that followed was swathed in white silk. That was all they saw. Whoever held the blade stayed concealed beneath the glassy waters.

Arthur looked at Merlin. "This is the sword you promised me?"

The wizard pointed again. Arthur pressed a hand to his mouth, disbelieving.

A woman walked across the lake, on the surface of the water. As her slippered feet stirred ruffles of foam, she was as unconcerned as if she strolled through some garden. Serenely beautiful with golden hair, she wore a seductive gown of flowing white silk. Roses perfumed the air, though there were none nearby.

Nimue sensed this woman was a sister to the unseen sword bearer. These two weren't alone. She felt many more presences amid the magic that weighed on her heavily now. These women would not allow a stranger to work any enchantment here.

Did they intend to seduce Arthur? Nimue could hear the rush of blood to the young king's manhood. Merlin couldn't be so foolish as to hand this sisterhood an unassailable hold over Logres' ruler? Or was he so arrogant that he believed he could impose his will on these lake maidens?

The woman halted a few paces from the shore. She looked at Merlin.

Brother.

She looked at Nimue.

Sister?

Nimue gripped her horse's reins tighter as the glamour surrounding the sorceress shimmered like heat haze. Seen clearly by her own kind, her features were sharper and her eyes were piercing. She moved like a predator, intent on the unsuspecting boy. Nimue refused to respond. The amused twitch of the woman's lips was as good as a shrug. Dismissing Nimue, she turned her attention to Arthur.

Merlin gestured. "Your grace, this is the Lady of the Lake."

So, the sorceress hadn't shared her true name with the wizard. Nimue also saw Merlin was prompting Arthur. They must have discussed what he must do and say. How many of her people's secrets had the king's wizard betrayed?

Arthur cleared his throat. "My lady, may I know more about that sword?"

The lady smiled sweetly, as far as any mortal gaze could see anyway. "That sword is mine."

Arthur's voice shook. "As you see, I carry no blade. I would very much like to wield that one."

The lady tilted her head, artlessly graceful. "You may have it, if you will give me a gift."

Nimue felt the air thicken with anticipation. The unseen presences drew closer, silently stalking the king.

"What would you ask of me?" Arthur sounded confident.

"Your promise to give me a gift when I ask one of you."

Nimue saw Merlin's shoulders stiffen, but he couldn't intervene before Arthur replied.

"I swear to give you the gift that you ask of me, in return for that sword."

"We have a bargain." Her voice was soft and musical, but for an instant, the lady's face was hard and triumphant. She had her claws hooked into her prey. "Row out and claim your sword. I will ask for my gift when the time is right."

She gestured, and Nimue saw a small rowing boat drawn up at the water's edge. Enchantments around the lake tried to convince her it had been there when they first arrived.

Arthur slid down from his bay horse, hurrying towards the boat. Merlin dismounted, and quickly tied both horses to a nearby sapling. His long dark robe flapped as he hurried after the king. Nimue watched them row across the still waters to the centre of the lake. The hidden maiden's delicate hand still held the sword aloft. The boat's wake cut a scar across the unsullied reflections that had been so beautiful.

Nimue knew the Lady of the Lake was watching her. As Arthur reached for the sword hilt, she looked straight at the woman in white.

What is this sword?

More exultant voices than she could count replied.

Excalibur
What is that?
The sword that will defend us against mortal attack.
Why should mortals–?

Too late. Arthur lifted the sword high above his head and the pale, slender hand slipped beneath the water. A wind sprang up to send waves scudding across the lake. Merlin fought to steady the little boat.

The Lady of the Lake was gone. No, she had not gone. She had never been there, the magic tried to convince Nimue. Those countless unseen presences had never been here either.

Arthur hurriedly sat down. He put the sword in the bottom of the boat and reached for the second pair of oars. Between them, he and Merlin fought their way back to shore. The hills and forests that ringed the lake were no longer the same. Everything looked meaner and ragged, even though every rock and tree was in exactly the same place.

Nimue expected the little boat to vanish as soon as Merlin and Arthur stepped onto the gravel shore. The boat stayed where it was, lapped by the unsettled waters. Lingering enchantment tried to persuade her there had never been magic here.

Arthur gleefully settled his new sword at his hip. The sword belt must have been in the boat, along with that scabbard of silk-smooth pale leather, banded and studded with bronze. Merlin was watching Arthur, smug with satisfaction.

Nimue snapped her fingers. Caught unawares, the wizard glanced at her.

Does he have any idea what he has done?
No, but when he does, he will consider the price worth paying.
What bargain did you make, to get her to give you that sword?

But Merlin walked over to the horses, checking his saddle's girth and doing the same for Arthur. The king remounted and Merlin was in his own saddle a moment later.

"We should get back to Camelot before we're missed." He kicked the black stallion into a trot.

"Let's go." Exultant, Arthur dug in his spurs.

The bay swiftly overtook the black. Merlin's horse broke into a canter, ready to make a race of it. Nimue's palfrey whinnied anxiously after her stable mates. Nimue gave the horse her head. She didn't want to get lost in these woods, even if they had left the hidden realm.

Or had they? As she rode after Merlin and the king, she sensed... something. Something like a snatch of melody half-heard amid gusts of wind. Like an unfamiliar taste in a mouthful of wine, washed away as soon as she swallowed.

Whatever was teasing her faded fast. In the mortal world, this lake wasn't far from Camelot. Sooner than Nimue expected, she saw the castle's tall, pale towers. She realised it was much later in the day. She should have remembered how time passed differently beyond the mortal realm.

The sentries on the wall walks saw them approach. The great gate opened, and men-at-arms spilled across the lowered drawbridge. As Arthur reached them, he drew his new sword with a flourish, deftly controlling his dancing horse.

The roar from the gathering was deafening, no matter whose blazon any man wore. Existing loyalties didn't matter. Whatever the king might say was irrelevant. As the blade shone silver in the sunlight, Nimue felt the lure of Excalibur's enchantments. The sword from the stone was a child's plaything by comparison.

Men clustered around Arthur's horse. No one took any notice of Nimue, and she was forced back as the crowd thickened between her and the king. Merlin went ahead of the throng, already disappearing into the shadows of the gatehouse.

The palfrey shied at the noise and the jostling. Nimue got the animal in hand, holding her back. By the time she rode into the castle yard, the throng had dispersed. She returned the horse to the stables and handed the reins to a stable lad who was grinning from ear to ear. "What makes you so cheerful?"

"It's a glorious day, mistress. The king will bring peace and prosperity to Logres."

Nimue sensed distant magic at work again. "How will he do that?"

Confusion flickered across the boy's forehead, then his smile returned. "You'll see," he said, as if that was the only answer anyone might need.

Nimue left the palfrey in his care. As she walked out of the stables, she saw Camelot's knights heading for the great keep. Arthur must have summoned them to show off his new sword. What would the young king say, when someone asked where he got the blade, and who had forged it? Men were fascinated by such details. She quelled a shiver of unease at the thought of more stories of magic spreading.

She was struck by the knights' expressions. She was used to these battle-hardened men looking grim-faced and, in unguarded moments, weary to the bone. Sir Ulfius wasn't the only one she had seen vent his fears and frustration on some undeserving victim. Now they were smiling, as if their worries had vanished like morning mist. They talked of sharing the thrill of the hunt, now that peace had come and prosperous days lay ahead. Yesterday they had been ready for war.

Nimue headed for the tower where the queen had her rooms, and walked up the spiral stair, thoughtful. In the sitting room, Ygraine and her daughters sat with their needlework. Nimue curtseyed to her mistress.

"Forgive me, your grace. I was detained." She hoped Ygraine had the sense to wait until they were alone before she asked any awkward questions.

Then she wondered if anyone had even noticed her enter. Morgause was talking to Elaine as Ygraine looked on. All three smiled with relief.

"I am so glad these old quarrels are behind us," Morgause said fervently. "We can look to our children and their future happiness."

Elaine nodded. "Nentres will tell Brittany's kings they have nothing to fear from our brother. They will make a lasting peace with Logres and send their sons to Arthur's court."

"Are you listening to yourselves?" Morgana was pacing to and fro at the far end of the room. "You think you can trust a Pendragon?"

"Your highness," Nimue said quickly. "If I may...?"

Morgana was swift to take the hint. "Of course."

She swept past the table where Elaine and Morgause were discussing how soon Gawain and Gaheris might visit Garlot, and when Prince Galeshin would be old enough to travel to Orkney. Nimue followed Morgana and closed the door behind them.

"Has everyone lost their wits this morning?" the princess demanded.

Someone else answered. "That remains to be seen."

Both women looked up the spiral stair to see a figure outlined against the brightness of a narrow window. Nimue felt the force of the stranger's magic like a physical blow. From Morgana's sudden pallor, so did she.

"Please, friend, if you know–" Nimue began.

"Know this," the figure told her curtly, "since you witnessed the deal struck with Merlin for that sword. We do not approve of unearned favours granted to mortal men. If our patience is abused further, we will redress the balance. Do not doubt it."

A gust of wind fresh with the scent of rain on stone left them shivering. The figure was gone.

"What is happening?" Morgana demanded, furious.

Nimue wondered if their mysterious visitor was still listening. Fortunately, that made no difference to what she had to say.

"I'm afraid Master Merlin may have overreached himself."

She realised with a sinking feeling that she was going to have to stay in Camelot, to see how this played out. She was devoted to Ygraine, but loyalty to her own people came first.

CHAPTER SEVENTEEN

A herald stood alone in Camelot's great hall. Gwynedd's ferocious lion snarled defiance on his tunic, but the youth was shivering, and not from the winter cold. Snow drifts lay thick on the ground outside, but the fire in the long central hearth burned fiercely and Merlin's magic carried the smoke away.

"So much for securing peace with your bargain." Unnoticed at the back of the dais, Nimue spoke for Merlin's ears alone. The wizard sat at Arthur's right hand, on a stool beside the king's carved and canopied throne. She saw Merlin's spine stiffen. Down below, the hapless herald swallowed hard and delivered the rest of his message.

"King Ryons of Gwynedd bids me say, he has defeated and shaved the knights whom you sent to force his allegiance. He trimmed his winter cloak with their whiskers, to keep himself warm. He has space for your beard, and he will take it along with your head if you continue to threaten his realm."

The herald stumbled over his final words and stared at the floor. His face was wretched. The boy expected to pay with his life for his liege lord's insolence. Plenty of the assembled knights were ready to hack the lad's head from his shoulders. Arthur inspired fierce loyalty, thanks to Excalibur.

Was she being unfair? The fighting that had plagued Logres had ended. Defiance melted like snow in the sun when Arthur rode into battle. Merlin had swiftly declared these victories proved he was destined to be high king of Britain, just as his father had been. Arthur was convinced that crown was now his birthright.

Ever cautious, King Mark of Cornwall acquiesced. Safe beyond the seas in Brittany, Nentres of Garlot and his fellow monarchs acknowledged Arthur's claims. That courtesy cost them nothing. Scotland's rulers followed Lot of Orkney's lead when he yielded.

Nimue couldn't decide if King Lot had succumbed to Excalibur's influence or if he had decided against making an enemy of Arthur. Orkney's king was older and wiser than he had been when he struck down Uther's ambitions. Now Logres' knights would march north if the young king summoned them instead of fighting among themselves to claim the throne. Besides, Gawain was Arthur's heir, with Lot's other sons to follow, at least until the king fathered an heir.

Nimue could see the four young men sitting at the lower table closest to the dais. They had been invited to stay for an extended visit, and they soon made their mark in Camelot's contests of skills. Before Lot and Morgause headed home at summer's end, Arthur personally honoured the Orkney squires with knighthood conferred by Excalibur's blade.

Only the Welsh kings still defied him. The sorcerous sword's influence could only change Ryons of Gwynedd's mind if he and Arthur met on the battlefield, as far as Nimue could tell.

Would Logres' forces march to war? The knights looked expectantly at the dais, where Arthur wore his father's crown. Like Uther, he had no squire, though for different reasons. Sir Griflet had barely escaped with his life after he had been cornered by Sir Pellinore's men, eager to hurt Arthur by killing those close to him. The king had sworn that would never happen again.

Nimue watched Merlin intently, ready to use her magic to hear anything the wizard might whisper. For now, the only sound was the chill wind howling around the keep's turrets.

"Take him away," Arthur ordered tersely. "I will consider how to answer such insult—"

As Sir Baudwin and two of his liegemen advanced on the

herald, the hall's heavy doors swung open. The iron-studded oak crashed against the stonework. Merlin sprang to his feet and Nimue felt magic shiver through the air.

A slender, golden-haired figure stood in the doorway. Nimue looked again. This wasn't the Lady of the Lake walking calmly towards the dais with flurries of snow curling around her bare feet. The maiden was equally beautiful though, and seemingly impervious to the bitter cold, wearing an ermine cloak over her ice-white silk dress.

The maiden halted and raised a hand. The hall doors closed behind her with barely a whisper. Uneasy murmurs rose and died. It was one thing for Merlin's magic to be openly acknowledged. He was Arthur's most trusted advisor. It was something else entirely to see such power wielded by an unknown girl.

"My lady." Arthur rose and walked to the edge of the dais. "Have you come to ask for the gift that I promised?"

Surprise coloured a fresh flurry of whispers. No one ever asked how Arthur had secured Excalibur, so that story had never been told.

The maiden halted halfway down the hall. She shook her shoulders and her white cloak slid to the floor. Her sleeveless silk dress clung to her seductive form. Nimue hid a smile. The assembled knights were more interested in the sword belt she wore. The leatherwork was exquisite, decorated with twisting, twining strands of silver. It carried a scabbarded hand-and-a-half blade with a gleaming hilt and pommel.

"I bring you a gift, your grace. The knight who wields this sword will never be defeated." The maiden raised a pale hand. "Such a gift is not lightly given. Only the purest of heart can draw it from this sheath."

Eagerness faded on the faces around her. At least some of these knights were honest enough to admit their sins, Nimue thought acidly. In the role she had claimed, as mistress of Camelot's maids, she knew what pleasures these men felt entitled to take, whether a girl was willing or not. In the absence of noblewomen in the castle, knights young and old forgot whatever manners their mothers and wives had taught them.

A faint scent caught her attention. The freshness of rain on stone. Hadn't the fragrance of roses surrounded the Lady of the Lake?

The maiden smiled at the closest knight. Her eyes were wide and innocent in her heart-shaped face. "Test the truth of my words."

She held her hand away from the sword. Sir Helynor grinned as he took hold of the hilt. He rested his other hand on the maiden's hip, to hold the sword belt. His smile faded. Everyone could see him trying and failing to draw the blade. Someone was surprised into a bark of laughter, and amusement spread. Sir Helynor retreated, forcing a rueful grin to share in the joke.

Nimue wasn't smiling. Something was very wrong, though she had no idea how to find out what that might be without revealing herself as far more than the mistress of maids. Only Merlin and the king knew she could work enchantments. The price of her silence about Excalibur was their silence about her.

Arthur took a pace towards the steps down from the dais. Merlin stood in his way. "You have no need of a new sword, your grace."

Was the king the only one who could draw this blade? If Arthur wasn't the purest of heart in Logres, he could probably claim that honour in Camelot. Nimue never heard complaints about him making unwanted advances. As far as she knew, Arthur was still a virgin, and that wasn't for lack of offers from the maids.

Merlin shouted, harsh. "Sir Balyn, come forth!"

The maiden was caught unawares. She turned to see a young warrior reluctantly make his way from the back of the hall. His blazon was a black boar framed by three blue stars. The knights watched him with mingled pity and hostility.

"Sir Balyn has done daily penance for half a year, for killing a brother knight of Northumberland," Merlin told the beautiful stranger. "You will not find a man of purer heart here."

Nimue couldn't argue with that. Balyn spent endless hours on his knees before the crucified god's altar. He sought forgiveness for a quarrel that had ended in another man's death, though according to kitchen gossip, the sadly tangled story had rights and wrongs on both sides. Nimue wasn't surprised King Clariance had sent him to Camelot to face the high king's judgement, rather than see his own kingdom divided if he pronounced Balyn's fate.

He went up to the maiden. Nimue saw a flash of anger in the visitor's eyes. The knight reached for the sword hilt, half-doubting, half-hopeful. If he could draw this sword, everyone would see that his guilt was spent. The blade slid from the scabbard. Balyn smiled with delight and tried a few passes with the sword.

The knights at the closest table stood up to look more closely. One drew his own blade and stepped forward to feint and parry. Balyn hacked the knight's sword hand from his arm. With a twist of his wrist, he cut off the man's head. The corpse fell with a thud before his unsullied blade hit the floor. Blood flooded the tiles to lap at Balyn's feet. The young knight stared at the sword he held, aghast.

He looked at Merlin with desperate appeal. "I didn't – I swear it!"

The maiden's laughter was lost in the clatter and scrape of benches as men sprang to their feet. Nimue saw hands reaching for sword hilts. The scent of rain on stone overpowered the warm, metallic tang of spilled blood. Now the maiden's face was eerily feline, and her cruel smile mocked them all. Nimue summoned her magic.

Merlin was faster. "No!"

Every man in the great hall stood as frozen as the icicles hanging from the battlements. They were unable to move, but they were not insensible. The closest knights' eyes rolled frantically as they tried to see what was going on.

The maiden laughed again. Unaffected by Merlin's magic, she stooped to retrieve her cloak.

"Who do you serve?" the wizard thundered. "Tell me every detail of the curse forged in that sword."

Nimue's knees buckled under such compulsion, even though Merlin's spell wasn't directed at her. The maiden gasped and sank to her knees, but Nimue felt her fighting back. This stranger might look frail, but she was a powerful sorceress.

"I serve Viviane of the River," she said through gritted teeth. "She leads those who oppose you, wizard. Since the Lady of the Lake has chosen to help you, we choose to balance the scales. We will not see our people betrayed to those who serve the crucified god. We will not see our powers squandered to settle mortal squabbles. Your petty ambitions will not drag us down to ruin."

Her face twisted, ugly with hatred, as she defied Merlin. Nimue felt his spell force the maiden to continue. She panted like an animal, but she couldn't stay silent.

"Whoever holds that sword will slay anyone who approaches with a blade in hand. He will cut down anyone who tries to take the sword. One day, when he least expects it, he will kill whomsoever he loves most in this world. He won't even know what he has done until it is too late."

Nimue shared Merlin's shock at such comprehensive malice. Arthur's rule could not have survived the slaughter that would have followed, if he had taken hold of the sword. A moment later, the wizard's magic faltered and the maiden sprang up.

"A curse fit for a king. Ah, well." She reached out to reclaim the lethal blade. "Stay vigilant, Master Merlin."

Nimue guessed whoever had created the curse sought to entangle Merlin too. Only magic could restrain Arthur, caught in that enchantment's grip. Camelot would have been defenceless against other hostile spells.

But the maiden didn't know about Nimue. If Viviane of the River was the enchantress who had threatened her and Morgana on the stairs, she had forgotten to warn her underling. Nimue summoned swift enchantment to bind the sorceress's hands and feet before she could pluck the hilt from Sir Balyn's helpless hand. The maiden gasped, horrified.

Merlin released Sir Balyn. His eyes were glazed with madness as he raised the cursed sword. He struck the maiden in the angle of her neck and shoulder. The blow nearly cut her in half before the blade stuck fast in the bones of her spine. Sir Balyn wrenched his arm back and her corpse slipped free to fall on the fur cloak. She lay butchered, with her blood pooling red on the white pelts. Balyn collapsed to his knees, distraught.

"Sheathe that blade," Merlin commanded.

Nimue felt the wizard's magic surround the sobbing man, but whoever had forged that blade didn't understand mortals. Sir Balyn didn't need forcing to stop further bloodshed. He cleaned the vile blade on an unsullied edge of the maiden's cloak and rammed the sword home in its scabbard. Getting to his feet, he raised his hands shoulder high and hung his head, utterly defeated.

"Do not approach Sir Balyn with a blade, if you value your life." Merlin's spell holding the knights melted away. Every man within arm's length of Sir Balyn hastily retreated. So did the ones behind them, even though they were well beyond the cursed knight's reach.

"Sir Balyn!" Arthur barked. "Will you follow Sir Kay to the cells beneath the gatehouse, so you may be locked in there, to ensure everyone's safety?"

The wretched knight answered with a nod.

Sir Kay was already stripping off his sword belt and blade, handing them to his squire. As seneschal and keeper of Camelot's keys, his authority was second only to Merlin's after the king. He walked towards Balyn, grim-faced and halted ten paces away. "Do you consent to follow me, knowing I mean you no harm?" Sir Kay's voice was admirably steady.

"I do." Sir Balyn's answer could barely be heard, even in this silence.

His steps echoed Sir Kay's as they walked towards the door. The men they passed shrank back, keeping their hands well away from their swords. Ahead, two quick thinkers hauled the great doors open. Swirling wind swept snow across the threshold as Sir Kay's squire darted out to shout a warning that no one approach the two knights. Sir Baudwin and his men followed, dragging the king of Gwynedd's whimpering herald.

Arthur didn't say a word as he walked towards the door at the back of the dais. Like his father, he valued swift access to his private chambers.

"Get that mess cleaned up," Merlin spat at the closest knights before he stalked after the king.

Sir Helynor and several others came forward, only to halt, uncertain what to do. To their visible relief, a squire appeared with a cloak he had found somewhere. Staying as far as they could from the butchered maiden, they rolled the slain knight onto the sturdy wool. A weeping greybeard gathered up the dead man's head and hand, and set them on his chest. More men stepped up to carry the gruesome burden out of the hall. Knights and squires filed after them. Nimue guessed they would lay the dead knight before the crucified god's altar until someone told them what to do next.

The dead sorceress lay sprawled on the gory tiles. Nimue moved quickly, stepping down from the dais without bothering with the stairs. She sensed a faint scent of rain amid the reek of spilled blood, and used that to weave a swift enchantment to send the dead maiden back to wherever she belonged. That was taking a risk, but it was preferable to one of the sorceress's sisters coming to see how their plot had fared. Hopefully, Viviane of the River would take her messenger's gruesome fate as a warning. Ideally, she would think twice before attacking Camelot again.

As the dead sorceress and her bloodstained cloak vanished, Nimue heard gasps in the doorway. A gaggle of maidservants huddled together, some with buckets and mops in hand. Nimue allowed herself a moment of satisfaction that one of her subordinates had considered such practicalities.

"The dead witch's magic has carried her evil far away." Nimue clapped her hands. "Quick as you can, wash this floor. Nothing here can hurt you now."

The maids came closer, reassured by her familiar authority. All the same, Nimue didn't wait for someone to ask what else she knew of such wicked magic, and how. She hurried through the door that opened onto Arthur's library. His collection had yet to rival Uther's long-since plundered and scattered treasures, but he was adding books at every opportunity.

"I don't believe she'll try another rash venture," Merlin assured the king as Arthur paced to and fro beneath the tall window.

"What can we do for Sir Balyn?" With no one to see, Arthur didn't hide his fear and revulsion.

Merlin looked at Nimue. "Have you—?"

"Got rid of the carrion? Yes, and that blood is on your hands," she told him bitterly. "You say you must save Logres from wild magic, but this Lady of the River only attacked because you're so quick to use enchantments to get your own way."

"I will have an answer!" yelled Arthur. "I am your king!"

Nimue swallowed her instinctive denial of such allegiance and focused on the problem in hand. "Can you lift the curse on that sword?" she asked Merlin. "Because I cannot."

She had no idea how to shatter such convoluted magic.

"No, but perhaps we can turn this to our advantage," the wizard said slowly.

"How?" the king demanded.

"Sir Balyn is a skilled and valiant warrior," Merlin observed. "Indeed, I would guess his hand and eye are faster than before, thanks to the magic bound into that sword. He will be a very hard man to kill."

"So, I send him into battle ahead of the front rank, and hope he only kills my enemies?" Arthur was ready to tear that idea to shreds.

"Let him carry your answer to King Ryons." Merlin smiled coldly. "No one will draw a blade against Sir Balyn if he travels under a white banner as your herald. Not until he throws your answer in the king of Gwynedd's face."

Arthur cocked his head. "When he tells Ryons to yield or face me in battle?"

Merlin shrugged. "We tell Sir Balyn to kill the Welsh king. We say this is his penance for shedding innocent blood in Camelot's hall. This courageous act will save his brothers-in-arms from death and injury. With Ryons dead, there will be no more war."

Arthur was tempted, but Nimue saw doubt in the young king's eyes.

"We will be sending Balyn to his death. Even wielding that cursed sword, he is only one man. Gwynedd's knights will cut him down, no matter how many he kills."

"How else is he to be freed from this curse?" Merlin rose from his seat. "I will ask him to do you this last service, your grace."

The wizard left the book-lined room.

Nimue would have followed, but Arthur stopped her. "Mistress."

"Your grace?" Reluctant, Nimue turned back.

"King Ryons' herald cannot travel with Sir Balyn. He saw everything that happened. He heard the witch confess the workings of that curse. Tell Sir Baudwin he must be kept confined. Not in chains," Arthur added hurriedly, "and not in the dungeons. He can be guarded in a decent chamber and treated with the courtesy owed to a herald. He just can't be allowed to leave. Not until King Ryons is dead. Then the boy can carry our promise of peace to Gwynedd, with my oath that no more men need die."

Nimue wondered how far treating the herald well would ease Arthur's guilty conscience over sending Sir Balyn to his death. At least that meant one life would be saved from this wretched day. Better yet, now she had an excuse to follow Merlin to the cells. She was carrying a message from the king.

She curtseyed. "I will tell him, your grace."

She headed for the gatehouse tower. To her annoyance, Merlin was already leaving. Sir Balyn looked up as Nimue peered through the iron grate set into the door of his cell. Even in the dim light, she saw the gleam of desperate hope in his eyes. What had Merlin told him?

She remembered Merlin had avoided a reply, when she had asked if he knew how to break this curse. She recalled his words to Arthur. How else might Balyn be freed? He had posed the question without answering it. Merlin knew a lot more than he was telling. Nimue was convinced of that.

CHAPTER EIGHTEEN

Nimue sighed as, yet again on this interminable journey, an unknown knight lay dead at her feet. Safe behind Camelot's walls, she hadn't realised how many masterless men roamed Britain's forests and byways. Men who knew nothing but killing after decades of endless battles. Did Arthur realise these warriors had nowhere to go, when their liege lords were killed, and their lands were seized by the crown to be granted to loyal knights? Did Merlin know? Did he care?

Those were questions for another day. She looked around with the sight of her people. As she followed Sir Balyn into the northern mountains of Wales, Nimue felt an eerie sensation of being watched. Did Viviane of the River want to know what had become of her sword? Was the Lady of the Lake curious about her rival's ploy? There was no scent of rain though, nor of roses. Once, Nimue thought she smelled a fleeting hint of musk and metal, and wondered if Merlin was scrying for her, despite her veiling enchantments. Perhaps he was keeping track of Sir Balyn. Perhaps she had imagined it, alone on this desolate road, fearful of lurking danger behind every tree.

Well, one less armoured and desperate man would be menacing the hapless peasantry. She waved a hand and the frozen ground opened up beneath the corpse. Winter might be turning to spring, but deathly cold still gripped Britain. The shifting earth buried the man who had challenged Sir Balyn. Nimue wondered if he had hoped to kill and rob the cursed knight, or if he sought vengeance. Could he be the brother or son of one of Balyn's earlier victims?

No, Nimue decided. Sir Balyn was just as much a victim of the sword's curse. As far as she was concerned, the blood of every dead man between here and Camelot was on Merlin's hands.

She shrouded the grave with frosted, fallen leaves, and turned her attention to the masterless knight's horse. Balyn had left the animal grazing after searching the bags tied to its saddle. Food and drink won from these unsought victories saved him from having to approach villages or farms where the curse might seize him, driving to cut down some innocent. He refused to be a horse thief though, and he never took coin or other plunder.

That was all very honourable, but these poor animals could hardly be left to their own devices in these wolf-haunted wilds. Exasperated, Nimue stripped off the horse's harness and searched the saddle bags. She tied the coin she found into a scrap of cloth and secured that under the horse's mane. She drove the saddle, the bridle and the dead knight's gear deep into the loosened earth of his grave. Now nothing could identify the horse.

She wove an enchantment to take the patient beast safely to the nearest smallholding. If anyone came looking for the horse and the peasant surrendered it, she hoped they would at least keep the silver coin they should find when they groomed the beast. No one could say whose hands such pennies had passed through.

Nimue drew a deep breath. One way or another, this unwanted quest would soon be over. The cursed knight was within a day's travel of Caerhun. A merchant on the road who thankfully felt no need to draw a warning blade, had told Sir Balyn that King Ryons was holding his court there. This road would take them to the coast, crossing the river that brought snowmelt down from the mountains.

Nimue summoned an enchantment to carry her after the knight, as light as a breath of wind, and just as invisible. She had travelled like this since leaving Camelot. She didn't want the encumbrance of a horse, and she didn't want Sir Balyn to know she was following him, in case that cursed sword decided she was a foe and forced him to attack her. If that happened, Nimue could escape injury, but if she had to flee, she wouldn't see what became of Merlin's plan.

She soon caught up with Balyn. He had taken care to rest his horse on this journey, but the poor animal was nearly spent. It plodded along the rutted road with its head low. Sir Balyn slumped in his saddle with the reins loose in his hand. Even the comet-tailed dragon pennant on his lance drooped beneath the white linen that marked the knight as an emissary. He favoured a helmet without a visor so Nimue could see his face, gaunt and hollow-eyed.

A church bell rang out ahead. The horse snorted and its ears pricked. Hoping for fodder and a stable, it broke into a heavy-footed trot. Sir Balyn straightened his back and braced his lance in his stirrup. Arthur's dragon snapped in a breeze that carried the salt scent of the distant sea. Nimue's magic kept pace with the knight, carrying her unseen over reed beds between the river and the road.

The pale sun rode high in the blue sky. Caerhun came into view. Earthworks marked out a great square enclosure where the road forded the river. Sturdy grey walls looked down from those banks, across a deep ditch defying any attackers. Rounded towers at each corner meant the king's sentries saw travellers in good time to sound a warning. A horn call soon proved that.

Nimue wondered how fast the Welsh king's sharp-eyed sentries would identify the blazon the knight carried. How would King Ryons react? Her heart sank as Caerhun's great gates opened and an armoured host appeared. Every surcote bore Gwynedd's ferocious lion. Worse still, the snarling beast clawed the air on the standard held high in their centre. King Ryons rode out with his men.

The horsemen approached the knight. If Merlin had given Sir Balyn a message for Gwynedd's king, that was forgotten. As soon as Ryons' knights drew their swords, the curse seized him.

Nimue had seen Sir Balyn struggle against the malevolent enchantment so often on this nightmarish journey. This time, he held off the magic until he tossed his lance aside. Whatever else, he wasn't going to defile the white flag of truce. Then Nimue saw his anguish fade as his face slackened into a dead-eyed mask. Balyn spurred his poor horse mercilessly as Gwynedd's knights charged on their fresher mounts.

Balyn wasn't encumbered by a shield, and he didn't have to fight while mastering his horse. The weary beast barely shied at the clash of swords or the hot reek of blood as Balyn cut down Gwynedd's knights. King Ryons' men were soon as frantic as their steeds, forcing their mounts between Sir Balyn and their liege lord. Welsh voices yelled defiance and abuse while their horses whinnied their protests.

Silent, Balyn hacked a man's hand from his arm. He swept the cursed blade back to strike another man's throat, knocking him out of his saddle. If the blow hadn't crushed his victim's windpipe, the man was dead once he hit the ground, trampled by iron-shod hooves. Welsh blades hacked at Balyn only to slide across his armour or to miss their strike entirely as he dodged and swayed in his saddle.

The cursed knight thrust his sword's tip into the next Welshman's face. The evil blade wrenched the helmet's visor aside and tore into the Welshman's cheek. He recoiled, choking on blood streaming from his wound. Balyn drove the sword into the man's eye. The dead knight toppled from his horse. Balyn's path to King Ryons lay open.

Balyn levelled the cursed blade at the king's face. Ryons met the threat with a deft parry. Balyn attacked again, intent on cutting the king's head from his shoulders. Ryons foiled the killing blow, but the heavy strike hit his elbow. The king's sword arm dropped, limp and useless. Ryons fumbled to pass his blade to his other hand.

Balyn raised the enchanted sword, but his horse collapsed under him. Nimue glimpsed an unknown knight on foot in the melee. His bloodied blade showed he had hamstrung the cursed knight's steed. The animal fell to thrash helplessly on the ground.

Balyn landed on his feet as horses around him reared away, defying their riders. The unknown knight parried once, twice. His sword broke. Balyn ducked low and the cursed blade cut the knight's legs out from under him. The Welshman fell, screaming as loudly as Balyn's wounded horse.

Ryons' standard dipped and swayed. A shout ordered retreat to Caerhun. Several riders succumbed to their fears. They wrenched their horses' heads around and fled. King Ryons' bodyguard was in utter disarray.

Nimue darted forward, still invisible. She laid a hand on the cursed knight's stricken horse and a thought ended its agony. She had no time to see if the unknown Welsh knight could be helped. A long stride carried her over the vicious skirmish to land beside Ryons' horse. Nimue seized the animal's bridle and shed the magic that hid her.

"What–" The king looked down, disbelieving.

Nimue muffled the dreadful noise of battle. "Surrender or he will kill you."

A muted scream told them both another Welshman had died. Nimue held Ryons' gaze. "He carries a cursed blade. He will kill any man who holds a sword."

Another knight fell in a crash of armour. Nimue could see that King Ryons had no idea who she was, but he had seen her step out of nowhere to warn him about evil magic. He could see for himself that his valiant liegemen stood no chance against this onslaught.

The king of Gwynedd threw down his sword and dragged off his helm. "I yield," he bellowed. "Yield! Yield, by my command. Drop your blades. We cannot defeat this sorcery."

Nimue's swift magic carried Ryons' words to every man in the melee. She saw they didn't understand, but they didn't want to die. More than that, they trusted their liege lord implicitly. Swords thudded to the ground.

Sir Balyn strode forward, spattered with dead men's blood. Scarlet drops fell to stain the dust as the evil sword shed its burden. As the spotless steel gleamed with deadly menace, Sir Balyn blinked and understanding kindled in his eyes. Seeing the carnage along the road, his face crumpled with immeasurable grief.

Wretched, he looked at Nimue. "He said if I killed Gwynedd's king, the enchantment would be broken. If Ryons lives, I am still cursed."

"Merlin told you that?" Nimue was appalled. Surely, that couldn't be true. Merlin could have no idea of the sorcery woven into Viviane of the River's spell.

"Who are you," Ryons of Gwynedd barked, "and what is this vile magic?"

"King Arthur sent me. Your herald brought your message to Camelot." But Sir Balyn didn't know what else to say.

King Ryons glared. "Your king sent you to kill me with a cursed sword? That was Arthur's answer?"

Nimue was glad that Gwynedd's furious ruler was still on his horse, clutching his injured arm with his empty hand. If Ryons had been on foot, he would have reached for his dropped sword with no thought for the consequences.

"This was his counsellor's plan," she said sharply. "Blame Merlin."

"Merlin the wizard." The word was a curse on Ryons' lips.

"Oh, come now." Merlin strolled into the empty space beside Balyn. "How many of your loyal men have been saved today? Granted, Gwynedd will grieve for the fallen, and rightly so, but how much more sorrow would have followed a pitched battle with Logres' mighty army?"

No one answered. Merlin smiled with satisfaction, as if their silence was agreement. He bowed to King Ryons. "You yielded to Sir Balyn and that was wise. Do you yield to King Arthur, your grace? Will you have peace between Gwynedd and Logres?"

"When the alternative is facing murderous magic?" Ryons said through gritted teeth. "I yield. Tell your master. I will tell my allies of your work this day."

Gwynedd's king gathered up his reins and wheeled his horse around. He did not look back as he rode for Caerhun. His few unwounded knights went to help the injured. Nimue hurried to the knight who had so courageously felled Balyn's horse. To her sorrow, she found him dead in a welter of blood.

Furious, she looked for Merlin. How dare he make such callous calculations with innocent men's lives? The wizard was talking to Balyn. The knight's shoulders slumped, and the cursed sword was slack in his hand. He barely seemed to be listening, staring into the distance with unseeing eyes.

A moment later, grim purpose replaced his desolation. Balyn sheathed the murderous blade and ran for the nearest loose horse. The knight mounted and kicked the beast into a canter. He headed back down the road towards the mountains.

Nimue took a long stride and accosted Merlin, grabbing his black sleeve. "What did you say? Where is he going?"

Merlin scowled as he shook her off. "Must you always meddle?"

"You accuse me?" His arrogance left her breathless. "When your scheme has killed so many?"

Merlin raised a hand to silence her. "Sir Balyn slew these unfortunates, here and on his journey. I had no part in that."

Nimue stared at him, incredulous. "You think that excuse will save you, when you are called to pay the threefold price for the harm you have done?"

"Everything I do is for the greater good." Merlin shrugged. "I've not been called to account as yet."

"That day will come," Nimue assured him. "I hope I am there to see it."

For an instant, Merlin looked uneasy. That dampened her anger a little, and Nimue decided his fate could wait. Her immediate concern was Sir Balyn.

"Where is he going?" she demanded. "What did you say?"

Merlin smiled with infuriating arrogance. "I told him I knew how he could break the curse."

Nimue fought an urge to slap the wizard. "Do you know, or did you tell him more lies? I know you deceived him into trying to kill King Ryons, saying that would set him free."

Merlin narrowed his eyes. "Since you are so concerned with his fate, follow him and find out."

He vanished, leaving Nimue surrounded by grieving men struggling to help their wounded brothers-in-arms. She looked towards Caerhun and saw a huddle of women coming through the gate. She could already hear their laments for the dead.

Nimue could help. Enchantments could nudge the wounded towards healing and ease the suffering of those past saving. She could help without magic as well. If she took turns tending the survivors, these women could find a little time to grieve.

What would become of Sir Balyn? Where had Merlin sent him, and who might stray into the knight's path and die a needless death? Nimue had followed him to try to stop such calamities. If she failed, she could at least bear witness and add such deaths to the tally of bloodshed Merlin had caused. Deaths that the wizard must pay for, if there was any justice in the mortal world or the hidden realm.

She turned her back on Caerhun. Sick with guilt, she focused on Sir Balyn. If she was going to find out what Merlin had told him, she would have to travel alongside him by more normal means. Nimue summoned a loose horse with a soft whistle and kilted up her skirts for riding. As soon as she was mounted, she used her heels to stir the horse to a trot. The beast whinnied with surprise when it arrived behind its stable mate after a bare handful of paces.

Sir Balyn's horse answered with a whicker. The knight looked around to see who was following, and there was no hint of the curse's madness in his eyes.

Even so, Nimue raised her hands to show she carried no weapon. "I want to help you."

"You're from Camelot." Balyn forced a heartbreaking smile. "Please, go back and stay safe, mistress."

"I have magic of my own." Telling him her secret was easier than she expected. "How else could I have followed you?"

"Do you honestly think you can help me?" Balyn shook his head in denial.

"I will try–" Nimue broke off as she realised the mountains ahead were taller and sharper. The river beside the road foamed and glittered with eerie light. The road itself was smooth and unmarked by hooves or wheel ruts. Somehow, in this short distance, they had ridden out of Gwynedd and into the hidden realm. What was Merlin up to now?

CHAPTER NINETEEN

Sir Balyn looked at Nimue, wary. "What's wrong, mistress?"

"What exactly did Master Merlin tell you?"

"That he would set me on the right road to find the witch who cursed this sword. The only way to free myself is to kill her." Balyn grimaced, clearly reluctant to slay a woman, even a sorceress.

Nimue didn't imagine he would get the chance. Though she was surprised Merlin had told the truth. If Viviane of the River died, her magic would die with her. If.

"Let's see what she has to say for herself. I'll lead the way." Nimue nudged her horse past Balyn's, holding the beast to a walk. She had no idea how far they might have to go, and she had no desire to ride into unexpected trouble at the gallop.

The river foamed beside the road, filling the air with the rush of water. It was the only sound to be heard. No birds chirped and squabbled in the trees or flew across the meadows where the grass was far too lush and green for this season of the year. Their horses' hooves were silent on the hard, dry earth.

"Mistress," Balyn asked uneasily. "Where are we? This isn't the road I followed to Caerhun."

Nimue twisted in her saddle to answer and saw there were no hoof prints in the pale dust. Anyone ahead of them on this road wouldn't leave a trace either. She should remember that.

"Thanks to Master Merlin, we have walked into a realm of magic. Few things will be what they seem. Be on your guard, but don't do anything rash." Though that was a vain hope, if someone or something attacked them.

"I only want to find this witch, kill her, and leave." Balyn's certainty faltered. "You know how to leave this place, don't you?"

Nimue nodded and turned back to urge her mount towards the sharp-edged mountains rising ahead. A nod wasn't lying, not exactly. She knew how to return to the mortal world. She just wasn't entirely sure she would be able to take Sir Balyn with her. But there was nothing to be gained by telling him that.

They rode on in silence. Some while later, for the second or perhaps the third time, Nimue jerked awake as her chin sunk towards her breastbone. The air here was warm and still after the aching cold of the journey from Camelot. Her horse's steady pace and the river's soft whisper were lulling her into a doze.

Really? She squared her shoulders and looked for any sign of her kindred working magic to send her to sleep. No, there was no one. She was simply weary to the bone. That was all well and good, but even a moment's inattention could be disastrous. She forced herself to stay vigilant as they rode on. Soon after, she saw movement in a cluster of trees whose vivid red and orange autumn leaves had somehow omitted to fall. She halted her placid horse.

"Mistress." Balyn urged his mount between her and whatever was out there.

"Let's not be hasty." Nimue noted the knight's blood-soaked surcote and armour were clean again. Had he noticed?

"I see a rider." Balyn stood in his stirrups.

"Is he armed?" Nimue wracked her brains for some way to stop Balyn reaching for that cursed sword.

"He wears a blade, but he hasn't drawn it." Balyn sank into his saddle, relieved.

A knight emerged from the autumnal trees and halted a

polite distance away. His horse was well-groomed and his gear was well-tended, though he wore no blazon on his surcote and his shield was plain white. His most notable feature was his magnificent black beard, and he appeared to be much the same age as Sir Balyn.

"Good day," he called out. "My name is Sir Herlews. May I know who you are, and where you are travelling?"

Nimue saw Balyn stiffen as he recognised the name. It meant nothing to her. Balyn glanced over and she nodded, prompting him to answer.

"I am Sir Balyn." He faltered and Nimue hid a grin as she realised he couldn't recall her name. He continued resolutely. "We do not know precisely where this road will take us, but when our business here is done, we will return to Camelot."

Sir Herlews shook his head. "I do not know where that might be, but may I ride with you? I was searching for a lost maiden, and I lost my way." He looked at them helplessly. "I beg you."

Balyn glanced at Nimue. She could see he had something to tell her, but that could wait. Her people's sight showed her Sir Herlews was a mortal man, no more and no less.

She answered him. "You are welcome to ride with us, sir knight. I have only one condition. You must not draw your sword. The blade my companion carries is cursed, and it will kill you."

She expected him to question that, and she was ready to speak over Sir Balyn before he offered too many answers. Just because Sir Herlews was mortal, that didn't mean he could be trusted.

"I give you my word." The bearded knight walked his horse past her to take his place a few paces behind Sir Balyn.

Nimue wondered how long he had been trapped in this realm, and what he had seen, if a murderous enchanted blade was so unremarkable.

They rode on, following the road beside the foaming river.

The eerie silence hung around them. After they had covered what felt like a good distance, Nimue pulled up her horse and waited for the two knights to draw level.

She nodded towards the mountains. "Do you think we're getting any closer?"

Balyn's bemusement turned to unease as he studied the grey-blue crags lightly dusted with snow. "They look as far away as ever."

Nimue looked up at the clear blue sky. "We should be seeing some hint of twilight by now, this early in the year."

Sir Herlews shook his head, despairing. "I fear I have led you astray."

"I hardly think so, since we haven't left this road." Nimue looked around. "But I think this is where we need to take another path."

It was always possible that whatever magic had trapped Sir Herlews here, like a fly in amber, was hampering her and Sir Balyn. She hardened her heart. If they couldn't make any progress as long as the bearded knight travelled with them, he would have to leave.

"What other path is there?" Balyn was baffled.

As soon as he spoke, a flower-dotted meadow opened up between the river and the road. The dusty road carried on towards the mountains, while the foaming river curled away towards the – was that the east? No sun shone overhead to give Nimue a bearing, although the blue sky was still as bright as noonday. No matter. If Viviane was mistress of this river, they should go upstream to its source.

"Let's try over there." Nimue urged her horse off the road. Sir Balyn rode with her. After a few moments she heard Sir Herlews muttering as he followed. Sir Balyn kicked his horse into a trot. Nimue did the same. They might as well reach wherever they were going a little faster now.

The meadow grew broader and away in the distance on either side, gentle hills rose, thickly forested. Now the river was broad and slow, curling through this vale in lazy loops. The long grass whispered as their horses walked through the dry stems, and flowers crushed beneath their hooves perfumed the air. Nimue glanced over her shoulder to judge how far they had come and saw the snow-capped mountain peaks were barely visible on the horizon.

She reminded herself to concentrate on whatever might lie ahead and searched the vale with the sight of her people as they rode on. Nothing caught her eye. She couldn't decide if that was good news or bad.

Galloping hooves thundered across the meadow behind them. Nimue hauled on her reins to turn her horse around. Both knights did the same, despite their startled steeds' protests. There was nothing to be seen. Balyn stared at Nimue. They could still hear a horse bearing down on them, but there was no sign of the beast.

Sir Herlews screamed in agony. A colossal impact drove him out of his saddle. The bearded knight flew through the air, his arms and legs flailing helplessly. A mortal wound blossomed bloodily red beneath his breastbone. He crashed to the ground as the hammering hooves faded into the distance.

Nimue was out of her saddle and running through the long grass. A glance told her Sir Balyn was still on horseback, looking in all directions for an enemy to fight. His hand hovered by his sword hilt, but with no foe to be seen, the blade's curse didn't seize him. That was something to be grateful for.

Nimue sank to her knees by the stricken knight. Now she could see what had hit Sir Herlews. A spear was thrust clean through his body, piercing his breastplate and the chain mail beneath it. His surcote was sodden with blood. There could be no surviving the wound, but he wouldn't die quickly or easily.

Nimue seized his hand as Herlews writhed in agony. The knight's face told her he knew he was dying. Even so, he sucked down desperate gulps of air as his body fought to live. Tears trickled down her cheeks. It would be so easy to end his suffering, but she resisted the temptation. There was still a chance that whoever was watching wasn't sure who she was. The longer they underestimated her, the better. If she used her magic in this enchanted place, they might decide she was a threat.

Sir Balyn ran to join them, still empty-handed.

"Tell me," he begged the dying knight. "Who has done this? Do you know?"

"Garlon." Sir Herlews coughed up a mouthful of blood. "Sir Garlon."

The name meant nothing to Nimue. She gritted her teeth as Sir Herlews' death grip crushed her fingers. Her pain was nothing compared to his. The knight's heels gouged scars in the earth as his breaths came shorter, bubbling deep in his chest. Scarlet foam trickled from his mouth and blood gushed from his wound. Nimue felt warm wetness soak through her gown beneath her knees. He coughed weakly one last time and his agonizing hold gave way. Nimue folded his hands on his chest. She closed his eyes and straightened his legs.

Sir Balyn's face twisted with rage, but this wasn't the sword's curse. He was simply furious as he twisted the spear's haft and wrenched it free of Sir Herlews' chest. The knight's corpse vanished. The blood on Nimue's clothes and hands was gone, and nothing had crushed the flowers and grass.

Sir Balyn stared at Nimue. Disbelief warred with fear in his eyes.

She realised the dead knight's horse had disappeared as well. "Who was Sir Herlews? Who is Sir Garlon?"

Sir Balyn shook his head, mystified. "They were knights who fought against Uther Pendragon and were defeated long ago. Neither had a noble reputation. How did they get to this place? Why couldn't they get home? Why couldn't we see Sir Garlon if he truly killed Sir Herlews?"

"I have no idea." Nimue wondered who had been left to grieve for these men, never knowing their fate. Who had been

left undefended? Wives, sisters, daughters? Had they longed to
see the knights return, or had they dreaded the prospect?

She stood up and held out her hand. "May I see that?"

Balyn stared at the spear as if he had no idea why he held
it. He handed the ash pole over. Nimue took it slowly, ready
to drop it if his hand moved an inch towards that sword hilt.

He stood there. "Well?"

"Can you cut the spearhead off this? I would like to have a
staff." She wasn't going to take a weapon into Viviane of the
River's presence. A simple wooden staff might be overlooked.

Something else occurred to her. At Camelot, the maiden had
said anyone carrying a blade stirred the curse on Balyn's sword.
It seemed a spearhead didn't count. Was that some oversight?
Precise wording was important when working complex magic.

Sir Balyn drew his sword and the cursed blade's impossibly
sharp edge cut cleanly through the ash wood. The spearhead
hit the ground and vanished.

"What now?" he demanded.

"We go on." Nimue went over to her horse, grazing a short
distance away. Once she was mounted, she tucked the spear
haft between her knee and the saddle, resting it against her
shoulder and bracing the end in her stirrup.

She didn't hear what Sir Balyn said as he headed for his
own horse, and she decided not to ask. She was pretty sure it
would be far from courteous.

They rode on. The vale stretched out ahead. The river
meandered between its grassy banks. The sky overhead was an
untroubled blue. Nimue grew steadily more irritated. Viviane
of the River must know they had brought her cursed sword
into the hidden folk's realm. Wasn't she in the least curious?

Hooves sounded loud behind them again. They whirled
their horses around. Sir Garlon – who else could it be? – was
nowhere to be seen. This time Balyn had drawn his sword. The
knight bared his teeth in a feral snarl that told Nimue the curse
had seized him. He spurred his horse into a sideways leap and

brought the blade down with a sweeping stroke. The blow hit home and for an instant, Nimue glimpsed a shadowy figure.

The hoof beats faded. Then they returned. Sir Balyn was ready. He hacked at empty air and the clash of steel on steel rang out. Nimue caught sight of Sir Garlon, only for the knight to vanish. She heard his horse carry him away.

Awareness returned to Sir Balyn's eyes. "He cannot kill me, but how can I kill him?"

They heard a galloping horse. Nimue saw the light of sanity in Balyn's eyes fade. Sir Garlon came nearer. This time, she was ready.

Sir Balyn's sword shot forward and parried Garlon's blade. Nimue forced her horse towards the uncanny battle. Balyn swept aside another blow. As their swords met, Sir Garlon could be seen once more. Nimue hit him hard between the shoulder blades with the spear haft. The blunt wood could do no damage. She wasn't even sure the knight would feel it. That didn't matter. The blow made Garlon visible.

Sir Garlon raised his sword for a murderous thrust at Balyn's face. The knight dodged to avoid the blow and drove the point of the cursed blade under Sir Garlon's hand. The bright steel plunged into his armpit, and Sir Garlon's sword fell from nerveless fingers. He swayed in his saddle, clearly visible. Like Sir Herlews, his surcote bore no blazon and the shield behind his saddle was white without any design.

Sir Balyn wrenched his sword free of Sir Garlon's body. The dying knight toppled off his horse. He disappeared as soon as he hit the ground and so did his steed.

Cheers and applause deafened Nimue. A great crowd surrounded them, too many people to count. Young, old, they were dressed in every sort of garb from silks and satins to peasant rags. They were clapping as if Sir Balyn had just provided some great entertainment.

Behind the onlookers, men and women strolled to and fro, holding goblets and flagons, laughing and chatting. Music from lutes and flutes floated through the air, and the breeze was fragrant with mouth-watering scents of roasting meat. The long flower-bright grass had vanished, and brightly-coloured tents stood on short emerald-green turf. A dais with a throne had been set up in front of the grandest pavilion.

An ageless woman relaxed in her seat, sipping from a silver goblet. She made no pretence of mortal beauty to soothe men's anxieties and spark their desire, or to prompt women's despairing jealousy to distract them just as effectively. The symmetry of her features and the satin perfection of her skin were equally unnerving. Her blue eyes were as brilliant as they were piercing.

A circlet of pearls swept long black hair back from her face. Her tresses flowed over her shoulder and past her waist to pool on the polished wood by her satin-slippered feet. Her gown was grey silk shot with blue, decorated with tiny pearls in swirls like drifts of foam. There could be no doubt who she was. They had found Viviane of the River.

Sir Balyn gripped the cursed sword and strode towards her. Men and women stood aside to let him through, still smiling, unconcerned. Viviane was smiling too as Sir Balyn stalked towards her with murderous intent. She gestured lazily with a silver-ringed hand and an armoured knight appeared in Balyn's path. He wore no blazon on his blood-red surcote and his helmet's visor concealed his face. Like Balyn, he carried no shield, and he held a single hand-and-a-half sword.

"This is my champion, the Knight of the River." Viviane's lilting voice carried clearly over the heads of the cheerful crowd. "Defeat him and you will have the reward you seek."

CHAPTER TWENTY

The knight of the river raised his sword hand shoulder-high with the blade angled down across his body. Sir Balyn struck hard and fast with a downward blow that should have smashed through his enemy's guard to bury the cursed sword in his head. The knight of the river darted forward and brought up his blade to block Balyn's strike. He used his empty hand to force Balyn's sword hand aside. In the same fluid movement, Viviane's champion brought his sword around to hit Balyn hard on the side of his helmet.

Nimue saw blood seep onto Balyn's forehead and felt a chill of apprehension. In every fight she had witnessed, Sir Balyn had come through unscathed. Both knights retreated. They circled slowly, alert for an opening. Nimue's concern grew. The cursed sword wasn't driving Sir Balyn into the usual frenzied attacks.

The knight of the river swept a high stroke around to cut off Sir Balyn's head. The cursed knight moved fast, retreating a pace. First, he swept the blow aside. Then he stepped behind the knight of the river's sword arm. Before his enemy could bring his blade back, Sir Balyn hacked at his knees. The knight of the river's legs were armoured, but Viviane's champion staggered as the blow landed. Limping, he retreated.

The knight of the river took up a guarding stance and waited for Sir Balyn to attack. The cursed knight feigned a full-bodied blow, only to pull back his hand as his enemy went to parry. With a twist of his wrist, Balyn attacked the knight of the river's sword hand.

Viviane's champion wasn't fooled. He snatched his sword hilt away. With the cursed sword meeting no resistance, Sir Balyn stumbled forward, just a pace. That was enough. The knight of the river brought his blade down hard on Balyn's forearm. Nimue saw blood seep through the links of Balyn's chain mail where the skin beneath had split.

He retaliated swiftly with a thrust at the knight of the river's shoulder. The force of the blow drove Viviane's champion back. Balyn pursued him with a flurry of brutal strikes. The knight of the river parried and rallied. He countered with rapid attacks of his own, forcing Sir Balyn onto the defensive. Nimue couldn't recall the cursed knight fighting anyone whose skills so nearly matched his own.

The battle went on. Each man landed bruising, wounding blows. Sir Balyn's chain mail was soon smeared with blood from an ominous tally of unseen wounds. The knight of the river pierced his guard and hit his helmet again. More blood mingled with the sweat trickling down Balyn's face.

Viviane's champion's red surcote made it harder to see how badly he was bleeding. He was certainly limping. Increasingly, he kept his off-hand elbow pressed tight against his side. Nimue guessed his ribs were injured.

The onlookers were unconcerned. They cheered when either knight landed a blow. Some strolled off in search of other entertainment when the pace of battle slackened as both men fought to catch their breath.

Nimue looked at Viviane of the River, ready to use her own magic to wipe any smirk off the sorceress's face. But Viviane sat forward, watching intently and gripping the carved arms of her throne.

The end was brutally sudden. Sir Balyn swung at the knight of the river's head. Viviane's champion swept up his blade to block the cursed sword's strike. Balyn was already sweeping a vicious cut downwards. He hacked at the knight of the river's unwounded knee.

The red knight's leg buckled. Sir Balyn stepped in to land a killing blow. The steel bit deep into the gap between the knight of the river's helmet and the neck of his armour. But Sir Balyn's weariness had betrayed him. As the cursed blade struck, the knight of the river thrust his own sword under the edge of Sir Balyn's hauberk and deep into his killer's guts.

The dying men collapsed to lie tangled together. Their blood flowed and mingled on the green grass. The men and women still watching gave a desultory cheer and wandered away. Merry music floated over the meadow.

Sobbing with fury and grief, Nimue dropped the spear haft and ran to the fallen men. As she reached them, a blazon appeared on the knight of the river's surcote. The black boar was identical to the one Sir Balyn wore, except his was framed by three blue stars.

Sir Balyn groaned. With an agonizing effort he dragged himself free of his defeated foe. The knight of the river's sword slid out from beneath his hauberk. Nimue braced herself for the fatal gush of blood that would end the cursed knight's life. Instead, Balyn looked up at her, puzzled. There was no trace of madness in his eyes.

"Who – who have I been fighting?" He forced himself up onto his hands and knees. Seeing the blazon on the dead knight's surcote, he howled with such anguish the whole vast gathering fell silent. Everyone watched Sir Balyn crawl over and remove the knight of the river's helmet. He cupped the dead man's face in his hands and his tears washed speckles of blood from his last victim's face.

"My brother Balan." He looked up at Nimue, heartbroken. "We were born in the same hour."

Balyn was the elder twin, she realised. That's what those stars signified.

"He will kill whomsoever he loves most in this world." Viviane had come down from her dais and strolled over to join them.

"He won't even know what he has done until far too late."
Nimue recalled the words of the curse. She shook her head,
vehement. "No, you have done this. Their blood is on your hands."

"Really?" Viviane asked, faintly mocking. "I thought you
blamed Master Merlin. As you should. He has sent countless
knights to plague my lands as he strives to further his ambitions
for the mortals he favours. I merely sent one of my daughters
to bring this mortal here, and I have only done that to teach
Merlin a much-needed lesson."

Balyn struggled to his feet, startling them both. Nimue saw
his brother's sword had passed right through his body, just
above his hip. The wound would be the death of him, but what
was he going to do with the little life he had left?

"I will kill you for this," he assured Viviane, breathless.

"Really?" Her fallen champion's sword flew into her hand.
"Are you sure you can?"

Balyn looked at the blade he held, and his bloodied brow
creased in confusion.

Nimue was equally at a loss. Why wasn't he attacking the
sorceress, unable to stop now that she held a sword?

"I told you," Viviane reproved him. "Defeat my champion
and you will have the reward you seek. You came here to
break the curse."

Balyn stared at her in utter desolation. Throwing his useless
sword away, he collapsed to his knees and gathered his dead
brother in his arms. His racking sobs ripped through the silence
in the meadow.

Nimue looked for the spear haft she had dropped. She
wouldn't use steel against one of her kin, and in any case, she
was no swordswoman. All the same, she was ready to give
Viviane a thrashing the sorceress wouldn't forget.

She saw Merlin standing by the riverbank with his arms
folded and a slight smile on his angular face. Now Nimue was
torn between two targets for her wrath. "How long have you
been there?" she spat.

"Long enough." He bowed to Viviane. "Well played, my lady of the river."

Viviane acknowledged his compliment with a satisfied smile. Tossing away the red knight's sword, she snapped her fingers to summon a lackey. A boy hurried forward with three ornate glass goblets on a silver tray. He offered the first to his mistress and the next to Nimue.

She shook her head, though only because she couldn't decide who deserved to have the golden wine thrown in their eyes. Was Viviane or Merlin the greater villain here?

Merlin accepted the goblet he was offered. "Can I expect you to send more such distractions to Camelot?"

Distractions? Devoted brothers lay dead and dying in this unspeakable tragedy. Nimue longed to challenge such callousness. Instead, she stayed silent to see what she might learn to use against both Merlin and Viviane.

The lady of the river waved a hand and the crowd, and the tents, disappeared. Sir Balyn knelt on the turf, cradling his dead brother as he silently wept. Only his shaking shoulders told Nimue he still lived.

As Viviane sipped her wine, her blue eyes never left Merlin's face. "I keep to my own lands and yet your selfishness constantly interferes with my affairs. You use your magic to sweep obstacles from your chosen pet's path, and you don't care that his people see your sorcery at work. You think they are left cowering in awe? Not at all. Thanks to you, greedy mortals hunt for enchantments to use for themselves. My people live in constant fear, pursued and forced to work magic if they are caught. Well, I can terrify your king's people in return. This is only the start."

Merlin met her gaze, but he didn't reply. Viviane threw down her goblet, furious.

"You don't give our kindred a second thought. You're obsessed with your petty ambitions in the mortal realm. You have defied our people's age-old customs and persuaded our sisters of the lake to give your favourite not one but two enchanted swords, since your boy was careless enough to lose the first. What have you promised the Lady of the Lake in return? She has long sought advantage over me and influence over my people. Was that her price? Tell me!"

"No," Merlin said quickly. He paused and considered his words carefully before he went on. "She knows that mortals have whispered about our magic for generations. She knows it's better to have allies than enemies. If she puts a sword in Arthur's hand, she can expect him to protect her and her people."

"She's a fool if she thinks any mortal will save her and her sisters. The maidens of the lake will suffer with the rest of us, thanks to you," hissed Viviane. "Your arrogance has betrayed us all."

Nimue shivered as she felt the chill of the sorceress's contempt. The grass crisped and silvered with frost. She heard a loud crack and shards of ice swirled in the river's eddies.

Abruptly, Viviane shrugged. "If you choose to meddle in mortal matters, why can't I? Why shouldn't I show your boy king that magic is a two-edged blade? Perhaps he will think twice about relying on your counsel as his people pay a high price in blood and sorrow for every unearned boon your enchantments grant him. Let's see if the maidens of the lake are so willing to help you when I repay any move against me with threefold vengeance on them."

Merlin pursed his lips as he contemplated the contents of his goblet. Ice tinkled against the glass. "Very well. I will not use my magic in mortal affairs, as long as you do the same."

"Then we are agreed. Do not test me again," Viviane warned ominously.

She vanished. Merlin and Nimue were left standing on either side of Sir Balyn, motionless on his knees and still cradling his brother. With a pang of grief, Nimue saw the wounded knight had died unnoticed while Viviane was talking. They were no longer in those perilous lands ruled by the lady of the river. The blunt, grey Welsh mountains rose above a muddy pasture beside a noisy stream. Merlin heaved a sigh as he took hold of Balyn's shoulders and eased the corpse to the ground.

"Are you going to tell King Arthur what your magic can cost an innocent man?" Nimue demanded. "That it's your fault Sir Balyn was cursed to kill his brother? What will Camelot's loyal knights think of that?"

Merlin ignored her, unbuckling Balyn's sword belt and scabbard. Seeing the cursed sword lying on the rough tussocks of grass a short distance away, he walked over to pick it up.

"What are you doing?" Nimue asked sharply.

Merlin examined the blade. "Sir Balyn may have broken the curse that drove him to kill, but this is still a weapon forged with sorcery. Only the pure of heart can draw it from this scabbard. That hasn't changed. In the right hands, this will be a mighty blade."

"And you will choose those hands?" Nimue stared at him, disbelieving. "When you just promised Viviane of the River you would stop using magic in mortal affairs."

"I didn't make this sword. I need not use any sorcery to find a knight worthy of carrying it."

"You think Viviane will consider that keeping your word?"

Merlin studied the sword, his eyes distant in thought. Nimue guessed he was contemplating which knight he might choose to wield it. What would the bloody price of that be?

"You know she will believe she's been deceived when she sees another knight using her sword." Precise words were important in their people's dealings. Nimue remembered exactly what the wizard had said. "She will send another warning, another threat, to King Arthur, and that will free you from your agreement. That's what you want, isn't it?"

Merlin didn't reply, but he couldn't hide a secretive smile as he sheathed the blade.

Nimue glared at him. "I will go back to Camelot and tell

Arthur what your help costs his men in grief and pain. I will tell him you left this brave knight and his brother as carrion to be eaten by crows."

Merlin scowled at her. "They are dead. What does the fate of their bodies matter? Or have the crucified god's priests convinced you with their tales of some life to come?"

"I may not share their faith, but those in Camelot do," Nimue retorted. "I will tell them they can expect such callous dishonour if they die in Arthur's service. How many will stay loyal then?"

Merlin glowered. "These brave knights can have a fitting memorial, if you insist."

The ground shivered, and the muddy grass where the dead men lay shimmered with pale light. In the next moment, the slaughtered brothers rested on a pristine white marble slab. More enchantmcnt solidified, building swift courses of stonework to hide the bloody corpses from view. A few moments later, and the tomb had a roof, elegant in its simplicity. All the evidence of those brutal deaths was hidden away.

Merlin's forefinger drew swift shapes in the air. Letters appeared on the marble, deeply incised and gilded.

Here lies Sir Balyn the Savage, Knight of Northumberland and Camelot.

Here lies Sir Balan, Knight of Northumberland. Pray for our souls.

"Satisfied?" Merlin demanded.

Making this tomb meant nothing to him, Nimue saw. These deaths were acceptable losses as he focused on his ultimate purpose. What was his aim anyway?

"Shall we put their family blazon on the side?" he sneered.

That would serve no real purpose, Nimue realised. Even if they recognised the black boar, no one who stopped to marvel at such a memorial in this remote place would have any idea of the undeserved fate that killed these two men. No one would ever know the anguish of Sir Balyn's last weeks or the heartbreak of his final moments. She was the only one who cared.

She could still feel the magic thrumming through the ground beneath her feet. Merlin had summoned the stone for this tomb from the far south of Logres. He had stripped the marble of its intricate patterns and colours to leave this bleak whiteness. This memorial was like a blank page in some book where he could write his version of events. She was the only one who could say different. She was the only one who could do more than stand witness to the truth.

Merlin raised his hand, intent on the smooth white stone. Nimue didn't know what he planned and she didn't care. She snatched the cursed sword from his unsuspecting grip, and hurled it at the tomb, scabbard, belt and all. Her magic made the white marble as insubstantial as fog. The evil blade vanished into the mist. A moment later, and the stone was impenetrable once again. The sword would lie with the men brought to their deaths by its sorcery.

"What are you doing?" Merlin was outraged.

Nimue seized his arm and plunged them both into the turmoil of magic far below. Merlin fought to free himself, but he had drawn deep on his power, first to come to Gwynedd, then to reach Viviane of the River's realm, and finally with this profligate display. He could not break her hold.

Nimue sensed his growing unease as Merlin found he was weaker than he expected. More than that, the wizard realised Nimue was far stronger than he had assumed. His disquiet turned to apprehension.

What are you doing?

Our people have always held aloof from mortals and for good reason. I see that now.

Nimue focused on tracing the ripples of the wizard's enchantments as he had forced the aeons-old rocks to do his bidding to build Sir Balyn and his brother's tomb. Merlin's magic had come surging back as the lands beyond Logres refused to yield to such mistreatment. Nimue found what she sought in the far west of Wales. The blue stones of those ancient hills had defied Merlin's arrogant sorcery most fiercely of all.

Nimue didn't attempt to force the rocks to obey her. Instead, she searched for a void. She found a crevice, then a wider chasm. It led to a cavern untouched by daylight. The still pool of water within had never felt the brush of a breeze. She slid through the gap, dragging Merlin with her.

As soon as their feet hit the cave's uneven floor, he fought his way free of her hold. He was physically taller and stronger now that they had form and substance once again. The darkness was absolute, but that was no hindrance to their kind. "You will regret this."

Nimue allowed him his moment of triumph. While he was distracted, she wove the spells that would keep him here. "Too late."

"What are you talking about?" He looked around the cavern. "Where is this place?"

"This is your future. I will not let you bring disaster down on our people."

Merlin laughed, scornful. "I think not."

His magic reverberated around the cavern as he tried to step through the darkness. Tried and failed. These hills would not allow Merlin to leave. The land knew he was their enemy.

"Now I understand why you see wild magic threatening Arthur's future," Nimue told him. "You are the reason. Your interference has caused the grief that's plagued Logres and the isles of Britain since you first contrived Uther's victories in battle. You should have left well alone. You should never have drawn the Lady of the Lake and her sisters into your schemes. If you had not made that alliance, Viviane of the River would have no reason to fear her rival's ascendancy. She would have no reason to attack Arthur."

"You have no idea what you're talking about." Merlin walked in a slow circle, studying the walls of the cave.

"I realised something else. Viviane said she will repay the

maidens of the lake threefold for any harm done to her people.
I've been waiting to see you pay the price for your offences,
without ever wondering who would exact such a penalty. Now
I see we are all responsible for keeping the peace between our
kind and mortals."

"You dare to judge me?" scoffed Merlin.

"I do," she said, steadfast. "And I say you must be stopped
from meddling in mortal affairs."

Merlin whirled around. Nimue was ready. She had seen his
face harden as he completed his circuit and seen the truth.
There was no way out of this cavern for him unless Nimue's
magic died with her.

Merlin's body contorted as he sprang at her. He took on a
great hound's form, heavy enough to knock her off her feet.
He snarled, showing teeth that would crush her bones and tear
her flesh. Nimue dropped to her hands and knees. Now she
was a hare, nimble enough to dart around the hound, too fast
for him to catch.

As she crouched in the shadows, she saw Merlin change
into a long-legged courser. Lithe, he bounded towards her
with murderous intent in his dark eyes. Nimue sprang for the
edge of the pool. She leapt and before her paws touched the
water, she was a small silver fish.

She swam into the depths. The waters roiled as Merlin
plunged into the pool. Looking up, Nimue saw he had become
an otter. His sleek, muscular body undulated as his blunt head
swept from side to side. His whiskers bristled as he sought out
the slightest vibrations that showed where she was.

A drop of water fell from the roof of the cave. As it struck
the pool, Merlin darted towards the ripples. The distraction
gave Nimue her chance. With a beat of her tail, she raced for
the surface. She was already changing shape as she left the
water, growing azure wings and a beak like a dagger as she
soared for the cavern's heights.

Merlin emerged from a surge of bubbles as an agile hawk.

Grey-backed and pale-bellied, he had broad, blunt wings and a squared fan of long tail feathers. He darted this way and that, searching for his prey.

Nimue clung to the rough rock with her claws. She had left the water as a kingfisher, but as soon as she felt Merlin's magic transform him, she swapped her form for another. Before he had those hawk's sharp eyes, she became a tiny bat, dark-furred on silent wings. As long as she didn't move, as long as she stayed hidden in this convenient cranny, she was as good as invisible against the dark stone. She drew all her magic inward, to bolster her sense of self against the bat's nature and instincts.

Merlin persisted, searching the cave in the form of the bird. Eventually he tired. Falling through the cool, still air, he landed on the uneven floor. He still didn't resume his human shape. A heavy-bodied hound with long ears and drooping jowls quartered the cavern to find Nimue's scent.

Much good that would do him. There must be a maze of tangled trails in the darkness. She waited patiently. Some interminable time later, Merlin's magic was finally exhausted. He appeared as a man and sat by the mirror-smooth pool, hugging his knees and brooding. Eventually he slumped to the floor and slept.

Nimue climbed higher up the crevice using her tiny claws. At long last, she eased herself into a nook where she felt a thread of air coming down from the world above. The stones let her pass. She had never abused them with her enchantments. Still in her bat form, she worked a swift and subtle enchantment to carry her back to Camelot.

BOOK THREE

CHAPTER TWENTY-ONE

Nimue's magic carried her to Camelot, still transformed. Dusk was drawing on and that was a relief. No one would think twice to see a bat flit around these lofty towers and battlements. Moments later, her relief turned to concern. The castle looked very different, and not only because winter's snows had melted.

How long had she been gone? Nimue smelled rising sap and fresh growth on the breeze. This could not be the spring after the winter when Sir Balyn had been cursed and died though. Even in this dim light, she saw stains of lichen on masonry that should still be pristine. Moss softened the cobbles of Camelot's yard. The wood of the doors, gates and drawbridge was no longer the fresh gold of newly sawn timber, but weathered to silver grey.

She flapped her translucent little wings harder, flying higher with increasing unease. Rising above the great curtain wall, she saw a substantial village beyond the dry moat. The track that had once led to this remote place was a broad road. Great tracts of the forest had been cleared for crops and grazing.

Use your magic sparingly, and always with caution. You can never know what consequences could follow.

Nimue fought a surge of panic. How many years had passed? How could she explain her absence? How would she explain her return? What answers could she possibly offer when Arthur asked where Merlin had gone? Was Arthur even still king?

She swooped lower on silent, leathery wings. Her magic was very nearly exhausted. She had to find a safe place to land and resume her human form before the bat's nature overwhelmed her. But which form should that be? Youthful Nimue or an aged facsimile? She had no idea.

Fighting a surge of panic, she realised she was close to the tower where Ygraine had lodged during that long-lost summer. Nimue saw a shutter was ajar, opening onto the spiral stair. Small and deft, she slipped through the gap and let her enchantment unravel. As her feet touched the stone steps, her body slumped, impossibly heavy. She could barely move her clumsy limbs. Stricken with dizziness, she clung to the wall to save herself from a fall, but her fingers were blunt and useless, not tipped with needle-sharp claws.

Somewhere below a door opened. A sharp voice echoed up the stairwell. "Who's there? Show yourself!"

"Morgana?" Nimue summoned up the last of her magic to take on the appearance she had worn when they had last seen each other. She felt more at home in this body now, but she still dared not move, unsure of her footing on the stairs. "Is that you?"

"Who–?" The voice broke off.

Nimue heard footsteps and Morgana appeared, holding a lantern high to banish the shadows in the stairwell. "It is you. I thought I felt–" She shook her head. "Come quickly, before anyone sees you."

Morgana turned around. Nimue followed her cautiously down the steps into what had been Ygraine's sitting room. Comfortable chairs for conversation over needlework or a glass of wine were long gone. A long table dominated the centre of the room flanked by sideboards against the walls. One was stacked with books while the other was crammed with what looked like an alchemist's apparatus. Evidently Morgana's studies had gone far beyond simple herbal cures.

Nimue assessed the table with a housekeeper's eye and

judged it hadn't seen polish for months. Upright chairs that diners might have used were stacked against the end wall, dull with dust. The tapestries were stained with soot. She glanced up. The ceiling had been recently whitewashed, but a hint of a dark shadow remained above burn scars on the table.

"I never thought I would see you again." Morgana walked to the far end of the room.

A brazier glowed beside a sloped desk set by the window to gather daylight for reading or writing. Morgana set the lantern on a small table cluttered with pens, ink, and parchment. Taking a spill of wood from an earthenware pot, she poked it into the smouldering charcoal. As she used the flame to light the beeswax candles on the branches of a tall stand, Nimue saw her clearly for the first time.

How many years had passed? A decade? A dozen? Morgana was a mature woman, poised and confident. A woman of status indicated by her gown of rich green velvet and emerald earrings. Such opulence looked incongruous in a room devoted to arcane pursuits.

Was she married? Morgana's dark hair was hidden by an ornate headdress draped with a gauzy veil, but Nimue didn't think so. She couldn't imagine any knight of Logres tolerating a wife more interested in her studies than serving his needs. Though there must be men transfixed by her beauty, who longed to claim her for their own.

Nimue wondered what had happened in the years she had lost. Morgana's eyes were knowing and wary as she sat on the chair by the desk and waved Nimue towards a stool. "Where have you been?" There was an accusing edge to her voice.

"Keeping Master Merlin from making more trouble by working enchantments to further Arthur's ambitions." Nimue saw she would have to be honest if Morgana was going to trust her.

"How?" Morgana demanded.

Nimue realised with a pang that her word was no longer

enough. "Have you heard what happened to Sir Balyn, when a strange maiden brought a cursed sword to Camelot?"

"No." Morgana was mystified.

Nimue told her the whole tragic tale. Outside the window, the evening darkened into night.

Morgana's smile was brief and humourless when Nimue finally fell silent. "So, I have you to thank for Merlin's absence. What became of the cursed sword?"

"It is beyond anyone's reach. Has there been any trouble from..." Nimue couldn't think how to ask if Viviane of the River had kept her word, or if she and the Lady of the Lake had blighted the mortal world with their renewed quarrel. "Has there been more trouble?"

"No, and Arthur has flourished despite the loss of his counsellor."

The sourness in Morgana's words worried Nimue. "How long have you been at Camelot? Why did you come here anyway?" Clearly that had happened some while ago. Sudden dread tightened her throat. "Your lady mother?"

Morgana's face softened and Nimue was briefly reminded of the little girl she had known. "She is cherished in Garlot, though she is frail with age. She and Elaine pay no attention to Logres."

She glanced at the sideboard cluttered with alchemical glassware. Nimue was astonished to recognise the silver scrying bowl from her own still room back in Tintagel. This wasn't the time to debate Morgana's use of magic to keep watch on her family overseas though. She repeated her earlier question. "What brought you to Camelot?"

Morgana shrugged. "I came here after Sir Pellinore killed King Lot. Not that I was given much choice. As the king's unmarried sister–"

"Wait." Nimue raised her hands, aghast. "Lot of Orkney is dead?"

"These past nine years." Morgana looked at her steadily.

"After Merlin vanished, Arthur mustered Logres' army to crush
Ryons of Gwynedd. The other kings of Wales joined Gwynedd
to defy him. By the time those wars were done and Wales was
crushed, the Scots had risen to fight. They joined forces with
Ryons' brother who refused to yield, even though Ryons had
been captured. King Lot led Orkney's host, acclaimed as leader
by the other kings of the Scots. When the final battle came, the
fighting was fierce and bloody. Who might win was always in
doubt, until Sir Pellinore fought through the ranks to attack
Orkney's standard. He cut down Lot's horse and split the king's
skull with his sword. The Scots threw down their weapons
after that."

She narrowed her eyes, suspicious. "Was there some sorcery
at work, even with Merlin gone? What do you know?"

"Nothing at all. Forgive me. I am simply shocked by such
grievous news."

That was true, though not the whole truth. Nimue finally
knew why Merlin had spared Sir Pellinore's life on that day
in the forest glade so long ago. Merlin must have known that
Lot of Orkney would never call Arthur high king. If Arthur
had killed him though, he would have cut down his sister's
husband, and the father of his own heirs. How many knights
would see that as a stain on their king's honour? Merlin would
much rather see King Lot dead at someone else's hands. He
must have foreseen some possible future where Sir Pellinore
did the deed and hoped to secure that by sparing the rebel
knight. The consequences of Merlin's enchantments had
persisted long after Nimue had trapped him in that cave.

Morgana was studying her intently. Nimue gestured.
"Please, go on."

After a long thoughtful moment, Morgana obliged. "When
we were forced to conclude you were lost to us, I travelled
from Brittany to Orkney. Elaine and Mother had no more
need of me in Garlot, and I had no desire to be a marriage
prize for some prince seeking an heir. Morgause had five sons

to manage and was striving to keep the peace between her husband and our brother. She asked for my help."

Her eyes grew distant with recollection. "Arthur and Lot were at odds before Ryons of Gwynedd took up arms. Arthur had claimed the right to keep Gawain and his brothers here at Camelot. Lot wanted them home as soon as winter had passed. As far as he was concerned, Gawain would only be Arthur's heir until the king married and fathered a son. As for Agravaine, Gaheris and Gareth, their futures would be in Orkney, whatever might happen in Logres. Lot wanted to teach them to work together in the best interests of his kingdom."

"What happened to them when Arthur's army marched north?" Nimue wished she had known this was happening. If only she had gone back to Brittany with Ygraine, she would have been part of those conversations. But then, what else might Merlin have done, if she hadn't confined him in that cave? There were no easy answers, no obvious best course she should have followed, even with the benefit of hindsight. Only someone with Merlin's arrogance would think they could mould the future as they saw fit.

"Orkney's princes were confined to their quarters." Morgana shook her head. "Arthur insisted they were honoured guests. As far as Lot was concerned, they might as well have been chained in Camelot's dungeons. He was furious."

"And after their father was killed?" Nimue asked with growing misgiving. "Why wasn't Gawain crowned king of Orkney?"

"The princes swore allegiance to Arthur and agreed that he should act as regent. The other Scots kings did the same. What else could they do?" Morgana didn't expect an answer.

"Where are the princes now?"

"Here." Morgana seemed surprised that Nimue needed to ask. "They are loyal knights in Arthur's court, enjoying the pleasures and privileges that come with the king's favour. Only Mordred still lives in Orkney, and that's the best place for the deceitful wretch. I imagine he will be summoned to Camelot soon enough, to be educated as his uncle sees fit. We all know better than to ask when Arthur might give up his regency." Her voice was neutral, but her eyes were hard.

"What does Morgause make of this?" As soon as she spoke, Nimue guessed the answer. "That's why you're here. To watch over her sons."

Morgana nodded. "I do what I can to safeguard Orkney's interests, and Cornwall's. Arthur keeps his own counsel, ever since Merlin vanished, but from time to time I can drop a word in his ear. As the king's sister, I am his chatelaine, managing his servants and ensuring his comforts, so he can spend his days honing his skills with his brothers in arms."

She paused. "Of course, I am also another hostage to guarantee Morgause nods her head to whatever our royal brother proposes. Though no one is ever tactless enough to mention that."

A horn call interrupted her.

"What is it?" Nimue saw from her reaction that the sound was a summons.

"The court dines with the king each and every night." Morgana rose to her feet. "You may as well come too."

Nimue shook her head. "As soon as Arthur sees me, he'll ask what's become of Merlin."

"Not if you look like you did when I was a child. Arthur never knew you at Tintagel, and no one is so easily overlooked as an ageing woman."

Nimue wasn't convinced, but she had had sufficient rest to resume that long-ago disguise. "I still think I should stay here. I have no need to join the court."

"No, I want you with me." Morgana wasn't going to be denied. "Everyone will believe you've been my personal maid since I came here from Orkney. No one will have ever known different."

Nimue gasped as a powerful, eerie enchantment swirled around her. "Whoever taught you to do that?"

"You were gone, and we were defenceless. I had to find help wherever I could." Morgana was already walking towards the door.

Nimue took a moment to clothe herself in a mossy green gown and a modest wimple, and then hurried after her. Her affection for the girl she had known fought with apprehension. Where had Morgana found such spells? What other enchantments did this self-assured stranger have at her fingertips? Was this the wild magic that Merlin had foreseen leading to disaster?

Outside, the castle yard was busy as men appeared from other towers. Clearly Arthur still liked to have as many of his knights here as possible. Some things had changed. Nimue saw women, and not merely maidservants. Elegantly gowned and bejewelled wives were proudly displayed on their husband's arm, reminding her of prized and hooded hawks. Younger women walked together, hiding their smiles with coy hands and downcast eyes, while younger knights circled them like bees in a flower garden. She realised these maidens were heading their way.

"Who are they?" she asked quietly as she walked at Morgana's side.

"My ladies?" Morgana shot her a sardonic look. "I can hardly keep Arthur's court supplied with necessities and comforts without the assistance of well-born attendants."

"What do they think of your arcane studies?" Nimue wondered.

"They have no idea what I do in my tower and less interest in finding out."

Morgana grinned and Nimue caught a glimpse of the young woman she had known. Morgana's next words shattered that illusion.

"A simple enchantment ensures no one passing that door ever stops to wonder what's behind it. When I release the girls from their duties, they're only concerned with their flirtations. That's why their mothers strive for the honour of sending their daughters here. They could teach them to manage the mundane demands of a household, but these girls want to advance their family's power and prestige with an advantageous marriage. Where else could they catch the eye of one of Arthur's favoured knights?"

"As long as that's all they catch." The Camelot of Arthur's youth was still fresh in Nimue's memory.

Morgana's face hardened. "Every man from knight to lowest scullion knows not to risk my wrath. No woman under my protection will ever be forced to yield to their lusts, or to bear a child of rape against her will."

Nimue's blood ran cold at her icy tone. "What are they afraid you'll do?"

"They do not know, exactly. I scry them swapping rumours in stairwells and the stables." Morgana smiled, merciless. "Speculating keeps them honest. It stops them pestering me as well."

Nimue fell back a few paces as Morgana's ladies approached. She followed the gathering up the broad steps and through the tall doors into Camelot's high-roofed hall. The dais had gone, replaced by a vast round table on the same level as the trestles and benches. The ornate chairs around it were identical. There was no throne where the king would sit.

Morgana waved a hand. Everyone halted, as dumb and unseeing as figures on a tapestry. Echoing silence replaced the noise and bustle as Nimue felt the passage of time stilled. Only she and Morgana were immune.

"Arthur likes to claim he and his knights are equals. This round table has no head and no foot, so no seat is more honoured than any other." Morgana arched her brows at Nimue. "He claims this was Merlin's suggestion. Was it?"

"I have no idea."

Morgana pursed her lips. "Arthur likes to claim the wizard's authority when he does something unexpected. As far as he's concerned, that ends any discussion."

Their moment out of time was over. Morgana led the way to the long table closest to Arthur's innovation. Her chair was at the head, and her nod told Nimue to take the place on the benches at her right hand. The other ladies took their seats in an established pecking order. No one spared Nimue more than an incurious glance.

. Several young women carried spring flowers. Some had single blooms while others held small posies bound with ribbons. As they laid them on the table, where plates, knives and goblets were set ready, discreet teasing prompted blushes and giggles. Nimue saw Morgana didn't miss a thing.

The other tables filled up. Knights and their squires sat side by side on the long benches. It seemed everyone served themselves these days. Chatter and laughter grew louder until every voice fell silent as Arthur and his retinue walked up the central aisle to the great table. As soon as the king was seated, conversation resumed.

Maidservants carried platters of squabs and other delicacies to the round table. Salt beef stewed long and tender with spices and dried fruit arrived for Morgana and her ladies. Lackeys followed with baskets of fine white bread and tall jugs of wine.

Nimue was unexpectedly hungry and thirsty. As she ate and drank, she covertly studied the men at the other tables, but she didn't recognise any faces. She saw the knights, young and old, glance in Arthur's direction from time to time, and their fleeting expressions hinted at resentment and envy. So much for Logres' king sitting as the first among equals. Arthur had created an inner circle of favourites which excluded everyone else. Though not every seat at the round table was taken. The chair at the king's left hand was empty.

Nimue realised Morgana was watching her. She nodded discreetly at the vacant seat. "Who's missing?"

"Merlin." Morgana answered, low-voiced. "Arthur is convinced he will return one day. No one else believes it, though they don't say so in the king's hearing."

Her tone was neutral. Nimue wondered if Morgana would see the wizard's return as a challenge to her power, or as an opportunity to learn whatever sorcery he might be persuaded to teach her. She desperately wanted to know who had taught Morgana her magic. Had the girl gone looking in Brittany's thick forests, or in the storm-tossed waters that surged around Orkney's isles? Perhaps she had found an ally closer to Camelot on the shores of a lake. Not that Nimue intended to ask, warned off by her reserve. There was a hardness about Morgana now.

Nimue couldn't blame her. The bold young woman she had known had found herself alone and friendless, sent on lengthy journeys as other people decided her fate, always at the mercy of her brother's decrees. With her family either distant or dead, no wonder that girl had sought out enchantments to protect herself at Camelot.

How had Arthur changed? Nimue looked at the king. He was heavier boned and solidly muscled, which strengthened his resemblance to Uther. Still, Nimue saw Ygraine in his smile as he joked with his chosen companions. She wondered if anyone else in this hall or castle would recognise such hints of his parentage. Apart from Morgana, of course.

The princes of Orkney might remember meeting their grandmother on that fateful visit to Camelot so long ago in their short lives. Where were Morgause's children? As Nimue looked around, she met Morgana's gaze.

"He keeps my sister's sons close. Sir Gawain is still his heir."

As Nimue looked at the round table, she wondered when Morgana had become so astute at reading people. Or had she somehow learned to read minds?

Lot of Orkney's heirs sat in the circle of favoured knights. Like Arthur, they had grown into muscular young men with neatly trimmed beards and close-cropped red hair. Gawain's resemblance to his father was more striking than ever. Agravaine brought Lot to mind too, though no one would mistake him for his brother. Gaheris and Gareth were still so similar that they could be taken for twins, though they resembled their mother rather more.

Nimue watched Gawain and Agravaine gesture as they interrupted and spoke over each other. From the sharp glances they exchanged, their rivalry looked undiminished. Gaheris and Gareth swapped wry glances, so evidently their old alliance held true.

The meal went on. The platters and serving bowls were replaced with dishes of elegant confections. Those looking towards the round table betrayed some impatience. Arthur and his chosen knights were oblivious, relaxing with wine and conversation.

At long last, Arthur pushed his goblet away and stood up. A burst of conversation drowned out the sound of the hall doors opening, until Arthur's hand cut through the air. The doors slammed shut and everyone fell silent. Servants stood motionless, as surprised as everyone else.

Arthur knew all eyes were on him. He grinned, handsome and charming. Even the men fidgeting on their benches couldn't help an answering smile.

"My friends." His words carried to the far corners of the hall. Nimue heard distant echoes of Uther's voice with a shiver of apprehension.

"I have momentous news," Arthur announced cheerfully. "A letter from King Leodegrance, my noble ally and the staunchest guardian of the Welsh marches."

Nimue recalled a man with shrewd eyes and a measured voice, lean and bald. Leodegrance ruled a fiefdom that bordered the southern lands of Powys. He had been allowed to style himself "king" in return for unquestioning loyalty, first to Uther and then to Arthur.

"As you know, he has a daughter. Guinevere was a child when I first saw her, when we fought to defend her home from Ryons of Gwynedd's attacks. Now she is a woman, and a beauty. King Leodegrance has given his blessing to our marriage, and my bride and her father will arrive some time after noon tomorrow."

Stunned silence answered him. Then someone on the far side of the hall stood up to shout congratulations. Soon every man was on his feet, clapping and cheering. The ladies around Morgana's table remained seated, applauding with more decorum. Nimue saw their keen interest, rather than disappointment openly admitted or unsuccessfully concealed. Had Morgana talked these women out of ambitions to wed the king themselves?

"Friends, friends." Arthur's voice commanded silence again. "Thank you for your good wishes. I have always known those who have urged me to wed have only ever had my best interests at heart."

Arthur sounded wholly sincere. Nimue saw men nodding, though those assuming the king had finished were wrong.

"Naturally, a castle can only have one mistress, and my queen must hold her own keys. My beloved sister will be freed of such burdens and rewarded for her years of service. Your highness, if you please?"

Morgana's chair had its back to the round table. As the king spoke, she rose and turned.

"You have more than done your duty to me and to Camelot," Arthur assured her. "Now you will be a cherished and honoured wife. King Urien of Gore sought your hand in marriage, and I have agreed. He is travelling with King Leodegrance. Your wedding will follow my own, and we will share a feast to celebrate."

More cheers and applause rang around the hall, though this time they were less prolonged. Morgana curtseyed gracefully, and for a moment, Nimue thought she would resume her seat. Instead, she strode from the hall without a word. The women around the table swapped discreetly apprehensive glances.

Nimue glanced at Arthur. For an instant, he looked bemused,

even angry. Then his knights surrounded him, offering renewed congratulations. The king accepted their good wishes, laughing and smiling. Nimue hurried after Morgana. The princess's hesitating ladies were no concern of hers.

CHAPTER TWENTY-TWO

Nimue went straight to Morgana's tower. Evidently the spell convincing people to ignore the sitting room door didn't apply to her. The princess wasn't in her sanctuary. Nimue hurried up the spiral stair to the bedchamber, but Morgana wasn't there either.

Nimue sat on the bed, uneasy. Where had the princess gone? What could she say, as Morgana's attendant, if someone came looking for her mistress? *When* someone came looking. If Arthur didn't summon his sister to rebuke her for ingratitude in private, Morgana would be expected to greet Arthur's bride-to-be tomorrow, as well as her promised husband Urien.

Camelot's servants would look for the chatelaine's guidance well before then. Rooms must be prepared for these unexpected guests. Feather beds would be unrolled, while linens were aired, and furniture was polished. Clearly Arthur had given no thought to such tasks as he kept this news secret to enjoy springing his surprise.

If Arthur expected a great wedding feast, endless questions needed answers. How many were the kitchens to feed? As well as noble guests who must be royally entertained, humbler folk would gather at the castle's gates expecting bread and ale as they wished the brides and grooms well.

Where was the food to come from? Spring leaves and flowers might be bright in the forests and meadows, but storerooms and cellars were nearly empty after the dark, hungry days of winter. Harvests were months away and few beasts could be spared for slaughter. Doubtless some merchants could help. Canny traders held back supplies to demand the highest prices at this time of year, but where was the silver to pay them to come from? Nimue had no idea what to do. She halted by the shuttered window, feeling utterly useless. Magic couldn't help her now.

"How dare he?"

Morgana was standing by the bed. Nimue hadn't heard her enter. Had she even used the door?

"If I argue against this match?" Morgana went on with quiet fury. "He will be hurt and disappointed. He will swear he seeks my best interests and my future happiness. That I have earned my leisure after serving him here? Surely, I must long to fulfil my destiny as a wife and mother? What woman doesn't?"

She shot a scorching glare at Nimue. "Why would I ever want to wed, to be subject to a man's whims and commands? As for bearing a child to bind me to its father lifelong? I will never offer up such a hostage to the twists and turns of fortune."

Nimue picked the question she hoped was least likely to provoke Morgana's ire. "What do you know of King Urien?"

"Urien of Gore." Morgana's scorn was withering. "Ruler of a petty little realm that makes Leodegrance look like a mighty king." She snapped her fingers. "Of course. Urien's lands border Leodegrance's, along the Welsh Marches."

Now Nimue remembered who the man was. "When Leodegrance was loyal to Uther and then to Arthur, Urien of Gore supported Ryons of Gwynedd's rebellion. Though he surrendered pretty swiftly, as I recall."

Morgana nodded. "Lot of Orkney reckoned his defiance was driven more by his rivalry with Leodegrance than by any commitment to Gwynedd. Once it was clear that Ryons' army wouldn't ride to help him seize his neighbour's lands, Urien yielded to Arthur, or at least to Excalibur."

So, Morgana was aware of the sword's influence. When had she discovered the blade was enchanted and how? Nimue asked a different question.

"What are you going to do?"

Morgana surprised her with a defeated sigh. "What can I do? I assume Arthur fears Urien's loyalty will be strained by seeing his neighbour become father to the queen. The next best favour Arthur can bestow to keep Urien sweet-tempered is his unwedded sister's hand. If I protest, he'll tell me I must not be selfish," she said bitterly. "That I have a duty to the kingdom, to keep the peace."

"Could Urien be a threat?" Nimue wished she knew what alliances and rivalries swirled around Camelot these days.

"Would he take up arms against Arthur?" Morgana shook her head. "No, but if he sees Leodegrance spending time at Camelot, serving as the king's counsellor? Urien might make overtures to the vassals who hold lands along their border, maybe lure them into swapping allegiance. Some trivial dispute could become a skirmish. We know how seldom men back down. All the while, the Welsh will be watching. They yielded to Arthur when Ryons was defeated, but that doesn't mean they accept Logres' suzerainty. They could strike a blow in hopes of winning back their freedom."

Her face was bleak and her dark eyes glistened. "I cannot be responsible for some spark that sets old quarrels and hatreds ablaze. I will not be the reason why widows weep and children mourn their fathers."

A sudden memory of Ygraine at Tintagel putting her people's interests above her own pierced Nimue like a knife to the heart.

"Besides, Arthur's right," Morgana said with sudden briskness. "I'll have no role at Camelot when his queen warms his bed and ensures his laundry is done. I may as well make the best of my life as queen of Gore. We should get to bed. We won't have a moment to ourselves tomorrow."

The princess was right. An apologetic steward knocked on the bedchamber door before first light. They were already up and dressed. After a brief breakfast, Morgana led the way to an audience chamber in the neighbouring tower. She told Nimue everyone was accustomed to find her here, as she managed the castle's day-to-day affairs.

They instructed maidservants and lackeys to make the necessary preparations. Such practicalities hadn't changed since Nimue had been in charge of the household and Morgana had every detail of Camelot's resources at her fingertips.

Everything was well in hand by the time Morgana's attendant ladies presented themselves in twos and threes. They were eager to know who would have the honour of waiting on the soon-to-be queen, seeking to advance their own claims to precedence with at least an appearance of modesty.

These young noble women were focused on the future, when Guinevere's favour would count in Camelot. Nimue saw the veiled glint of anger in the princess's eye as Morgana turned their questions away with non-committal replies, allocating trivial tasks suitable for girls' rank. Some persisted more doggedly than others.

"You see, since my father is Sir Sagramore–" A horn call outside the castle walls interrupted the determinedly demure maiden.

Morgana looked up from the table strewn with writing slates covered in notes and calculations. "They can't be here already."

"I'll go and see." Nimue hurried from the chamber.

The castle's entrance stood open with the drawbridge lowered over the dry moat. One of Morgana's girls had told Nimue loftily that King Arthur decreed his subjects, however humble, should always be able to approach their king. Besides, she added more practically, any enemy would be seen in plenty of time to secure Camelot's defences.

A mere handful of knights with a few attendants and pack animals were approaching the castle. They had halted where the road reached the meadow between the village and the moat. Carpenters and labourers were busy setting up the lists for a joust. Arthur had given no thought to how his guests might be fed, but he had ordered the elaborate preparations for a celebratory tournament. Nimue set that irritation aside as a young man with flaming red hair passed her.

"Gaheris! Sir Gaheris of Orkney." She hastily corrected herself as he stopped and looked at her, startled. She must remember that Lot's sons were grown men, not the callow boys she had known.

Thankfully, he didn't seem offended, though he gave no hint that he recognised her. "May I be of assistance?"

"If you please, good sir." Nimue curtseyed, to be on the safe side. "Do you know who those knights might be? Are they expected?"

Gaheris shaded his eyes with a hand as he peered at the newcomers. He stiffened like a hound catching a scent. "I believe that shield with the three red bands belongs to Sir Lancelot. There have been rumours he'd crossed the seas from Brittany."

"From which kingdom?" Nimue wondered if the visitor might have news of Garlot.

Gaheris shook his head. "His father was King Ban of Benoic which is a realm between Brittany and Gaul. Claudas, the king of the Franks, killed his father and seized those lands when he was a child. Lancelot grew up in exile, moving from place to place as different royal courts sheltered him and his mother."

Nimue couldn't recall any mention of these unfortunates when she'd lived in Garlot, but King Nentres had no obligation to offer aid without ties of marriage or blood. He would have had no other interest. A young man dispossessed of his inheritance wouldn't be a remotely suitable match for his daughter Elaine, or even for Morgana.

Gaheris of Orkney looked avidly at the strangers. "He has a fearsome reputation in tourneys. I wonder how he'll fare against Gawain."

His eagerness suggested that would be a close contest. Nimue wanted to ask the young knight about his eldest brother, but that risked betraying her ignorance. She would be familiar with the sons of Orkney and their reputations, if she was Morgana's long-standing attendant.

Gaheris hurried away with long-legged strides, presumably heading for the tower where he and his brothers were quartered. Nimue waited as the horsemen approached. The bare-headed knight with the red-banded shield paused to talk to the sergeant of the guard, leaning down from his tall white horse. Whatever he said was satisfactory, and the sergeant waved the small party on through the gate.

The visitors rode past without giving Nimue a second glance. Everyone in the castle yard stopped to stare. Lancelot was strikingly handsome with golden hair and alluring blue eyes. He was lightly armoured for travelling, though Nimue guessed the width of his shoulders and his muscular thighs would make any thief think twice before trying to rob him. He was a handful of years younger than Arthur, as best she could judge. His companions were more obviously exiles, with worn gear that had never been anywhere near such good quality as Lancelot's. Being born a prince counted for something, even in exile.

But where were half a dozen more men and horses to be housed with so many guests expected? Nimue hurried back to tell Morgana the news.

"There are rooms set aside for such visitors." Morgana reached for a slate and rubbed out sums with a damp cloth. "Every bold youth across these islands and beyond knows they can expect a welcome, and an invitation to take to the lists at Arthur's next tournament if they're proficient with lance and sword. Logres may be at peace, more or less, but masterless manors are in the king's gift so taxes and tithes can be gathered and used for the good of the realm."

They were alone in the audience room so Morgana could speak freely. "Arthur says he's more than repaid for his hospitality with the information he charms out of such strays. My brother listens to every whisper on the wind, to be ready to forestall discontent. As for these tournaments, if a man's skill at arms earns him a fiefdom, Arthur wins a proven warrior's loyalty for life."

Nimue must remember that Arthur was no longer an inexperienced young king. His style seemed very different to Uther's heavy-handed rule. Had Sir Ector taught him the value of building friendships and loyalty? Or had Arthur realised he couldn't ignore dissent and enforce his will without Merlin's magic?

"Who shall I tell about these new arrivals?"

Morgana was checking another list. "Ask for Enid in the kitchens."

Nimue found a sturdy matron supervising a cluster of maidservants with a broad smile and a reassuring air of competence. She greeted the news of more unforeseen arrivals with a robust laugh that suggested few things could put her off her stride. Satisfied, Nimue went back to Morgana.

Camelot's royal guests arrived as the afternoon light turned golden and the spring air grew a little chilly. King Leodegrance and King Urien rode together at the head of a long column of riders and wagons, chatting with every appearance of civility.

Even so, neither man yielded precedence to the other. They rode over the drawbridge, stirrup to stirrup. Both wore substantial crowns and long velvet cloaks that flowed over their horses' rumps. Nimue wondered which of them had been first to call for his regalia.

Eagle-eyed sentries had given Camelot plenty of warning. The castle yard was thronged with Arthur's knights and the ladies of the court had gathered by the great hall. The king waited halfway up the steps with Morgana at his side. Arthur wore a pale grey tunic embroidered with the comet-tailed red dragon and his father's crown. Morgana wore the delicate gold diadem that Uther had decreed for Ygraine, with gold necklaces and bracelets shining bright against her dark grey gown.

Arthur smiled as he spread his gold-ringed hands wide. "You are welcome, my dear friends. I hope you had an easy journey."

Leodegrance dismounted with an ease that belied his age and left his horse without a backward look to see who came forward to hold the beast. Advancing up the steps, he claimed a kinsman's embrace from Arthur. He looked much the same as Nimue remembered, though older and more wrinkled. His eyes were still as shrewd.

Urien stayed in his saddle rather than follow Leodegrance and stand waiting to be noticed. At his signal, Guinevere's carriage advanced. Nimue studied the king of Gore as everyone waited to see Arthur's bride. Urien must be nearly twenty years older than Morgana. He was broad shouldered and thick-set, still dark of beard and hair, with heavy brows that shadowed his eyes. The squire who resembled him so strongly must be his son. An acknowledged son and heir, since he wore fine leathers for riding and a black velvet surcote with an embroidered white shield, with three ravens around a stark black chevron.

It hadn't occurred to Nimue this might be King Urien's second marriage. Had Morgana acquiesced to Arthur's decree, knowing she wasn't expected to produce an heir? Then Morgana could use her knowledge of herbs to stay childless, as she clearly wished to be. The people of Gore would commiserate, but her position as queen would remain secure.

Guinevere's carriage drew up and a groom jumped down to open the door and unfold the step. Leodegrance's daughter emerged to shouts of welcome, smiling sweetly and blushing scarlet.

Guinevere was younger than Morgana had been when she and Nimue had been safe in Brittany. To Nimue's eye, she was pretty rather than beautiful, whatever Arthur had said. Slightly built, her head would barely reach the king's shoulder. Though the soon-to-be queen must be more resilient than she looked. There was no sign that the jolting carriage ride had prompted the nausea that plagued so many travellers.

The sinking sun lent her soft brown hair a sheen of gold. A rose velvet band embellished with seed pearls held her long tresses off her face, and her long-sleeved, round-necked gown had been sewn from the same rich fabric. A broad embroidered belt emphasised her slender waist. The glint of gold and garnets suggested the lean golden leopard on her father's black shield, with its vivid red tongue and claws.

Arthur walked down the steps to greet his bride. He reached out and she took his hands. Arthur drew her closer and kissed her fingers. As their eyes met, a cheer rang around the castle yard. Guinevere gazed at Arthur, biddable and adoring. The king's smile widened with delight. Then Arthur escorted Guinevere to her father's side. Leodegrance tucked her hand through his arm with satisfaction as Arthur turned to the king of Gore and bowed, low and respectful.

Urien's son came forward to hold his father's horse as the heavy-set man dismounted. Arthur turned to Morgana with his hand outstretched. She stepped forward and curtseyed to Urien with her gaze modestly lowered. The people of Camelot cheered for their lady and affectionate calls wished her well. Urien looked content with whatever bargain he and Arthur had struck.

The king led the way to the great hall, with Leodegrance and Guinevere on one side and Morgana with Urien on the other. Nimue joined the ladies of the court as they followed the king and his guests, with Camelot's eager knights crowding behind them.

Arthur headed for the round table, deep in conversation with Urien. Leodegrance was quick to notice Morgana going to her customary seat. He unhooked his daughter's hand from his arm and pushed Guinevere towards the women's table. She hesitated, uncertain, until the sharpest-eyed of Morgana's maidens hurried over to their soon-to-be queen, surrounding her with smiles and kind words. Visibly relieved, Guinevere allowed them to escort her to the tall chair at the foot of the table.

Morgana had sent Nimue to the hall's steward earlier to make sure that was where Guinevere would sit. She and no one else would choose when she relinquished Camelot's keys.

As soon as Arthur and his knights were seated, maids and lackeys served the meal. Truth be told, given the short notice, the dishes were little different to the night before. With Morgana's permission, the cooks had done what they could to hint at extravagance with flourishes of spice and decoration.

The chair at the king's left hand was still left empty, but Urien had been given the next one, and Leodegrance sat at Arthur's right. Urien's son had been honoured with an invitation to the king's table, as well as one of Leodegrance's retinue wearing the black blazon with their liege lord's golden leopard. Nimue could pick out the four princes of Orkney by their bright red hair, but she still couldn't put names to the other knights around the king's table. She didn't recognise half the blazons she saw worn around the castle, and plenty of those she expected were inexplicably absent.

Well, she had only been at this strange new Camelot for a little over a night and a day. There wasn't much point in learning names, when she and Morgana would soon be heading for Gore. They would be on an equal footing there, needing to find out who might be an ally, and who would need watching.

She spoke to Morgana, low-voiced. "Have you and Arthur agreed on a day for the weddings? How soon should I start packing for the journey?"

Morgana was watching Guinevere, intense and unblinking. Nimue felt a faint thrum of enchantment, and realised Morgana was using magic to listen to the conversation at the other end of the table. Then she looked at Nimue.

"What did you say?"

Nimue started to repeat herself, but Morgana cut her off.

"Forgive me." An eerie echo after her words told Nimue no one else could hear them, despite the noise filling the hall. "You cannot come with me to Gore."

"Surely–?" Nimue was lost for words.

Morgana nodded at Guinevere. "She's sweet-natured and decorative, I grant you, and I'm sure she'll please Arthur in bed as he ploughs her furrow, but can you see her as mistress of this castle? Can you see her managing the stores and the kitchens, the maidservants and the lackeys, never mind keeping the peace between these silly girls with their feuds and bickering?"

She looked at Nimue. "We can hope she will learn quickly, but she'll need your help every day until she does. Once her belly swells with Arthur's sons, she will need you even more. The realm needs to see her brought safely through childbed and raising his children. Arthur's dynasty must secure Logres' throne to stave off the chaos that ravaged the land after Uther's death."

She shook her head, decisive. "You have to stay. Besides, one of us has to be at Camelot in case Merlin ever does return. You don't want him filling Arthur's head with schemes and dreams of conquest any more than I do."

Nimue's heart sank. Morgana was right. She could not be certain that Merlin would not reappear. Her spell should be strong enough to hold him under the earth until every mortal had forgotten his name, but the Lady of the Lake was still out there, and Viviane of the River ruled over her hidden realm. Passing years made no difference to them. One of them might seek out the wizard, looking for an ally in some quarrel between them.

CHAPTER TWENTY-THREE

Nimue woke early, but had no immediate need to get out of bed in her private chamber. Her days of sleeping on a pallet on the floor were long gone, and not only because she still wore the guise of Morgana's faithful retainer, grown old in her service. This past year, she had been Guinevere's constant companion as the new queen learned how to manage Camelot's many demands. Nimue had been impressed with the young woman's quick wits and her determination to succeed. She had also been grateful for the excuse this gave her to go everywhere and ask endless questions as she reacquainted herself with the household.

She would wager the king and his knights hadn't noticed the change in Camelot's guiding hand. The maidservants and lackeys certainly had, along with the cooks and the women who brewed the ale and baked the bread. So had the merchants and the farmers who supplied the castle's needs. Morgana had commanded their unquestioned respect. Guinevere effortlessly won their affection.

These days, the queen rarely needed advice. Even so, no one suggested Nimue give up her room in the great keep, on the same floor as the king and the queen. She listened for any sound of them stirring as she got ready for the day.

As she emerged from her bedchamber, a laundry maid left the queen's room, carrying a basket of bundled bed linen. This wasn't the usual day for such tasks and Nimue saw a tear on the girl's flushed cheek.

"The queen?" Though every woman in Camelot and far beyond knew the rhythm of Guinevere's womb by now, and probably most of the men.

The girl nodded. She scrubbed her cheek against her shoulder to wipe away fresh tears.

"Go on with you." Nimue let the girl head for the stairs before she knocked on the queen's door. She didn't wait for an answer. Guinevere stood over by the window. She must have woken, realised what had happened overnight, and sent the maid who spent her nights on a pallet by her door to summon a laundress.

The queen still wore the chemise she had slept in, stained with the bloody bad news. Yet again, her pretty face was stricken with grief for what would never be. Nimue went over and put her arms around the young woman. Guinevere wasn't weeping. She never did these days, though Nimue felt her stiffness yield as she took some comfort from the embrace. Neither woman spoke. Everything had already been said far too often.

Nimue scoured her memory for any herb lore she might have overlooked. She had used every tincture and infusion she knew of to help the queen conceive and bear a healthy child. Not for the first time, she wondered if the fault lay with Arthur.

Guinevere stepped away. "So that's that, for this month at least. We must hope and pray for some future blessing."

"Indeed, your grace." And Nimue would dose Camelot's priest with a purge to keep him in the privy for days, if he dared repeat his hints that the queen must have displeased the crucified god somehow, to still be barren.

A knock at the door turned their heads. Nimue reached for the queen's chamber robe, though doubtless the laundry maid had already spread the sad news.

"Enter. Oh."

Like Guinevere, Nimue expected a maid with hot water so

the queen could wash and dress. Instead, Arthur stood on the threshold.

"Your grace." Seeing the bloodstains, the king couldn't hide his disappointment. A moment later, he addressed her politely. "Which of your ladies will award the prizes at the tournament today?"

"Elaine of Lystenois. Sir Pellinore's daughter," Guinevere added, seeing Arthur's uncertainty.

He forced a rueful smile. "So many girls share that name."

"Indeed," Guinevere agreed.

"I will see you at the joust." Arthur bowed and retreated. He hadn't glanced at Nimue. He seldom did unless he had some question or instruction for her.

Guinevere stared at the closed door. Nimue didn't need magic to know what the queen was thinking. For the first months of their marriage, Arthur had shared her tears and disappointment. He had hugged her, offering comfort and hope. Those days were gone, along with the bright-eyed passion he had brought to his new wife's bed. He still came of course, dismissing her maid every third night or so, but he no longer brought each evening's drinking around the round table to an early halt, prompting chuckles from the assembled knights. Nimue no longer heard sensuous laughter or languorous love-making long after midnight. Arthur seldom spent the night in Guinevere's bed. Once he had done his duty, he preferred to sleep in his own chamber.

She glanced at Nimue. "Has he–?"

"No."

Arthur wasn't taking any other woman to his bed. Nimue had scryed after the king often enough to know he kept the vows he and Guinevere had exchanged. In that at least, he was not his father's son. He didn't surround himself with trusted knights either, demanding the unquestioning approval that Uther had craved. These days, Arthur even kept Sir Ector and Sir Kay at arm's length.

Another knock rattled the door and a maid brought hot water and fresh underlinen. Nimue fetched the rags that would save today's velvet gown from stains. She wished it were so easy to spare the queen the humiliation she must face without ever letting anyone see anything amiss.

Guinevere tucked an errant wisp of hair into her jewelled headdress and settled the gauzy veil around her shoulders. Only Arthur wore a crown in Camelot. As a married woman, the neckline of her pale blue gown was low and wide, all the better to display her ornate necklace of silver and sapphires. Last of all, she fastened the plain belt of narrow steel chain that held her dangling keys. She couldn't stop people hoping to see her waist thickening before they looked at her face, but she need not draw attention to her flat stomach.

"Let's go to breakfast."

"Your grace." Nimue followed the queen down the great keep's stairs. As they crossed the castle yard, Guinevere wished a smiling good morning to everyone from a grimy scullion carrying a bucket of scraps to Sir Pellinore, newly arrived to see his daughter honoured at the tournament. The knight was bald now and wrinkled, but he still rode a horse rather than travel in a carriage and moved with no sign of stiffness.

"I hoped you slept well," Guinevere asked, solicitous. "Is everything in your chamber to your liking?"

"It is indeed, your grace, and thank you."

As Guinevere and Sir Pellinore exchanged courtesies, Nimue saw the young ladies of the court making their way to what was now called the Queen's Tower. Morgana had insisted on breakfasting alone, but Guinevere started her days with this gathering. She was adept at managing the petty rivalries that flared up between these young women, far from home and burdened with their family's expectations. Guinevere knew how that felt and managed her match-making duties accordingly. As a result, she regularly received letters from contented brides. More recently, she sent generous christening gifts when Arthur's knights sent their liege lord word of their newborn heirs. Only Nimue saw her tears afterwards.

Sir Pellinore went on his way. Nimue and Guinevere had barely walked ten paces when they heard raised voices. On the far side of the castle yard, a handful of young men were squaring up to each other. Those redheads could only be two of Morgause's sons, but Nimue couldn't put names to the others.

Guinevere glanced at Nimue. She headed across the cobbles while the queen went on alone. As she got closer, she saw Gawain and Agravaine standing shoulder to shoulder. That was no surprise. Agravaine was rarely far from a quarrel, as a participant or an onlooker. Gawain was less inclined to start arguments, but he was one of Camelot's most eminent knights. Nimue guessed some newcomer must have made the mistake of challenging him, thinking his reputation was exaggerated. Gawain never hesitated to prove such fools wrong. Agravaine was clenching sizeable fists. He and Gawain were fierce rivals in Arthur's tournaments, but however often they clashed, Lot of Orkney's sons backed each other against anybody else.

Nimue recognised the other knights and walked more quickly. Sir Aglovale and Sir Lamorak were Sir Pellinore's elder sons, and their family resemblance and the blazon they shared meant the third must be their younger brother. Guinevere was honouring their sister Elaine today to mark Sir Percival's arrival at Camelot.

"Call my father a traitor again and I will thrash you like a dog," Gawain promised the young knight with soft menace.

Sir Percival swallowed, sickly pale. "I only meant–"

"Your father took up arms against the king," Agravaine snarled. "Who was the traitor then?"

"King Arthur met our father in the lists as an honoured equal." Wiry and weather-beaten, Lamorak challenged the younger man. "Our family has served our liege lord faithfully. No one had to lock us up at Camelot."

Agravaine looked ready to punch Lamorak. Gawain looked

ready to let him. Aglovale was poised to retaliate. Percival looked horrified.

This was not the first such clash Nimue had seen. Sir Pellinore's sons were among Camelot's most eminent knights, but they resented the younger men's status as Arthur's heirs. Orkney's princes still grieved for their father. Since they couldn't blame Arthur, Gawain and Agravaine had turned their hatred on the man who had killed King Lot. Gareth or Gaheris usually played peacemaker, but neither of them was here.

"Good sirs. Is there anything you need?" Nimue offered Sir Percival a kindly smile. "Her grace is delighted to honour your charming sister today."

"Thank you – that's to say – I am honoured. I mean – Elaine is honoured."

As Percival stammered, Nimue looked at Aglovale and Lamorak.

"Surely you cannot wish to cast the shadow of a brawl over your sister's day?"

"Let's go, Percival." Lamorak led his brothers away.

Agravaine watched them, triumphant. Before he could open his mouth and reignite the quarrel, Nimue snapped her fingers at him.

"Are you determined to embarrass your uncle the king, and his queen?"

Agravaine scowled and walked off.

"I beg your pardon." Gawain ducked his head, contrite, and followed his brother.

Exasperated, Nimue went to the Queen's Tower. Pink with excitement, Elaine of Lystenois was the centre of attention. Girls who had already enjoyed their day in the sun as the queen of a tourney offered kind advice. Those who awaited their turn were sweetly encouraging. If any of them envied Elaine, they didn't let that slip. Guinevere rewarded sly spite with a long wait for preferment.

The young women were eager to look their best for the knights who might come courting them, so no one lingered over the soft white bread and sweet preserves. Once the audience chamber was empty, Guinevere turned to Nimue with a pained expression.

"Your grace? Do you have cramps? Shall I make you a soothing tisane?"

"What? Oh, no." Guinevere shook her head. "Elaine of Lystenois begged to speak to me in private earlier. Her brother Percival has heard troubling rumours from Gore."

"About Morgana?" This wouldn't be the first time.

"It's said that she's taken a lover. I know she hasn't been happy with Urien, but if she openly dishonours him…" Guinevere shook her head. "King Urien will be furious if everyone sees him humiliated. He'll punish Morgana, and Arthur will have to back his ally or excuse his sister's behaviour."

Nimue hated to think what Morgana might do if Urien tried to exact some penance for her supposed offences. She wondered what wild magic the princess – no, Gore's queen – might have learned from some hidden teacher in the Welsh marches. She had not forgotten Merlin's prophecy.

"My father won't be able to resist goading Urien and that will make everything worse." Guinevere loved her father, but they both knew Leodegrance held a grudge. He had expected his daughter's marriage would make him Arthur's chief counsellor. It had not.

"What do you want me to do?"

"Mingle with our visitors and see what they're whispering. If this isn't true, we must consider what Sir Pellinore might gain by spreading lies."

Guinevere seldom spoke at court gatherings beyond gracefully accepting compliments. That left her free to listen. She had become an astute observer of the shifting alliances and currents of intrigue in Arthur's court.

"Of course, your grace." Nimue rose. "Is there anything you need from me first?"

"I have my ladies to call on." Guinevere waved her on her way.

Nimue left the tower. The castle yard was thronged with guests and their servants, as well as resident knights fetching their horses from the stables. She saw the back of Sir Lancelot's golden head as he rode towards the gatehouse and the meadow beyond the drawbridge. He had swiftly established himself as one of the few knights whose skills rivalled Gawain. He also had a knack of easy friendship that prompted admiration rather than envy. Arthur had soon invited him to take a seat at the round table.

Nimue headed for Morgana's workroom. Whether her magic lingered, or Arthur thought he owed her the courtesy, this tower was reserved for the king and queen of Gore's use even though they had never visited. One enchantment definitely held true. No one ever disturbed Nimue when she came here to scry, using the ancient silver bowl brought from Tintagel.

Water wrung from the air filled the bowl on the scarred table. Nimue's gesture uncorked a bottle of ink and summoned a drop to send ripples across the bowl. The dark shimmer of enchantment spread.

Then the magic was gone. Nimue tried a second time, and a third. Each time, Morgana's sorcery scattered her spell. Nimue wondered why she had expected any different. Morgana had done this since her arrival in Gore.

They had exchanged letters and Nimue had asked why, in suitably veiled terms in case Urien insisted on a husband's right to read his wife's correspondence. If Nimue had read Morgana's answer correctly, she wished to hide from any scrying by the Lady of the Lake or Viviane of the River. Nimue could hardly blame her for that, though she doubted that was the whole truth. When the first rumours had reached Camelot of friction between King Urien and his queen, Nimue had written again, discreetly offering help. Between the lines of her reply, Morgana insisted nothing was wrong.

Now Morgana was accused of infidelity. Guinevere might hope Sir Pellinore was spreading falsehoods, but Nimue had lived among mortals long enough to know such smoke seldom spread without fire. But why would Morgana be so reckless? Had she been overwhelmed by love or lust? That seemed unlikely. When had she ever been unable to master her emotions?

Nimue waved a hand and the water disappeared. She left the tower and the castle yard, heading for the tournament field. The jousts had already started with the most junior knights testing their skills. The seats of honour were high on a canopied wooden platform on the far side of the lists. Arthur sat with Pellinore, deep in conversation. Beside her father, Elaine of Lystenois perched on the edge of her chair, watching Sir Percival as he tried to settle his lance while controlling his mettlesome horse. On Arthur's other side, with her ladies behind her, Guinevere watched the other knight make ready. He was one of the Gauls who had followed Sir Lancelot to Camelot.

A sizeable crowd had gathered, even though the round table's most famous knights wouldn't joust until later. Then there would be the great melee which was as close as these knights came to warfare while Arthur's peace held across these isles.

Nimue wove a subtle enchantment to allow her to slip unnoticed though the onlookers. She listened for any mention of Morgana or Urien. All she heard were wagers on contests and promises of opportunities that surely would beggar the unwary.

Horses' hooves thundered over the turf. Nimue watched Sir Percival ride at the Gallic knight. Percival's lance struck his foe's shield with a glancing blow. The Gallic knight hit him hard and true. Percival fell from his horse to lie ominously still.

Nimue looked at the seats of honour. Elaine of Lystenois stared down, white-faced. Her lips moved as she clasped her hands, praying to the crucified god. Sir Pellinore looked on, impassive, though Nimue felt the chill of his fear. Men died in these jousts from time to time. She always made sure the tournament stewards were well-supplied with bandages and salves to treat cuts and bruises, and she was ready to reset broken bones.

Percival was stirring. His brothers helped him to his feet, and back into his saddle. Both knights readied themselves for the second of three passes they would make with the lance, before competing on foot to see who could land three blows with a sword. Idle conversation resumed as Nimue went on her way.

Sir Percival fought valiantly, but he was defeated. The Gallic knight received his prize from Elaine with a charming smile, and the next combatants prepared to fight. Nimue noticed Guinevere lean forward to talk to Sir Pellinore while Arthur watched the knights getting ready. One was Sir Miles, an excellent match for Elaine. Doubtless the queen was telling Sir Pellinore about him, doing her duty to her ladies and her king.

Sir Miles was victorious, and Elaine blushed prettily as she gave him his prize. Sir Pellinore nodded with approval. The jousts continued, and as the day wore on, more eminent knights took to the lists. The crowds grew bigger and noisier, raising raucous cheers as Sir Gawain and Sir Agravaine won their contests. So did Sir Lamorak and Sir Aglovale, to equal acclaim. Sir Pellinore's smile grew broader as he joked with the king.

Nimue made her way to the village where every household had thrown open its doors, selling meat, bread and ale to visitors from towns and villages many days walk away. She heard no mention of Morgana or Urien. Everyone was discussing the forthcoming melee. As Arthur had explained to Guinevere, the tourneys weren't only a way for his knights to hone their skills. If humbler folk were kept entertained, they were less likely to dwell on any grievances, real or imagined.

The day grew warmer and the tang of sweat joined the scents of woodsmoke and griddled sausages. Nimue went back to the tourney field where the jousts had finished. Up on the canopied platform, the king and queen and their favoured guests had been served a sumptuous meal with plenty of wine. Nimue had relayed Guinevere's instructions to the kitchens to arrange every detail days ago.

The tournament ground was prepared for the great melee. The crowd were speculating who would fight on either side. Newcomers were surprised to learn that Arthur didn't simply pitch Camelot's knights against the rest. Instead, he gave guests from further afield the chance to fight alongside the castle's warriors. Arthur studied such unknowns' potential. Promising young swordsmen would be invited to spend time at his table. Any knight who might nurture some dissatisfaction had the opportunity to see how the king's forces would crush rebellion.

The two forces were drawing up, Nimue still hadn't heard Urien's name or Morgana's on anyone's lips. She breathed a little easier. Whatever the problems might be in Gore, it would be far harder to placate King Urien if he was widely mocked as a cuckold.

A trumpet call cut through the air and the melee began. Forty or so knights on either side advanced towards each other. Men spread out across the field as the front ranks drew closer. Now the warriors could identify their opponents' shields, weighing up what they knew of each man's reputation or recalling some previous encounter. Some yelled insults while others shouted encouragement to those who flanked them. In reality, friends and foes were unlikely to hear much through the padding beneath their helmets.

In theory, the knights should advance together, to force the opposing ranks to wheel and break. In reality, the battle lines ebbed and flowed. Some warriors retreated from opponents they had no wish to face. Voices in the crowd mocked such craven behaviour. Others cheered as a lone swordsman advanced on a foe he was confident he could defeat. If a knight yielded on the tourney field, he must pay his opponent a handsome sum to redeem his honour.

The first clash of steel sparked an ecstatic roar from the crowd. Combat began in earnest. Some men were fighting duels, one on one. Elsewhere, twos and threes pursued a single foe, at least until allies came to his aid. Larger groups were skirmishing, seeking to trap their opponents in a crush where they had no option but to surrender. The victors would share the spoils.

Nimue had no interest in who might end the day richer. She watched for signs of serious injury. These swords might be blunted, and the knights were supposed to use the flat of their blades, but when a man's blood was up, blows had a tendency to land harder than intended. She listened for high-pitched cries of sudden agony amid the belligerent roars and the din of clashing metal, sword on sword, sword on shield, sword on armour.

On the far side of the field, a ferocious fight caught her eye. Nimue stiffened as she recognised the knights' blazons. Bright gold on a purple ground, the double-headed eagle of Orkney was Gawain. Agravaine carried the same device crossed with a band of green. Gaheris' shield bore the family crest with a silver border, while Gareth's was marked with a diagonal band of red. They were fighting Sir Pellinore's sons who carried the Lystenois pattern of golden crosses on different coloured shields. Nimue didn't know which of them carried which hue and she didn't care.

Arthur was well aware of the bad blood between the families and his tournament stewards made sure they never faced each other in the joust. Nimue suspected they had seized this opportunity to settle a few scores themselves. Agravaine was hot-headed enough to start a fight, and Lamorak had a vicious temper when provoked.

Reprimands could wait. Their brutal blows were more and more savage. Someone had to stop this before one of the young idiots was killed or maimed. What could she do though? If she used magic to trip someone or make a sword slip in a hand, that risked an attacker landing a murderous strike.

A knight with a white shield banded with red forced his way into Agravaine and Lamorak's private battle. A handful of others followed Lancelot. These new arrivals drove Sir Pellinore's sons and the princes of Orkney apart. Now Lancelot was battling with Gawain, driving him backwards, step by step.

The danger passed. The knights who had intervened scattered across the field. Onlookers around Nimue praised Lancelot's intervention, while others openly wondered who would have died first: one of Sir Pellinore's sons or some prince of Orkney.

The melee reached its conclusion well before sunset. Arthur had no interest in hosting brutal tourneys that only ended with every man too exhausted to raise a blade. The knights on this field knew it. Once it was clear which side would win the day, those still fighting broke apart by mutual consent, retreating with honours even.

Nimue ducked under the perimeter rope and assessed those carried off the torn and bruised turf. Satisfied that no one needed her healing skills, she went on towards the canopied stand as those weary warriors still able to stand gathered to salute the royal couple and their honoured guests. The day's prizes for valour would be awarded before the king and queen returned to the castle for the evening's sumptuous banquet.

Nimue wanted to reassure Guinevere that Morgana's supposed sins weren't common gossip. She made her way to the grass behind the seats of honour, where tables held silver jugs of wine, goblets and plates of dainties, in case some lord or lady called for refreshment. The castle servants were packing baskets to carry everything back to the kitchens.

A hand landed on Nimue's shoulder. She turned, expecting some lackey or maid with a question. Instead, she saw the king.

She was startled into a curtsey. "Your grace."

"Pack whatever the queen needs for a journey of at least a month. We are going to visit the kingdom of Gore and then we will visit Leodegrance. We leave at first light tomorrow. I expect you to make Morgana see sense. You will use whatever arts you must."

He turned away, grim-faced, and went back up the steps to his throne once again. Nimue hastily got her thoughts in order. Sir Pellinore must have told Arthur that Morgana had taken a lover. It seemed the king believed it.

That wasn't Nimue's greatest concern. Arthur had looked her in the eye. He had recognised her. He must have known who she was ever since she reappeared at Morgana's side. He knew that she had magic to call on. Was he going to ask her to find Merlin?

CHAPTER TWENTY-FOUR

The weather stayed dry for their journey to Gore, so the roads were firm. There was peace in the land, and so many knights escorted King Arthur and his queen that sensible bandits would have headed for the Welsh hills.

Nimue would have remarked on such things, to while away the hours of tedium in the trundling carriage. But courtly manners decreed that she and today's two noble young ladies take their lead from the queen. Guinevere had no inclination for small talk.

She had not wanted to come on this royal progress. She had begged Arthur to excuse her. Nimue had shared his astonishment, in the queen's chamber, late in the evening after the tournament. Guinevere had never questioned the king's most trivial wish.

Arthur gave her no chance to explain. "I need you at my side to quell gossip. This must be seen as an unremarkable journey to visit my sister and your father."

"That's not what people will say." Guinevere wrung her hands, white-faced. "They will think we're going to tell them I am with child."

Clearly, that hadn't occurred to Arthur. He strode out of the room, slamming the heavy door. Guinevere didn't say a word as she got ready for bed. Later, Nimue heard her sobbing.

The following morning, the queen had been as composed as always, choosing which of her ladies would accompany them. Half a dozen young noblewomen followed in another carriage drawn by two placid horses.

Today, Elaine of Lystenois sat at Guinevere's side. Nimue and a newcomer called Linet were opposite them in the carriage. The rumble of wheels on the beaten earth filled the silence. Outside, Nimue could hear horses' hooves, though she couldn't see who was escorting them. The leather curtains at the windows were lowered to stop dust blowing in.

Arthur would have ridden on ahead, with Sir Owain of Gore showing the king and his knights the route to his father's castle. Sir Pellinore's three sons were in Arthur's retinue while Sir Gawain and his brothers stayed behind. Nimue assumed Arthur was determined the families shouldn't come to blows while he was away. He could have brought the Orkney princes, but she guessed he didn't want Morgana to claim them as allies when he confronted her.

Nimue still had no idea what might await them in Gore, or what Arthur might expect her to do. She had wrestled with these conundrums, but she was no closer to finding answers.

"I barely know Morgana." Guinevere broke into her fruitless musing. "What do you think she will do when the king demands an explanation?"

Elaine and Linet looked horrified. They had scrupulously avoided mentioning the reason for this journey, though Nimue was sure there was endless speculation in the other carriage.

"I honestly cannot say."

Morgana might simply deny the accusation. She could challenge Arthur to prove she had been unfaithful. That would put him in a very awkward position. There would be no sparing Urien's humiliation if the king was forced to drag the sordid details of her adultery into the light for all to see. Was that what Morgana wanted?

Would she admit the affair? Did she want Urien to repudiate her, to demand that their marriage was dissolved? Who was her lover, anyway? None of the rumours could agree on his name. That was no great surprise, Nimue thought sourly. Those relishing a scandal leered after the women involved, whether they were guilty or innocent.

Was Morgana unfairly accused? If so, by whom, and why? King Urien's son, Sir Owain had no reason to resent their marriage. Even if she bore his father a child, his position as first-born son and heir was unassailable. Unless the young knight was jealous of anyone who replaced his mother, but Nimue had seen no sign that he was so mean-spirited. Besides, he was living at Camelot, so how could he conspire against Morgana in Gore?

Nimue wondered if Urien wanted rid of a wife he found too strong-minded. That was the most likely explanation she had found. But what might Morgana do, if her husband and her brother decreed she should be punished for her offences, real or imagined. Nimue couldn't see her meekly retreating to a convent, to sit and weep at the feet of the crucified god. Not with the enchantments she could call on, and whatever newer magic she might have learned.

A horn call sounded in the distance. The rumble of the wheels on the road soon gave way to the hollow sound of planks, then they were jolted by cobbles. They heard the driver praise his horses as the carriage halted amid the familiar bustle of a castle. A groom opened the carriage door.

Guinevere squared her shoulders, preparing herself yet again for the assault of curious eyes and avid whispers. No knight armed for battle ever showed such courage, as far as Nimue was concerned. She alone was close enough to see the shadow in the queen's eyes, as Elaine and Linet got out of the carriage first.

"Thank you." Guinevere gave the boy her practised smile. She accepted his offer of a helping hand and stepped down to a warm welcome.

Nimue followed, disregarded, and saw King Urien's vassals had been summoned to see him honoured by Arthur's visit. The castle yard was crowded, though it wasn't particularly large, certainly not for anyone accustomed to Camelot. Only the outer defences and the tall keep were built of stone. Sir Lamorak, Sir Aglovale and the other knights who accompanied the king would be housed in wooden halls by the curtain wall. The noble young ladies would stay with the queen, of course. Until they returned to Camelot, Guinevere wouldn't get a moment to herself.

Arthur had dismounted and was waiting with Sir Owain of Gore. As their horses were led away, he offered his arm to his queen. The royal couple smiled at each other, and Nimue hoped no one else noticed Arthur avoiding Guinevere's gaze. The queen had been right. Whenever they halted on this journey, she had run the gauntlet of barely concealed speculation over when her supposed baby would be born. Nimue was still waiting for Arthur to acknowledge his mistake.

The king and queen walked towards the castle's round keep. It was built in the older style with a single broad room on each upper floor. Wide steps rose to the doorway that led to the banqueting hall on the lowest level. It was only a little after noon, but savoury scents suggested a feast was ready to be served. Guinevere wouldn't get any respite and Nimue would have to wait to talk to Morgana alone.

At least Gore's queen wasn't locked up in disgrace, confined in that keep. Morgana stood on the steps at her husband's side. Both were richly dressed in russet velvet, though only Gore's king wore a crown. Morgana's dark hair was plaited and coiled beneath a net of gilt thread and a silken veil secured with pins. Her hand was tucked through her husband's arm and Urien smiled fondly at her. He said something and Morgana's lips curved with amusement. Nimue couldn't recall her ever looking so carefree.

King Urien extended his free hand. "My liege. Your grace. You are most welcome to our home." His voice was strong and confident, and he smiled at Morgana once again.

Arthur and Guinevere exchanged embraces with their

hosts as the onlookers cheered. Relief on Arthur's face warred with irritation as he suspected he had made this journey for nothing. Guinevere was still braced for the inevitable, kindly queries that assumed she carried Arthur's child.

Urien's brow was unfurrowed and his smile never wavered as he greeted his king. Nimue felt a prickle of suspicion. She hadn't spent much time around the king of Gore in the month he had spent at Camelot while preparations for the great double wedding were made, but from what she had seen, and what other servants had said, Urien was an exacting, even demanding master. He was reputedly conscious of his status and swift to resent any perceived slight. Today he looked as placid as a favourite uncle enjoying a warm seat by the hearth.

Morgana was as hard to read as ever. When she stepped aside as Urien embraced his son, her gaze met Nimue's. Morgana's eyes were coldly implacable.

Leave well alone. This is no business of yours.

Nimue's suspicions hardened into certainty. Morgana had done what she was accused of, and more besides. She needed to know why, and what Morgana planned to do next.

The moment passed and they walked into the keep. Arthur and Guinevere were granted time to wash away the dust of the road and to change out of their travelling clothes. Urien's servants showed them to the great chamber on the keep's fourth floor, while those who had come from Camelot ferried chests and baskets up from the luggage carts.

Arthur swiftly made himself presentable and headed for the door. Nimue saw Guinevere's lips thin, but with so many strangers coming and going, she could hardly call after her husband to ask where he was going.

The queen looked at her instead. "See what his grace might need."

Her eyes said different. Guinevere wanted to know where Arthur was going and why. Nimue went after the king. As she crossed the threshold, she reached for a swift enchantment.

Those within the royal guests' chamber would have seen her leave, but no one on the stairs would see her appear. She hurried after Arthur, doing her best to keep out of the way. As long as no one actually bumped into her, her presence would go unremarked.

He had only gone to the floor below where Morgana and Urien shared the chamber. The door stood ajar as servants came and went. Nimue caught a glimpse of Morgana sitting at her ease with a goblet of wine. There was no sign of Urien.

Arthur snapped his fingers at the maids. "Leave us. I wish to speak to my sister." As soon as the maidservants left, he pushed the door to and secured the latch. Nimue had no chance to slip inside.

Not that it mattered. She knew Morgana would see through the magic that hid her. Would she realise Nimue was listening out on the stairs? She had no sense of Morgana working an enchantment, but that was no guarantee, given the subtlety of the younger woman's magic. If she did suspect Nimue was spying on her, would she care? Since she had no way to know, Nimue hid herself in the shadows and waited to learn what she could.

"Good day, my liege," Morgana said meekly. "May I offer you some wine?"

"Thank you, no." Arthur's voice was harsh. "Tell me the truth. I am told you have a lover. Have you dishonoured my ally and threatened my kingdom's peace?"

Arthur was in search of a target for his anger. As they travelled, he had heard the same incautious remarks anticipating an heir. Nimue had seen him pretend not to notice, unable to vent his frustrations without inviting questions he had no wish to answer.

"Forgive me," Morgana begged with a catch in her voice. "I have been foolish – but no, please believe me, I have not been unfaithful. You must believe me, dearest brother. I was lonely, I confess that much. My husband's lifelong passion for the hunt took him from my side day after day, even when we had not long been married. I resented his absence, though I knew I was being selfish. I fell into an idle flirtation with a young knight who passed this way and begged shelter for a little while. He was handsome and ardent, and I was flattered and charmed. I paid no attention to the gossip that followed, and I was at fault."

Was that an actual sob, before Morgana continued?

"I made no effort to make friends here, even though I am now Gore's queen, and I have paid for my mistake. Those who didn't know me were ready to think the worst. Rumours reached my husband's ear, and he challenged me to explain. I realised what I had done, and I threw myself on his mercy. Urien has been gracious enough to forgive me, and to admit his own part in our estrangement. We have committed ourselves to each other anew. He spends less time with his hounds, and I am more mindful of my duties as his queen. I believe we will find true affection in the days and years to come."

"Oh." Arthur didn't know what to say.

Nimue wondered, if she opened the door, if she would see Morgana on her knees, or with her hands clasped beneath her chin in entreaty. She was almost tempted to do it, to see if Urien's apparently remorseful queen could keep a straight face when she saw Nimue.

In that month before Morgana's marriage, Nimue had learned the noble ladies of Camelot enjoyed stories of fraught romance and chivalrous courtship. Merchants brought small, exquisitely illustrated books from Brittany and elsewhere overseas. The ladies sipped the sweet wines the merchants also sold while one of them read the latest breathless tale aloud.

Morgana excused herself from such gatherings, claiming her duties as chatelaine called her elsewhere. In private, as Nimue assisted her with the seemingly endless wedding preparations, she mocked these implausible adventures and ruthlessly dissected their heroines' follies. Now her ladies' love of those passionate stories had served Morgana well. This yarn she had spun to disarm Arthur could have come straight from one of those volumes of over-elaborate verse.

The king cleared his throat. "Thank you for your honesty, sister. As long as your husband has forgiven you, nothing more needs to be said."

"Thank you, my liege," Morgana said humbly. "May I finish dressing for the feast?"

"Of course. I will see you there."

Nimue stepped deeper into the shadows as Arthur left the room and headed down the stairs. She was ready to confront Morgana, but the queen of Gore rang a silver bell to summon her servants. All Nimue could do was return to Guinevere's side.

The feast to honour the high king and his queen was lavish. The food was excellent and fine wines were poured generously. Skilled minstrels played neither too loud to hinder conversation nor so softly that they were wasting their time. King Urien of Gore was amiable, even jovial. Morgana hung on his every word, gazing at him, adoring. He fed her sweetmeats from his plate, and she offered him sips from her goblet.

Arthur relaxed in the seat of honour while Urien boasted of the stags that could be hunted locally and of the quality of his hounds. The conversation turned to Sir Owain's skills in the joust and the melee. The knights in the king's escort were quick to praise Urien's son. Urien's vassals were interested to learn how a warrior might win a prize in a tournament.

The noble ladies of Gore listened patiently and smiled at Guinevere. Their sons exchanged discreet smiles with the young noblewomen attending the queen. No one was interested in Nimue in a seat at the far end of the high table. She wondered why she warranted this honour, until Morgana glanced at her. Her gaze was steely.

Leave well alone. This is no business of yours.

Nimue looked down, spreading butter on her bread. So that

was her answer. Morgana wanted to be sure she wasn't asking questions around the kitchens or the laundry while everyone else was occupied. She wasn't going to get the chance today to learn whatever Urien's queen didn't want her to know.

The feast eventually ended. Below the dais, the trestle tables and benches were carried away and the floor was swept clear for dancing. The minstrels seized their chance for some refreshment and Nimue saw Guinevere rise from her seat. She hurried to the queen's side.

"I am tired from the journey," Guinevere was saying to Arthur before she turned to her ladies. "Nimue can see to my needs. Stay here and enjoy yourselves. If our gracious host will excuse me."

She smiled sweetly at King Urien, but she didn't wait for his answer. Nimue followed as Guinevere walked swiftly to the door to the stairs. Not swiftly enough to avoid hearing a noblewoman of Gore recall her own weariness in the early months of pregnancy. The queen flinched as if she'd been pricked with a pin.

Guinevere didn't speak until they reached the guest chamber, now cluttered with pallet beds. Nimue clapped her hands and dismissed the servants busy with linen and blankets.

"Thank you. Camelot's ladies can see to these things for themselves."

The servants hastily left. Guinevere took off her earrings. "Did you hear what Morgana told Arthur?"

"I did." Nimue relayed the story of the supposed misunderstanding.

"Arthur will accept that because he believes what he wants to hear." Guinevere wasn't remotely convinced. "Have you any idea what Morgana is up to?"

"At the moment, no," Nimue admitted.

Guinevere sighed. "Let's see if we can learn more tomorrow."

CHAPTER TWENTY-FIVE

The next day started with commotion out in the castle yard. Snarling and barking threatened a dog fight. As everyone in the guest chamber stirred, Nimue sat up to see Arthur was already out of the curtained bed, getting dressed in his travelling clothes.

"Your grace?" Guinevere brushed stray curls out of her eyes as she rolled over to see where he might be.

"Uricn and I are going hunting. He suggested it after you retired last night." Arthur gathered up his sword and belt. "It will be an excellent opportunity for me to become better acquainted with his vassals. Morgana can entertain you."

"I wish you good fortune," Guinevere said dutifully. Behind Arthur's back, she shot Nimue a determined look. They could pursue their own quarry.

Elaine, Linet, and the other young women on the pallets were sitting up and yawning. Nimue dressed quickly. "I will call for hot water."

She hurried down the stairs. As she reached the floor below, she saw Morgana's door was ajar. Gore's queen was already dressed and jewelled for the day. The scabbarded sword in her hands looked thoroughly out of place.

Nimue went in and closed the door. "What are you doing? Don't imagine I believe that tale you spun for Arthur."

Caught unawares, Morgana laughed. Nimue felt the heaviness in the air that ensured their conversation wouldn't leave this room.

"You heard that, did you? I should have expected as much, and no, I would never think I could fool you."

Nimue ignored that admission or compliment, whichever it might be. She recognised the sword in Morgana's hands. "What are you doing with Excalibur?"

Morgana's smile vanished. "This is no business of yours."

"It is, if you're using magic to throw the realm into chaos."

"When the enchantment in this blade is the only thing that sustains Arthur's rule?" Morgana gripped the sword hilt harder. "When that sorcery gives him the right to hand me over to a boorish old man who sees me as no more than some prized mare in his stables or a bitch with good bloodlines in his kennels?"

She laughed, bitter. "Not that Urien can play the stud, no matter what he tries. Do you know why I barred you from scrying here? I didn't want you to see my nightly humiliation. Urien orders me to strip naked of all but the jewels he thinks can buy my affection. Since I've been paid like some whore, I'm expected to lie back as he slobbers and licks my breasts and sniffs between my thighs, in hopes of arousing his manhood long enough to spill his seed. When he can't manage more than a handful of thrusts, I'm the one to blame. So he says, anyway. I can assure you that is not the case."

Nimue felt sick as she saw the defiance in Morgana's eyes. "So, it is true. You took a lover."

"I have a lover who worships me," Morgana said swiftly. "He is young and virile and the slightest touch of his hand thrills me beyond imagining."

Why did every generation think they were the first mortals to discover sex? Nimue considered telling Morgana she had known dizzying passion with her human lovers in the course of her long life. But this was a distraction and they both knew it. "Why have you taken Arthur's sword?"

"You imprisoned Merlin to remove magic's influence from mortal affairs." Morgana shrugged. "I am doing the same."

"Really? You must have used enchantment to shield yourself, to keep everyone else asleep, when you crept up the stairs and swapped that sword for whatever counterfeit Arthur's wearing."

Unnerved, Nimue realised that spell must have been both subtle and strong enough to catch her in its coils as well as the mortals in the room. That was a problem for later though. She challenged Morgana. "You're using enchantments to dupe your husband so you can betray your wedding vows."

"Vows made under duress," Morgana hissed. "Like my mother, forced to wed *his* father."

The venom in her words shocked Nimue. She had missed so much in the years she had been trapped in that cave, hiding from Merlin. When had Morgana's amused disdain for Arthur curdled into this hatred? But that was another distraction.

She nodded at Excalibur. "Arthur will search this castle from cellars to rafters once he realises the sword on his hip isn't his own."

Morgana said nothing. Nimue studied her face.

"But he won't, will he? You're sure of that. Why? What have you done?"

Morgana had recovered her poise. "Go back to your mistress. She will need you before the day is out. Tell her I bear her no ill-will. I'm sure Gawain will treat her kindly when he is crowned king."

Nimue felt a chill of foreboding. "Gawain will only become king when Arthur dies, and only if Arthur dies without a son."

"I can see Guinevere isn't pregnant, whatever the rumours hope." Morgana lifted her chin, defiant. "Arthur's line is dead, even if he still lives. Everyone knows the truth, even if they haven't got the courage to admit it. Uther would have been the last Pendragon if Merlin hadn't helped that pig rape my mother. My sister's line, our father's blood, will secure a peaceful future for Logres, and for every other kingdom in these isles. There are five princes of Orkney, who will likely be as fertile as their parents. Gawain's rule will offer a lasting future built on solid foundations, not this quicksand of enchantments. Can't you see how much better that will be?"

Nimue refused to be drawn, no matter how much she might agree. "You said Guinevere will need me before the day is out. What did you mean?"

"Arthur has forced my hand by coming here. I can dupe Urien with my spells, but I know someone will seek to win the king's favour, or Sir Owain's, by sharing my lover's name. Even without proof, Arthur will exile my beloved or maybe even execute him, and I will be alone again. So be it. Before sunset, the queen and I will both be free." Morgana vanished.

Nimue swallowed a vile curse. She looked around and spotted a shallow silver bowl heaped with enamelled pins to adorn Morgana's hair. Nimue wasn't fooled. That was a scrying bowl. Dumping the contents on the floor, she wrung water from the air to fill it, and bit the side of her thumbnail for a drop of blood.

She didn't bother scrying for Morgana. Whenever she had gone, she would be hidden. Arthur was the one in danger, even if Nimue had no idea what the threat might be.

The water shimmered and rippled and her spell showed the king in a forest glade. Arthur knelt beside Urien who was lying on the ground. Nimue frowned. It didn't look as if Urien had fallen from his horse. Gore's king was comfortably settled, lying on his back with a rolled cloak for a pillow. His clasped hands rose and fell on his belly, and as she watched, his feet shifted a little.

Even so, Arthur couldn't rouse the older man. Nimue watched him shake Urien's shoulder, once, twice and a third time. Urien didn't stir. That wasn't the only thing amiss. Nimue couldn't see anyone else, even when she drew her magic out wider until Urien and Arthur were no bigger than the illustrations in those books of verse from Brittany. Where were the other knights, the huntsmen and Urien's prized pack of hounds?

Never mind that. Nimue moved fast. She closed the window shutters around the wide room. In the gloom, she returned to the scrying bowl and summoned the image of Arthur again. She focused on the shadows behind a holly thicket not far away from the king. Summoning her magic, she stepped into the void between time and place.

For an instant, she was unable to move, or to see or hear. She couldn't even breathe. Then her feet found solid ground and she gasped with relief. Around her the holly trees rustled, knowing the risk she had taken and shaking their branches with disapproval.

Nimue hid herself with an enchantment. She had no wish to try explaining herself to Arthur. What could she tell him anyway? She had no idea what Morgana intended, though only widowhood would free her and Guinevere from the shackles of marriage. Nimue must watch and wait and hope she could thwart Morgana's murderous plan, whenever that might be revealed.

Would Gore's unwilling queen truly intend to use magic to kill the king? When they had lived in Brittany, Nimue had told her often enough that any pain she inflicted using sorcery would come back to her threefold. Nimue wished she had known Morgana had been driven to such desperation. She wished she had asked her for help.

Nimue reproached herself. Why should Morgana think anyone could help her? Her childhood happiness at Tintagel had been destroyed, when Morgana had lost the father she loved with brutal suddenness. As she grew older, she learned that however much her mother and sisters loved her, she would always come second to their husbands and sons. Nimue had vanished from Morgana's life without a word of warning and years had passed before she returned. No wonder the princess had concluded she must act alone.

Even so, killing Arthur was utter folly. If he died a mysterious death in Gore's forests, blame and counter accusation would see bloody chaos tear the realm apart. Why couldn't Morgana wait? If Arthur was indeed the last Pendragon, the people of Logres would see Gawain or his son take the throne in the fullness of time, when the old king died childless. Though that condemned Guinevere to a barren marriage and years of undeserved grief, Nimue thought with a qualm.

She looked at Urien. Despite Arthur's exasperated efforts, he was still lost in enchanted sleep. Was he going to sink into stupor and death, or did Morgana have some worse fate in mind for this man who had mistreated her?

Movement on the far side of the glade caught her eye. A young knight walked out of the trees. Armoured for a tourney, he held a drawn sword. Nimue frowned and looked more closely at the blade, and at the scabbard on his belt. This stranger was armed with Excalibur.

Nimue looked at the blade Arthur carried with the sight of her people. She saw it might be identical, but that sword was no more than a skilled blacksmith's work.

The unknown knight must be Morgana's lover, since he was carrying the magical blade. The scabbard held some sorcery as well. Nimue had never realised that before. It didn't matter. Deprived of Excalibur, Arthur would be no harder to kill than any other warrior. This knight was presumably a skilled swordsman, and he would have Excalibur's magic to help him. Did Morgana think she would escape the threefold debt as long as she used no sorcery against Arthur directly?

Nimue looked at Urien. Magic must have made him lose his way in the forest and fall into this deep sleep. The law of the land would condemn him though, as well as the fury of Camelot's knights, if he was found lying senseless beside Arthur's butchered corpse with a bloody sword in his hand. He would lose his head for killing his king, with or without a trial by his peers. Was that how Morgana hoped to win her freedom without paying a hideous price for murdering him?

"Sir knight!" The newcomer hailed Arthur with a warning, not a greeting.

The king abandoned Urien and stood up. Seeing the other man's naked blade, he drew his own sword. "I am your king, and you will address me as such."

"You are no king of mine." The newcomer approached with his sword – with Arthur's sword – clearly prepared to strike.

"You are in my realm. To attack me is treason, whoever you may be." The king raised his own blade in a defensive stance. "At least give me your name."

The stranger acknowledged that request with a brief salute. "I am Accolon of Gaul."

So, he wasn't one of Arthur's subjects. Nimue wondered if his accent had reminded Morgana of happier days long ago in Brittany, when she sought illicit comfort to relieve her misery here.

Accolon launched an attack. Arthur parried. Accolon struck again. Arthur turned the blade aside. They circled each other, looking for an opening, alert for any sign of a weakness in the other man's skills. Accolon feinted. Arthur retreated. Accolon swept Excalibur around with a twist of his wrist and lunged forward. Arthur's counterstrike robbed that blow of its power, but the edge of the steel bit into the king's arm. Hunting leathers would only protect him from thorns and perhaps a thrashing stag's antlers. Accolon wore a chain mail hauberk, vambraces and greaves.

Arthur backed away fast. He went on the defensive, batting Accolon's blows aside rather than trying to attack. Nimue had heard plenty of Camelot's knights discussing tactics for getting the better of every imaginable foe. Arthur hoped to tire Accolon out, burdened as he was with his armour. Morgana's lover showed no sign of flagging. He pursued Arthur with strike after strike. Soon the king was bleeding from a handful of wounds on his arms and thighs.

Nimue saw the pain on the king's face. She saw something

else too. Before she could identify it, Arthur surprised Accolon with a ferocious assault. As his enemy recoiled, Arthur took a swift sidestep. The king's blade curved down and around to bite deep behind Accolon's knee. Nimue winced. Hamstrung, Accolon would fall to his knees, and Arthur would hack off his head. A sword didn't need to be Excalibur to do that.

But Accolon didn't even stagger. He spun around and launched a murderous blow at Arthur's back. The king darted out of the way, but the tip of Accolon's blade cut a deep score across his shoulder. As Arthur retreated, Nimue saw his naked fear. Now she had seen the sorcery that the scabbard carried at work.

The king's stroke should have crippled Accolon, but Excalibur's sheath didn't only protect the blade. The Lady of the Lake had been thorough when she devised her magic. This enchantment on the scabbard saved whoever carried her sword from any other blade's bite. Arthur had known that, Nimue realised. So he had known something was wrong when Accolon's blade had first cut him. Now the king knew the full extent of his peril. Even if he got past his enemy's guard, he wouldn't even be able to wound him.

A lesser man might have despaired. Such a man might have yielded, thinking surrender would save his life. Arthur went on the attack. He was his father's son, and Uther had been no coward. Besides, what did he have to lose? He could see Accolon was here to kill him.

Arthur smashed Accolon's blade aside. He stepped in, as close as he could. Inside the arc of the enchanted sword, he brought his own hilt up and around. Instead of using his blade, he smashed the pommel into the side of Accolon's helmet. If Arthur couldn't cut his enemy's head off, he could knock him senseless.

Morgana's lover staggered away. Arthur pursued him, merciless. Accolon recovered to swing Excalibur at the king. They circled each other once again and battle resumed. Arthur dodged and weaved, keeping his distance when he must, darting forward when he could. He was intent on cracking his enemy's skull, but now Accolon knew what the king intended. He gave Arthur no opportunity to repeat that strike at his head. His deft strikes cut more bloody gashes on Arthur's arms and legs.

Both men were tiring. The weight of Accolon's armour was sapping his strength as Arthur hoped. On the other side of those scales, the king had lost a perilous amount of blood. The fight would be lost now, rather than won. The only question was, which man would make the fatal mistake?

Arthur got inside Accolon's guard. He brought a hammer blow down on the knight's helm. Accolon went sprawling, but Arthur's blade had snapped where the steel met the cross-guard. Arthur was left with only the hilt in his hand. He stared at it, aghast.

Accolon lay flat on his back, only stunned for a moment. He swept Excalibur up to threaten Arthur. "Yield to me and give up your throne!"

Arthur used his cross-guard to turn the blade aside as he sprang backwards. "I will live, or I will die a king. Dishonour yourself if you must, killing an unarmed man.

If he thought he could shame the knight into retreating, he was mistaken. Accolon got back on his feet and attacked with a rain of blows that Arthur could barely evade. Then Accolon launched a strike that was sure to kill the king.

Nimue would not stand to see Arthur murdered. She gestured and Excalibur twisted out of Accolon's hand. The sword fell to the ground. That should end the fight.

Arthur moved fastest. He threw away his broken sword's hilt and snatched up Excalibur. He had not forgotten Accolon was still wearing the enchanted sword's scabbard. As Accolon brought up his vambraced arms to ward off a blow from the sword, Arthur seized hold of the knight's crossed wrists with his free hand. Leaping into the air, Arthur used all his weight to force Accolon's arms down. In the same move, he smashed Excalibur's pommel into the knight's forehead. Accolon fell to the ground like a poleaxed bullock, bleeding from his mouth and his nose.

Arthur knelt on his chest, pinning him to the ground. His face twisted with fury. "Who gave you my fucking sword?"

Accolon choked on blood filling his throat and shook his head. Arthur was about to ask him again, when Nimue heard loud voices calling out for the king, and for Urien. Dogs barked in triumph as they found whatever scent they had been given.

The magic that had trapped Arthur in this glade was unravelling. Morgana must have fled. Nimue berated herself. She should have realised the younger enchantress would be here. She must have had some scheme to get Accolon away, to make sure he was never suspected of any part in Arthur's death. Now Morgana would need a new plan and now she would be truly desperate.

The hunting party drew closer. That must mean Arthur was safe. Nimue waited until she saw movement among the trees. As she heard the first cries of relief, of alarm, and of utter confusion, she left.

Stepping through the shadows to return to the castle, she arrived in the room Morgana shared with Urien. She was ready to use her own magic to stupefy some hapless servant, but there was no one to be seen. Nimue looked again, using the sight of her people. There was still no sign of Morgana. Shaking, Nimue went to find Guinevere.

CHAPTER TWENTY-SIX

By the time the hunting party returned, Nimue had searched every nook and cranny of King Urien's castle. Morgana was nowhere to be found, by spells or any other means. When she heard the harsh call of horns beyond the curtain wall, she hurried back to the guest chamber where Guinevere and her ladies were occupying themselves with some desultory needlework.

Guinevere glanced up from her embroidery. "Have you come from our hostess?" Her eyes asked a slew of other questions.

The young noblewomen looked at Nimue with varying degrees of impatience. This was not how they expected to spend their day when they had dressed each other's hair in flattering styles this morning and chosen their finest jewels.

"The hunting party is returning, your grace." Nimue tried to convey a warning that Guinevere should prepare herself.

Guinevere held her needle motionless, then stabbed it into the decorated linen. "I would have expected his grace to spend longer at the chase. Let us hope nothing is amiss."

She handed her embroidery hoop to Linet. The other girls stowed away their own work. Guinevere ignored their whispers as she joined Nimue at the door. They headed quickly down the stairs to seize what little privacy they could.

As they reached Morgana's door, Guinevere grabbed Nimue's arm. "Where is she?"

"I have no idea. She seems to have fled."

"Why?" Guinevere was baffled.

Morgana's misery and treachery wasn't Nimue's to betray. Fortunately, commotion as the castle gates opened interrupted the queen's questions. Guinevere hurried out of the keep to wait on the steps. Nimue followed. King Urien's household appeared from the wooden buildings that ringed the castle yard as the drawbridge was lowered. Confused questions grew louder as the gate opened.

Arthur was the first to appear, swathed in a cloak as if this was mid-winter. He spurred his horse towards Guinevere. Nimue thought he was going to force the beast up the steps to confront her until the animal baulked.

"Where is my sister?" he yelled at the queen.

Everyone fell silent. Wide-eyed glances shared consternation. Guinevere shrank from his anger. "I have no idea."

As he got the fractious horse in hand, Arthur's gaze fixed on Nimue. For one heart-stopping moment, she thought he was going to denounce her as an enchantress in front of everyone here.

"Find her." His scowl was dark with unspoken threats. Use her sorcery to do what he wanted, or the consequences would be dire.

"I have looked." Nimue forced herself to speak calmly. "She isn't here."

"We haven't seen her all morning, your grace." Guinevere had no idea what was going on, but she wouldn't let Nimue stand alone.

Arthur's lip curled, but before he could speak, fresh cries of alarm startled his horse. King Urien's people lamented as their liege lord was carried through the gate. He lay senseless on a rough litter of cloak-draped poles cut from the forest. That was slung between stocky ponies who should have returned with freshly killed venison.

Ashen-faced, Sir Owain followed. "Take my father to his chamber."

He could barely force out the words, strangled by his distress.

The castle's men and women crowded around the ponies. Countless hands reached for the litter. Nimue and Guinevere stepped aside as Urien was taken into the keep. No one spared them a glance. No one paid any attention to Arthur, still in his saddle and surrounded by Camelot's grim-faced knights.

"My king," Guinevere cried with sudden alarm. "You're wounded."

Arthur's cloak had fallen away, revealing the bloody gashes in his leathers. Nimue saw his high colour had faded to unhealthy pallor. Morgana's plan might still succeed if the king succumbed to blood loss or if those deep cuts festered.

"Your grace," the queen said, pleading. "You need rest, and your hurts need tending."

Arthur scowled, but he couldn't deny it. All the same, he made no move to dismount. He jerked his head towards the gateway and looked hard at Nimue. "Find somewhere to put this traitor. He attacked me out in the forest."

An anxious groom led one last pony into the castle yard. A man wearing only his shirt was slung across the animal's back, face down with his arms and legs hanging limp. Ropes lashed his ankles and wrists together and another length had been passed under the beast's belly.

Nimue made sure not to show that she recognised Accolon, stripped of his armour. "Of course, your grace."

Arthur nodded curtly, dismounted and walked stiffly towards the keep. He grimaced as he accepted the offer of Guinevere's arm. They walked slowly up the steps, followed by Sir Aglovale and Sir Lamorak. Elaine, Linet and Guinevere's other ladies had gathered in the doorway. Arthur shooed them away with a flick of his hand.

Nimue turned her attention to Accolon. She was startled to see that he still clung to life. She pushed through the men and women milling about, to reach the groom clutching the pony's halter rope.

"Where are Camelot's knights lodged?" Nimue knew Arthur

would want his own men guarding his attacker, even if there was no possibility the captive could escape.

"This way." The groom led the pony towards the closest wooden hall.

A steward emerged from the doorway as the stableman untied the prisoner's ropes. That was a relief. Nimue couldn't move Accolon herself without using magic.

"Please carry him inside. Where can I tend him privately?"

"Follow me." The steward hauled Accolon off the pony, slung him over his shoulder and carried him inside.

Nimue followed. There were two smaller rooms at the far end of the hall. The steward kicked open a door and dumped Accolon on the long table within. He clearly thought the knight was as good as dead. "Mistress?"

"I need hot water and rags. Please find me some blankets."

The man nodded and left. She soon had the things she needed. Urien's people were well-trained. Not that anything could change the outcome here. Nimue soon knew she could not save Accolon without sorcery. Even if enchantment ensured he would live, he would never be the man he once was. After she had washed his face and head clean, Nimue could feel his skull was cracked above his shattered nose. Dark bruises behind his ears showed her blood was seeping from his brain and pooling beneath his skin. He might linger for hours or days, but his death was certain.

It was more merciful to let him die. Even if she revived him, using her skills, he faced savage execution for trying to murder Arthur. The penalty for such treason was to be partly hanged, then drawn and quartered. That atrocity would stain everyone who witnessed it.

She turned to the door and nearly dropped the basin of bloody water and rags. Arthur stood there. He wore a long-sleeved tunic and thick hose, and Nimue saw the bulk of bandages beneath the finely woven wool. She resisted the temptation to look beneath them to see how well his wounds had been cleaned. She would do what she could to heal Arthur later on, whether or not he was willing.

The king nodded at Accolon. "Wake him."

His hard gaze dared her to refuse. She turned back to the table, put down the bowl, and laid a gentle hand on Accolon's forehead. Rousing him would hasten his death, but that would only be a blessing. The dying knight opened his eyes, and the whites were scarlet with blood.

Soft-footed, Arthur stood at Nimue's shoulder. He spoke quietly, calm. "Morgana gave you my sword. What did she hope to gain by my death?"

Accolon stared blindly at the rafters, his words barely a whisper. "I love her, and she loves me. She can do wondrous, marvellous things. We moved through the castle unseen to spend our nights in each other's arms. She could turn away suspicion if anyone saw us kiss. She said Urien would soon die, and I would marry her to become king of Gore. But when you came, you had to die because you would never allow us our happiness. Your father destroyed her mother's happiness, and she would be avenged."

The dying knight's eyes closed. Nimue saw the faint shimmer of his life dwindling faster.

Arthur sighed heavily. "Then she really can work enchantments."

Nimue braced herself, expecting him to demand she tell him everything she knew.

Instead, he shook his head, looking down at Accolon. "She used magic to deceive this poor fool. How could he be king of Gore while Sir Owain still lives?"

Nimue kept quiet. She thought it was at least as likely Morgana had been deceiving herself. Perhaps she had truly believed that Gawain would grant her lover this boon, once he was crowned ruler of both Logres and Orkney at Camelot. Everyone from the humblest knight to the rulers of these petty realms held their lands at the high king's pleasure.

"Perhaps her dupe can do some penance for his treason."
Arthur looked more like Uther than ever. "If she knows he's
still alive, she may try to save him. If she comes here, use your
magic to hold her or you will answer to me."

He strode from the room. Nimue watched him go. Then
she found a stool and sat down to wait. Arthur using Accolon
as bait was revolting, but if there was any chance she could
talk to Morgana, Nimue would take it. Whether she could or
would hold Morgana against her will, to answer to the king?
That remained to be seen.

No one came into the hall. Nimue guessed Camelot's knights
had been told to stay away, like hunters keeping clear of a
dead-fall trap. Outside, the bustle faded. Tense stillness settled
over the castle like a threatening storm, even though the sky
through the shutters was cloudless blue.

Some while later, the hall's outer door opened. Nimue's
heart beat faster, though she didn't expect to see Morgana.
She would come and go unseen, if she came at all. Some other
disaster could still be looming.

Sir Owain entered the small room. He didn't even glance at
Accolon.

"Mistress. I'm told you are a noted healer. I beg you, my
father–" He swallowed, struggling to hold back his tears.

"Of course." Nimue could do nothing more for Accolon
except witness his death. She might be able to save Urien if
she could unravel Morgana's enchantment, and there was no
one else who could even try.

She followed Owain to the keep, past people waiting with
anxious faces. Whatever the king of Gore's faults as a husband
might have been, his son and his people valued him. They
entered Urien's chamber, where a priest knelt in prayer at the
king's bedside. He broke off and at Owain's gesture, he rose
and left. Nimue moved closer and was relieved to see Urien
still taking deep and regular breaths.

Gore's king looked old and diminished, lying stripped to

his shirt in the wide bed. She had not realised how thin his hair was when he wore his crown, or seen the spots of age on the backs of his hands. Had he really wanted to be married to Morgana? Perhaps he had been comfortable suiting himself since Owain's mother had died, but he dared not refuse the king. Morgana said he had abused her. True, but had that been malice? Nimue wondered if Urien was only guilty of desperately trying to rouse his flagging manhood to pleasure a much younger woman as a dutiful husband should. Perhaps he was afraid that humiliating whispers of impotence would cost him his people's respect.

"Is this truly some vile sorcery?" Owain was fighting not to lose hope. "Perhaps he has been poisoned? Is there some medicine that might rouse him?"

"Perhaps." Nimue would have to tread carefully, if Urien's people suspected magic was at work. "Let me look more closely."

"There is no need."

Owain gasped as Morgana stepped out of the shadows cast by the curtains drawn back at the head of the bed. Her long hair hung loose to her waist. She was dressed in mourning black, and her face was deathly pale. A sword in her hand shone steely in the light falling through the window.

The faintest rasp of metal told Nimue that Owain had drawn his own blade. She took a pace forward to stand between Urien's wife and his son, though she wasn't certain which of them she was protecting. Morgana could still kill Gore's king if she chose, but she would have to come within arm's reach of Nimue. Would she take that risk, knowing the older enchantress's magic would carry them both away?

"Please," Owain begged, anguished. "If you kill him, I will have to kill you."

Clearly, he didn't understand Morgana's magic could kill him before he raised his hand. Would she do that? Was she truly a killer?

Nimue looked at the younger woman. "Urien must have done something good to earn his son's affection. What has Owain ever done to you, to deserve the grief of seeing his father die? You know the depths of such sorrow."

Tears welled in Morgana's eyes. A drop escaped her lashes to trickle down her cheek. She vanished and Owain gasped. Nimue did her best to look equally startled.

"Where has the witch gone?" Owain looked in vain for someone to tell him.

"Your father. He's stirring."

Nimue stepped aside so Owain could take his father's hand. Urien was by no means awake, but his head moved from side to side and his mouth opened.

"If she is gone, so is her sorcery." Owain heaved a heartfelt sigh.

Nimue knew different. In the instant before she fled, Morgana had unknotted the enchantment holding Urien. If she hadn't, he would have died slowly and painfully, wracked by hunger and thirst. Nimue had seen enough of the spell to know she had no hope of breaking it. Morgana had been merciful. Nimue hugged that knowledge close. Not all hope for her was lost.

Owain pressed his father's hand to his lips, weeping with relief. Nimue heard movement by the door and saw the priest and several others trying to see what was happening.

"I will fetch a strengthening cordial for his grace," she said to no one in particular.

Those crowding the door entered the room. Owain hastily got to his feet and scrubbed his face free of tears, giving brisk orders.

Nimue hurried up to the guest chamber. She would fetch a tincture for Urien if she had time, but she wanted to find Arthur. She had just reminded Morgana of her grief after Gorlois's death at Pendragon's hands. Would she go to seek revenge on Uther's son?

Upstairs, Elaine, Linet and the other girls were sitting on stools in a circle, not even pretending to be sewing. Some looked bored, others were irritated, and the rest wavered in between.

Nimue clapped her hands. "Where is his grace? Where is your queen?"

The girls looked at Elaine, who blushed scarlet at being appointed spokeswoman. "I have no idea where his grace might be, but the queen has gone to see if anything can be done for the wounded knight."

Nimue hurried back down the stairs. If Morgana couldn't find Arthur, she might try to save her lover instead. What would she do if she found Guinevere with him?

News that Urien had woken was spreading. Nimue skirted his people sharing their relief in the castle yard. The hall where Accolon lay was still empty though. She guessed Camelot's knights must be with Arthur, wherever he might be.

It seemed no one was paying any attention to Guinevere. Nimue heard soft conversation in the little room. Her blood ran cold as she recognised the queen's voice and Morgana's. Her magic muffled her steps on the wooden floor and a wisp of enchantment helped her hear what they said.

"You have to stay." Guinevere's voice trembled. "You must answer to your brother, to your king."

"Why? Arthur knows he's won. He always wins," Morgana said bitterly. "He has Excalibur again and the man I love is dead. Isn't that punishment enough?"

"He is your king." But Guinevere sounded less certain.

"If I leave, will you tell him I was here? If I swear to never return? If you will never see me again?"

Nimue waited for Guinevere to ask how Morgana possibly thought she could get out of the castle unseen. Or did the queen already know that she was talking to an enchantress? What had Morgana told her, while the two of them were here alone?

Finally, Guinevere broke the silence. "I will tell no one. Go and find whatever peace you can."

"Thank you. I am in your debt."

Nimue hid herself as Morgana strode out of the room. It didn't matter. Morgana was fading from mortal sight with every step. Before she reached the outer door, she had vanished utterly. Nimue hurried into the little room. Guinevere sprang up from the stool in the corner, looking as guilty as a child caught in mischief.

"Did you see–?"

"The king will never hear this from me." Nimue promised.

The queen stared at Accolon's pallid corpse. "To risk everything for love. To lose his life for her sake. To throw away her throne and her family. To be so wretchedly, so desperately unhappy."

She didn't seem to expect any response, which was a relief because Nimue could find nothing to say.

Heavy footsteps in the empty hall startled them both.

"Your grace!" Arthur bellowed.

"I – your grace – I am here." Guinevere hugged herself, frightened. She hurriedly gestured towards the table as Arthur strode into the room. "The treacherous knight has died, your grace."

Arthur's eyes narrowed. "Go to your ladies, your grace. This is no place for you."

To Nimue's surprise, the queen didn't move. "Will he be buried with the rites of the church? Will you show him that much mercy, whatever his sins may have been."

Arthur stared at her, taken aback. "What?"

"Will he be buried in sacred ground?" Guinevere's voice shook.

"Yes, of course. Now rejoin your women." The king glowered at her.

Guinevere hurried away. Nimue would have followed, but Arthur grabbed her arm.

"Where is she?"

"I don't know."

As Arthur released her, Nimue flinched. Exhausted as he was, Arthur looked angry enough to hit her out of sheer frustration. Instead, he flung a hand at the bowl she had used to wash Accolon earlier. Someone had emptied it and set it at the end of the table with a fresh ewer of water, a pile of clean rags, and a folded length of linen. The old women of the castle knew that Accolon's corpse must be laid out and shrouded.

"Find her with your magic," Arthur snapped.

Clearly, he had seen Merlin scrying often enough to know how it was done. Nimue half-filled the basin from the jug. She thought about asking Arthur to fetch her some ink. If she could get him out of the room for a few moments, if she could scry for Morgana unobserved...

Arthur held his hands out over the bowl, using the tip of a gleaming dagger to prick his own thumb. A scarlet bead of blood dropped into the water. Now Nimue really wanted to know what Merlin told him about scrying, but this really wasn't the time or place to ask. She focused her magic on the bowl.

"She may well be concealing herself," she warned.

Arthur grunted sourly.

Nimue was briefly tempted to cloud her spell, but she guessed Arthur would insist she try again and again until he got what he wanted. In any case she wanted to see for herself where Morgana had gone. Magic rippled across the water. Nimue felt Morgana's own enchantment trying to hide her, but something unexpected was at work. Arthur's blood lent strength to Nimue's spell. No, not Arthur's blood. Ygraine's blood linked her children.

The scrying showed them Morgana standing on a rocky headland with wind tearing at her unbound hair. The coastline was low to the sea and the treeless shore was veiled with spray. Arthur knew where she was before Nimue could begin to guess.

"Orkney. If she thinks I won't pursue her there, she is very much mistaken."

"Why?" Nimue demanded.

"What do you mean?" Arthur didn't understand.

"Why pursue her?"

"She tried to kill me."

"And she failed. It was all for nothing."

He shook his head, stubborn. "She must be punished."

"She has lost the man she loved." Nimue jabbed a finger at Accolon's corpse. "The people of Gore believe she tried to kill their king with magic, so word of her sorceries will spread far and wide. She is homeless and friendless now."

"Hardly," Arthur snarled. "She fled straight to her sister."

"Do you think Morgause knew anything about this? Do you think Morgana would put them both at such risk, by telling her what she had planned? When you have Morgause's sons in your care?"

For the first time, Arthur hesitated. Nimue followed up her advantage.

"Are you going to muster Logres' army and march north? Will you make war on Orkney on no more than suspicion? Do you think the other Scots kings will stand idly by? How many men will die this time? How can such deaths possibly benefit you? Far from it." She went on swiftly, before he could reply. "You are acclaimed as a great king because we have peace across these isles after generations of bloodshed."

She saw that made an impression.

"What will happen at Camelot, when Gawain and his brothers learn you intend to wage war on their homeland? Will you tell your knights that your heirs cannot be trusted because their aunt Morgana somehow stole Excalibur, even though they knew nothing about her plans? Will they see that as justice from their king?"

She waved a hand at Accolon's body again. "Do you want your enemies to hear how he used Excalibur against you? Do you want everyone to know how much your rule relies on that sword and its enchantments? Aren't such things better kept secret? Whatever this poor wretch knew died with him and no one will believe a word Morgana says, after Sir Owain and King Urien accuse her of witchcraft."

Arthur opened his mouth, but closed it again, scowling.

"Besides," Nimue concluded, "let's be practical. You cannot believe Morgana will still be on Orkney by the time you arrive, even if you take a fast ship and travel with a bare handful of men. She can scry to see you coming and she can cross a hundred leagues in the blink of an eye."

"Whose fault is that?" Arthur was glad to have a new target for his anger. "She was your pupil!"

Nimue shook her head. "I have no idea who taught Morgana the magic she used today. I wasn't at Camelot when she learned such things."

"No, you weren't." Arthur stared at her for a long moment. "You disappeared not long before Merlin left me without a word. Do you know what happened to him?"

"I cannot say, your grace." Nimue could see he was suspicious. Her heart pounded as she waited for him to ask a question she could only answer with an outright lie. "But he warned you that wild magic would threaten to destroy your kingdom. If you pursue Morgana, you could bring disaster down on your own head. Perhaps this is what Merlin foresaw."

She had no idea if that might be true, and she was hardly going to go and ask the imprisoned wizard, but if the possibility could save Morgana, that would suffice. Breathless, she waited for the king to speak. The silence lengthened.

"I will offer you a bargain." Arthur's face was hard and unforgiving. "I won't pursue Morgana if you use your magic in my service as Merlin did. To keep the peace across Logres."

Nimue nodded reluctant agreement. "To keep the peace across Logres."

It wasn't as if she could help Morgana now. As long as she

was at Camelot though, she could watch over Morgause's sons, Ygraine's grandsons. She would do what she could to help Guinevere too, for the queen's own sake as well as to keep the promise she had made to Morgana. Nimue had no intention of using her magic with Merlin's reckless arrogance though, whatever Arthur demanded.

CHAPTER TWENTY-SEVEN

A month later, and they might never have been away from Camelot, as far as everyone else was concerned. Distant cheering floated through the open shutters. The castle yard was busy with preparations for a tournament.

All the same, Nimue saw lingering consequences from their trip to Gore. Arthur hadn't come to see the queen this morning, not before they joined her ladies for an early breakfast, nor when they had come back afterwards to adorn her with jewels for the day. On the other hand, the king had dutifully visited Guinevere's bed every night since their return. Not that either of them seemed to get any pleasure from it.

Standing by the window, Guinevere looked out at the castle's towers. Coloured flags flew from each turret identifying the visitors. "He suffered so many wounds and yet not one has left a scar. Your skills as a healer are remarkable."

Nimue was tidying the queen's jewel coffer. "I'm thankful for the wisdom of so many women who came before me."

That was more true than Guinevere knew. As well as salves to stop Arthur's wounds festering, Nimue had used subtle enchantments learned long ago to ensure the king's forearms and thighs healed without a mark. She didn't want him seeing those angry, red reminders of his grievance with Morgana every time he undressed.

The breeze disturbed the gauzy veil hanging from the queen's headdress. Guinevere smoothed the delicate silk. "We had better take our places at the joust."

Nimue locked the little chest. "There's no hurry, your grace."

Guinevere shrugged. "People will stop to stare at my belly whenever I appear. Undue delay will start rumours of morning sickness again."

Nimue offered what little comfort she could. "Let's hope they're more interested in discussing Arthur's reasons for honouring Sir Gawain and his brothers."

Any hope that Morgana's scandalous behaviour could be left behind in Gore had been in vain. Rumour and exaggeration had flown on ahead down the road to Camelot and spread from there across Logres. Nimue was hardly surprised. The knights who travelled with them must have been besieged by their comrades eager for the gory details. Those young nobles doubtless felt honour-bound to share such news in letters to their fathers. The queen hadn't even attempted to stop Elaine, Linet and the other girls telling those who had stayed behind at Camelot what they had seen and heard.

Arthur was finally forced to admit such gossip could no more be stopped than an arrow from a bow could be recalled. The next day he announced this tournament. Whatever Morgana might have done, the king was going to show everyone his nephews and heirs were still loyal and trusted.

Guinevere smiled briefly. "There's that, I suppose, and hopefully we'll see if Linet shows a preference for Gareth over Gaheris by this evening – or the other way around."

"Indeed." Nimue had been wondering why the queen had chosen the girl for the seat of honour today. Well, wedding either of Morgause's younger sons would be a good marriage for her. If the match was made with genuine affection, so much the better, as far as Guinevere was concerned.

Nimue followed the queen down the great keep's stairs and they made their way towards the gatehouse. Well-wishers stopped Guinevere to exchange courtesies, hoping to draw the queen into some incautious remark about events in Gore. Guinevere smiled sweetly and offered nothing of consequence.

One knight was provoked into incautious exasperation as he walked away. "I know Arthur married her for her beauty not her brains, but can she really be so dull-witted?"

Nimue was tempted to trip the arrogant noble into a pile of dung left by some knight's steed. Before she allowed herself that satisfaction, a howl rose from the crowd in the meadow watching the day's early jousts.

Guinevere looked at her, alarmed. "Something's wrong."

Nimue agreed. That wasn't the typical cheer when a knight unhorsed his opponent, or the groan of commiseration when a rider took a heavy fall. She heard outrage as well as visceral fear, and the uproar wasn't subsiding.

The two women plucked up the hems of their skirts and hurried out over the drawbridge. Beyond the moat, in the meadow, the crowd parted to let two armoured men run towards the castle. Sir Aglovale and Sir Lamorak were both bareheaded. Aglovale was furious. Lamorak was distraught.

They ran towards the queen. No, Nimue realised her mistake. They were looking at her.

"Mistress," Lamorak gasped. "We need a healer."

"With your permission, your grace," Aglovale growled.

"Of course." Guinevere assured him.

Nimue looked at the knights. "Who's hurt?"

"Our father." Lamorak choked on his fear.

"Sir Pellinore?" Guinevere was already hurrying towards the lists. "Has he suffered some seizure?"

The knights didn't hear her, already running back to their father. As Nimue and Guinevere followed, men and women doffed their caps or curtsied to their queen. The commotion subsided to ominous murmurs threaded through with apprehension as the crowd parted.

"Sir Pellinore was jousting?" Guinevere stared at the meadow in disbelief.

A knight in full armour lay flat on his back, unmoving. A lance with the blue and yellow pennant of Lystenois was discarded on the turf. Beside the groom holding Sir Pellinore's horse, Sir Percival clutched his father's shield. Lamorak offered his younger brother a reassuring hand. Percival flinched and turned away.

Sir Aglovale dropped to his knees by their father. He reached for the fallen knight's helmet.

"No!" Nimue shouted. "Leave that alone!"

She ran forward and seized Aglovale's shoulder, dragging him away. She didn't care if her unexpected strength startled the knight. If Sir Pellinore was to survive, the greatest care must be taken. If he wasn't already dead.

As Aglovale retreated to join his brothers, Nimue knelt by the motionless knight. She found the catch to unfasten his helmet's visor and raised the pierced metal as gently as she could. Sir Pellinore's faded eyes were wide open, unseeing in his wrinkled face. Someone stifled a sob behind her as she held her open palm over his mouth and nose. She couldn't feel the faintest hint of breath.

Nimue felt for the beat of Pellinore's heart in the side of his neck. No blood moved beneath her fingertips. More than that, as her senses reached deeper, she realised his neck was broken. The bones where his spine met his skull had been ripped apart. No flicker of life remained.

She looked up at Sir Aglovale. "Your father is dead, my lord. He will barely have known what happened and I promise you he felt no pain."

"I will kill him." Aglovale stormed away with his sword already half-drawn.

Lamorak stepped into his path, seizing his brother's shoulders. "You cannot–"

"I will!" Aglovale yelled.

Nimue got to her feet and looked down the lists to the far end of the meadow. Another trio of knights clustered around a fourth mounted on an unperturbed horse. Her heart sank as she recognised Orkney's double-headed eagle. The variations on their shields identified all four of Morgause's sons.

"Who did Sir Pellinore meet in the joust?" Guinevere asked with trepidation.

"Sir Gawain." Now that Sir Percival's worst fears were realised, he was oddly calm. "His lance struck first, and it struck hard, but not true. The end slipped upwards to hit my father under his chin."

That might have been enough to break Pellinore's neck, Nimue judged, or the fall might have done the damage. Not that it mattered.

"He did that deliberately!" Aglovale was trying to evade his brother. "He murdered our father."

"You cannot say that for certain." Lamorak forced him back with a mailed hand.

Aglovale wasn't listening. "I will have our revenge!"

"You will not!" Arthur's shout silenced them both.

Nimue hadn't seen the king come down from the platform. She hadn't even noticed him up in the seats of honour.

"See to your ladies," Arthur snapped at Guinevere.

Nimue saw the girls were split into two factions. Elaine of Lystenois was surrounded by her friends. Linet stood with a handful of others, clutching a scarf dyed with Orkney's purple. Guinevere hesitated.

"Go!" Arthur could barely keep his temper in check.

White-faced, Guinevere walked quickly away.

The king rounded on the hapless groom holding Sir Pellinore's horse. "Fetch men and have him carried to the chapel. He is to be laid with all honour before the altar."

As the lad scurried off, Nimue hoped he had the wits to summon older women from the kitchens to take care of more mundane and disagreeable necessities.

Arthur glared at Sir Pellinore's sons. "Wait in the chapel until I send for you."

He didn't move until they obeyed him. Percival wiped tears

from his eyes as he stumbled away, still clutching his father's shield. Lamorak was watching Aglovale warily. For a moment, Nimue thought Pellinore's heir was going to defy Arthur. Then Aglovale ducked his head and walked towards the castle. Lamorak followed his brothers.

Nimue would have gone after them, but Arthur shot her a piercing look. "Come with me."

He strode across the meadow, and she dutifully walked a few paces behind. The hum of speculation in the crowd grew louder.

Sir Gawain dismounted as Arthur approached. Looking more like his father than ever, his expression gave nothing away. Sir Agravaine's face was defiant, verging on triumphant. In sharp contrast, Sir Gareth and Sir Gaheris were openly distressed.

Gawain dropped to one knee. "Forgive me for my part in this tragedy, my liege."

Arthur glared at Agravaine. "Wipe that smirk off your face or I will do it with the back of my hand."

Taken aback, Agravaine hastily knelt beside his brother. "Forgive me, your grace."

Unsure what else to do, Gareth and Gaheris took a knee too. Nimue caught the dubious glance the younger brothers shared. She was sure Arthur saw it as well.

The king's lips were pressed tight together, and Nimue wondered what he might have said if so many onlookers hadn't been present.

He dismissed the princes of Orkney. "Go and wait in my hall."

"Of course, my liege." Gawain rose and bowed before he led his brothers away. The other three bowed as well, though Nimue saw Agravaine gloating when he thought no one else could see.

Arthur was looking around for the castle's stewards. One ran up, summoned by the king's gesture.

"The tournament is over." Arthur might have said more, but commotion erupted in the seats of honour.

Elaine of Lystenois rushed at Linet with her fingers hooked like claws. Incoherent with tears, she screamed some accusation. Linet shrieked, protesting, stumbling backwards. Her few friends rallied around her, aghast. Elaine's supporters tried to hold her back. Guinevere stepped between the girls, raising her hands. Nimue took a step, ready to go and help.

"No. You're with me." Arthur walked away.

Nimue looked at the queen. Guinevere turned her head as she spoke to one group and then to the other. Elaine had collapsed, sobbing as her kneeling friends hugged her. Linet was still on her feet, though she swayed like a tree in a gale with her face buried in her hands.

Trumpets sounded in every direction as Camelot's stewards relayed the king's command to abandon the tourney. The crowd's tone turned to barely veiled dissatisfaction. They had no idea why their entertainment had ended so suddenly. Commoners drifted away towards the village while noble guests made their way back to the castle. Knights who were Sir Aglovale's friends stood vigil near Sir Pellinore's body, waiting for the servants to carry the corpse to the chapel. Nimue saw Sir Lancelot deep in conversation with Sir Kay. Grave concern furrowed their brows.

Arthur left the meadow, ignoring the clamour of questions as no one dared address him directly. Nimue hurried to catch up. The king ignored everyone as he entered the castle yard and climbed the keep's steps to the great hall. Sir Gareth and Sir Gaheris were sitting on a bench beside a lower table. Gawain was in the middle of the aisle with his back to the door. He was facing Agravaine, who stood behind his customary chair at the round table, ready to pull it out and take his seat.

"I don't see why–" Agravaine said, belligerent.

Whatever he saw in Arthur's face gave him his answer. He hastily joined his younger brothers. Gawain did the same.

Arthur walked past the four of them. He rested his hands on the round table, looking straight ahead. Nimue wondered if Arthur was regretting doing away with the hall's dais and his throne. A confrontation like this would be easier from an undisputed position of authority.

The king turned and Sir Gawain sprang to his feet. "My liege, I–"

"Why did you joust with Sir Pellinore?"

Agravaine answered. "He challenged–"

"Silence," hissed Arthur.

Gawain gave his brother a searing look before he answered the king. "Forgive me, your grace. Sir Pellinore challenged me. I would never go against your wishes and face Sir Aglovale or Sir Lamorak in the lists, but I did not think I was forbidden to meet their father."

"Really?" Arthur's sarcasm rang to the rafters.

Sir Gawain reddened, but he met the king's gaze. "I swear it."

"They said–" Agravaine began.

"Leave. One more word and I will have you whipped." Arthur didn't even look at Agravaine as he glared at Gareth and Gaheris. "What have you two got to say for yourselves?"

The younger knights stood up as Agravaine thought better of arguing and walked towards the door.

Gaheris answered the king. "Sir Lamorak and Sir Aglovale often boast of their father's skill at arms, knowing we will hear them. They tell their friends of the battle where he killed our father, when they know that reminds us of our greatest grief. We have heard different stories of that day and we have shared them from time to time, to honour our father's memory. Sir Pellinore must have heard such talk."

Sir Gareth spoke up. "Sir Pellinore issued the challenge, I swear it, your grace. He boasted he could easily defeat Gawain. He said he would prove he was a better man than our father had ever been. He – he dishonoured our father's memory with foul insults."

Arthur raised a hand before Gareth shared whatever Pellinore had said. He looked hard at Gawain. "Where is the honour for you in defeating an old man? Did you not think how easily he might be injured?"

"He challenged me. If I refused to meet him, I would be dishonoured." Gawain was unrepentant. "He chose to risk life and limb. We all take our chances in a tourney, whatever our age."

Arthur could hardly deny it. He shook his head even so. "Go to your quarters and stay there till I send for you."

He walked out of the hall. Nimue followed a pace behind. She still wasn't sure what the king wanted from her, but she wasn't going to risk his wrath.

Arthur headed for the chapel. "Were they telling the truth? What does your sorcery tell you?"

Thankfully everyone was keeping their distance, so there was no danger of them being overheard.

"They spoke honestly, though I doubt that was the whole truth."

"You doubt? You don't know?" Arthur glanced at her, dissatisfied.

"I cannot see into unspoken thoughts. No magic can."

Arthur grunted. They reached the chapel tower and climbed the short stair to the gloomy vaulted room. The jewel colours that stained the window glass behind the altar muted the daylight and none of the usual candles were lit.

Nimue was relieved to see a handful of women washing Sir Pellinore's corpse, laid out on a bier. The crucified god's priest was muttering and bowing with a silver vial in one hand. Intent on whatever he was doing, he didn't notice the neat stack of armour. He knocked something with his foot and metal clattered across the stone floor. The dead knight's sons winced, standing by the door with their heads bowed.

Arthur paused in the doorway and took in the scene. Nimue wasn't sure how far the king could understand the bereaved men's grief. He had never known Uther, and Sir Ector who had raised him was still hale and hearty. How much had he lamented Merlin's loss, she wondered suddenly.

"Your grace." Sir Aglovale's rage had subsided. Now he simply looked sad.

"Did your father challenge Sir Gawain to the joust?" Arthur asked.

Sir Lamorak answered for his elder brother. "He did, but he was sorely provoked."

"The princes of Orkney always deny he killed their father in a fair fight." Sir Percival swallowed fresh tears. "Ever since Father arrived for the tourney, we heard their insulting whispers night and day."

"Father could not let such accusations go unanswered," Aglovale insisted. "Not without being dishonoured."

Lamorak's temper flared. "Gawain is your heir, but he talks as if he already wears a crown."

Arthur's face hardened, but he ignored that, still addressing Aglovale, Sir Pellinore's heir. "Do you want your father buried here, or will you lay him to rest in Lystenois?"

Aglovale answered for the three of them before Lamorak could say something else unwise. "We will take him home."

"Father Thomas will arrange whatever you need." The king left the chapel. As they went down the stairs and reached the castle yard, he looked at Nimue. "Well?"

"They are telling the truth as they see it–"

"But not the whole truth." Arthur shook his head, frustrated. "What use is your magic to me? You had no idea of Morgana's treachery in Gore, and now you can't unravel this tangle."

He didn't expect an answer, so Nimue followed him wordlessly back to the keep. All the same, she knew what she wanted to say.

Perhaps if Arthur had asked Morgana before he handed her over to Urien of Gore, that calamity might have been avoided. If he had asked older, wiser knights for their advice, he might have seen the need to mediate between Pellinore's sons and the princes of Orkney. If he hadn't taught those who sat at his round table to prize their personal honour above all else, his chosen companions might not be so quick to take deadly offence.

But Arthur took no one's advice, not since Merlin had vanished. Nimue realised she had deprived him of more than the wizard's enchantments to bolster his rule. Merlin had been the one person who could make Arthur listen. Perhaps if the wizard had been here these past ten years, the tensions between Gawain and Aglovale would have been addressed instead of being ignored.

Use your magic sparingly, and always with caution. You can never know what consequences could follow.

Arthur headed for his library behind the great hall. Guinevere was waiting. She rose from her seat at the reading desk.

"Your grace. I have spoken with my ladies. Faults on both sides led to today's tragedy. You wished to honour Orkney's princes, to show the lords of Logres that you don't believe Gawain or his brothers had any part in Morgana's treachery, but Sir Pellinore's sons have always resented seeing them shown any favour. They murmured to their friends that perhaps their loyalty wasn't so certain. Lot of Orkney rebelled against you, and Morgana had always been close to his sons. Gawain and his brothers sought some way to retaliate. They have always wanted to make Sir Pellinore pay some price for cutting down their father in battle–"

Arthur pounded the table with his fists. "What makes you think I want to hear pointless gossip from stupid girls?"

Guinevere paled. "Your grace–"

A knock on the door interrupted her.

"Enter!" Arthur barked.

The door swung open. Sir Lancelot and Sir Kay stood on the threshold.

Arthur beckoned them in before turning to Guinevere.

"See to our guests, your grace. Everyone will need food and wine."

He might have been dismissing a servant. Nimue saw Sir Lancelot's hastily concealed surprise at seeing the queen treated so discourteously.

Guinevere's cheekbones reddened with humiliation. "Of course, your grace."

She walked to the door and Nimue followed just as swiftly. She was ready to defy Arthur if he called her back, but he was already deep in conversation with Lancelot and Kay.

"Who is backing Gawain, and who is on Aglovale's side?"

Nimue hurried after the queen as Guinevere went up the stairs to her chamber.

"Your grace?"

Guinevere sat down at the writing table set near the window to catch the light. "Tell the kitchens to serve the refreshments intended for the tournament in the great hall instead. Make sure our guests are informed. The cooks can go ahead with the plans for the feast tonight, though the minstrels must be told to play sombre tunes out of respect for Sir Pellinore."

She opened the box that held pens, ink, and neatly trimmed sheets of vellum. "Find a messenger to carry a letter to my father, to tell him to expect me. Pack everything I will need for a week's visit, perhaps longer."

"Your grace?" Nimue hadn't expected this.

Guinevere looked at her, resolute. "We were supposed to visit my father after we left Gore, but Arthur came back here instead. My father didn't deserve such discourtesy. More than that, as Urien's nearest neighbour, he should hear the truth from me instead of wild rumours on the wind. He should hear what really happened here today. If the king wants his nobles reassured, who better to do that than my father?"

Clearly, these were the arguments she intended to use if Arthur objected to her plan.

Nimue curtseyed. "By all means, your grace."

As she headed down the great stair, she wondered if Arthur would be convinced. Then she wondered something else. If the queen left Camelot like this, how long might Guinevere stay away?

CHAPTER TWENTY-EIGHT

Arthur's price for allowing Guinevere to visit Leodegrance was Nimue staying behind. She wondered how much he truly wanted her at Camelot, in case he needed to call on her magic. How much was he punishing the queen for leaving his side by depriving her of her trusted attendant?

Perhaps she was being unfair. Nimue wondered, as she crossed the castle yard to what had once been Morgana's tower. She couldn't decide, so she focused on more immediate concerns. The sun was rising, and it wouldn't be long before the king demanded her presence, but Nimue started each day making sure the queen was safe. All being well, Guinevere should reach Leodegrance's castle before dusk tonight.

Her departure had given Camelot's rumour-mongers fresh meat to chew on, as the prospect of open strife between the princes of Orkney and Sir Aglovale and his brothers faded. Arthur had Sir Lancelot to thank for averting that disaster, together with Sir Kay. Both knights convinced the nobles supporting the rival factions to keep the peace in the aftermath of the ruined tournament. Gawain had seen the sense of not celebrating his victory, and he, Gareth and Gaheris had convinced Agravaine to keep his mouth shut until the Lystenois knights left to escort their father's body home.

Their sister Elaine had gone with them. That made Nimue's life easier as she supervised the queen's ladies. Guinevere had refused to have any of them accompany her, prompting agitation that still hadn't subsided. The girls asked Nimue every day how they could possibly have offended the queen. Nimue suggested that Guinevere might wish for silence and solitude after so many recent shocking events. The girls didn't bother lowering their voices as they shared their disdain for that suggestion. What could a servant know of a noblewoman's finer feelings?

Nimue wasn't offended. As they devoted their days to their needlework in order to gossip undisturbed, she was pleased to see these girls had no idea an enchantress was sitting beside them. She was discreetly amused to hear them discuss the rumours of Morgana's magical powers. According to their chatter, at least half these noble young ladies had seen something to arouse their suspicions, though naturally they hadn't spoken of it. Nimue didn't believe a word.

She opened the door to the spiral stair and wondered when Arthur would turn his attention to this tower. She couldn't imagine Urien of Gore or his son would visit Camelot any time soon. At least her magic had been of use to Arthur there. Her scrying had reassured him that the petty king was fully recovered from whatever enchantment Morgana had used to strike him down.

Arthur would most likely ignore this tower until he was forced to make some decision. Until then, she would make good use of Morgana's workroom. Her old silver scrying bowl was on the table. Water filled it as she walked over. Nimue gestured at the jar of ink and a drop spread across the water's surface. Her spell strengthened and Nimue saw the queen's carriage by the side of the road.

Her shock shivered through the spell, twisting and distorting the vision. Nimue forced herself to concentrate and the picture became clearer, though no less ominous. Guinevere's carriage was toppled on its side. Drag marks cut across the ruts in the road where her chests of belongings had been hauled away. There was no sign of the harness horses, living or dead, but the men-at-arms who should have guarded the queen had been murdered. They sprawled on the blood-stained earth. A raven perched on one, digging out his eyeballs with beak and claw. Another had been mauled by wolves.

Where was Guinevere? Nimue tried to release the spell to send her magic searching for the queen, but this unexpected horror had too strong a hold on her. Then the awful vision vanished and a face appeared in the water. Nimue clasped the sides of the bowl and stared.

Morgana? She hadn't even tried to find her since she fled from Gore. She wanted to be able to tell the king truthfully that she had no idea where his sister might be. Besides, Nimue had assumed Morgana would hide herself as thoroughly as she had done before.

A faint, sweet chime rang through the room. Startled, Nimue looked around for the source of this new enchantment. Golden light shimmered in a dark corner as if a shaft of sunlight had struck the small bronze bell hanging from a hook on a fine chain. Nimue realised Morgana had fetched more than the scrying bowl from Tintagel, as the younger enchantress's voice floated through the air.

"Sir Meliagant has seized the queen and he is carrying her off to his castle. He is son to Sir Bagdemagus who was banished from Camelot several years ago. I have no idea what revenge he plans to take, so you must act fast. I will watch over Guinevere, but I cannot do more than that. Arthur must send men to reclaim her, as soon as he can."

Even through the spell, Nimue could hear Morgana's agitation.

"Why have you been scrying for the queen?" Her question went unanswered. The glow in the corner of the room faded and the scrying bowl held nothing more than water.

Nimue reached for the tattered quill stuck in the jar of ink. But if she scryed for Guinevere, there was no telling what she might learn. Some things might be better left unseen, for the moment at least. She drew her hand back and stepped through the shadows instead, to stand at Arthur's bedside.

As always, he slept alone. Nimue looked down at the king. Deeply asleep in a tangle of blankets, he looked much more like the unsure youth she had met in Westminster, before he pulled that first enchanted sword from the block of marble. Did he ever wish he had left that blade alone? That's what he had said he wished for, all those years ago. But that was then, and this was now, and Guinevere was in danger.

"Your grace, wake up."

Arthur's eyes opened instantly. "What is it?"

"The queen has been abducted by Sir Meliagant."

Arthur was already pulling the shirt he had slept in off over his head. "Meliagant? What does he want?"

"I have no way to know."

Arthur tossed the bundled linen to the floor. "How do you know this has happened?"

"I may not be at the queen's side, but I can still watch over her." Nimue tried not to make this a rebuke.

Arthur had other concerns as he got out of bed. "When did this happen?"

Nimue pictured the dreadful scene. Wolves would have waited for cover of darkness before they approached the bodies. "By my best guess, last night at dusk. Though I did not know until this morning."

"Has she been violated?" Arthur asked distantly.

"I have seen nothing to say so," Nimue replied firmly, fervently hoping that was the truth.

The king took a fresh shirt from the linen press, looking thoughtful. "Sir Meliagant, you say?"

"I believe so." She really hoped Morgana was right. "Why was his father banished from Camelot?"

"Who told you that?" Arthur scowled. "Sir Bagdemagus left of his own accord. He declared to anyone who would listen that he had been intolerably insulted when he was passed over for a seat at the round table." He got dressed. "Can his son possibly imagine I will trade that honour for the queen's safe return?"

Nimue was relieved to see Arthur was thinking out loud rather than asking her a question. If she answered, she would have to ask the king if he was willing to offer such a deal.

"You must send a trusted messenger, someone you trust to be discreet, as soon as possible. Once we know what Sir Meliagant hopes to gain, we can convince him of his error."

"Must I? No, I will wait for Meliagant to send word, or Bagdemagus, if he has the audacity to be part of this." Arthur's contempt promised nothing good for father or son.

"Your grace?" Nimue protested. "The queen will be terrified."

"There's nothing I can do about that." Arthur looked momentarily shame-faced. "There is more at stake here. We must consider how this will look to the lords of Logres."

"Your grace?" Nimue hid clenched fists in the folds of her skirts.

"You say she was taken last night? She has been at Meliagant's mercy ever since. Who can say what has happened?"

Arthur's tone made Nimue uneasy. "He would be a fool to lay lustful hands on her, your grace. He must know that would mean his death, rather than whatever he hopes to win from you."

Arthur folded his arms. "The king's wife must be above suspicion."

"That's all the more reason why she must be rescued quickly and discreetly," Nimue retorted. "Your grace, this is none of her doing."

Arthur scowled, stubborn. Nimue stared at him, appalled.

"You think this will give you an excuse to set her aside. What will you do with your loyal, blameless wife? Send her to a nunnery?"

Arthur reddened. "You don't think my most loyal knights have suggested I do exactly that, more than once? As every season passes without her giving me an heir to continue my line?"

Furious, Nimue stormed out of the bedchamber. The king

called her back, irate. She ignored him, waving a hand to slam his door with a resounding crash. She left the keep and headed for Morgana's tower, for the scrying bowl. Once she knew where Guinevere was being held, she would devise some plan–

"Mistress? What's wrong?" Out in the castle yard, Sir Lancelot stepped into her path, clearly concerned by whatever he saw in her face.

Nimue hadn't even seen him approaching. "The queen has been abducted." The words were out before she could stop herself.

"Abducted?" Lancelot looked over her head at the keep. "What does the king command?"

"He needs her rescued, at once and discreetly. Will you do this for him?"

Lancelot stopping her had broken her furious chain of thought and given Nimue a moment to think. If she rescued the queen by means of her magic, she would have a lot of explaining to do, to Guinevere most of all. If Camelot's most eminent knight returned with the queen, that would merely be another triumph of his skill at arms.

"Me?" Though Lancelot clearly didn't doubt he could succeed. "Of course. Where has she been taken?"

"A knight called Sir Meliagant has her. Do you know where to find his manor?" Nimue had to hope it wasn't too far.

To her relief, Lancelot was nodding. "I will rouse Sir–"

"No," Nimue said quickly. "We must go alone, just you and I. We must leave at once and travel light. The king commands it."

She heard the sour note of that falsehood in her voice, but the handsome knight was frowning over something else.

"You are coming with me?"

"I am the queen's personal attendant. She cannot travel unescorted." She sent him on his way with a shove. "Get your horse and your gear. Remember, tell no one about this. I will meet you outside the gatehouse."

Thankfully Lancelot was used to travelling light, or at least he had been in his wandering days. Nimue wanted him on his horse and out of the castle before anyone questioned what they were doing. Before Lancelot asked her anything awkward, come to that.

She hurried back to the keep to pack the few things she might need. Her heart raced as she found riding boots and a cloak thick enough to do double duty as a blanket. She expected Arthur to appear at any moment. The king's door was still closed when she reached her bedchamber, but that was no guarantee of anything. She decided not to risk the stairs a second time and stepped through the shadows to a dark corner of the stables. Her arrival startled the closest horses, but as a stable-boy came to see what was amiss, she was saddling the palfrey she rode most often.

"Fetch me a bag of fodder for a short journey," she ordered before the boy could speak.

He was too lowly to now think of challenging his elders, so he did as he was told. Nimue was soon mounted and riding for the gatehouse. The few people in the castle yard paid her no attention. They were looking at Sir Lancelot, cloaked and up on his horse with his red-banded shield slung across his back. He was talking to the sergeant-at-arms in charge of the gate.

As Nimue approached, the sergeant nodded. At his signal, the gate opened, and the drawbridge lowered with a rattle of chains. Naturally. No one would question noble Sir Lancelot when he said he must leave the castle on urgent business. Nimue urged her horse on with a kick and followed the knight out of Camelot and across the moat.

CHAPTER TWENTY-NINE

Sir Meliagant's modest fiefdom was several days' ride away. Nimue and Sir Lancelot travelled without talking, unless brief conversation was necessary. As they drew closer, Lancelot asked what might lie ahead. Evidently, he thought Nimue knew what they would find, that one of the queen's retinue had escaped the attack and brought this dire news to Camelot.

Nimue didn't correct his assumptions. By then she had seized every opportunity to scry for Guinevere in the small silver platter she carried, after Lancelot had fallen asleep, or when she was supposedly finding a place to piss in the morning. To her profound relief, the queen still seemed unharmed. Guinevere was evidently treated with respect by the old woman who brought her food, though Nimue could see she was wretchedly unhappy. She had no way to hear what Sir Meliagant hoped to gain though. Nimue simply saw him pacing to and fro, waving his hands as he harangued the queen.

"So, there are only two ways in and out?" Sir Lancelot asked again. "The main entrance and this narrow gate tucked away beside the barn?"

They were within half a morning's ride, sheltering in a hazel thicket. Lancelot had woken her at first light. They were eating the cold remains of the rabbits he had snared while Nimue foraged for greens when they halted the day before.

Lancelot had used the charcoaled ends of half-burnt sticks to draw an outline of Meliagant's castle on the bare earth. The dwelling barely deserved the name. A wall of roughly dressed

stone joined a gatehouse of timber and brick to a modest
thatched hall. A stable, a tithe barn and a kitchen had been
built within the irregular enclosure. That didn't mean rescuing
Guinevere would be easy.

"That's right." Nimue tossed a rabbit bone into the dew-
soaked ashes of their fire.

Lancelot stared at the black lines and the fragments of bark
he had used to signify buildings. "The queen must be in the
hall."

"She must be." Nimue's scrying had invariably shown
Guinevere in an upper room with moth-eaten tapestries and a
bed stripped of its curtains.

"Meliagant will have perhaps a dozen men-at-arms to call
on," Lancelot mused. "Men who have only done their lord's
bidding. I have no wish to kill them for his crime. Besides, the
more of them I fight, the greater the risk that one lands a lucky
blow. If I'm wounded, this rescue is over."

"What are you going to do?" Nimue wondered if she was
going to have to use her magic to defend him.

"I'll challenge Meliagant to single combat." The knight
gestured towards the neat stack of armour topped with his
breastplate and helmet. Nimue had become used to helping
him don the array each morning. "He can't refuse me without
dishonour that will follow him for the rest of his life."

"Of course." Nimue wondered how many men had gone
to their deaths for the sake of honour. Though she would use
a little magic to secure Lancelot's victory if necessary. He was
far more skilled than Meliagant, but as he said, the other man
might get in a lucky strike.

The knight walked over to his hobbled horse. The peacefully
grazing animals raised their heads, ears pricked. Lancelot
looked towards the road and Nimue heard a laden cart's
trundling wheels.

"Wait here." Lancelot hurried towards the highway.

Nimue waited until he vanished from sight, then followed,

veiled with a brief enchantment. Lancelot had halted a cart piled high with firewood and drawn by a rough-coated horse. He was deep in conversation with the carter. Before Nimue could summon a spell to hear what they were saying, Lancelot smiled, charming, and shook the man's hand. He headed back to the hazel thicket at a jog, and Nimue barely had time to return the remains of the fire.

Lancelot went over to his armour and unrolled his chain mail hauberk. Threading his hands through the sleeves, he held the weight on his forearms for a moment before ducking his head as he lifted the hauberk high. The mail slithered down his body, over his long, padded tunic. After a swift shake of his shoulders to settle the links, he picked up his sword, belted it tight and found his purse in the bag tied to his saddle. "That cart of firewood is going to Meliagant's castle, and the carter will let me hide under his load for a handful of silver. Once I'm inside the walls, I can go straight to the hall and find the queen. If Meliagant is with her, he can fight me and die, or he can surrender with no one to see it and call him a coward. We may even be able to leave through that sally gate before anyone else realises what's happening."

"You're only taking your sword?"

Lancelot saw Nimue's astonishment and grinned.

"I can hardly climb in and out of a wood cart unseen wearing a full suit of armour. I'll fight and win when I have to, but if I can rescue her grace without bloodshed, so much the better for everyone."

"Indeed." This was far better than Nimue could have hoped for.

"Can you manage both horses and follow some distance behind the cart?" Lancelot carried his saddle and bridle over to his horse. "The carter tells me there's a lightning-struck oak at a crossroads not far from the castle. We'll come and find you there."

He had no doubt that he would succeed. That suited Nimue.

This plan would make it far easier for her to use enchantments without the knight or the queen noticing something uncanny.

"I'll find it." She saddled her own horse. "Go on, before the carter changes his mind."

Lancelot headed for the road. Nimue gathered up his armour. Strapping the shield to the saddle was simple enough. Securing everything else between breastplate and backplate was another matter entirely. There were sabatons for the knight's feet, greaves for his shins, cuisses to protect his thighs, and the flexible tassets that covered the gap between those and the bottom edge of his breast plate. Nimue tucked Lancelot's gauntlets inside his helmet, along with the gorget that protected his throat. Pauldrons protected his shoulders with rerebraces and vambraces for his arms, and the smaller pieces for elbows and knees that she could never remember the names of. She still found it remarkable that a man could move, much less fight in such encumbrance, but assisting Lancelot on this trip had shown her how the weight of well-fitted armour was shared between a warrior's shoulders and hips.

Thankfully Lancelot's steed was a placid beast, well used to the clatter and sheen of so much expertly crafted steel. It waited content until Nimue mounted her own horse and led it to the road with a halter rope. She kept the cart within sight until she reached the crossroads with the stricken oak. Close by, a stretch of grass ran down to a small stream in a gully. Nimue left the horses surrounded by an enchantment to stop them from wandering, unlikely as that was with fodder and water within easy reach. More importantly, the spell would also hide the valuable animals from anyone passing by.

She veiled herself with magic and followed the road to Meliagant's castle. Every stride she took covered a bow shot's distance. The trees and bushes alongside the road blurred into a shapeless mess at the edge of her vision. What had been a mild breeze became a vicious wind cutting right through her. Nimue gritted her teeth and ignored the discomfort. She need not endure it for long and she could endure it for Guinevere's sake. As soon as she caught up with the cart, she was able walk unseen behind the stack of split branches at a normal pace. She looked, but she couldn't see any sign of Lancelot beneath the firewood.

The woodcutter was evidently known to Sir Meliagant's guards, who ushered the cart through the gatehouse. Nimue didn't follow. She took a step that carried her to the top of the castle wall. There was no walkway for sentries and now she saw the renegade knight's residence was even shabbier in reality. Old cracks gaped in the plaster covering the kitchen and the stable doors were raggedly rat-gnawed.

Instead of some watchful cohort of men-at-arms, she saw a trio of servants in tattered tunics, too old or too young to be labouring in their liege lord's fields. Shovelling dung and hauling water from the well, they ignored the wood cart as the sturdy horse plodded around to the back of the kitchen. Nimue had been wondering how Lancelot expected to get out of the cart unseen. The woodcutter must have said where he would dump his load.

She resisted the temptation to go closer, to see what the knight was doing. Up here on the wall, she could keep watch on the gatehouse and the hall. If Sir Meliagant appeared, she would find some way to hinder him.

The thuds as the firewood was thrown into a heap slowed and stopped. A few moments later, the wood cart headed back to the gate and departed. A little while longer, and Sir Lancelot appeared at the corner of the kitchen. One of the dung shovellers saw him and gaped like a simpleton. Lancelot didn't challenge the old man, but his meaning was clear as he laid his hand on the sword at his hip.

The greybeard hadn't grown old by being foolish. He dropped his dung fork and raised his hands. The gangly boy at his side did the same, eyes huge in his thin face. Lancelot nodded approval and ran for the steps up to the raggedly thatched hall's arched door.

Nimue frowned. As soon as the knight disappeared, the dung shoveller and his apprentice hurried to the well. The woman hauling buckets of water had been winding the handle with her back turned. The dung shovellers told her what had happened. Nimue didn't need to use magic to hear what they said. The woman gestured, agitated, as they tried to decide what to do.

The boy was running for the gatehouse when Lancelot appeared at the hall door, leading Guinevere by the hand. The queen's gown was creased, and her face was drawn, but she moved without stiffness or hesitation that might suggest she had been abused. Lancelot's sword was drawn, though Nimue couldn't see blood on the blade. Had Meliagant surrendered, or had Lancelot found Guinevere alone?

Questions would have to wait. They still had to get out of the castle. The old man and the woman stood motionless by the well. Lancelot barely spared them a glance. He had heard the gatehouse door open. A handful of men emerged from the brick and timber archway, wearing chain mail and gripping swords. Even so, they didn't look eager to attack this tall stranger with his gleaming blade.

Lancelot came slowly down the steps, keeping Guinevere behind him. Nimue saw him speaking to her. Guinevere glanced over her shoulder and nodded. Lancelot must be telling her to head for the narrow gate behind the tithe barn.

They reached the bottom of the steps. Sir Meliagant's men advanced slowly, brandishing their blades and shouting threats. Their master must not be here, Nimue decided, to goad them into risking injury or death. As long as they agreed on their story before he returned, who could deny they had yielded in the face of overwhelming force?

Guinevere was hurrying towards the narrow gate, looking in all directions for anything unexpected. Lancelot followed, walking backwards to watch the men advancing across the muddy, rutted yard. The trio of servants retreated to the other side of the well.

The queen reached the narrow gate. As she laid a hand on its heavy iron ring, Nimue focused every magical sense she possessed upon the lock. The metal itself would resist her enchantments, and she had no time to bend that to her will, but the old, weathered wood of the frame was hers to command. Unseen, the socket holding the bolt secure crumbled As Guinevere twisted the handle, the spar holding the hinges splintered. The whole gate sagged.

Guinevere threw her weight against it. The gate swung open so easily she nearly fell through the narrow arch to tumble down the steep bank outside. Her yelp of surprise startled Sir Lancelot. He glanced over his shoulder. Seeing the gate was open, he ran after her.

The men-at-arms found some scrap of courage. They broke into a run. Nimue was ready. Three men staggered as snaking ruts tripped them and sudden slick mud betrayed the other two. By the time they scrambled up, Lancelot and Guinevere were through the gate. Lancelot shoved the sagging wood backwards, though he didn't pause to try and secure it. His aim was escape.

No matter. Nimue wove the splintered wood back together to secure the hinges. She reminded the old, dry timber that it had once been green and flexible, vigorous as it grew in a forest. She drew moisture up from the earth to bolster the memory of the tree these chiselled lengths had once been. On the other side of the gate, the wood above and below the wobbling lock began to swell and shift, quickly restoring what she had destroyed. Within moments, the narrow gate was impassable. The first man to arrive rattled the ring with impotent rage. The last was sent running back to the gatehouse, presumably in search of the key.

Nimue stepped lightly down from the top of the wall and looked along the grassy bank outside the castle wall. Would Lancelot and Guinevere circle around this way? They might head right away from the castle. Lancelot knew to expect pursuit from the gatehouse, and he would assume those men were close behind them.

Enchantment carried her quickly back to the placidly grazing horses. Nimue dug the silver plate out of the pocket inside her cloak. She soon saw the knight was indeed taking a circuitous route back to the crossroads. She watched and waited, ready to repel any of Sir Meliagant's men heading this way. Nothing happened. Lancelot and Guinevere soon arrived. He was grinning from ear to ear at his triumph.

"Your grace!" Nimue ran to embrace the queen.

Guinevere managed a faint smile before she burst into tears. Lancelot hurried into the gully to tend to his horse.

Nimue held the queen tight until her sobs slowed. "Your grace, I must ask," she murmured for Guinevere's ears alone. "Are you hurt? Have you been mistreated?"

If so, she would make Sir Meliagant regret the day he had been born. But Guinevere shook her head. As Nimue released her, she wiped her face with a crumpled sleeve.

"He didn't lay a finger on me. Well, not beyond tying my hands and ankles once he had me on his horse."

"What happened?" Nimue handed her a linen kerchief.

"We met Sir Meliagant and his men on the road, quite by chance, I think. He seized his chance to appeal to me. He was certain I could persuade the king to recall his father to Camelot. He wanted an invitation to the king's tournaments for himself. I tried to tell him he was mistaken, that I have no say on such things, but he called me a liar."

The queen was growing angry. "He called me arrogant and selfish. He said I was condemning him and his father to poverty when they had done nothing to deserve such scorn. The captain of my escort warned him to mind his manners, and Sir Meliagant cut him down. It was over so fast. No one expected to be attacked." More tears threatened as she recalled those deaths, but Guinevere wiped her eyes. "He said if I refused to help him, he would use me to force Arthur to hear him."

"Where is he now?"

"The serving woman said he had been summoned to explain himself to his father. She said he was furious." The queen was torn between satisfaction at the thought of Meliagant facing Sir Bagdemagus's wrath and apprehension. Then a different thought struck her. "My father! What–?"

Nimue interrupted her. "We must get back to Camelot as soon as we can."

"I agree." Sir Lancelot approached, now that he saw Guinevere was no longer weeping.

"Mistress Nimue?" He gestured towards his armour. "Will you help me? It will make anyone tempted to delay us think twice."

They were soon on the road. Sir Lancelot led the way, armoured and with sword and shield ready. Guinevere rode pillion on the palfrey behind Nimue. Other travellers stepped aside to let them pass. Lancelot kept up the best pace that he could without tiring the horses, and they rode late into the twilight.

Nimue was growing impatient by the time the knight called a halt. She was weary to the bone after working so much magic, but she still needed to scry. She had to know if Meliagant had come home to find his captive fled. Was the renegade knight pursuing them? Sir Lancelot was only one man. They wouldn't be truly safe until they reached Camelot.

The knight found a sheltered hollow and unsaddled the horses. Nimue helped him out of his armour while Guinevere fetched water from a nearby stream. The queen had barely spoken all day. That suited Nimue. She was trying to work out how to explain herself, when Sir Lancelot learned he hadn't been sent on this quest by the king.

"What did Arthur say?" Guinevere asked suddenly when Nimue joined her at the stream. "When he got Sir Meliagant's message?"

Nimue had been dreading this question too. How could

she have known where the queen was being held before Meliagant's herald had even arrived? She hesitated.

"He didn't say anything, did he?" Guinevere studied Nimue's face. "He was going to wait to see if Meliagant would make good on his threats. Showing that the king will not be bullied was more important than whatever might happen to me."

Nimue didn't know what to say. She wondered what threats the renegade knight had made.

Guinevere watched Lancelot as he tethered the horses beneath a broad oak. "Why did he defy the king? He's one of Arthur's most loyal knights."

"Forgive me, your grace. I deceived him. He believes he rode out with Arthur's blessing."

Nimue waited, apprehensive, but the queen didn't say anything more. She walked over to sit and watch Sir Lancelot build a small fire inside a ring of stones. He struck a spark to light the tinder, as competent with flint and steel as he was with sword or lance.

He looked at the two women. "I can offer you biscuit and dried meat, my ladies."

"You can?" Nimue was astonished.

He grinned. "I never travel without some supplies. Our time was better spent on the road today instead of hunting for something to eat. It's meagre fare, but if we ride at first light and travel late, we should dine in Camelot tomorrow."

"Whatever you have to share will be most welcome," Guinevere said politely.

Lancelot fetched the food from his saddle bag. They shared water from the pewter flagon he had given Nimue on their first day. Lancelot had been well-equipped in his wandering days. After they had eaten, she picked up the empty flagon. "I'll refill this."

She left them sitting by the fire. Down by the stream, she worked her scrying swiftly. Following the highway back along their route, she saw no sign of pursuit.

Nimue sent her questing spell all the way to Sir Meliagant's castle and saw a great deal of activity. Torches burned in brackets on the gatehouse and far more horses than the rundown stables could accommodate were picketed in the castle yard. Servants came and went from the kitchen while the hall's long windows glowed with light.

Had Sir Bagdemagus come to beg the queen's forgiveness, to plead on bended knee for his foolish son's life? Or was Sir Meliagant desperately seeking some plan to get himself out of this mire? She decided it didn't matter. By the time Meliagant caught up with them, even if he set out at first light, she and Guinevere would be close enough to Camelot to ride on ahead while Sir Lancelot held the road behind them.

She went back to the fire and was surprised and relieved to see Guinevere smiling at something Sir Lancelot had said. The knight saw Nimue approaching and rose to his feet.

"You had better get what rest you can." He fetched his cloak for the queen. "This will soften the ground a little, your grace."

"Thank you." As she took it, she looked at him, uncertain. "But won't you be cold?"

He shook his head with that charming smile. "I'll keep watch and feed the fire. Don't worry. I can sleep when we're back at Camelot."

Relieved, Nimue rolled herself in her own cloak, and lay down on the other side of the fire from Guinevere. By now she could barely keep her eyes open. She drifted off to sleep, hearing Lancelot exchange a few words with the queen.

Some while later, much later, a different sound roused her from sleep as deep as dark water. By the time she realised Guinevere was crying, Lancelot was kneeling at the queen's side. Before Nimue could sit up, he had gathered Guinevere in his arms, whispering reassurance. Nimue closed her eyes. Seeing she was awake would only embarrass them both and add to the queen's distress.

Nimue fell asleep again. When she woke, the fire had died

to dull embers, but that didn't matter. She could see all too easily what was happening.

There was no way to know if Lancelot had offered the queen more than a comforting embrace, or if Guinevere had surprised the knight with an unexpected response to his kindness. Whoever had made the first move, they had both surrendered to passion. Neither spoke, only offering murmurs of encouragement. Beneath Lancelot's cloak, and under the cover of the velvet darkness, they were moving together in a rhythm as instinctive as it is unmistakable.

Nimue kept her eyes closed, and wished she could plug her ears, but someone needed to stay alert in case some night-time thief stumbled across them. Lancelot was in no position to defend anyone.

Soon, though not too soon, she heard the queen's stifled gasp of ecstasy swiftly followed by the knight's groan of release. A few moments later, Lancelot walked away into the night. Guinevere settled down to sleep wrapped in the warmth of his cloak.

Nimue was wide awake now. It seemed it wasn't only using magic that could lead to unexpected consequences.

CHAPTER THIRTY

They reached Camelot at dusk the following day. They had ridden as fast as they dared for as long as they could. Their valiant horses were tiring fast when the castle's towers appeared over the treetops.

Sir Lancelot allowed his mount to slow and the palfrey drew level. "I told you we would dine here tonight."

The knight had treated the queen with the same courtesy as always, when she and Nimue had woken just before dawn to see him saddling both horses. Nothing Lancelot had said or done gave the slightest indication that anything unforeseen had occurred.

"Let's see if the king has his usual appetite," Guinevere muttered as the weary horses walked on.

Nimue wasn't sure what she meant and decided not to ask. The queen had been preoccupied all day, and Nimue was hardly about to ask why. She had her own concerns. She was going to have to answer Arthur for her defiance now.

They approached the village outside the castle. A swineherd recognised Sir Lancelot with a shout. He sent his boy running for the nearest house. Faster than Nimue expected, a man on a plough horse was hurrying down the road.

"It seems we have a herald," Lancelot said drily.

When they reached the market place, villagers lined the road and greeted them with joyful commotion.

"Hurrah for Sir Lancelot!"

"God bless you, your grace!"

"Thank the Lord that you're safely returned to us!"

The palfrey was too tired to take kindly to such noise. Fortunately, it barely had the energy to shy sideways with a disapproving snort, so the queen wasn't dumped unceremoniously on the ground.

The villagers fell back as they reached the meadow. Ahead, Camelot's drawbridge was open and a dozen or more knights rode out. Sir Gawain led them with Sir Agravaine close behind. Gawain's face was hard to read, but Agravaine was scowling. Nimue reminded herself that Agravaine could always find something to displease him.

As they arrived, Gawain bowed to Guinevere from his saddle. "Your grace, thank God you're safe."

Guinevere cleared her throat. "Thanks to God, and to Sir Lancelot."

Her rescuer had ridden on ahead, laughing as the other knights congratulated him. He didn't look back. As they entered the castle yard, knights and ladies, maidservants and scullions cheered and applauded. Lancelot raised his gauntleted hand to acknowledge their praise as he rode towards the stables.

The palfrey wanted to follow its stable mate towards water and hay. Nimue sympathised, but turned the animal towards the keep. The king stood on the steps. He came down to meet them and the throng cheered when Arthur reached up and lifted Guinevere down from the horse.

Stiff and tired after the long day's ride, her knees buckled when her feet touched the ground. Arthur scooped her into his arms. Guinevere buried her face in his chest. As the king carried the queen up into the keep, Nimue saw women and men alike smiling fondly. Camelot still believed in Arthur and Guinevere's mutual devotion. Who would the people blame if that changed?

"Mistress Nimue?" Linet approached with the other noble young ladies.

"Send word to the kitchens for hot water so that her grace

may bathe," Nimue said briskly. "The queen needs quiet and rest tonight. She will see you in the morning."

She dismounted and handed the horse's reins to the closest man who might know where to find the stables. She was weary to the bone, but she couldn't let Guinevere face Arthur alone. She hurried after them. The great hall was deserted, so she headed up the staircase. As she reached the upper floor, she saw Guinevere's door was open. She went towards it, but Arthur's voice stopped her.

"Mistress Nimue, if you please."

The king stood in his doorway. He turned, expecting her to follow. Reluctantly, Nimue did so.

"Close the door." Arthur stood by the window, looking down. The crowd below were in no hurry to stop celebrating.

Nimue decided she had nothing to lose by speaking first. "What did you tell them?"

"That the queen had been abducted. That I had sent Sir Lancelot to rescue her. It was obvious what you had done, when I heard you had ridden out together." Arthur shot her a scathing look. "No one asked how I knew what had happened to the queen. I am the king, after all."

"Where is Sir Meliagant's messenger?"

"Chained in the dungeons below the gatehouse." Arthur glowered. "Now everyone has seen the queen is safe, he can take word of her return to his master. Along with news of my decree that Meliagant's lands are forfeit to the crown, and so is his life, to anyone who cares to take it."

Nimue wanted to ask why the king wasn't pursuing the man guilty of such a grievous offence against his queen. She wondered what Arthur would have done if Guinevere hadn't returned. Looking at the king's face, she doubted he knew the answer.

"May I go to the queen?"

"Was she – is she – unharmed?" demanded Arthur.

"Yes." Nimue was glad she could say that with certainty.

"I am thankful for it." Arthur managed a painful smile. "Whether or not you believe me."

"I believe you, your grace." Nimue curtseyed. "May I go to the queen?"

Arthur waved her away. Nimue crossed the landing to find Guinevere's chamber full of maidservants setting up her bath. The queen lay on her bed, still wearing her travel-stained clothes. Her eyes were closed, but Nimue didn't think she was asleep. As soon as the servants were done, Nimue shooed them away and took off the queen's shoes. Guinevere sat up and Nimue helped her undress. Neither of them spoke. As Guinevere sank into the steaming, herb-scented water, Nimue gathered up her discarded linen and gown.

"Burn everything," the queen said abruptly. "I never want to see that gown again."

"Yes, your grace." Nimue bundled up the clothes and headed for the door. There were no marks of mistreatment on Guinevere's pale skin, but she had been through a terrifying ordeal. She wouldn't want any reminders.

"Wait." Water sloshed as Guinevere sat up in the tub. "How did you know what had happened to me? From what those kitchen girls said, you and Sir Lancelot rode out before Meliagant's messenger even reached Arthur."

Nimue confessed as much of the truth as she could. "Morgana told me, your grace, by means of some enchantment."

Guinevere stared at her.

"She said she owed you a debt."

Guinevere nodded slowly. Her eyes were distant, but she wasn't thinking about Morgana. "So, Arthur was given this news twice, and he still chose to leave me at Sir Meliagant's mercy."

There was nothing Nimue could say to that. "Shall I fetch food and wine, your grace? You must be hungry." The last of Sir Lancelot's supplies had made a meagre noonday meal split between three.

"Fetch enough for us both. Oh, and make a tea to help me sleep. Something blended with raspberry leaves, I think, in case my legs cramp in the night after so much riding." Guinevere sank quickly under the bathwater to avoid any awkward questions.

Nimue went on her way. She would fetch hot water from the kitchens, and make the queen's tea in her own chamber, from her own supply of herbs. That would avoid unhelpful gossip. While raspberry leaves assuredly promoted sleep and countered cramps, such a tea could also prompt a woman's womb to cleanse itself. Most women learned that once they were old enough to bear a child. Nimue thought it was highly unlikely that Guinevere had conceived, but evidently the queen sought to avoid fathering Lancelot's bastard on Arthur.

She waited in the kitchen for the cooks to prepare a tray of delicacies. Carrying the food back to the keep, she paused briefly in her own room to select the herbs she wanted. In Guinevere's chamber, the bath had been removed, and the queen sat wrapped in a chamber robe, combing her wet hair and looking thoughtfully into her mirror.

Nimue set down the tray. Guinevere avoided her gaze as she drank the fragrant tea. They ate in silence, though the queen seemed to have little appetite. As soon as Nimue had eaten her fill, Guinevere dismissed her with a courteous good night.

"Sleep well, your grace." Nimue had no choice but to leave her. At least her magic had shown her Guinevere's womb was indeed empty.

She went to her own room, and once she had washed off the dust of the road, she settled down to sleep. Tired as she was, sleep was slow to come. Nimue realised she was listening with half an ear for the king going to his wife's bedchamber. She heard nothing. The queen might be back at Camelot, but she had come home to the same problems that beset her before.

* * *

Dawn came, and Nimue had only managed a little fitful and unrefreshing sleep. She forced herself out of bed and went to the window. She expected to see dark clouds threatening thunder. Instead, the clear, pale sky was sprinkled with the last fading stars. If the weather wasn't causing this sense of dread, what was wrong?

The light strengthened, and the castle's day began with the humblest and youngest servants hauling wood and water. Some lad passed close by the keep whistling a snatch of melody. As far as these people were concerned, the queen had been brought safely home and all was right with the world.

Camelot's towers warmed from ivory to gold in the sunshine. A maid brought hot water. Nimue washed and dressed and made a cup of strengthening tea. Fear still surrounded her like fog, as frustrating as it was oppressive. Every time she came close to grasping some explanation, her reasons thinned to nothingness.

She put the clothes she had worn ready to be collected by the castle's laundresses. She hung her warm cloak on its peg and assessed how best to clean the mud off the sturdy woven wool with a stiff brush and a damp cloth.

The silver plate she had used for scrying weighed down the pocket. Should she look just a little way into the future? If she was forewarned, perhaps she could steer the king and queen away from the unknown disaster she was convinced loomed over them. Unless of course, her meddling unwittingly brought that catastrophe down on their heads.

She heard the queen's door open and close. Nimue hurried over to her chamber. Guinevere wore a fresh linen chemise as she selected gold and coral jewellery to adorn a rose-pink gown laid ready. She waited for the queen to say something, but Guinevere accepted her help to dress in silence, until she sat in front of her mirror.

"If you could see to my hair, please?"

"Of course, your grace."

As Nimue reached for comb and pins, she saw the queen's eyes were distant and pensive. She plaited and coiled Guinevere's soft brown locks, ready to offer advice, but Guinevere kept her own counsel. As soon as Nimue secured a fine silk veil to her headdress of starched linen shot with gilt threads, the queen stood up.

"Let's join my ladies for breakfast."

"By all means, your grace."

As they went down the stairs, Nimue wondered if Guinevere had decided to put that silent encounter in the night on the road behind her. That would surely be best for everyone.

When they reached the queen's tower, the noble young ladies were already present. Amid the murmur of avid speculation, several didn't even notice when Guinevere entered the room.

"It was Sir Gawain's duty to support the king, whether or not the queen was restored to us. There can't be any doubt he will be the heir when–"

The girl beside Linet poked her in the ribs with a frantic elbow. Several girls blushed guiltily.

Guinevere smiled without looking at anyone in particular and took her seat at the head of the table. "I've been thinking," she said conversationally as she reached for a bread roll and a dish of honey. "We should embroider a new altar cloth for the chapel. What designs might we consider?"

Whatever the girls might have expected her to say, this took them completely by surprise. They looked under their lashes at each other as Guinevere gazed around the table. Her half-smile was as kind as ever, but the quicker-witted girls saw a hardness in her eyes and recognised this warning not to discuss anything else.

One of the numerous Elaines spoke up. "Are you thinking of an altar cloth for some particular season or saint, your grace?"

"That's a good question." Guinevere approved. "What do we think?"

The other noble maidens offered suggestions, hesitant at

first, then more quickly, as they considered this new challenge. Nimue didn't follow the ins and outs of the debate. She never bothered with the shifting dictates of the crucified god's priests through the year. She studied the girls' faces instead. More than half were clearly relieved not to hear distressing details of Guinevere's ordeal. If such an outrage could befall the queen, then none of them were safe. That prospect was too horrible to contemplate.

By the time they had finished eating, they had agreed the new altar cloth would show a lamb in a meadow of spring flowers. Now suitable linen must be found, and coloured wools. The different flowers and the holy lamb must be sketched to everyone's satisfaction on vellum, which would be pierced and pounced to transfer the design to the cloth beneath. Guinevere allocated the necessary tasks and walked out into the castle yard with her ladies.

As the girls dispersed, the queen didn't return to the keep. Instead, she went to the crucified god's chapel. Nimue followed. Perhaps Guinevere wanted to remind herself of the altar's dimensions. Perhaps she wished to offer up some prayer of thanks for her safe return. This altar cloth would be an offering to show her gratitude, as well as a way to avoid revisiting recent events to satisfy anyone's curiosity.

Unless... The sense of dread that plagued Nimue returned, redoubled. Did Guinevere intend to confess what she must see as her sin? Such confessions were supposedly sacred and secret, but Nimue had no faith in that. If Camelot's priest learned the queen had shared her body with another man, surely he would tell Arthur?

Could she persuade Guinevere not to do this? How could she even raise the subject without revealing that she knew what had happened? Would that cause a rift between them? Nimue searched in vain for answers. Then she saw Sir Lancelot walking up the steps to the chapel ahead of them.

Guinevere's pace quickened. Nimue realised the queen had

seen the knight before she had. So, she was following him. What did she want to say to Lancelot? Nimue's head ached with apprehension as the knight entered the chapel.

Guinevere halted at the top of the steps. The chapel door was in a deep recess, with the spiral stair that led to the tower's upper floors to one side. A broad stone ledge served as a bench for those waiting to be admitted to the sanctuary.

"Wait here, please." She wouldn't meet Nimue's eyes, but she was the queen. Nimue had to obey her.

"Yes, your grace." She sat and folded her hands in her lap.

Guinevere went into the chapel and closed the door. That was of no consequence. Nimue sharpened her ears to hear what was said inside.

"Your grace." Lancelot greeted Guinevere with his usual courtesy.

The queen wasted no time. "We must decide what to do."

"I ask for no reward. I was doing my duty to my king," he assured her. "His praise and that of my fellow knights is worth more than any silver."

Nimue felt Guinevere's confusion through the solid oak planks.

"That's not what—"

"Nothing has changed, your grace," Lancelot assured her.

"How can you say that?" Guinevere protested. "Everything—"

"Everything is just as it was, your grace." His politeness was implacable. "I was honoured by the gift of your gratitude, truly, but what's done is done and that night should be left in the dust of the road. We are back at Camelot. The king is your husband, and he is my liege lord. I will not betray his trust. I sit at his right hand at the round table—"

"And you won't risk losing that honour or the high regard of your fellow knights for the sake of a foolish woman." Guinevere's scorn was withering, though Nimue couldn't tell if she was more disgusted with Lancelot or herself. "Forgive me, I thought you had seen my unhappiness. I thought you were offering me some hope of escape, of love for my own sake, not for my value in an alliance or as a means to secure a son. I thought you had come to my rescue, defying the king who was ready to leave me to my fate at Sir Meliagant's hands. Clearly, I was mistaken. You only sought renown for yourself, and you only saw me as a cunt to fuck."

Nimue didn't need her spell to hear the knight's shocked gasp at the queen's brutal words. Guinevere's swift steps came towards the door. As she struggled to open the heavy oak, Nimue hurried to help. She caught a glimpse of Lancelot standing by the altar, slack-jawed and lost for words. Nimue thought she saw shame in his eyes, but in the dim light, she could be mistaken.

White-faced and dry-eyed, Guinevere crossed the castle yard to the keep, oblivious to greetings and blessings on her safe return. Nimue could only smile apologetically at the bemused men and women staring at their queen's back. Guinevere even walked straight past the king. Arthur was too astonished to be affronted.

"The queen has been through a dreadful ordeal, your grace," Nimue said hastily. "She found herself overwhelmed–"

"See that she rests and recovers. Tonight, we will celebrate with a feast to share our joy at her safe return." Arthur's brief smile didn't reach his cold eyes.

Nimue's head ached worse than ever as she hurried to the keep. She would have followed Guinevere into her chamber, but the queen had slammed the door. Nimue heard the key turn in the lock. A moment later, she heard the queen sobbing with anguish only equalled by her fury.

CHAPTER THIRTY-ONE

Nimue left Guinevere undisturbed for as long as she dared. She intercepted maidservants appearing to do their daily tasks. Several of the queen's ladies arrived, keen to show Guinevere their plans for the new altar cloth. Nimue turned them away with regretful smiles. The queen had a merciless headache after the strain and exertion of the past few days.

As the daylight dimmed, Nimue's foreboding persisted. She couldn't ignore the bustle in the great hall below. Minstrels rehearsed sprightly music for the celebrations, but the melodies irritated her like the scrape of a knife on earthenware. She reached for the small silver plate on her side table, only to draw back her hand, as she had done several times before. She knew where the queen was, and what could watching Sir Lancelot tell her? If one of those noble girls walked in, this was no time to risk an accusation of witchcraft so soon after Morgana's desperate, murderous folly.

When Arthur came up the stairs, Nimue went to her doorway, ready with excuses. The king didn't acknowledge her as he went into his room, followed by a lackey with a jug of hot water. A maidservant who followed turned towards the queen's door. Nimue hurried to meet her.

"Let me have that." She took the steaming ewer from the woman and waited until the maid had gone down the stairs. She knocked gently on the queen's door, her voice low.

"Your grace?"

There was no reply. Nimue resolutely rejected her worst

imaginings and wondered how to force her way in without making a noise that would disturb Arthur. Confrontation with the king wouldn't help anyone, especially not if he summoned men to break down Guinevere's door.

She brushed the latch with her fingertips but held off using any magic. It would take some effort to force the lock to eject the key, then she would have to persuade Guinevere that she had failed to secure the door. She whispered more urgently. "Your grace?"

The key turned in the lock. Guinevere opened up and turned away. Nimue hurried inside, pushing the door closed behind her.

"There is to be a feast, your grace." She took the hot water to the washstand.

"I will play my part." Guinevere sounded utterly defeated.

As the queen washed her tear-stained face, Nimue wished she could offer some comfort, but she dared not speak in case that provoked another storm of weeping. She only hoped they could get through this evening. Then she would try to guide Guinevere through tomorrow, and the next day, and the one after that.

The queen had torn off her headdress and her rose pink skirts were badly creased. She stripped off the gown and sat on the stool to allow Nimue to pluck the remaining pins out of her hair and comb through the tangles.

Keeping an ear open for any sign that Arthur was ready, she fought the urge to hurry. "Which gown will you wear, your grace?"

"The purple velvet, with the amethysts set in silver," Guinevere muttered.

Nimue found the gown. The queen dressed and put on her jewels, pale but calm. She reached for the cosmetics she rarely used and hid the shadows under her eyes. Nimue bound her braided hair with a headdress and veil bright with silver thread. When Arthur knocked on her door, Guinevere was a picture of regal beauty, ready to present a serene face to Camelot.

"Your grace?" The king was dressed in black with the comet-tailed dragon embroidered on his tunic. He wore his father's heavy crown.

"Your grace." Guinevere tucked her hand into his elbow, and they walked down the great staircase together. Nimue followed a few paces behind.

The king and queen entered the great hall and a cheer rose from every table. Arthur escorted Guinevere to the queen's chair, kissed her hand and went to join his waiting knights. Those who had already taken their seats at the round table stood up. As Arthur greeted Sir Lancelot with a kinsman's embrace, Camelot's approval was deafening.

As soon as the king sat down, the minstrels struck up a lively tune. The castle's servants appeared carrying food and wine, and the hum of conversation rose around the hall.

"Your grace?" Linet smiled brightly. "We have made some progress on the altar cloth designs."

"Please, go on," Guinevere invited her to elaborate.

Other noble young ladies chimed in, and the queen barely had to say a word. Even so, Nimue couldn't relax. Sitting with her back to the round table, she couldn't see the king or his knights. She could see several girls discreetly studying Guinevere, and she wondered what their letters might say to their fathers and brothers. Had these young women noticed the queen was barely eating or drinking? Guinevere moved food around her plate but rarely lifted anything to her mouth. She seemed to take sips of wine, but when a lackey with a jug passed by, her goblet never needed refilling.

The evening wore on. Finally, the platters of roast meat were replaced by sweetmeats and fragrant wine. Nimue saw Guinevere eat a few of those and drink a little more. Soon though, the queen pushed her chair away from the table and stood up.

"I will retire." As her attendant ladies got to their feet,

Guinevere shook her head with a smile. "No, please, stay and enjoy the music."

"I will come with you, your grace." Nimue snatched a glance at the round table.

Arthur was deep in conversation with Sir Kay. The other knights were listening with close attention. Only Sir Agravaine looked around, presumably as he saw some movement in the corner of his eye. He looked back at the king just as quickly.

Nimue followed Guinevere out of the hall. They went up to the queen's chamber and Guinevere took off her jewels and headdress. She sat in silence, staring into the mirror as Nimue brushed her hair for the third time that day. The hopelessness in her eyes was painful to see. Nimue was trying to find the words to ask what Guinevere wanted to do, when a knock at the door startled them both.

"The king?" Guinevere looked up at Nimue, alarmed. "I can't–"

"I'll tell him you're sick." She headed for the door.

But Sir Lancelot came in, pushing Nimue out of the way.

"You will listen to me." Angry, he stabbed the air with his forefinger. "You're mistaken if–"

"Get out." Guinevere's voice shook.

"Not until I know what you're going to do." Lancelot scowled. "I won't be brought down by your folly."

Guinevere sprang up and hurled herself at the knight. She hammered at his chest with ineffectual fists as tears of rage spilled down her cheeks. Lancelot grabbed her wrists. Mistaking her rage for distress, he tried to fold her in his arms like a weeping child.

"Your Grace," he chided in soothing tones.

The opening door crashed against the wall. A rough hand shoved Nimue aside and ten or more men stormed into the room. Sir Agravaine grasped the sword hilt at his hip. The other knights were armed as well, even though they were dressed in their finery for the feast. The queen's chamber was spacious, but the room was uncomfortably crowded.

Lancelot pushed Guinevere away. Nimue ran to the queen, and they retreated to the window embrasure. Lancelot stood poised as he faced these intruders. He might be weaponless, but he would react to any threat, quick as lightning. Nimue had seen the knight fight and win in countless tournaments.

"Whatever you think you have seen, believe me, you are mistaken." His voice was too strained to be convincing. Several knights exchanged dour nods, as if he had made some damning confession.

"I order you to leave." Guinevere stepped forward, trembling despite her defiance. "At once. All of you. This is my chamber and–"

"We have the king's permission." Agravaine barely glanced at her, contemptuous. "I told him you are a faithless slut, and he told me to catch you in the act to prove it. I never thought you would make it so easy, you stupid bitch."

"What did you call me?" Guinevere was as shocked as if he had slapped her.

Agravaine ignored her as he addressed Lancelot. "I was in the chapel this morning, praying for my father's soul. I heard you there. I heard both of you. You never thought you might not be alone."

Now he was gloating. "You've always been an arrogant bastard, ever since the first day you arrived. No more than a beggar, with nothing to your name but your horse and your armour, but you still thought you were better than us. Well, now we know you're a fool."

Hatred and triumph warred in his words. "Now it all makes sense. Why else would you ride out alone unless you were desperate to rescue your whore? How long have you been spreading her thighs?"

"I have not–" But Sir Lancelot couldn't tell an outright lie. Everyone saw his hesitation. Worse, Guinevere blushed scarlet with humiliation.

"See the guilt on her face," Agravaine sneered, before

jutting his chin towards Lancelot. "I told my brothers you were a traitor, but they said I must be mistaken. They didn't want to go to the king. They didn't want to break this brotherhood we have forged in Camelot. I told them we have a duty as Arthur's heirs. I am loyal to my king. There will be no seat at his table for the man who defiled his marriage bed!"

His voice rose to a shout as he reached for his sword. Lancelot was already moving. He grabbed a blanket from the bed and swirled it around his arm. The closest knight drew his blade. Lancelot was too quick. He took a long stride and punched the man brutally hard in the side of his head. Sir Colegrevance collapsed, senseless or dead. Before he hit the ground, Sir Lancelot grabbed his sword.

He had to drop to one knee to do it. Agravaine's sword came down to hack off his head. Lancelot swung the stolen blade up with a two-handed grip. Their swords locked. Agravaine bore down with all his weight, spitting with incoherent fury. Lancelot forced their blades upwards.

Agravaine's resistance broke. Whether that was real or a feint, Lancelot was ready. He sprang up and lashed at Agravaine's face with the trailing edge of the blanket. The prince of Orkney recoiled, instinctive. Lancelot drove Sir Colegrevance's sword deep into Agravaine's chest.

It seemed to Nimue that time had stopped still, as if Morgana had worked her sorcery. Agravaine stared at Lancelot in disbelief. The other knights gaped, aghast. Guinevere pressed her hands to her face as she opened her mouth to cry out.

Agravaine's knees buckled. Lancelot ripped the blade free. Agravaine fell face down onto the floor, choking on a catastrophic rush of blood. The other knights fought to draw their swords, desperate to avenge him. Crammed together, they fatally hampered each other. Steel bit into flesh, and scarlet sprayed in the air, as Lancelot fought his way to the door. One young knight tried to bar his way, but Lancelot snared his sword with the blanket and shattered his hand with his ruthless blade.

The wounded knight staggered backwards. Lancelot reached the door. He ran for the stairs, and no one pursued him. Wounded knights cried out in agony. Several clutched their wounds in a futile attempt to stop their lives ebbing away. Others lay limp, ominously pale. The queen's chamber reeked like a slaughterhouse.

Agravaine lay dead in a pool of blood. Nimue remembered seeing him as a baby, when she had scryed across the countless miles that separated Garlot and Orkney. She remembered Ygraine's delight. How they had laughed together seeing little Gawain solemnly counting his new brother's fingers and toes. She recalled Agravaine as a growing boy; sometimes foolhardy, always brave.

As a youth he had been harder to love, lacking Gawain's earnest charm. He had excelled as a knight, but he always seemed to fear falling short of his rivals. That made Agravaine defiant, even aggressive, and won him few friends. None of that mattered any more. He was dead. Who would tell his brothers? Who would tell Morgause?

"No!" Guinevere screamed, as if denial could somehow do away with this horror.

The cry jerked Nimue out of her shock. She heard consternation surge up the stairwell. A moment later, the commotion moved outside. She ran to the window. Darkness and confusion hid Sir Lancelot from pursuit, but Nimue saw him running across the castle yard to the stables. As he disappeared, torches appeared. Firelight glinted red on the men's drawn swords. They circled and Nimue heard their uncertainty. Before they could decide where to look for the fugitive, Lancelot burst out of the stables, riding bareback on his white horse. He had only paused to bridle the beast before making his escape.

Iron-shod hooves clattered on the cobbles as Lancelot galloped for the gatehouse. No one had sent word to close the gate or raise the castle's drawbridge. Several men ran for the gatehouse tower, realising their error. They couldn't outpace the horse and the echoes of Lancelot's flight soon faded.

"Well." The king stood in the doorway. He surveyed the carnage and looked at Guinevere. Silent, she met his gaze.

"Your grace," Nimue began.

Arthur cut her off with a curt gesture. "Deal with this," he told Sir Kay who stood beside him, appalled. "I must speak with Sir Gawain and his brothers. Have her brought to the great hall."

Arthur walked away as Sir Kay began shouting orders. Knights and servants appeared, as confused as they were horrified. The wounded were carried from the room, whimpering as they were lifted. The dead followed, uncaring.

Deeply troubled, Sir Kay approached Guinevere. "Your grace."

Nimue saw that he at least knew of Agravaine's accusations against the queen.

Guinevere raised a hand to ward him off and walked towards the door. Kay followed close behind, keeping one hand on his sword.

Nimue went after them. She passed a lackey kneeling by a knight bleeding from a gaping belly wound. The boy looked up with desperate appeal. Nimue shook her head. She couldn't abandon the queen. Besides, Sir Meliot was past saving without powerful magic and using that would condemn her as a witch. Then Guinevere would have no one to help her.

Guinevere walked ahead of Sir Kay into the great hall. Goblets and jugs of wine stood abandoned on the long tables. Knights and ladies clustered in groups and broke apart just as quickly, as everyone asked questions which no one could answer. Some of the chairs at the round table lay toppled over as if those knights had sprung up and hurried away. Other knights were still seated, bemused.

Arthur stood a short distance from the round table, talking to the princes of Orkney. Sir Gawain gestured as he spoke. The seated knights saw Sir Kay following Guinevere through the hall. Out of habit, they stood up to acknowledge the queen's arrival. Every agitated voice fell silent.

Guinevere halted. Arthur stared at her, impassive. She gazed back with her head held high.

"What have you to say for yourself?" he demanded.

Guinevere didn't answer.

"Nothing?" Arthur pursed his lips. "Very well, your grace. You have been caught in adultery and that is treason against your king. According to the law of Logres, the penalty for treason is death. You have condemned yourself and you will die by fire at dawn. Take her away, Sir Kay."

His voice cracked as he turned away, though there was nowhere for him to go. Stunned silence filled the hall, followed by outcry.

"My king!" Sir Gawain's was the loudest protest.

Knights and ladies alike shrank back towards the sides of the hall, quickly hushing each other.

"You cannot condemn the queen on the accounts we have had so far," Gawain insisted. "Not until she chooses to speak. Not when Sir Lancelot isn't here to answer for his part in whatever may have happened."

"His part?" spat Arthur. "He just killed your brother!"

"And Lancelot must answer for that, but Agravaine was a fool to confront him." Gawain was grief-stricken but resolute. "When Sir Lancelot left this table, he was unarmed. We all saw that. We must hear what he has to say, on his oath as a knight before God, before we can know the truth. Agravaine may have misheard. He may have heard what he wanted to hear. God save my brother's soul, but we both know it wouldn't be the first time."

"You say *must* to me?" Arthur's face darkened. "I am your king and I have spoken. You *must* obey me, if you are true to your oath."

Gawain's mouth twisted with anguish. Everyone waited,

breathless, to see if he would challenge the king a second time. The prince of Orkney shook his head and hurried blindly out of the hall. Gareth followed, distraught. Gaheris went last, openly weeping. Everyone stared at Arthur. Guinevere hadn't moved. Her expression was unchanged.

"Take her away!" the king roared at Sir Kay.

Guinevere's face was eerily calm as she looked at the knight. He gestured helplessly at the great hall's door. Guinevere walked towards it. Nimue followed with meekly folded hands, looking at the floor as a good servant should. Her thoughts were in turmoil.

They left the hall and Guinevere continued walking towards the outer door and the steps.

"Wait." Sir Kay hurried to her side.

"Aren't we going to the gatehouse dungeons?" Guinevere asked acidly. "I have been condemned after all. Or do you expect me to sleep in the charnel house that Sir Agravaine and Sir Lancelot made of my bedchamber?"

Nimue could see Sir Kay was at a loss. "There's a suitable chamber for the queen in Princess Morgana's tower," she said quickly. "With a single spiral stair that's easily guarded."

Sir Kay nodded. "Go."

CHAPTER THIRTY-TWO

Thanks to Camelot's diligent servants, the bedchamber above Morgana's workroom was fit for guests. Nimue hurried to strike sparks into a scrap of tow, so she could light the candles. Sir Kay took the key and, locking them in, he left. Guinevere kicked off her soft leather shoes and lay down on the bed. She stretched her hands over her head and heaved a long sigh.

"Your grace?" Nimue gave up her struggle with the steel and flint. The wick flared at her touch, but she didn't care if the queen saw. She would have to use enchantment to get Guinevere away from here.

"Yes?" The queen asked as if this were any normal evening.

Nimue picked up the silver candlestick. "We must decide where you will be safest."

"Safe?" Guinevere laughed wearily. "There's nowhere safe for me, even if I could get out of this room. I can't go to my father. He handed me over to Arthur. He'll hand me straight back. Where else could I go? Who would take me in, knowing they're making an enemy of the high king? He has the might of Logres' armies to call on and he would pursue me, you know that. He couldn't be humiliated by a mere woman."

She sat up, serious now. "I won't put anyone here at risk by trying to escape. Arthur will be merciless. He'll condemn you and anyone else who might try to help me for treason too. I won't have your deaths on my conscience."

"You have to be alive to be guilty of a sin," Nimue retorted. "You'll be the first go to the executioner's pyre."

"Then at least this will be over." Guinevere's voice wavered. "I've done everything I can to serve Camelot and the kingdom, and I have nothing more left in me. I cannot give Arthur a son. Without that, I'm worthless as a queen."

"That doesn't make you worth any less as a woman," Nimue protested.

"What of it? Besides, I am guilty, even if I'm not going to give Arthur the satisfaction of confessing." Guinevere lay back down again. "I broke my marriage vows to the king, and that is treason, even if I was an utter fool to believe Sir Lancelot was any different to the rest."

Nimue tried again. "Foolishness doesn't mean you deserve this vile death. Your grace, you will be tied to a post with logs and brushwood piled around you. The fire will be lit–"

"Do you know why women are burned?" Guinevere stared up at the ceiling. "Instead of being hanged as men are?"

"What?"

"It's for modesty's sake. My nurse explained when I was a child, though I can't remember why. It's true," the queen insisted, although Nimue hadn't said a word. "If a woman is hanged high enough for her to die a quick death, men might see under her skirts. Can you believe it? The men who make these laws think that is worse than being burned alive."

"Presumably the men who build a pyre take steps to ensure the flames will be fierce enough to hide their victim's nakedness once her clothes have been seared away." Nimue was determined to shock Guinevere into understanding the fate that awaited her. Then she could offer her an escape by means of magic. However much the queen had been taught to mistrust sorcery, she would have to accept the lesser of these evils. "Though I don't suppose many men lust after screaming women seared raw with their hair ablaze."

Guinevere rolled onto her side and drew up her feet to curl into a ball. "I remember now, why we were talking about dying in a fire. A kitchen boy tripped and fell into the hearth.

His clothes caught alight, and nothing could save him, even after he was dragged out of the flames. Nurse said the pains he suffered before he died would lessen his time in Purgatory. My torment tomorrow will soon be done, and I will have paid for my sins. I will finally be free of all this."

Nimue could have believed the queen had drunk poppy syrup or some other apothecary's concoction to dull her wits. She decided the time for talking was over. She would simply take Guinevere far from here and explain what she had done afterwards. Brittany was far enough away that no one would recognise the queen, and they wouldn't seek sanctuary with King Nentres. She knew plenty of places where a spell could carry them unseen. They would travel on into Gaul and Arthur would have no trail to follow.

She approached the bed, ready to take Guinevere's hand and drag her into the shadows. She looked down with disbelief. The queen was so deeply asleep she was snoring. Well, Guinevere must be exhausted. She would have had little enough rest since Sir Meliagant seized her, and she'd had precious little to eat for these past few days. No wonder the queen was giving up hope. She must be light-headed from hunger.

Nimue set the candlestick on the table and sat on the edge of the bed. Guinevere might as well sleep. No one would come for them tonight. An execution by fire took time to arrange. A man could be hanged as soon as someone found a rope to bear the felon's weight and somewhere high enough to tie it. Though not for treason. A man would be condemned to being hung, drawn and quartered for such a crime against the king. Would that be Sir Lancelot's fate? Nimue decided she didn't care. Lancelot could look after himself. He had abandoned the queen.

Besides, not everything Guinevere had said was nonsense. Nimue needed a different plan. If they vanished from this room, Arthur would know she had used her magic, but she didn't imagine the king would confess he had knowingly sheltered an enchantress, not after Morgana's crimes. He could hardly keep Guinevere's disappearance a secret though, and he would need some explanation that Camelot would accept. So he would have to blame whoever had been set to guard them and Nimue would face the threefold punishment if those innocents were harmed.

How could Nimue get Guinevere away from Camelot without anyone realising magic was involved? Would people believe the queen had been utterly consumed by the pyre, leaving no trace of bone or teeth among the ashes? Perhaps. Women were so rarely executed that no one at Camelot had seen such a horror, as far as Nimue knew.

What enchantments would she have to work? She would have to shield the queen from the flames while raising her own wall of fire, whether that was real or illusion, to hide Guinevere from the crowd. She would have to step through the distance between them, grab the queen's hand, and carry them both far away. That would be far harder to do without any shadows to use.

If the crowd didn't believe the queen had burned completely away, they were bound to suspect sorcery, but no one would have any reason to suspect Nimue apart from the king. Perhaps Arthur would blame Morgana. She would make a handy scapegoat for years to come.

Nimue lay on the bed beside the snoring queen and closed her eyes. She would need all her strength to contrive such complex magics, and Guinevere wasn't the only one short on sleep.

A knock on the door roused them both. The dawn sky at the window was dull and grey. Nimue saw Guinevere's confusion. A moment later, the queen realised she hadn't woken from some foul dream. She was to be sent to her death. Guinevere's chin quivered and her eyes filled with tears. This morning, she wanted to live.

Nimue wanted to tell her not to lose hope, but that risked questions she couldn't answer. She settled for taking the queen's hand and holding it tight. Guinevere nodded as she blinked away tears, unable to speak.

The knock came again. "Your grace?"

That wasn't Sir Kay. Sir Gawain was at the door. Guinevere looked at Nimue, startled.

"One moment." Nimue hurried to find a comb in the small chest on a side table.

Guinevere sat on the edge of the bed. She laced her fingers in her lap and her knuckles whitened. "I hardly think I need to look my best."

"They can hardly start without you." Nimue began to tidy the queen's long hair.

Guinevere was startled into a laugh, though tears threatened to follow. As the queen sniffed inelegantly, Nimue bound Guinevere's soft brown hair with a black ribbon she had found in the coffer.

Sir Gawain waited silently outside. Guinevere stood up, found her shoes and smoothed her dress. The heavy velvet's weight pulled out the worst of the creases. "Let's get this over and done with."

Nimue heard an echo of last night's despair as the queen raised her voice. "We are ready."

The key turned in the lock with an ominous click. The door opened. Sir Gawain stood there with Sir Gareth and Sir Gaheris. All three were armoured as if they were going to compete in a tournament.

Gawain's face was impossible to read. "We are to accompany the queen, by order of the king."

Gaheris looked mutinous. Gareth was pale and hollow-eyed. Neither younger prince said a word.

"Very well." Guinevere nodded.

Silent, Sir Gawain led the way. Guinevere followed with Gaheris and Gareth close behind her. Nimue came last of all.

She allowed a little distance to open up as she wove a subtle enchantment. She didn't hide herself as people would expect to see her in attendance. Even so, she could ensure that once she was out of sight, as soon as her magic carried them away, everyone at Camelot would forget her.

She followed the three princes and the queen across the castle yard and out through the gatehouse. The sizeable crowd was intent on Guinevere. From commoners to knights and noble ladies, Nimue saw pity and disquiet on their faces rather than condemnation. An uneasy whisper followed the procession like the rustle of a breeze through reeds.

The pyre was ready in the meadow. A stake driven into the ground was surrounded by bundles of firewood, presumably taken from the local woodsmen supplying the castle's daily fuel. Some building project had lost laboriously split planks to make a platform for the queen to stand on. It wasn't enough that she must die. The people of Logres must see it.

The crucified god's priest waited close to the pyre, clutching his holy book. A hooded man beside him held a burning torch, its flames almost invisible in the sunlight. Nimue was tempted to remind everyone here that their holy book said "thou shalt not kill". Though presumably the men would say this was not their doing, but the king's decision. Arthur would claim he was only following the law of Logres. How was that justice, if no man took responsibility for the harm they did?

There was no sign of Arthur. Something else caught Nimue's eye. A lad was looking towards the trees on the far side of the meadow, where a sizeable stand of woodland offered shade for the knights and their horses in a tourney. Nimue recognised the boy from Camelot's stables. Why was he the only person not staring at the queen?

Hooves drummed on the turf, followed by shouts of alarm. An armoured knight on a white horse rode through the scattering crowd. His visor was down, but only Sir Lancelot carried that red-striped, white shield. He spurred his horse on, sword in hand, charging at the three men and the queen.

Guinevere stood still. Orkney's princes reached for their swords. Only Sir Gawain was fast enough to draw his blade. He braced himself, ready to fight. Lancelot wheeled his horse behind the queen. He had no intention of coming within Gawain's reach. He felled Sir Gareth with a swift blow to the head, and cut down Sir Gaheris with the backswing of the same stroke. Both young knights collapsed as Sir Lancelot leaned down. He hooked his shield-bearing arm around Guinevere's waist and threw her across the front of his saddle. Shouts and screams of protest from onlookers startled roosting birds from the trees.

Gawain dropped his sword. He leaped at the white horse's head. Grabbing a handful of mane, he seized its bridle with his other hand. The horse reared and tossed its head, fighting to get free. Lancelot fought to stay in his saddle, struggling to keep hold of Guinevere. Hampered by his shield, he could only press down on her back as she kicked and twisted. His other hand held his sword and the horse's reins, neither of them securely.

Guinevere fell. The crowd cried out and surged forward. Nimue cast a desperate enchantment to cushion Guinevere's fall and to save her from the plunging horse's hooves. Shoved and jostled, she lost sight of the horse and the knights amid the confusion. Then the throng retreated, as fast as a wave leaving the shore. Sir Gawain was on his hands and knees, his head hanging. Guinevere sprawled on the ground a few paces away. Sir Lancelot's bolting horse carried the knight away to disappear beneath the trees.

Guinevere was stirring. People around her dithered as Nimue ran to help her sit up and catch her breath. Arthur might not be present, but everyone was thankful that someone else had gone to the queen's aid. Nimue was relieved to find that Guinevere had only suffered bruises and bloody scrapes where Lancelot's shield had torn her velvet gown. She reached for the queen's hand, ready to carry them both far away. She would answer her questions afterwards.

But Guinevere was scrambling to her feet. She ran to Sir Gaheris and Sir Gareth. As she dropped to her knees, Sir Gawain stood up. He pressed a hand to his side, wincing. Whether Lancelot's horse had kicked him, or he'd been stuck by the knight's sword, Gawain was badly hurt.

The crucified god's priest hurried over, for all the use he might be. Nimue recognised the stillness of death as she looked at Gaheris and Gareth. Both young knights wore helmets, but in his haste and anger, Lancelot had hit them hard enough to crack their skulls. Such blows did untold, unseen, unintended damage.

The crucified god's priest closed Gaheris' vacant eyes with a gentle hand. Doing the same for Gareth, he began mumbling his prayers. Sir Gawain stared at his dead brothers with blank disbelief. Guinevere looked at him with tears on her pale cheeks.

Nimue stood frozen with horror. Who would tell Morgause that three of her five sons had died in less than a day and a night? What would this mean for Camelot? Some might think Agravaine had a hand in his own fate, but the younger boys were well-liked. All four of Orkney's princes had liked and admired Sir Lancelot. Nimue wondered if Lancelot knew he had killed them. Would he care?

A lone voice shouted. "Sir Kay!" Some of the crowd looked around for the seneschal, thinking he had arrived. Another voice cried out. "Send for Sir Kay!" The men who had gone in pointless pursuit of Lancelot halted, uncertain what to do until they had orders from someone in authority.

Gawain grabbed the queen's upper arm and forced her to her feet. Holding Guinevere tight, he began walking back towards Camelot's gatehouse, ignoring the milling onlookers' distress. He kept his other hand pressed to his side. Nimue pushed through the throng to follow them and hid herself with magic. People could think they had lost sight of her in the confusion. If they didn't, she really didn't care.

Sir Gawain marched Guinevere through the gatehouse and across the castle yard. Camelot's guards barred the way to anyone trying to follow, whatever their rank. Inside the keep, Gawain forced the queen through the echoing, empty great hall. Unseen and unsuspected, Nimue kept pace. Skirting the round table, Gawain threw open the door that led to Arthur's library.

The king stood with his back to them. "Is it done?"

"No."

Hearing Gawain's voice, Arthur spun around. Seeing Guinevere in her torn and bloodied gown, he gaped.

"Sir Lancelot tried to save her. He killed my brothers, hoping to carry her away." Gawain's words were bitter. "You said we must escort the queen to her death, to prove we are loyal. Are you satisfied now?"

"How–?" Arthur couldn't go on.

"Will you pursue Lancelot? Will you make him answer for two more murders?" Gawain demanded, merciless. "What will you do with the queen? She could have gone with him, but she fought her way free. Do you still condemn her as his lover? Shall I take her back to the fire or cut her throat for you here?"

Arthur couldn't meet Gawain's eyes. He looked down at a book on the reading desk. "Just take her away."

Guinevere turned and walked back through the great hall. Sir Gawain followed. Still unseen, Nimue flew on ahead. By the time Guinevere and Gawain reached the outer door, she stood at the bottom of the keep's stone steps, as if she had been waiting there all along.

Straight-backed and calm, Guinevere crossed the castle yard to Morgana's tower. She walked up the spiral stair and Nimue followed Sir Gawain. The queen paused in the bedchamber doorway and gestured at her ripped velvet gown.

"If I'm to be kept here until the king decides my fate, I need clothes and other necessities."

Gawain nodded. "Your woman can see to that."

"Thank you." Guinevere went into the room.

Gawain locked the door behind her. For a moment, he leaned his head against the dark wood, breathing heavily with his eyes tight shut.

"Your highness," Nimue began. "You're hurt–"

"What does that matter?" He pushed past her and went down the steps.

She waited until she heard the door below open and close. Then she went down the spiral stair herself. There were few people in the castle yard. No one could enter Camelot without a good reason today. No one spoke to her as she crossed to the keep. She hurried up to the queen's room where the air was still tainted with spilled blood. No one had tried to clean the stained floorboards or the spattered walls. There was no one to give such orders. How long before Arthur realised his castle was without a chatelaine? Who would ensure the work he never saw happen got done? The king would soon learn some hard lessons.

Nimue crossed to the queen's clothes chests and selected an armful of plain gowns in dark weaves. As long as they were still at Camelot, a show of humility would serve Guinevere better than defiant elegance. She found underlinen and stockings, but she left the queen's jewels alone. Arthur would have no excuse to pursue Guinevere as a thief when they fled.

Once darkness fell and the castle was sleeping, she and the queen would be gone. She wondered who Arthur would accuse of helping them. Sir Gawain? Sir Kay? Some hapless servant? Nimue could only hope whoever the king turned his anger on was able to prove they could not have been the one to betray him. She fervently hoped the bloody chaos out in the meadow had blunted Arthur's lust for vengeance. If not, Nimue would have to pay whatever price was demanded of her. There was no other option now.

She didn't want to think what that penalty might be, in case her nerve failed her. Nimue pictured Morgana's work room instead and considered what herbs and instruments she might take for her own purposes. She would have to pay their way with her skills as a healer as they travelled into Gaul.

"What are you doing?" Arthur stood in the open doorway.

"Fetching clothes for the queen, your grace." Nimue concentrated on rolling the queen's stockings into a ball.

"Tell me what happened out there."

"As Sir Gawain said, your grace, Sir Lancelot attacked him and his brothers, hoping to save the queen from the flames." Nimue chose her words carefully as she folded the gowns around the underlinen. If Arthur was thinking twice about condemning Guinevere, she mustn't provoke him into losing his temper.

"He knocked Sir Gaheris and Sir Gareth down and dragged her up in front of his saddle. She fought back and fell to the ground. Sir Gawain tried to bring down Sir Lancelot's horse, but the animal shook him off."

"Why wouldn't she flee, if she was guilty?"

To Nimue's profound relief, Arthur was asking himself, not her. He walked slowly around the room, looking at the bloodstains.

"Why do the people I trust always lie to me, and betray me? Sir Ector and Sir Kay lied for my whole childhood. Merlin swore he would never leave me, but he went away without a word. Morgana tried to have me killed, and she used witchcraft to do it. Did you teach her such vile magic?" He rounded on Nimue.

"No, your grace, I did not." She didn't remind him she had already told him that.

"How can I believe you? Can I believe anyone?" The king didn't wait for her to answer. "And now my queen may or may not have betrayed me, but I have no idea who's lying or telling the truth."

He fell silent for a long moment. Nimue concentrated on securing the bundle of clothes with a belt. She had never suspected Arthur's wounds went so deep. Wounds she had played her part in inflicting when she had trapped Merlin in that cave.

Use your magic sparingly, and always with caution. You can never know what consequences could follow.

"Now Lancelot has killed my heirs, my sister's sons. Lancelot, the knight whom I swore was the most honourable of us all. He has betrayed everyone in Camelot and made a fool of me." A fresh edge of anger in his voice sharpened with grief and wounded pride.

"We cannot be certain that Sir Lancelot intended to kill anyone," Nimue ventured.

"What does that matter? Gawain's right," Arthur said, resolute. "Lancelot must answer for his crimes. Wherever he's gone, my army will pursue him. Logres must see that I will not be defied. You will tell me where to find him. Your magic can do that much good at least."

"It can, your grace," Nimue said steadily. Saying so wasn't the same as agreeing to do what the king wanted.

Arthur strode away. Nimue waited a few moments, then picked up the bundle of clothes. She made her way cautiously down the staircase. Hearing men's voices in the great hall, she hurried out of the keep.

Reaching Morgana's tower, she went up the stairs. As she rounded the spiral, she stumbled backwards. Sir Gawain was sitting on the stone steps. He sprang up and grabbed Nimue's hand, saving her from a painful fall.

"Forgive me. I didn't mean to startle you." He was hoarse and his eyes were red with weeping.

"I'm the one at fault, my prince. I should look where I was going."

Gawain had shed his armour. He winced as he reached inside his tunic. Nimue really hoped that someone would take a look at whatever injury he had suffered.

As he held up the key to the bedchamber, he nodded at the bundle Nimue carried. "I'm a fool. You'll need this to take clean clothes to the queen."

"Thank you." She held out her hand for the key.

Sir Gawain held it out of reach. "I must have your word that you won't help the queen to escape. Your sacred oath, if you please."

Nimue realised that the knight had no idea what he was asking. He had no reason to suspect she could work magic. His simple and honourable request trapped her just the same. Once she made such an inconveniently binding promise, she and Guinevere were stuck here.

If she refused, she would be thrown out of Camelot. That wouldn't stop her returning, but what might happen when Guinevere was told her only friend had been banished? Would she break down and confess what she and Lancelot had done? Nimue couldn't take that chance. She would have to find another way out of this maze.

"I swear it." She took the key from Gawain.

CHAPTER THIRTY-THREE

Arthur and his knights had been gone for weeks. Nimue was leaving the kitchens when she heard a herald's horn. Her heart beat faster as she waited to see who rode through Camelot's gatehouse. Was the king returning with his army?

Nimue used her scrying bowl daily to watch them laying siege to Lancelot's castle. Arthur had granted him extensive, lucrative lands when he was the most admired knight at the round table. Many lords still admired him. A sizeable number had declared their support and joined Lancelot before Arthur's forces surrounded his castle. The threat of warfare hung over Logres again.

A handful of mounted men in travel-worn leather and chain mail rode into the castle yard, looking warily around. Their surcotes bore Orkney's double-headed eagle. The youthful rider whom they guarded carried a shield with the same device below a silver band. As he removed his helmet to talk to the sergeant-at-arms, he revealed dark locks and familiar features. Nimue saw his resemblance to his father as well as to his mother, even if he didn't have King Lot's red hair.

The sergeant-at-arms hurried over to her. "Prince Mordred has come to reclaim his brothers' bodies. He says their mother wishes them to be buried with their father. He says he has the king's permission."

The grey, pot-bellied old man looked anxiously at Nimue. This sergeant had laid down his sword years ago. He never expected to be recalled to the king's service because every younger, stronger man had marched off to fight. He had soon started bringing problems to Nimue. She was the queen's representative after all, even if Guinevere kept to the chamber where Sir Gawain had put her, even though no one locked the door. Nimue had taken charge of the castle's mundane affairs once again. Somebody had to. Arthur had left no orders for the household.

Nimue smiled, reassuring. "Show the prince and his men to the stables, so their horses can be tended. Tell him his brothers have been laid to rest in the crypt beneath the chapel. He is welcome to pray while rooms are prepared for him and his retinue. I will let him know when everything is ready."

Camelot could offer plenty of accommodation. Guinevere's attendant ladies had left the castle before the king and his knights departed. No one was sure if the queen had been pardoned or if her execution was merely postponed. She had certainly not been declared innocent, and as long as suspicion remained, she must be considered unfit to guide young maidens' morals.

Nimue didn't care. With the king away, Guinevere had peace and quiet to recover from her ordeal. She would find a way for them to leave for Gaul without breaking her word to Gawain, when the scrying bowl showed her Arthur was preparing to return.

"I will tell him." The sergeant hurried off towards the riders.

Nimue headed for the kitchen and gave brisk orders to make sure that Mordred's needs were met. Satisfied, she walked back to Morgana's tower. Guinevere must be told who had arrived.

As Nimue reached the upper chamber door, she heard voices inside the room. She realised the queen was talking to Mordred. Nimue heard echoes of his dead brothers in his voice.

"You are as beautiful as I have been told, your grace."

He lied easily, Nimue noted. These days Guinevere was pale and drawn in her plain, dark gowns, wearing her hair in a simple braid beneath an unflattering linen coif. Some whispers

saw this as a show of penitence and thus, an admission of her
guilt. No one imagined Guinevere was content to be free of the
demands of dressing like a queen.

Nimue wondered why Mordred had come here rather than
go to the chapel. She remembered Morgana's low opinion of
him as a boy. She decided to wait and see what she might learn
before a servant's presence curbed his tongue.

"I grieve for Agravaine, Gareth and Gaheris," Guinevere
told him, tense. "Believe me, I had no hand in anything that
happened."

"I know," Mordred assured her. "I have spoken to Gawain."

"At the siege?" Guinevere was surprised.

So was Nimue, until she recalled the gate sergeant had
said Mordred was here with Arthur's permission. He must
have secured that as well as finding Gawain in the army's
entrenchments.

"The king may not have cut down my brothers, but their
blood is on his hands." Mordred's voice was cold. "Arthur
broke the brotherhood of Camelot when he sent them out to
face Sir Lancelot."

"No one imagined he would return," Guinevere protested.

"Gawain won our family some measure of vengeance when
he killed Sir Pellinore," Mordred continued as if she hadn't
spoken, "but Arthur is ultimately guilty of our father's murder
as well."

"It's not for us to judge the king." Guinevere sounded
nervous. "His grace will answer to God, as we all will."

"Then let us pray he faces his judgement sooner rather
than later. Perhaps we can hasten that day. Don't you want
to be rid of him?" Mordred challenged Guinevere. "When he
has abused you so foully and imprisoned you in this tower?
When he has no idea of the treasure he has let slip through
his fingers?"

His tone turned caressing. Nimue's skin crawled.

"Father Thomas holds the keys to the crypt," Guinevere

said hurriedly. "Don't let me keep you from your duty to your brothers."

"You hold the keys to Camelot," Mordred said silkily. "Give them to me, give yourself to me, and I will give you revenge on Arthur."

"Get out!" Guinevere's shock nearly rattled the door.

"So coy, your grace?" Now Mordred mocked her. "We both know you were Lancelot's lover. What's one more slice from a cut loaf?"

Guinevere said nothing.

"Gawain may still cling to hope that you're innocent, your grace, but Agravaine was no such fool. Well, he was a fool," the prince allowed, "but he would have been certain about what he heard before he accused you. You can admit he was right. I won't tell anyone."

Guinevere still didn't answer.

"I knew it." Mordred laughed, triumphant, as if he had seen some confession in her face. "I don't care who else has had you in his bed. Your grace, don't you see? Sir Lancelot has abandoned you to whatever fate the king decrees. I'm here to rescue you. Give me Camelot's keys and Orkney's soldiers will seize this castle before the king returns. Marry me and I will claim the crown of Logres once Arthur lies dead on the meadow outside his own gates. I will rule the whole of Britain with you at my side."

"You have no claim to any throne," Guinevere's scorn was withering. "Sir Gawain is Arthur's heir as well as rightful king of Orkney."

"Gawain isn't here," Mordred said with sudden menace. "Who's to say he won't fall in battle just like our father. Now, you can give me what I want, your grace, or make no mistake, I will take it."

Guinevere screamed. Nimue threw open the door. Mordred had seized the queen with an arm around her waist. He wasn't trying to force kisses on her. His free hand hauled up her skirts while he used his greater height and weight to force her towards the bed.

Nimue's enchantment hit Mordred full in the chest. The force of her loathing threw him against the wall with a solid thud. As his feet hit the floor, his knees buckled. He crouched, gasping, with a hand pressed to the eagle on his surcote. As he caught his breath, he looked up at Nimue.

"So, Arthur does still have a witch." His dark eyes were calculating. "Morgana would never tell me who taught her, when I caught her working enchantments. I should have guessed, I suppose, but who pays any attention to old women who are always underfoot."

He got to his feet, wincing as he tugged his surcote straight. "Very well. I will have my vengeance on Arthur, even if I must find another way. Then you will have a choice." His glance took in Guinevere. "You can serve me, or you can both die, condemned as a whore and the witch who served her. Perhaps I'll burn you at the same stake."

He walked towards the door. Nimue stepped aside to let him pass. Mordred paused on the threshold.

"My brothers can rest in their coffins here for now. I will send them north to my lady mother once I am master of Camelot." He laughed as he walked away.

Nimue stood watching the spiral stair after he was out of sight.

"Was he–? Did you–?" Guinevere's voice shook.

Nimue turned to see the queen hugging herself in a vain attempt to stop trembling. She could tell Guinevere desperately wanted her to say that Mordred was lying, but the queen had seen him thrown across the room without a hand laid on him.

"It is true I have magic to call on," Nimue said steadily. "I strive to only use enchantment to save innocents from harm, and only when there is no other option."

Scrying to confirm to Arthur that Lancelot had indeed retreated to his castle might be testing the truth of that, but hurrying the king's departure from Camelot had surely protected Guinevere.

"I would have saved you from the flames," she promised the queen.

"I believe that, even if I don't know what else to believe." Guinevere managed a faint smile. "But Morgana...?"

"She saw me work magic when she was a child, but I never taught her to use sorcery to do such reckless harm. I have no idea where she learned such spells." Nimue decided against trying to explain the long history she and Morgana shared, or mention the hidden people and their wild magic. That risked Guinevere asking questions that demanded endlessly complicated answers.

The queen's thoughts were already elsewhere. "They said Arthur owed his crown to magic, or so the story went when I was a little girl. They said an ageless sorcerer served him, who had served his father before him, but Merlin disappeared long ago. Is that true?"

"It is, your grace." Nimue told herself she had no obligation to tell Guinevere any more of that truth.

"Arthur never spoke of such things, so I didn't ask. I never really believed in magic, until I saw what Morgana had done in Gore." Guinevere marvelled at her own naivety. "What enchantments have you worked that I never suspected?" The queen was half-curious, half-apprehensive.

Nimue considered what to tell her. "When I knew Sir Meliagant had taken you, I watched over you, your grace, to be certain you were safe. If he had tried to hurt you, I would have intervened. I opened that locked gate in the castle wall so you could escape. I barred it to the men who pursued you."

"I had no idea." Guinevere's face clouded. "What can your magic do now that Prince Mordred has decided he will possess me, as if marrying Arthur's queen will somehow make him Arthur's heir?"

She broke off as they heard shouts outside. Both women

went to the window. Looking down, they saw Mordred's men surround him in the castle yard. After a brief, angry conversation, the Orkney contingent headed for the stables.

"It seems we'll be rid of him for the moment at least." Guinevere shuddered. "Can you stop him coming back? Do I have to tell Arthur what that vile snake said? Will he even believe me?"

Nimue had no answers for her.

"What will become of me if Arthur dies in battle?" Guinevere was trembling again. "How many men will fight to claim me like meat torn between ravening dogs?"

"That depends who prevails. I'd back Lancelot in a fight against Mordred."

Guinevere stared at Nimue. Her face hardened. Now she was angry. Nimue was glad to see it.

"I will not be Lancelot's prize. I refuse to be anyone's spoils of war."

"Then don't be. Say the word, your grace, and whoever comes here to claim you will find us long gone. I was going to take you out of the fire and over the seas to Gaul."

"Gaul?" Guinevere was astonished, then intrigued. "Truly?"

Nimue wondered why she had dreaded the queen discovering her skills with magic for so long. "Truly, and now we can plan our journey and gather what we might need."

"And do the innocent people you'll leave behind deserve their fate?" Morgana asked from the doorway. "You know how they will suffer, the commoners and yeomen, the merchants and artisans, if war ravages Logres yet again."

Guinevere stifled a squeak of shock. Nimue wondered where Morgana had found refuge when she had fled from Gore. She was richly dressed and jewelled, and as self-assured as Nimue had ever seen her.

"If?" She challenged the younger sorceress. "Do you see some way to avoid such strife?"

"Perhaps." Morgana smiled, friendly. "Let's discuss this where we won't be disturbed."

She went down the spiral stair. Guinevere needed no encouragement to go after her. Nimue followed the queen.

Guinevere halted on the work room's threshold, marvelling. "I never thought to wonder what was in here."

"Do you imagine that's by chance?" Morgana walked around the table, looking at the walls and shelves to see what might have changed since she had left. "Magic's at its most effective when it's subtle and unsuspected. Nimue taught me that and I was a fool to forget it. So was Merlin."

"You knew Merlin?" Guinevere looked unnerved.

Nimue spoke up before Morgana could answer. "What brings you here, today of all days, your highness?" If Morgana was no longer a queen by marriage to Urien, she was still a princess by right as Gorlois's daughter.

"I owe Guinevere a debt." Morgana took a seat, and her gesture invited them to do the same. "I've been watching Mordred, just as I watched over his brothers."

"You knew what he intended?" Outrage momentarily overcame Guinevere's nervousness.

"No, I promise you that," Morgana assured her, "but I knew he would be up to no good. He was a sly child, always listening at keyholes and going behind his brothers' backs because he could never compete with them on equal terms. He has envied them ever since they came to Camelot. He felt snubbed when Arthur didn't summon him, once he was old enough to serve as a squire. His resentment turned to hatred, fed by endless stories of Orkney's betrayal told by old men who served his father. Morgause has done her best to counter their spite, but she is only one voice among many and a mere woman. The greybeards taught Mordred to ignore her."

"Did you hear what he said?" Guinevere pulled out a chair and sat down.

Morgana nodded. "It comes as no great surprise. He's always sworn to show everyone they're wrong to overlook him."

"Is there no end to this?" Nimue couldn't sit. She walked the length of the room, exasperated.

"Not while high kings and princes and knights decide everyone else's fate," Morgana said acidly. "Perhaps we should consider a world where they don't."

"That would be anarchy." Guinevere was shocked.

"Really?" Morgana leaned forward, intent. "Would the ordinary folk of these islands suffer if they were left to manage their own affairs without being dragged into arrogant men's quarrels? If their sons weren't sent to die to salve their liege lord's wounded pride? Would their lives be so different, day to day? They harness their oxen for ploughing, sow crops and reap their harvests without any noble knight's instructions. They tend their flocks and herds and take their goods to market without needing guidance – unless some lord's quest for vengeance destroys their livelihood."

Guinevere had no idea how to answer her. Nimue joined them at the table.

"A lord and his men keep the highways safe from vagabonds and thieves," she pointed out. "The king's authority upholds the common law which keeps men and women honest. His justice pursues those who murder or rape and sees them hanged."

"Can't the people do those things for themselves?" Morgana demanded. "In the name of the common good?"

"Perhaps." Nimue couldn't deny that the hidden folk managed their own affairs without bowing to kings. Though her people were hardly free of strife or rivalry.

"If wishes were horses, beggars would ride," Guinevere said tartly. "My father is a just and honest king. He rules in the best interests of the humblest as well as the highest, always mindful that he sits under God."

"He traded you to Arthur to rise above his peers," Morgana countered, merciless. "Whose interests did that serve?"

Guinevere's eyes filled with tears and she didn't reply.

"We have a chance to change everything now, don't you see?" Morgana pleaded with them both. "If Mordred kills Arthur–"

"So, for all your high-minded talk, you just want to see Arthur dead," Guinevere snapped. "To avenge your father, because Uther Pendragon slew him in battle? You're no different from Mordred, pursuing grievances down the generations."

Morgana's eyes narrowed. "Don't you dare–"

"Quiet." Nimue weighted that command with a little magic to give herself some time to think. Seeing it wouldn't hold Morgana for long, she spoke her thoughts aloud. "Leodegrance is a well-respected ruler, and so was Gorlois in his day. Other kings across these islands have rightly earned their people's loyalty. Maybe there is a better path, a way to live without kings, but let's not be too hasty. It's far easier to pull down a roof and walls than it is to build a house. It's best to have a plan before you demolish something."

"So your plan is do nothing?" Morgana rose to her feet. "I don't know why I bothered coming here."

Nimue raised a hand. "Hear me out. Uther's ambition to be high king is what started this mayhem. I was there. I saw it. Logres was no paradise before the war with the Picts, but by and large the realm was at peace. If some petty king got over-ambitious, the others would unite to keep him in his place. Uther did away with that unspoken agreement. That's why after he died, the lords of Logres fought to claim his place instead of returning to the cooperation they had known. Perhaps they would have done that in time, but Merlin put Arthur on the throne. He taught Arthur how Uther had ruled, through shows of might and the fear of the consequences of crossing him. That's all Arthur has ever known. But what would Logres be without him ruling from Camelot?"

"You want to kill Arthur as well?" Guinevere looked at her, aghast.

"He doesn't have to die to be defeated," Nimue said quickly.

"Merlin used magic to put Arthur on his father's throne, and used more to keep him there. Who told you about Excalibur?" she asked Morgana. "Why did you steal it for Sir Accolon to use against Arthur?"

"Viviane of the River told me he cannot be wounded as long as he holds that sword."

Nimue wanted to ask where and when the younger enchantress had encountered Viviane, and how she had learned the sorceress's name. That would have to wait. "Excalibur is far more than that. When Arthur rides into battle with that blade, his enemies lose heart while everyone else rallies to support him. Arthur has never earned the loyalty of Logres' lords, not truly, not for himself. Magic compels their devotion. What if that magic was gone? Such enchantments have no place in the mortal world."

"If Excalibur was taken away?" Morgana nodded slowly. "But how? I got close enough to steal it once, and that will never happen again.

"What if Excalibur was broken?" Nimue countered.

"What can break an enchanted blade?" Morgana drummed her fingertips on the table.

Nimue recalled Sir Pellinore breaking the sword drawn from the stone, but she wasn't inclined to rely on such luck this time. "Another enchanted sword would most likely succeed."

Morgana's fingers stilled. "Like the one Sir Balyn carried, when Merlin hoped to use him to kill Viviane."

So, she had heard that tale from the Lady of the River. Nimue was ready to wager that Morgana had fled to Viviane's lands from Gore.

Guinevere was desperately trying to follow their conversation. "I know that story. Sir Balyn was given a cursed sword that compelled him to kill anyone who came near him. You do still want to kill Arthur," she accused Morgana.

"Viviane said the curse was broken." Morgana clearly regretted that.

"But the sword is still enchanted," Nimue pointed out, "and I know where it is."

"Who's going to challenge Arthur with it?" Guinevere interrupted. "What if Arthur kills whoever is so stupidly reckless before Excalibur breaks?"

"Perhaps there's some way to use Sir Balyn's blade against Arthur's sword without actually coming to blows." Though Nimue had no idea what that might be.

"How can you be so sure what will happen, even if you succeed," the queen persisted. "If Logres' lords are no longer loyal to Arthur, what's to stop them fighting each other to become high king in his place?"

"Not what. Who. Gawain," Morgana said firmly. "He's well-liked and well-respected among Logres' lords, as well as by Britain's other rulers. They will listen if he says he won't demand fealty as high king if he inherits Arthur's throne. He could convince them their best path to peace is to rule their own lands without wanting more. Once Arthur's no longer acclaimed as high king but only as king of Logres, Gawain can return to Orkney and rule in his father's place. That will show everyone he means what he says."

"I don't think Prince Mordred will be happy about that," Guinevere said tartly.

"True." Nimue looked at Morgana. "What do we do about him?"

"We watch him," the younger enchantress replied. "We watch Mordred very carefully, while we look for our chance to shatter Excalibur."

Nimue nodded. "Then we need Sir Balyn's sword."

CHAPTER THIRTY-FOUR

At least travelling to the wilds of Gwynedd's mountains was a simple task, Nimue reflected, even if this hadn't been an easy journey. She hadn't dared to come straight here by means of enchantment. The risk of finding herself in Viviane of the River's territory was far too great. Her magic might go astray with the border between the mortal realm and the hidden lands so uncertain hereabouts. That or Viviane would draw Nimue into her presence deliberately, at best to ask what she was doing, at worst to trap her for her own amusement. Nimue knew the enchantress's power was far greater than her own.

She had used her magic to travel to the road which led to Caerhun, and come the rest of the way on foot. Finally, she reached the marble tomb Merlin which had built for Sir Balyn and his brother. The white stone was weathered and stained, while wind-blown dirt blurred the dead knights' names. She wondered if anyone who passed this way ever paused to wonder who these men had been.

She gestured and the once-cursed sword passed through the marble to fly to her hand. The weapon, its belt and scabbard were as pristine as they had been when she took the blade from Merlin. The same would hardly be true of the dead men, but Nimue felt no need to witness their decay. She looked around for some sign that Viviane was watching. The Lady of the River had made this sword. She would undoubtedly have an interest in what became of it.

Nimue was ready to remind the enchantress that she herself

had sought an end to magic's influence in mortal affairs. She would explain how they hoped to break Excalibur once and for all. She would look for any hint that Viviane had sent Morgana to Camelot with some outcome like this in mind.

A breeze ruffled the coarse grass. The brook chattered in its stony bed. There was still no sign of Viviane. Nimue wondered if anyone ever passed this way. She decided she wouldn't come here again. This time, if they succeeded – no, when they succeeded – she would find another way to put this last enchanted sword beyond everyone's reach, whether they were mortal or one of her own kin.

She turned her back on the lonely tomb and walked back up the road. Now she wondered what might be happening at Camelot. What might have happened while she was away? Abruptly, she decided she might not be beyond Viviane's reach, but if the enchantress was going to challenge her, she would have done so by now. Nimue headed for a stand of trees, and stepped through the shadows to arrive in Morgana's workroom.

She held up the sword. "I have it."

Guinevere and Morgana looked up from the scrying bowl. Their faces were grim.

Nimue felt a chill. "What's happened?"

"Mordred," Guinevere said with loathing.

"He arrived at the siege as we expected, but one of his men went straight to Arthur and accused Mordred of plotting treachery," Morgana explained. "The man said the prince had no intention of taking his brothers' bodies to Orkney. He said he only sought permission to enter Camelot to assess the defences. He told Arthur Mordred plans to seize the castle and make Guinevere his wife."

"One of his own betrayed him?" Nimue was astonished.

Morgana laughed, humourless. "Only because Mordred ordered it. Our treacherous princeling denies everything, naturally. He cut the man's throat, as soon as the poor fool reported back to him. So there's no danger of the man changing his story, and no one saw Mordred do the murder but us."

"He's told Sir Gawain that Arthur invented this story as an excuse to condemn him for treason, in order to have him executed," Guinevere said hotly.

"Why would Gawain believe Arthur would do such a thing?"

"Because the king has already heard that Mordred was wandering the siege lines last night, vowing to avenge his dead brothers, and naturally those rumours are true," Morgana assured Nimue. "Of course, Mordred swears to Gawain that he never meant treason, that he spoke without thinking, maddened by anger and grief."

"Reminding Gawain of his own anger and grievances." Nimue could have been impressed by Mordred's cunning if this deceit wasn't so vile. "What has Gawain made of this?"

"He and his men have packed up their tents and withdrawn from the siege. Mordred has gone with them, along with some other knights." Guinevere looked at her, anxious. "Arthur is furious."

"And he's ready to believe the worst of everyone, as we know all too well," Nimue said heavily. "Do you have any idea what will happen now?"

"Arthur has just sent a herald with a letter to Lancelot's gate under a flag of truce." Morgana saw Nimue's surprise. "Come and see for yourself."

Nimue laid the enchanted sword on the long table as she went to peer into the scrying bowl. A cluster of men wearing Arthur's comet-tailed dragon waited a respectful distance from the formidable gatehouse of Sir Lancelot's castle. The drawbridge was lowered, but so was the portcullis. Crossbowmen stood watchful on the battlements. The besiegers' defences were well beyond the range of those deadly bolts. Far too far away for Arthur's envoys to reach safety if Lancelot and his allies chose to answer the king's letter by attempting to break out of this siege. They would be the first to die.

"Where are the gaps in Arthur's ranks?" Lancelot's sentries must have seen Sir Gawain and his supporters leaving. How soon could the king muster more knights to replace those he had lost? Nimue wondered who might drag their feet, or even ignore his summons. Arthur's rule over Logres was crumbling. If they could deprive him of Excalibur, his reign as high king would be over.

"Wait. Look." Guinevere's finger hovered over the water.

Morgana gently moved the queen's hand away. "I wonder what was in that letter."

"I wonder." Nimue watched a knight on a white horse duck his head to pass under the slowly rising portcullis. Sir Lancelot's three-banded shield was unmistakable. He rode towards the heralds, and the portcullis crashed down behind him. Whatever Lancelot's fate might be, his castle wasn't about to surrender.

When the knight reached the heralds, he handed over a letter. One of Arthur's messengers ran for the besiegers' lines. Nimue, Morgana and Guinevere waited, silently watching. Outside the tower room, down in the castle yard, the sounds of Camelot's daily life carried on.

Eventually the messenger reappeared. A man on a horse rode behind him.

"Is that Arthur?" Guinevere asked, incredulous.

Nimue didn't reply, and nor did Morgana. The rider couldn't be anyone else.

"Are they going to fight?" Guinevere demanded.

"Surely he wouldn't be so foolish." Nimue couldn't believe Arthur had forgotten how single combat with Sir Pellinore had so nearly ended in disaster. Lancelot was twice the fighter Pellinore had been.

Morgana said nothing, focused on her spell. They watched Arthur ride to within a few horse's lengths of Sir Lancelot. The king gestured and the heralds retreated. Lancelot nudged his horse into a walk and drew level with the king. Both men removed their helmets.

"What are they saying?" Guinevere was frustrated.

Nimue looked over to the corner and the bronze bell. Before she could add her spell to Morgana's, Sir Lancelot offered Arthur his hand. The king took it gladly. More than that, Arthur drew the knight into an awkward embrace. If Nimue had worked some magic to carry the sounds of the siege into this room, she knew they would hear cheering. She could hardly blame the liegemen. Men on both sides had no wish to die fighting other men of Logres they had so recently called friends.

"Those letters must have been very persuasive." Morgana was sourly amused.

Guinevere stared at the scrying bowl. "So, their differences are forgiven and forgotten. What does that mean for me?"

"We will be long gone before they return," Nimue assured her. "We'll tell everyone you're retiring to a remote convent to live out your life in prayer. I doubt Arthur will pursue you, and even if he does, we'll be in Gaul."

"He won't want you back. He'll take a new wife who can give him a son," Morgana said, contemptuous.

Guinevere nodded. "I'm sure he can find a priest to give him dispensation to consider his marriage vows void." But her eyes were hollow with her own longing for a child.

"I have no doubt he'll wed again." Nimue despised the way the crucified god's priests found excuses for those they favoured to avoid laws they swore were hard and fast for everybody else. "But there's no guarantee he'll get her pregnant. A man can be barren just as easily as a woman."

On the other hand, if Arthur did take another wife, she would have to think long and hard about using her magic to ensure this unknown maiden gave the king an heir. Nimue always swore she used enchantment to save innocents from suffering. If she had intervened to help Guinevere conceive, so much anguish would have been avoided. If Arthur grew old and grey as king of Logres while Gawain ruled over Orkney, and both men passed their kingdoms to their sons, perhaps all the rulers across Britain's isles would grow accustomed to living in peace. Meantime, perhaps Guinevere would find a man who loved her for herself and raise a family with him.

Morgana stepped away from the table as her scrying spell faded. "I don't imagine Mordred will give Arthur any leisure to court a new wife. He's got what he wanted. Gawain has broken with the king, and they have a sizeable following of knights and their men."

"Won't Gawain simply return to Orkney?" Guinevere asked, hopeful. "Even if he was angry enough to defy the king after hearing Mordred's lies, surely the news that Arthur and Lancelot have reconciled will give him pause for thought once his blood has cooled?"

"Are they truly reconciled?" Morgana wasn't convinced. "Perhaps Arthur simply wants to avoid fighting two foes at once. He'll find it far easier to defeat Gawain if he has Lancelot and his allies at his side. Once that threat is settled, he can deal with Lancelot whenever he chooses."

She looked at the two of them, sardonic. "You forget I lived here with Arthur for ten years. I know him better than you think. He will never forgive or forget betrayal. Why else do you think I had to convince Sir Accolon to kill him, or at very least, to leave him for dead? It was our only hope of ever being free."

No one spoke for a long moment.

"What happens between Arthur and Lancelot is a problem for another day," Nimue said at last. "We have to find out what Mordred plans to do next."

"We must break Excalibur, above all else." Morgana waved a hand at the enchanted sword on the table. "If Mordred is intent on killing Arthur, perhaps we should put that blade in his hand."

"If Mordred breaks Excalibur on the battlefield, do you think he'll hold back from killing Arthur with his next stroke?" Guinevere shook her head. "We can't risk that snake in the grass claiming the throne of Logres."

"Agreed," Morgana conceded.

"Why should we give this blade to any knight?" Nimue said suddenly. "We can use it to break Excalibur ourselves. One blade striking another doesn't have to happen in a battle."

"True," Morgana nodded, "but how do we get hold of Excalibur?"

"We watch and wait to see if Arthur stays in his tent tonight, or if Lancelot invites him into his castle." Nimue nodded at the scrying bowl. "We wait until Arthur's asleep, then we steal it."

"And if he wakes?"

"I could distract the king." Guinevere stirred the empty water with a finger. "I'll be the last person he expects to see. I could insist on talking to him alone."

"He'll wonder how on earth you got there." Nimue tried to think this through.

"I'll tell him some story," Guinevere said, exasperated. "Does it matter? We only need to get him away from Excalibur long enough for one of you to take it. You can both pass unseen, can't you?"

Nimue looked at Morgana. "Will you do it? While I stay with the queen, ready to carry her out of danger."

"You'll need to be there unseen," Morgana pointed out. "Arthur knows you have magic to call on, and he knows you'll take Guinevere's side against his."

"True." All the same, Nimue couldn't resist a grin. "So, what are we waiting for?"

Morgana renewed her scrying spell. "Let's see what Arthur's up to."

"Oh." Guinevere looked into the silver bowl.

Morgana sighed. "It seems we must think again."

The besieging army had started striking their tents and dismantling their painstakingly built defences. Morgana sent her spell soaring over the walls of Sir Lancelot's castle. Inside, the yard looked like a kicked anthill, swarming with activity.

"They're pursuing Gawain and Mordred." Morgana looked grim. "They're not even waiting a day."

"Then we must watch and wait for our moment," Nimue said, resolute. "If we're going to save Logres from years of bloodshed, we have to break Excalibur before these armies come to battle."

CHAPTER THIRTY-FIVE

Nimue was tidying the queen's bedchamber when Guinevere opened the door. It was Morgana's turn to cast the scrying spell, but she had to do something to occupy her hands and her thoughts. They had been watching for days now as Arthur drove his men on a forced march westward pursuing Sir Gawain and Mordred.

"They're making camp." Guinevere hurried back down the spiral stair.

Nimue followed quickly. Until now, the army had only halted when darkness forced them, and the king had bedded down in the open alongside his knights. Nimue, Morgana and Guinevere had seen no possible opportunity to steal Excalibur. Today, the afternoon was barely half gone. Would this give them some chance, however slight?

In the room on the floor below, Morgana stood over the scrying bowl. The enchanted sword from the distant tomb lay on the table.

"Where are they?" Nimue couldn't see anything distinctive about the scrubby heathland where Arthur's men were setting up their tents and digging fire pits.

"This fiefdom is called Camlann." Morgana clasped the silver bowl between her hands as the distant image shivered. Powerful as her magic was, working these enchantments day after day had taken its toll.

"And Sir Gawain?"

Guinevere answered. "His forces are camped about three miles away."

"You think they'll do battle tomorrow?" Nimue searched for Arthur's comet-tailed dragon on the pennants being hoisted to mark each noble lord's tent.

Morgana nodded, certain. "Gawain has decided to make a stand. He's found a defensible slope with a stream on one flank. If he goes any further, there are much bigger rivers to cross and doing that will split his army. When Arthur and Lancelot's scouts see that happening, Gawain must know there's every chance the king will seize the advantage and attack."

"Arthur must know that too." Guinevere was puzzled. "Why doesn't he just wait until they reach the rivers?"

"He knows his men and their horses are tiring. Softer land by a river won't favour his knights nearly as much as this dry plain." Morgana shrugged. "Besides, if Gawain has decided to stand and fight, he won't go anywhere. Arthur must meet him on the field of battle now or retreat. If he does that, he'll be condemned as a coward to the end of his days. There won't be a knight of Logres who'll swear fealty to him ever again."

"Will Arthur still ride into battle once he realises Excalibur is gone?" wondered Nimue.

"If he does, is there a chance these knights won't follow him without the blade's magic?" Guinevere constantly found reasons to hope this strife could be resolved without bloodshed.

Morgana shook her head. "Sir Lancelot still rides at his side. He'll stay loyal to Arthur come what may. Doing anything else will see him denounced as a traitor for a second time. There will be no coming back from that, and Lancelot is here to reclaim his place as Camelot's greatest knight. The rest will follow him into battle even if their belief in Arthur has faltered."

"So they've made their choices and men will die whatever we do." Nimue could only hope she wouldn't be held to account for any of those deaths. "At least they'll get a good night's sleep with full bellies, if tomorrow is to be their last day. Where's Mordred?"

"Staying as close to Gawain as his shadow," Morgana said

with distaste. "I hate to think what poison he's dripped into his brother's ears. We must find some way to rein him in when this is over."

"Once the dust has settled and we see who's left standing." When Nimue would remind Morgana they had agreed to put an end to magical interference in mortal affairs. As soon as she had the princess's binding promise on that, she and the queen would leave for Gaul. The leather bags stacked under this table held everything they had decided to take with them.

"Perhaps some worthy knight will kill Mordred in the fighting," Guinevere said venomously. She wasn't opposed to all bloodshed.

Nimue looked at Morgana. "How close to the king's camp can you get us? Do you need to rest for a while first?"

The younger enchantress shook her head. "The sooner we do this, the better. There's a hazel coppice not too far away. I can get us there before Arthur's men start searching for firewood."

She held out her hand. Guinevere took it. All three women were dressed alike in drab gowns with their hair hidden by linen coifs. Nimue's enchantment should make sure they passed through the camp overlooked, but if something caused her magic to falter, humble dress was their next best chance of going unnoticed.

Nimue took Guinevere's other hand. Morgana still cupped the scrying bowl with one palm. Nimue fervently hoped the younger enchantress's confidence that she could get them to this unknown place was justified. It was too late for doubts though. She picked up the enchanted sword and gave Guinevere's hand a reassuring squeeze. Morgana's magic swirled around them and the tower room in Camelot vanished. Nimue wondered why she had been worried. The princess's power was astonishing.

That might be so, but she felt someone else's magic brush against Morgana's spell. It felt oddly familiar and at the same time, wholly strange. Before Nimue could grasp whatever memory that strange sorcery was stirring, the intrusive magic moved on. Morgana's enchantment carried them towards Camlann.

Before they reached the heath, the strange magic returned. This time the sorcery was far stronger. Nimue felt the enchanted sword in her hand thrum with the same resonance. She realised Viviane of the River was searching for her blade. Nimue had been right when she suspected Sir Balyn's tomb was being watched. Viviane had watched and waited while the three of them made their plans. Now the sorceress had acted.

Caught between rival enchantments, Nimue was weightless. She saw nothing, heard nothing. The only things she could feel were the sword she held in one hand and on the other side, Guinevere's fingers entwined with her own. She sensed the queen's growing panic. This wasn't the swift and seamless step from one place to another that Morgana had promised.

The magic in the sword grew stronger. The scabbard twisted in Nimue's grip. She tightened her hold. Whatever Viviane might want with this blade, whichever side she might favour in this battle, Nimue would not let the sorceress have the sword. She summoned her own power and lashed out. The intrusive magic recoiled. An instant later, it returned. Now Viviane was angry.

The sword grew searing hot. A vile image filled Nimue's mind's eye. Her scorched fingers were swelling and blistering. Her weeping skin split in countless places to reveal raw scarlet flesh beneath. Her palm was slick with blood. Only the magic that surrounded them saved her from choking on the stench of her own hand burning. The fire grew hotter. Her fingers were blackened bone and rags of shrivelled skin. Soon her whole hand would be gone, sacrificed to her folly. When Morgana's magic brought them back to the mortal realm, Nimue would feel the indescribable agonies of her injuries.

She could live without a hand, but soon her wrist would be

consumed, and then her arm. How could this sword be worth such mutilation? It wasn't as if she could keep hold of the blade once the splintered bones of her hand crumbled to ash. But perhaps not all was lost. As long as she was caught up in this enchantment, Nimue was neither in the hidden lands or in the mortal realm. Perhaps Viviane's all-powerful magic could restore what it had so easily destroyed...

Guinevere was gripping her other hand so tightly that Nimue's knuckles were crushed. That pain was real. Those bruises would linger, along with the red crescent marks where Guinevere's nails were digging deep.

Nimue struck out with her magic. The terrifying illusion vanished. Viviane was undoubtedly powerful, but there were limits to what she could do when they were without substance here in the void. Nimue felt the solid pressure of the enchanted blade's scabbard against her palm and her fingers again. She still had hold of the sword and her hand was still whole. The magic trying to take the blade from her faded away.

They were still very far from safety. Different sorcery attacked Morgana. This was a more subtle assault, trying to shred the princess's spell. Darts of insidious malice struck her from every direction. Morgana was trying to ward them off with what little magic she could spare. She was having scant success. As soon as she focused on one attack, that taunting enchantment vanished. Meantime other dagger-sharp thrusts tore at the spell that carried them.

Nimue had once seen a wildcat mobbed by crows. The animal could have killed any one of the birds with a swipe of its lethal claws, but the crows were well aware of that danger. They attacked the cat's tail and rump with their beaks and talons. As soon as the snarling beast spun around, the crows flew out of reach. Others who had been waiting their turn attacked the cat from behind. The animal was reduced to crouching in a gully, licking a dozen or more wounds while it flailed a desperate paw to keep the birds away. No single injury was enough to kill it, but its lifeblood was draining away. At least it had been until Nimue had intervened, healing the cat and carrying it far away from the crows and the nests they were defending.

She couldn't do anything to help Morgana. Nimue had to keep hold of the sword. Viviane's magic might have retreated, but the enchantress would sense any hint of distraction and attack her again. Nimue couldn't risk that, not when she must keep Guinevere safe in this turmoil. The queen had no magic of her own. If Guinevere's hand slipped from Morgana's grasp, only Nimue could save the helpless young woman and that would take all her strength. She felt Guinevere's terror growing. Soon she would panic and try to escape. That could mean disaster for the three of them.

Then Nimue realised this vicious new magic was being worked by many lesser enchantresses led by a cunning mind. The Lady of the Lake must have been watching them too, quite possibly ever since the day when she had given Arthur Excalibur. Whatever her reasons were for giving him that sword, Nimue guessed the Lake Maidens didn't want to see their enchanted blade broken.

She gripped the once-cursed sword's scabbard tighter. Feeling the hum of its magic, she sought out the answering rhythm of Viviane's distant sorcery. As soon as she sensed the enchantress, distant and watchful, Nimue let the jagged shocks of the Lady of the Lake's magic flow through her, passing from Morgana through Guinevere and on through the sword. Each stab was bitterly painful. She could feel the queen's confusion and agony. Nimue summoned her resolve. She must do this for as long as she could stand the torment.

Viviane's magic returned like a breaking storm. The enchantress attacked the Lake Maidens' sorcery. She ruthlessly stripped away each lesser working to expose and erode the magic at the heart of their onslaught. Nimue felt Morgana realise what was happening. The princess swiftly repaired her spell. Nimue lent as much as she dared of her own enchantment to carry them towards Camlann.

The Lady of the Lake attacked. Unerring, Viviane retaliated. The Lady of the Lake's magic retreated, though not because she was beaten. Nimue sensed her determination to save her strength for a better opportunity. She had no time to consider what that might mean. Her feet hit solid ground and daylight dazzled her. She staggered, nearly falling as Guinevere slumped to the trampled grass.

"Morgana?" Nimue blinked away tears. "Where are you?"

"Where are we?" The younger enchantress panted, on her hands and knees beside Guinevere.

"We're too late." Nimue looked at the slaughter surrounding them, appalled.

Somehow Morgana's spell had brought them to the final throes of the bloody battle between Arthur's army and Sir Gawain's forces. Viviane's attack, and the Lady of the Lake's assault must have held them in the void all through the day and night and well into the day that followed. The sun was sinking in the west in a blood-red sky.

Men lay dead and wounded as far as Nimue could see. The stink of blood and shit filled the air, where dying men had soiled themselves or had their bellies ripped open to leave them screaming as they died. Those who had been killed by a blow that split their skull or by a sword driven into their face lay still and mercifully mute. Many more writhed on the ground, clutching a shattered knee or some mangled wound inexorably oozing blood.

Morgana struggled to her feet. "Where is the king? Where is Arthur?"

Nimue searched in vain for any sign of the comet-tailed dragon. She could hardly make out any of the blazons that the dead knights and their squires bore so proudly on their surcotes. Cloth was torn and embroidered devices were lost beneath blood and filth.

"What happened?" Guinevere managed to stand. She was as pale as milk and her chest heaved as the stink made her cough, but her bruised eyes were determined.

"My magic was dragged awry." Morgana looked murderous.

"We came to break Excalibur," Nimue insisted. "That must be done, whether Arthur lives or dies. We have to find him. He'll have the sword."

"There." Guinevere pointed.

Nimue squinted. Far away, where the shallow slope ran down to more level ground beside a meagre stream, men were still fighting on foot. Their horses were either dead or fled from the turmoil. Nimue saw a white shield with three red stripes disfigured by splashes of blood.

"The king won't be far from Lancelot," Morgana said, breathless.

Nimue worked a swift spell to hide the three of them from sight. They hurried towards that final skirmish. She wished her magic could stop them seeing the pitiful wounded and muffle the desperate pleas and curses of the dying. The queen was weeping behind her. Morgana stayed grimly silent until they saw who was fighting Lancelot.

"Gawain." The princess choked on her anguish.

Orkney's prince was exhausted. His ragged feints and thrusts made a mockery of his hard-won skills. Sir Lancelot had barely any more strength left, but that was enough. He swung his sword up with a tearing groan and brought it down to land a crushing blow. Gawain parried but his blade slid away, useless. Lancelot's sword hit Gawain's head hard enough to dent his helmet.

Gawain staggered. His sword arm hung limp. Sir Lancelot drove a final thrust into Gawain's side. Gawain's armour turned the blow aside, but that didn't save him. He howled in agony and his knees buckled. Lancelot threw away his sword and caught Gawain as he fell. He pulled off the prince's helmet. Blood frothed on Gawain's lips. His face stilled and his gaze fixed on nothingness.

Nimue remembered how Lancelot had injured the prince in their struggle to save Guinevere. She guessed that last blow had struck an already-cracked rib. The bone had broken and torn a fatal gash in Gawain's lung.

"There's Mordred," Guinevere gasped.

Not far away and surrounded by corpses, the last prince of Orkney fought the king. Where was Excalibur? Arthur was armed with a spear. Mordred had a sword and his shield with the double-headed eagle scarred by countless blows. Mordred circled, looking for his chance to get past the menacing spearhead. Once he was inside the sweep of the polearm, Arthur would have no defence against his blade.

Arthur charged at Mordred. The prince raised his sword to hack the spearhead from its haft. At the last moment, Arthur deceived him. He sidestepped and thrust the spear under Mordred's shield. The prince's arm fell backwards. Arthur had known exactly where to strike. The spear's point slid under the lower edge of Mordred's breast plate, where the tassets, the lesser plates joined with rivets and straps, would flex as he rode a horse. The spear sank deep into Mordred's guts.

Arthur thrust again. There could be no surviving that wound. Even so, oncoming death didn't stop Mordred. Driven on by his hatred, he forced himself forward, step by impossible step. The spear found some path through his body and his armour to appear at his back, dripping with blood.

The king stood with his head hanging, both hands clutching the spear shaft, even when Mordred found the strength to raise his sword above his head. Arthur looked up like some unsuspecting animal before the slaughterman's poleaxe fell.

Mordred brought the blade down. Arthur's helmet strap must have broken, or perhaps it had never been fastened. The blow dragged the helmet from his head. The king's face was covered with blood. Perhaps Mordred saw that before he died. Arthur let go of the spear shaft. Mordred toppled sideways to lie face down and unmoving in the foulness of the battlefield.

Now all five of Morgause's sons had died violent deaths like their father, Nimue thought with piercing sorrow. Ygraine's son would soon join them, fallen in battle like Uther before him. As Arthur collapsed to his knees, she saw the wound to his head was lethally deep. Some vicious edge of metal had torn through skin and scalp to gouge into his skull. As blood streamed down his face, Arthur raised a gauntleted hand to his cheek. He lowered it and stared at the reddened steel.

Guinevere wept beside her, wracked with grief for the husband she had known in better days, in those early months after their wedding when they thought a contented lifetime together lay ahead.

"What happens now?" the queen choked.

"I don't know." Nimue owed Guinevere the truth.

"Perhaps they can tell us." Morgana pointed towards the little stream that bordered the battlefield.

The water was stained red with blood and choked with corpses. A moment later, and the dead men were gone. What had been a meagre stream was far wider and deeper. Weeping willows clustered along the banks and a white-sailed barge came gliding towards them.

The Lady of the Lake stood in the prow. Now she had no need to soothe mortal men's fears with a semblance of sweet, biddable beauty, her face was fiercely intent. She was tall, leanly muscular and her eyes glittered, hard as diamond. The Lady's maidens were gathered behind her, dressed in mourning black, cloaked and hooded. They were looking this way and that, and as one turned her head, Nimue glimpsed her true form. The Lady had found her allies among the lurking shadows that fed on mortal nightmares. Her magic hid their lipless mouths and sunken cheeks, their burning eyes and crooked, taloned hands. They repaid her with their power.

The vessel drew closer. Its billowing sails were filled with enchantment. As the twilight deepened, no breeze stirred across this field of dead and dying men.

"We have to find Excalibur." Nimue moved quickly to search the ground where Mordred's body lay. She found the sword he had dropped, but it wasn't the one she sought.

Arthur was still kneeling motionless, staring at nothing. If the wound to his head hadn't been bleeding, Nimue would have thought he was already dead. He couldn't live much longer. The light of his life flickered wildly, fading fast. She had seen him born into this world, squalling and red. Now she could only watch him die.

Steeling herself, Nimue approached the stricken king. He wasn't wearing a sword belt. So that was why Excalibur's scabbard hadn't been able to save him from Mordred's fatal blow. But what had happened to the enchanted blade? Had Arthur lost his sword in some mishap or had someone else stolen it away?

She looked at the meagre stream that had become a river. The white-sailed barge reached the bank and the Lady of the Lake stepped ashore and strode towards them. Where she had been meek and graceful before, now she was confident and dangerous. Three maidens followed her, their gaunt faces hidden by their hoods and their clawed hands tucked inside their sleeves. None of them glanced at Nimue or at Guinevere and Morgana. They were intent on Arthur.

Nimue stepped between the lake maidens and the king. "Did you have a hand in this slaughter?"

Viviane of the River appeared and laughed. "Oh, she would have, if she hadn't been trying to stop you coming here."

Morgana stepped forward, shielding Guinevere. "What were you going to do, if you succeeded in taking that sword from Nimue? Why are you here now?"

Viviane ignored the princess, addressing Nimue. "These men brought this fate on themselves. Their armies drew up to fight not long after dawn. Even so, the king and his most loyal knight met with Gawain and his brother, to see if they could come to terms. They might have found a path to peace, but some fool drew his sword to kill an adder when the creature struck at his foot. Mordred had warned his men to be alert for treachery. As soon as they saw a naked blade, they thought the worst and attacked." She shrugged. "Mortals are foolish."

Nimue tightened her grip on the enchanted sword. "Answer the question. What brings you here?"

The sorceress gestured at the weapon. "I came to retrieve that blade. You may have changed your mind, but I hold to my agreement with Merlin. Magic has no place in mortal affairs."

"Merlin used his magic to stop bloodshed such as this. His magic and mine." The Lady of the Lake raised her hand and Excalibur flew from wherever it had lain, lost or stolen. Deftly, she caught it and smiled.

"There has been peace without magic's interference for long years now," Viviane countered. "Mortal passions and follies caused this strife."

Nimue wasn't having this. "Old grudges and inherited quarrels brought these men to their deaths, but magic played its part in causing those quarrels, thanks to Merlin's meddling."

Viviane nodded as if Nimue had agreed with her. "We see yet again we should leave mortals to manage their own fates, for better or for worse."

"I choose to offer them hope." The Lady of the Lake narrowed her eyes, menacing. "And I will do as I please."

Viviane looked at Nimue. "Then you may keep that blade. Find a worthy champion to wield it and I will ensure it shatters Excalibur when your knight meets whatever tyrant uses such undeserved power to rule over these isles. Who will you curse with your favour next?" she asked the Lady of the Lake. "Few of these poor fools will live to see another dawn, and I don't believe they will have any appetite for more war."

The Lady of the Lake's lip curled, but she didn't answer.

Viviane surveyed the battlefield with mild interest. "Will that bold knight pick up Pendragon's standard, now he realises he has slain a man he once considered a friend as close as any brother?"

Sir Lancelot staggered to his feet. Looking at Sir Gawain's corpse, he began stripping off his own armour. He threw away each skilfully crafted piece, not caring where it fell. Where a strap or a buckle stopped him, he sliced through leather with a dagger. He didn't care if he cut himself. Bending double with his arms outstretched and shaking himself like a dog, he shed his chain mail hauberk. Rips in his padded tunic beneath blossomed with scarlet. Lancelot stripped that tunic off as well, tossing it aside like a garment crawling with lice. Last of all he hurled away his dagger to be lost among the dead.

Wearing only his bloodstained shirt, he stumbled away. Even if magic hadn't been hiding them, Nimue didn't think he would have noticed the women by the stream. The knight's handsome face was desolate as his blank eyes saw only the horrors of this day.

The Lady of the Lake laughed. "I need no new champion. I will take Arthur to Avalon and heal him. He will be even deeper in my debt when he returns to rule."

"You will not," Viviane said ominously.

The three maidens had moved closer to Arthur. They halted, hearing Viviane's words. Nimue saw that blood had stopped flowing from the king's deadly wound, but she could see a last stubborn spark deep within him as he clung to life. It would take long and complex enchantments to restore him, but the Lady of the Lake had the magic of her maidens to help her.

Nimue looked at Morgana and saw her own unease reflected in the younger enchantress's face. Using the once-cursed sword to break Excalibur was one thing. Putting Viviane's blade in some unknowing king's hand and watching him lead more men to their deaths wasn't what they wanted. But they could hardly let the Lady of the Lake rule Logres through Arthur.

"How dare you condemn the innocent people of these

islands to endless war?" Guinevere stepped out of Morgana's shadow. "Why can't you leave us in peace?"

"This isn't my doing," Viviane said swiftly. "She chooses to find a new champion to wield Excalibur. I only seek to stop her."

"By putting magic in mortal hands," Morgana retorted. "When you claim to want the opposite."

"Fine words from a woman who uses magic as easily as breathing," scoffed Viviane.

"I am impressed, your highness," The Lady of the Lake said drily before turning from Morgana to Viviane. "I cannot recall when a mortal last learned how to wield magic and did not kill themselves inside a year. You are to be congratulated on your pupil's diligence."

"Enough!" Nimue had been searching her recollections of the day when Arthur had been given Excalibur, and of the day when she had trapped Merlin in that cave. Something had occurred to her. The Lady of the Lake must know where the wizard was imprisoned. She had made no attempt to free him. Nimue would have known if she had tried.

She challenged the sorceress. "You gave Excalibur to Arthur in return for a gift you would name some day. What do you want from him?"

"I want him in my debt to protect my people," the Lady of the Lake said angrily. "Merlin never cared that mortals saw his magic put Arthur on his father's throne. He broke our people's age-old customs whenever he pleased, not caring that he put the rest of us in danger. We are still in danger. Mortals seek us out, wanting the power Merlin had. They try to trap us or trick us, lusting after magic to win them wealth or advantage."

"But Merlin is gone," Nimue protested. "There has been no wild magic seen in Logres for years now."

"But you are here, and so is she." The Lady of the Lake glowered at Morgana. "I saw your reckless magic when you tried to have Arthur killed. How much death and grief did that bring you?"

Morgana didn't answer, red-faced with humiliation. They stood in silence only broken by the croaks of the ravens flocking to feast on the carnage.

Nimue looked at Morgana. "Would you swear a binding oath to never use your magic again? If I did the same." She turned to Viviane and the Lady of the Lake. "If we do that, will you take these swords out of the mortal realm, and swear to stay within the borders of your own lands? Then there will be nothing for you two to quarrel over."

Viviane looked thoughtful, then she shrugged. "I will, if she agrees. I have little interest in mortals."

"I will not agree," spat the Lady of the Lake. "Even if you two give up your magic, mortals know such power is there to be found. Stories of Merlin's sorcery are told in every tavern and market place. Such tales cannot be untold. Ballads cannot be unsung."

Morgana found her voice. "As long as these are only stories, what harm can they do? As long as the curious and the greedy can't find your kin to teach them magic as I did, won't such fables fade away?"

"Could you convince our people to stay out of the mortal realm?" Nimue asked Viviane. "For their own sake? To keep the peace."

Viviane nodded. "I can only speak for those within my lands, but I believe that most will listen."

"I do not." The Lady of the Lake was adamant.

"Then what do you propose?" Morgana snapped. "If you have any interest in ending this cycle of death and grief."

"Do tell us," Viviane invited.

Now the Lady of the Lake looked uncertain. One of her maidens shooed away a raven that looked far too eager to try plucking out Arthur's glassy eyes.

"I will offer you a bargain," the sorceress said slowly. "You may take it or leave it, but I will accept nothing less. I will take Arthur to Avalon and heal him, and I will take Excalibur and I will keep them there. Mortals can kill each other from sunrise to sunset for all I care. But they will still lust after magic, mark my words, and some of them will find it, no matter how many of our people forswear this realm. She is proof of that." She flung an accusing hand at Morgana.

"Sooner or later, the day will come when some mortal will seek to use sorcery to rule over the rest," the Lady of the Lake said with absolute certainty. "Or they will cross the borders of my realm in search of plunder or greater magic. I will not see my people left undefended. I will send Arthur to drive back those invaders with Excalibur in his hand. I will set him on his father's throne to lead mortal men once again, to keep me and my kindred safe. If I must, I will release Merlin from his imprisonment too."

"But only if you see some tyrant use magic to seize power in this mortal realm," Morgana said quickly, "or if someone invades your lands with evil intent. For no other reason."

"That is what I said." The Lady of the Lake looked at her, irritated.

Viviane of the River spoke up. "I will agree to such terms."

Both the mighty sorceresses looked at Nimue and Morgana.

"Will you two truly give up your magic?" The Lady of the Lake clearly had her doubts.

Nimue saw the desperate appeal in Guinevere's hollow eyes. She looked at Morgana.

Morgana nodded. "I will. Enchantment cannot give me what I want."

"Then you have my word." Nimue was about to offer her binding oath, but Viviane of the River disappeared. The Lady of the Lake vanished as well, together with her maidens and her barge. The broad, glassy river hung with willows was a meagre stream fouled with corpses once more. Arthur was gone, to whatever fate awaited him in Avalon.

"So, what do we do now?" Morgana looked around.

"We leave before we're asked too many questions." Nimue pointed at distant figures barely visible in the dusk. "Without my magic, I don't want to face the people who come to plunder the dead after a battle." Knowing she was truly defenceless was a most unwelcome feeling.

"Which way is it to Camelot?" Guinevere made a brave attempt at a smile. "How long a walk will that be?"

"Surely, we–" Morgana shook her head. "No, we can't, can we? I wonder if we can catch some loose horses."

"It's that way." Nimue hadn't lost her ability to read directions by the sun's place in the sky. She started walking. The other two walked with her, one on either side.

"I'm going to Orkney," Morgana said abruptly. "Someone must tell Morgause what has become of her sons."

"Do you suppose there's anyone left alive to tell the true story of this battle?" Guinevere glanced at the path Lancelot had taken. He was nowhere to be seen.

Morgana had already moved on. "I'm more concerned with those stories of Merlin and his magic. The Lady of the Lake was right about that. Words have power, even when they're not crafting spells. The lazy and feckless will always long for shortcuts to undeserved advantage."

"Then let's craft stories of our own." Nimue walked steadily onward. "Let's tell tales of tragic folly when mortals get entangled with magic. Let's show how unearned power deceives and corrupts even those who have the best intentions. Let's convince the people of these isles and beyond to look to their own strengths and to work with each other. To be the masters and mistresses of their own fates rather than blindly following the loudest voice."

"That will take some doing." Though Morgana sounded ready for the challenge.

"It'll give us something to do," Guinevere agreed, "on the journey to Gaul."

For a moment, Nimue was surprised. Then she realised the

queen – no longer a queen – was right. There was nothing for them in Logres. There was no one left to claim Arthur's chair or any other seat at the round table in Camelot. The castle that Merlin had crafted for him would soon be deserted. The walls would be robbed of useful stone to build homes and barns and stables, leaving the rubble to crumble into dust. Meantime, someone should carry word of Viviane's agreement with the Lady of the Lake overseas, if the mortal realm was to be truly sundered from those who could work magic, wherever they might be found.

Despite the deaths she had seen, despite the grief and loss that weighed her down, Nimue felt a new purpose. She might have laid aside her own magic, but she would still have the long, long life of her people. She would have plenty of time to shape at least some of the myths that mortals would tell each other about Arthur.

ACKNOWLEDGEMENTS

An author writes the words, but it takes a good many people and their skills and hard work, to put a book into a reader's hands.

I am immensely grateful to Chris Panatier for his splendid artwork, and to Alice Coleman for the cover design.

My sincere thanks to the Angry Robot team. As well as commissioning editor at large Simon Spanton, who got this project started, thank you to Gemma Creffield, editor; Caroline Lambe, publicity; Amy Portland, marketing; Desola Coker, publishing assistant, and Eleanor Teasdale, publisher.

My agent Max Edwards has been invaluable as always, with the able assistance of Tom Lloyd Jones checking the fine detail on the paperwork, and Gus Brown providing administrative support. My thanks to them and everyone at Aevitas Creative Management.

Last but by no means least, I am very grateful for my fellow authors, the keen readers and eager booksellers who have been encouraging me with their interest since this book was first announced.